Trust in Tomorrow

Dana Sweeney

Cover art by Andrei Dragomir

Contents

Previously on...

Have you read Lust for Tomorrow? If not, I really recommend reading it, not only because I wrote it and am proud of it, but because this book will probably be more satisfying that way, being a sequel and all. But hey, I grew up before DVRs, box sets, and streaming services, plus I'm a huge comic book fan, so I respect the choice to dive right in and figure it out as you go!

Even if you have read Lust for Tomorrow, here's a refresher on some of the basics of this world, just in case.

In the recent past, the zombie apocalypse hit. The world is a total wreck. In the Pacific Northwest exists a walled city called Illustris, built by the fabulously wealthy. It's fully equipped for long-term safety and survival. As the apocalypse refugees began to descend on it, Illustris rebranded as the Stronghold and started a rigorous system of intake testing to ensure only the ideal newcomers were allowed in.

Most refugees are admitted specifically to serve in the military. Female soldiers are encouraged to see their service as temporary, with the expectation that they will choose to marry and start having babies to regrow the population.

To *encourage* this process along, there are rules in place around relationships: If two soldiers develop a strong emotional connection, they will no longer be allowed to go on patrol together but must be separated in the interest of team solidarity; if they remain unmarried, they must both continue to serve.

Upon admittance to the Stronghold, each resident is given a biotech implant. It provides birth control, among other things.

Nina, the heroine of Lust for Tomorrow, was deeply resistant to the Stronghold's plan for her as a woman. Falling in love with Tom gradually wore her down, particularly seeing how much he worried about her. She accepted his marriage proposal, triggering her immediate retirement from the corps.

On her first day as a civilian, she was approached by Commander Maxwell, a military leader who'd taken an interest in her. Maxwell informed her that her post-retirement "implant calibration appointment" was a farce; the Stronghold pretends to bring people in to adjust their implant settings in person to conceal the truth that the implants are controlled remotely and can be adjusted without warning. Nina's birth control has been off since the marriage paperwork was signed.

While Nina was reeling from this, Maxwell invited her to join his resistance movement.

The timeline overlaps as follows: Events in Chapters 1-5 of Trust in Tomorrow happen during Chapters 12-17 of Lust for Tomorrow.

Content Notes and Warnings

Trust in Tomorrow is a dystopian sci-fi romance with a HEA. It is an open-door romance with explicit and enthusiastic consent throughout. In a post-apocalyptic dystopian society, expect some discussion of somber topics such as personal loss and grief, as well as systemic oppression and exploitation.

In this story, the hero and heroine both suffer from trauma, and their coping mechanisms are a significant element in the narrative.

For a full list of potential thematic triggers and intimate acts portrayed, visit https://www.danasweeney.com/content-notes

For my daughter, who deserves the best of all possible worlds.

Chapter One

The Exhibitionist and the Voyeur

Stella

Like most bad habits, Stella Vernon's eavesdropping would start out innocently enough.

The library is her domain, gifted to her in a rare moment of largesse by her fiancé. Greg is a very busy, very important man. He took pity on Stella, trapped in the Gennero mansion with his mother, Celeste. Trapped in a mansion. What a thought. A horrid, ungrateful thought. Stella pinches herself.

In the early days of the end times, the library was briefly shuttered. It was a luxury, after all, and the male head librarian was conscripted. Had he returned from the fight to resume his position, would Stella languish still in that cold place, all day, every day? Her heart rate accelerates at the thought of that alternate life. She reminds herself she is a monster, seemingly grateful for a man's death. She pinches herself, hard, three times in succession for good measure, her eyes flaring at the galvanizing pressure.

It's a place where a bruise won't form. A place where one can pinch over and over and over, finding a tender nerve bundle ripe for retribution every time. She blinks rapidly as her pulse returns to a steadier pace.

Stella loves her days at the library. Pathetically grateful to be placed here, she knows there are a million ways she might fail and lose this gift or make Greg regret bestowing it. The first hurdle turns out to be how people react to her. Something about her makes them flinch or cringe. Why? She is desperate to please, to welcome, to help and accommodate. She is obsequious and quick and so, so quiet. But when she makes eye contact with a guest, they flinch, as if she were a predator.

Perhaps, she thinks, they resent her for being here instead of her predecessor. Was he popular, even beloved? Greg certainly wouldn't have known if that were the case. The Genneros would never have set foot in the library unless it were a gala venue. Awful, ungrateful. *Pinch*.

If they dislike her merely for not being Emmett, that hardly seems fair. Not that much about the world could be characterized as fair these days anyway. But Stella isn't responsible for his death or conscription. She certainly can't be blamed for the zombies.

Her breath hitches, holding involuntarily before resuming in a shaky recovery, an equally involuntary assertion of the unconscious will to live. She can be blamed for so much else. Not that anyone knows it.

But if they don't know it, then why? Why do people seem so uncomfortable around her? Do they see her as an interloper, an outsider? Too newly minted, a likely counterfeit?

I'm just like you! she wanted to scream, her eyes wide, desperate, fearstruck like a prey animal. But it's not true, of course. She's not like any of them, and that's the point.

She's not Illustrian elite by birth or achievement but by marriage, the impossibly rare Cinderella story. A story bookmarked and set on the shelf, at that. Things are still settling in, and Greg is so busy, and it would be unseemly. She's still a Vernon, not a Gennero, not quite yet.

She's not Illustrian proletariat either. She was an outsider until far too recently, and there were no homegrown Cinderella stories in this place. They are well within their rights to resent her. If only they knew—but self-pity is a wicked indulgence under the circumstances. *Pinch.*

A moment of dazzling clarity arrives one bright day as winter staggers bitterly into early spring.

Wandering aimlessly, studying the shelves, noting the gaps in the collection, Stella ponders whether private libraries might have anything worth seizing for the public good. Illustris' library exists as a concession to classic notions of civility, not because the founders cared overmuch or intended to use it. After all, books and research materials were all available via the cloud, which would certainly never cease to rain down on them at will.

Yet, everyone has favorites, those titles they simply have to have, if only to showcase and admire. The Genneros' shelves feature several dozen titles, not all of which are represented here. And the Basher mansion, she recalls suddenly, is home to a colorful selection that surely won't be missed.

It's a good idea, she thinks. Private collections moldering on dusty shelves should be surrendered to the library. They'll be read once or twice in a lifetime as it stands, yet they could be enjoyed by the populace. She'll bring it up to Greg, next time he's in a good mood. A shiver overtakes her for a moment, and her eyes unfocus, so she closes them.

The sound of the main door brings her back to the here and now. She whirls automatically toward the whoosh of displaced air, bracing herself.

A man enters without apparent discomfort and heads for the classics. Stella takes her time about returning to the desk so she can assist him when he's ready to check out, and their interaction is perfectly pleasant. Satisfied at this small sign that people might be adjusting to her presence, Stella sits in the tall chair behind the desk and looks around her library with a gently hopeful smile.

The door opens again, and Stella whirls, back on high alert, as if her moment of peace had been a daydream. She sees the alarm mirrored on the face of her guest. And suddenly, she knows.

It's her. Not dislike or distrust as she uncharitably assumed, but a fairly natural reaction to her skittishness. She's thought they perceived her as fearsome when they've been understandably discomfited by someone so visibly fearful.

Her eyes quivering, she holds herself to account for her failures. She was offered this wonderful gift, stewardship of this sacred space in a tumultuous time. People need and deserve a sanctuary, and that is what a library must be. Realizing how close she has come to inadvertently shattering this sanctuary renews her drive to do better. If she can't take proper care of this place, she will lose it. She can't lose it.

Stella hasn't always been this person. Rabbity, timorous. Stella Vernon was a person capable of great things. A person who strove, engaged with superiors as if they were all potential mentors, asked endless thoughtful questions, argued her points with vibrant enthusiasm.

It's moot, of course, to think about what changed. It hardly matters, does it? What matters is only that Stella cannot lose her library. Not yet. Not like this.

When she was among the stacks, out of the way, she didn't trouble the man who walked in. That's sufficient data to work with, she decides. Who needs a chair anyway? Why tie herself to a desk? Stella spins a pencil on the desk and walks in the direction it points.

This new practice transforms the library over the days to come. Stella's heart is lighter, at least while she's here. That lightness gives her something to hold onto at night and a reason to be happy she awakens in the morning. And for a time, that is enough.

Always on the move, still imbued with her prey animal energy, Stella is light on her feet and oh-so-quiet. She doesn't intend to listen in on anyone. Certainly not the first time it happens, anyway.

"—think he is now?" The woman's voice, though hushed, is mournful enough to carry across the aisle to where Stella now pauses.

"I think you should get used to not knowing," another woman says, her voice hardened against a loss she has clearly decided to be done feeling so deeply, a topic she'd prefer her companion to stop raising.

"But I thought we'd hear updates—"

"Would that make you feel better? If someone told you a lie and you could choose to believe it? I could tell you anything you want. Jimmy's watching TV in his hospital room. Jimmy's in a meadow somewhere, staring up at the stars. Jimmy got sent to a farm upstate. Jimmy—"

A strangled chirp and a flurry of footsteps. A sad sigh, then resigned footfalls as the second woman follows, perhaps to comfort and apologize to the one who fled.

Stella isn't entirely sure what horrible fate this Jimmy may have suffered, though she has a couple of strong guesses. She leans against the shelf and presses her forehead against the backs of her hands, the hard edge of the wood biting into her palms.

Her eyes closed, she recalls an old calming technique that worked for her when she was stuck in traffic, in what feels now like a former life. Alone in the car, she used to recite poetry.

Talking to oneself while alone in a car was one thing, though. Here, now, she will not so much as whisper the words. Her lips barely move, in fact. William Carlos Williams wrote so many peaceful, brief poems. They remind her of simpler times. They soothe her spirit. She recovers and returns to her wanderings.

"—rumors?"

"Please, there's nothing *but* rumors. Who can decide which ones to even listen to?"

"How can you not want to—"

"I want, okay? Of course I want to know what's happening, I just don't believe any of the gossip. Everyone's bored and nervous, and maybe they know something, and maybe they're making shit up or imagining things!"

"You heard about Erin Watkins?" the first woman says sadly.

The other pauses. "Yeah."

"You believe that, so why not—"

"Ugh, fuck's sake, Jenna. Someone dies, I believe it, okay? It's not the same as whether spies are being sent out or there's a secret, super-quiet helicopter taking people in and out at night, or there's an exciting new life path called being a concubine."

"I guess. Still, if that concubine thing is true, there are a few guys I wouldn't mind—"

"Ew, please stop talking. And you're dreaming if you think you'd get to pick."

The two women move on. Stella waits in place as their voices and footsteps fade. Funny how even though the gossip topics are unmistakably horrifying, end-of-the-world matters, the act of gossiping sounds the same. There's something so normal and human about it. It gives her hope in a way. People are still just people, aren't they? At least, these people are. It's been soul-crushing to spend so much time with only the Genneros and their ilk. How dare you think that way of your hosts? *Pinch*.

"—just creepy," the young woman complains.

"Get used to it," the man answers, his shrug both audible in his tone and visible from Stella's vantage point two rows away, peering over the tops of the books.

"It seems like—like they shouldn't be allowed? Or something?"

"What's the difference?" he says, bored.

"In the old days, no one walked around with masks on everywhere they went. Okay," she amends, and based on her tone, Stella imagines the man raised an eyebrow in challenge, "maybe sometimes when the wildfires were really bad or the occasional bad flu or whatever, but those were little masks. You could still see people's eyes. You could still know who they were."

He adjusts to face her fully. "Who cares who they are? They're soldiers. From outside. Not like you'd recognize them or whatever."

"It's creepy," she says again, a little petulantly.

He moves closer, and from the motion of his shoulder, Stella imagines he's put a hand on his companion's hip.

"I'll protect you," he flirts.

She giggles and tilts her head to kiss him. Stella smiles and moves on quietly to give them some privacy now that this has turned physical. While hearing people talk has been making her feel less lonely of late, watching them kiss feels like a genuine intrusion she has no right to.

They were talking about the Helmet contingent, she muses. She's familiar with them in concept, of course, but she has yet to see one in person.

By the time she sights a Helmet up close, she has heard a great deal of chatter about them. They're a strange mix of elite and outcast, not unlike Stella herself in a way. The military is gradually being replaced as newcomers transition from quarantine to training to active duty, allowing Illustrian citizens to return to their old lives, insofar as those lives still exist, or at least to relative peace and safety.

During their training, the soldiers are tested, and those who show sufficient aptitude are eligible for the Helmet corps. They have a minor leadership role, as Stella understands it, and they wear the headgear Greg helped design. Her pulse flutters when he tramples across her thoughts. Another person might call it love. She did, once upon a time.

The library is shuttered again, very briefly. Numb with apparent grief, Stella implores her benefactors to allow her to maintain her routine. Even Celeste doesn't argue. And why would she? Celeste barely tolerated Stella when it was still understood that Stella would bear her grandchildren; she would surely have even less good will to spare for her erstwhile daughter-in-law-to-be.

There are empty apartments and even houses in the city. Why would the Genneros keep her at all? With a dire chill, she realizes she might still bear their grandchildren... she imagines they might be keeping her around long enough to be sure.

Once this question has been answered conclusively, Stella realizes she is far too afraid to ask the other question that eats at her: Why won't you let me go?

In truth, she fears they would take her up on it and punish her ingratitude at the same time. The Genneros are the lesser evil compared to exile beyond the wall. Their son chose her, and he's gone. It's possible her very life depends on their belief in her love for him. And, well, she had loved him once.

The Helmets turned out to be fonder of their gear than expected; they don't seem to take it off much. She's gotten used to the occasional sight of a helmeted soldier tromping by in the distance outside. Mostly, though, she hears people discussing them. They're *new*, after all. And in a world of content-addicted people whose content hoses were recently shut off for good, novelty is worth a great deal of attention.

The Illustrian attitude toward the Helmets is largely negative at first, suspicious. How dare these people conceal their faces? Who are they really? How can we trust them?

Gradually, the sentiment softens to curiosity.

"They can't be bad, really, or they wouldn't be here."

"If they passed the psych evals, we shouldn't distrust them... exactly... still, it's weird, right?"

"What do you think that one looks like? He's tall, and those broad shoulders... I'd climb him like a tree."

"Oh my god, stop it!"

"You think I'm kidding? I would, I'd—"

"He could be a total goblin under that helmet, you know, Lise."

Among the military, the curiosity phase is skipped. The rank-and-file soldiers seem to go directly from suspicion to derision when it comes to their helmeted counterparts. They assign nicknames, mocking and cruel.

Stella sees a different side. Literally.

One day, a Helmet is a few rows away from Stella in the stacks. She isn't paying too much attention, as they don't often speak to anyone. But between glances in his direction, something changes, and she does a doubletake.

Where a moment before had been a shiny black helmet, there is now a scarred, bald head. She stares, now transfixed, as he selects a book from the shelf and opens it.

Shortly, the door's whoosh alerts him to replace the book on the shelf and the helmet on his head, and he leaves quickly.

In the weeks that follow, this sort of thing happens several times with different Helmets. Sometimes, a Helmet enters the library, selects a book, and leaves with it. But when they want to browse, they always need to remove the gear. Stella forms a theory: They can't read with that thing on, at least not comfortably. She feels bad for them.

Over time, she picks up on who is who to some extent. Having heard the nicknames, she matches them to the real names used to check out books, and in some cases, the faces she's glimpsed.

Bruno, the bald man, is clearly Bruto to his fellow soldiers. He likes comedic mysteries in the vein of Carl Hiaasen. Graves has to be Grace, the one who likes lyrical novels and poetry.

Alpha takes longer to figure out, since it doesn't follow the usual rhyming pattern. *But of course*, she realizes one day after hearing someone mocking an English accent. *Tom.*

He's the one who discovers a workaround for the helmet discomfort. One day, she watches as he selects a pile of books, proceeds to a table in the main atrium, and stows his helmet underneath. He sits for a long while, relaxing with his books, reading a little of each until he determines what to take with him. He waits until he is alone (save Stella) before putting his helmet back on and standing up.

Clever, she thinks.

Perhaps Tom advises other Helmets of his discovery, or perhaps they observe and follow suit. Grace sometimes sits with a volume of poetry, her eyes welling up with tears that never manage to spill over, reabsorbed perhaps in the drought of her sorrow. Bruno's resting face is severe, but when his book makes him chuckle, he gains a momentary boyish charm. No one would speak ill of them, surely, if they could see what Stella sees.

Tom spends a lot of time here. Sometimes he peruses books like that first day, but other evenings he just sits and reads for long periods. She likes to imagine they have something in common. After all, why read here instead of his quarters? He must be lonely. She knows that could be projection, the abyss of her own solitude calling out for a mirror if not a fellow traveller.

It feels plausible though. Just as Stella listens in on the conversations around her not out of nosiness but longing. She is adjacent to the world now, out of sync. These are stories she's listening to, nothing more.

She is a sleepwalker, and the library is filled with lovely dreams; that they are not her own makes them safer by far.

Like her, Tom loves stories. He could read in privacy; therefore, he sits here to be among people, even if he doesn't want to interact with them.

His inclinations notwithstanding, though, it seems he is about to find interaction unavoidable.

While Stella mills about nearby, listening to a table of women reminiscing about a favorite sitcom, a tall, dark-haired man walks into her library and makes a beeline for Tom.

Following an instinct that this may be a better show than the one the women are discussing, Stella surreptitiously makes her way through the stacks.

The stranger's back is to Stella, conveniently blocking her from Tom's view through the shelves as she moves into range, catching the newcomer's voice midsentence, "—see her the other day.

Sounds like she's healing up all right. Thought you'd wanna know, seeing as you're probably the reason she's alive."

"Yes. Thank you for the update," Tom says crisply, but the terseness of the reply is undercut by the sound of his breath just before he speaks—the smallest sigh of relief.

"You know," the stranger continues in a conspiratorial tone, "I've been with my share of women. More than my share, actually. Nearly every woman in the corps. I'm not trying to brag, just sayin'."

An echo in Stella's memory: *human shields... let them eat, drink, and be merry.* It hardly matters that this voice is not her own; she bears the weight of it. The anchor's rusty chain is lodged in her heart and drags heavily with the tides.

"But Nina... she's been kind of elusive. Hard to get. Not like a tease or anything, more like a shy, blushing virgin. And I *love* to make her blush. Get under her skin. Turn her on and watch her struggle with it. I bet she's got a wild side."

Stella creeps along the row for a new angle, curious to see Tom's reaction. Perhaps that will tell her how to feel as well. There's something so strange going on here, something almost taunting in the lewd, gauche speech.

Tom's face is impassive, but the tension around his mouth speaks of impatience or irritation. Is he annoyed by the uncivilized behavior? Does he just want to be left alone? Stella risks moving a little faster to find a new position that will give her a look at the stranger. Maybe his face will be easier to read.

Oh, my. Easier to read remains to be seen, but he's certainly easy on the eyes. Not that Tom isn't good-looking... but *a hawk and a peacock are both birds,* she thinks, and pinches herself for objectifying them.

Allowing herself to stare at the too-handsome man, she sees a kind of searchlight intensity in him. He seems to be studying Tom. He reminds her of a poker player, supremely confident of his hand.

"She was fucking someone for a while, I'm pretty sure. But a month's a long time to cool off. I figure she comes outta quarantine a free agent. No way she's lying there pining over some guy, right?" His eyebrows cock, making Stella even more confident of her read on the situation: He is priming Tom for some kind of reaction. "She almost died! She'll be looking to live life to the fullest. I'm gonna take another run at her." He purses his lips and rubs his hands in a parody of sin. Another hard stare, waiting for Tom to fold whatever hand this man clearly believes he's holding. In response to Tom's stubborn silence, he goes on with lascivious glee, "A month in a box, getting lonely and horny... And I helped you save her! Might as well collect my reward—"

"She's mine, Demetri!"

The words burst out in a hushed snarl. From her vantage point, she can't see the rage in Tom's face, but there's no mistaking the rigid muscular set of his arms and shoulders.

In the quiet moment after Tom's outburst, Stella barely allows herself to breathe, afraid the slightest motion will give her away. Eyes wide, she watches the handsome man—*Demetri*—as his face begins to tremble. He doesn't seem frightened, certainly, or chastened, as one might expect... The set of his lips, the twitch in his cheeks—is he laughing?

Just then, he loses the struggle and stops trying to conceal his amusement. A boyish laugh rings out in the hollow atmosphere of the high-ceilinged room, and Stella feels something like a dusty, out-of-tune guitar string twanging in her chest.

"You knew," Tom quietly observes.

Demetri nods cheerfully, his eyes gleaming, his lanky frame quaking with mirth.

"So just now, you were—"

"Fucking with you?" Demetri supplies. "Oh, yeah."

Tom takes a measured breath and glances from side to side. "You risk drawing attention. Take a walk with me."

To Stella's disappointment, they both stand. *Show's over,* she thinks.

But as they walk away, Demetri looks over his shoulder, makes eye contact with her, and winks.

Chapter Two

The Supplicant and the Sleepwalker

Stella

Walking back to the mansion that night in the crisp winter air, Stella watches her breath form loose white plumes. Another month and those plumes will be firmer, tighter. She remembers the progression of the wintry phenomena. More than a year has passed for her in this place. More than a year since the world ended, starting with her own.

If asked how deeply and for how long she might mourn her fiancé, Stella would profess shock at the very question. She would declare her undying love and devotion and swear that life was empty without him.

She had always been very good at giving the right answer.

And yet, when the news of his sudden, violent demise reached her in the frigid early spring, there had been no need to feign a reaction. She fell to her knees. She wailed as if her own life had ended. Again. And yes, she wept—wept until she was gasping for air, near hyperventilating.

Her world just kept ending, didn't it? The shattered illusion of her happy, loving family. The loss of her mother. At least those had not been her fault... But then came Greg, and cuts that were un-deniably self-inflicted: the abandoned achievements and discarded dreams. The fairy tale she should have known better than to believe in. Felt in retrospect that she *had* known better and had chosen to ignore her instincts. She blames herself for all of it. For the sacrifice of her former self: the self she'd learned to adjust where possible, to subsume where necessary.

When Greg was suddenly gone, what was left? She'd replaced so much of herself with him, she was Theseus' ship, now also lacking a captain.

And now she's a pathetic, lonely shell of a woman who spies on people. It's all fine and well to say she innocently observes their lives like stories... until you get caught. The shame is somehow both in-vigorating and mortifying—complementary feelings which ought perhaps to cancel each other out, but her heart races, and her face burns against the bracing chill in the air.

As much as she might not prefer to dwell on this embarrassment, his wink requires interpretation. Was he inviting her into the joke? No. That seems unlikely, their being complete strangers. Letting her know he was aware of her presence? That could imply some degree of threat if she were to speak of this, but he didn't seem particularly intimidating. Taunting her? The mortification rolls over her again—did he think she was mesmerized by his good looks? And in truth, wasn't she, a bit? The admission halts her forward motion.

Damn her curiosity! Damn her loneliness. In the lower left quadrant of her vision, the diamond on her hand throws little flares of light, its natural twinkle enhanced by the tears suddenly swimming in her eyes.

She's mine, Demetri. The passionate declaration of a man in love. She'd never seen that kind of fire in Greg; he had an icy ferocity, certainly, but it had been directed *at* her, never *for* her. The love she'd observed between her parents so long ago had been cordial and companionable and nowhere near strong enough in the end.

But there is love in the world. Love is felt and fought for, even in this place. Her own empty fate aside, this thought soothes her nerves a bit.

Seeing who has walked into her library for the second night in a row, Stella braces herself. Whatever the meaning of that wink, she is about to find out.

Demetri appears at the end of the row and strides toward her with purpose, but she notes something different in his bearing. Last night, he was confident and amused, looking to play a game. This time, he seems to hold no cards.

As he comes near, a megawatt smile transforms his face from handsome to *unreasonably* handsome.

"Hey," he says intimately, as if this is a date.

Stella's expression turns utterly blank, as if her facial muscles have received a command to relax all at once. It's been some time since anyone tried to charm her, and deep down, she's been afraid to discover that she truly learned nothing. But perhaps her experience has inoculated her. Far from blushing at his casual sensuality and affected interest, she finds herself disgusted by the bullshit attempt to influence her.

Good for me, she thinks sadly, then turns and walks away, dismissing him without a word.

"Hey!" He sounds surprised and a bit desperate as he follows her.

She turns to look at him again, impassive, unreadable, yet privately intrigued. After all, nothing he said last night was damaging to *him*, and yet he's plainly distressed, which implies he is here acting on someone else's interests. Not that she cares, exactly, but it is a story.

"Listen, the other night... I was being an asshole, okay? It's like, this guy, he's so uptight, and I thought it would be funny..."

He nervously thumps his palm with his fingertips. The gesture recalls her self-inflicted pinch, and she wants to tell him to stop talking, but her voice isn't responding to the impulse. He clearly worries she'll repeat what she heard, but a sleepwalker would never think to trouble the waking world with the inconsequential substance of their dreams.

"I didn't know it would go down like that. I thought he was just buttoned up, but maybe he's more high-strung?" He pauses, searching her eyes for some hint she might be softening toward him, then plows ahead miserably, "See, I saw you and I should've stopped talking. But I got carried away, I don't know. I was having fun or something, it was stupid and careless, and it was like the middle of the night before it hit me about the ramifications, and how I could've hurt my friend—"

"He's your friend?" Stella maintains her neutral gaze, affecting disinterest even as the question betrays the curiosity that loosened her clenched vocal cords.

Demetri pauses, frowning at the question as if it requires further examination. "I don't—maybe. Regardless, I wouldn't wanna fuck up his life, and it's not just about him. I don't know how much you know about our rules and—being a civilian, you might not know—"

Stella nods, and he falls quiet. Of course, she knows. Maybe everyone does, but she *knows*. It's a stupid, incomprehensible rule, and an innocent person might assume that meant it was above their paygrade and therefore worth enforcing, just in case.

"I only care about the library. I would never threaten it by betraying its secrets."

She turns to walk away again, assuming his concerns have been sufficiently addressed. He surprises her by trotting after her a second time.

"Thanks. I also wanted to say, um... I was *really* full of shit the other night, you know? I wouldn't want you to—I mean, I wouldn't want *anyone* to think I'm *that guy*." Lightly punching the palm of his hand, inclining his head in a vaguely submissive posture, he seems genuinely dismayed at the idea that his over-the-top lothario act could be taken at face value.

Stella feels a kind of reflexive twinge just below her cheekbones, the smallest indication of a smile threatening to form.

"It was clear that you employed hyperbole to some extent. But the most convincing lies are rooted in truth."

He squirms, clearly at a loss dealing with someone so resistant to his charms. It's somehow satisfying, but she isn't a cruel person, so she throws him a bone.

"They make a cute couple."

His eyes widen. "You've seen them together?"

"No," she says simply, letting the moment drag out, letting him wonder if she will say anything further; she really isn't cruel, but she is enjoying herself. For all this is a game, it's also the most genuine interaction she's had in recent memory.

She confides at last, "You said her name. I knew who you meant. And it made sense to me, the two of them. They like the same books."

Demetri's face warms then in a slow smile, not ostentatiously wide or deliberate. He clearly considers at least one, if not both, of these people his friends and is happy for them. Stella meant what she said about lies being rooted in truth. She has no reason to care which elements of his ruse were the seeds of fiction and which the firm, fertile ground. If he isn't quite the shallow cad he portrayed, that shouldn't matter to her.

"That's nice," he agrees quietly. "I'm Demetri, by the way."

"I know. 'She's mine, Demetri,'" she reminds him dryly.

"Right," he acknowledges with a sheepish skyward glance. "And you are?"

"Stella." She still hasn't so much as smiled at him throughout their conversation, but all the tension has mysteriously evaporated from her shoulders.

He gives a little nod of gratitude and goodbye, then disappears from the library into the night.

She'd never seen him before last night, which means he isn't a reader. Now that their business has concluded, it's safe to assume she'll never see him again. Her throat feels strangely thick. The sensation passes almost as soon as she acknowledges it, to her relief. She settles back into her routine, watching the world from within a dreamy haze. Perhaps by the time the Genneros decide what to do with her, she will have simply disappeared.

When Demetri comes in to see Tom again a few nights later, Stella feels a quixotic joy. She holds it in her hands to examine it. Why should his return mean anything at all? She's happy for him, she decides. He was uncertain if he and Tom were friends, and this seems to indicate that they are. She's happy for Tom, too. The loneliness of the so-called helmet heads speaks to her, and to see one develop a friendship—even fall in love as Tom apparently has—is a small glow of hope in this dark place.

Yet she finds herself frustrated and annoyed. It's like staring at a bowl of her favorite potato chips and being unable to grab a greasy, crunchy handful. Demetri knows about her shameful little habit. She will simply have to remain in plain view while he's here, no way around it.

She putters around the desk, tries to read a book, and does her best to avoid watching the conversation she desperately wants to hear.

And then, insult to injury, Demetri walks right up to taunt her about it after Tom has gone. Walks? No. Saunters. The insufferable handsome jerk. He leans on the counter at her, even licks his lips before speaking.

"Sorry you had to miss the show. You'da loved it. Very salacious. We coulda had a podcast back in the day, him and me."

It's on the tip of her tongue to tell him he is being unfair, but she can't lie to herself that way, and she doesn't care to lie to him. It's entirely fair. She deserves it. She deserves worse.

Perhaps the fall of her face makes him want to take it back; his insouciant smile drops away.

"I'm sorry, Stella. That was uncalled for. I came over here to say hi or whatever, I wasn't planning to be an asshole, but sometimes it just pops out. Guess I should leave the funny stuff to the comedians."

He was trying to be funny? Not cruel? The lump mercifully clears from her throat.

"Think there are any left?" she ventures cautiously.

He blinks and their eyes meet as they smile at each other in relief.

"That's what I was hoping to see. And I'm taking partial credit for it," he adds meaningfully, raising an index finger like he's proving some kind of point.

"What?" she asks, confused.

"You. Smiling."

A bright sheen of tears gathers in her eyes. He quickly retreats, giving a little wave by way of a farewell. Is it an act of kindness not staying to gawk at her emotional display, or did he flee in discomfort? Will he come back again? Why does it matter?

When, for the first time, Tom and Demetri show up at the library together, Stella notes the development, happy for them both. Definitely friends, then. They find a table and huddle in conversation as she makes an effort to avoid paying attention. The frustration finds her picking miserably at a dry edge of cuticle, and she frowns at the newly exposed underlayer of skin. She deserves this little bit of pain, no doubt. It is only fair that she suffer in flesh as well as in feeling over her thwarted desire to spy on perfectly nice people, hardworking soldiers who help keep her safe, caring friends who protect each other's—

Allowing herself the occasional glance, she is startled by the sight and forgets to look away as quickly as she intended. Whirling around to face the back of the room, her face burns in dismay at the private public moment she just witnessed. Demetri... crying? No. That must have been laughter. The same as the first night, no doubt, when his shoulders shook and his face trembled—that had been his attempt to suppress a burst of laughter. Surely this was the same.

She carefully turns, finding a perpendicular angle to where they sit, then letting her gaze drift along the line of her shoulder—

Crying. His face is splotchy, his expression screwed up tight with the effort of control. Is he mourning someone from before? Overcome with fear or regret or loss? It's so easy to be swallowed up by the trauma of their inconceivable reality. Her chest aches, and her hands restlessly flutter across the books in front of her.

She wants to comfort him. Cross the room and lean beside him, pull his head to rest against her, let him find safety in the gentle cushion of her breasts. He would wrap his arms around her hips as he wept into the gray fabric of her dress. She would stroke his dark hair and hold him to her as his tears soaked through and left her skin wet underneath.

But that isn't where she suddenly feels wet. Her eyes wide in horror, she shuts down this absurd fantasy with a vicious pinch. Is she that pathetic and lonely that a handsome man in pain opens a secret well of lust inside her? She should be ashamed. She *is* ashamed.

It's easier to resist looking over again, and under the circumstances, she doesn't expect him to stick around and tease her again. Still, she finds herself saddened to realize he slipped out without so much as a smile or a wave.

Tom walks in with Demetri in tow once again, and Stella smiles to herself, thinking that while they bear no particular resemblance to one another, they somehow look like brothers. Tom is older, more serious; Demetri is younger, eager, sticking close and paying attention. Tom has the brisk stride of a man who knows where he needs to be and will waste no time getting there, while Demetri's casual, aimless lope speaks of energy to spare—together, they remind her of an engineer walking a youthful golden retriever.

Later, the library has emptied out but for the three of them, the two men conversing quietly at a table near the center of the room. Stella fusses with things behind the desk and pretends inattention as usual.

In her vague, peripheral attempt at not staring, Stella sees Tom stand to go, apparently leaving Demetri behind. It's a relief to drop the pretense of distraction when his purposeful stride carries him out of the library.

Stella turns back toward their table and starts at the sight of Demetri right beside the desk. Had she thought of him as a golden retriever? The man could move like a cat when he wanted to.

He smiles, plainly amused by her reaction but in a guileless and benevolent way. "Sorry. I didn't mean to startle you."

"That's okay," she says, neither smiling back nor frowning. Something about him leaves her uncertain how to respond.

"I think they're gonna get married," he says. The non sequitur sends her mind searching for context, even as the warmth of his smile distracts her from the task.

Touched, Stella suddenly intuits his purpose in coming to talk to her: He's happy for his brother, and he wanted to tell someone. Owing to the odd circumstances of their acquaintance, she counts in his mind as someone who knows—and respects—the secret. It's almost like having a friend. It's been so long since she's felt like a person.

"Good for them." Marriage is a complicated topic in the Stronghold, but that's very much beside the point, not that she could talk about it anyway.

"Yeah," he says, seeming not to notice Stella's reticence. "They really love each other. It's like, the world fell to pieces, and we're all just getting through the days and nights. Sometimes, it's kinda like, what's-it-all-for, you know? But life can still surprise you."

She blinks. *He's* surprising. There's something ingenuous about him that pries at the heavy lid tamping down her emotions.

"That's sweet," she says vaguely, unwelcome emotions competing to move her. "It's nice that you come in to visit your friend—"

"And you," he teases, and a neon light seems to flash at the outer edges of her vision.

"—but why didn't you ever stop by before?"

"Why are *you* always here?" he counters playfully.

A bittersweet, inward smile settles onto her face. "I'm happy here. And I don't really have anywhere else to be."

With a comical expression of vicarious pain, he slaps a hand over his heart and exclaims, "Ouch! Don't let your husband hear you say that."

At her blank look, he gestures toward her left hand.

"Oh. He's not... We were engaged, but—"

Demetri looks stricken, recoiling with guilt. "Shit. I'm sorry, I should've—"

"No," she rushes to assure him, "it's okay. I'm not..."

...in mourning? ...sad? ...sorry he's gone?

"The truth is, I live with his parents. I'm not sure how they would react if I stopped wearing the ring. But it's not a... fresh wound or anything. Please don't feel bad."

"Thanks for trying to make me feel better when I was just totally shitty," he mutters, chastened but grateful.

A real smile confuses the muscles of her cheeks. "You weren't."

"I was though. I should've thought about it. It's not like I don't know what our world is. We've all lost so much, and I—"

Reaching for his hand where it leans, just to reassure him, she says, "Stop. You have nothing to apologize for. I promise."

There's a long, quiet moment, and the air feels cleaner somehow. Like the tiny spark of static electricity of fingers barely brushing is a sudden summer storm that leaves the world fresher for a time in its wake.

That was the first I've spoken of Greg outside his family home.

The first time I've acknowledged to anyone that I'm okay.

Chapter Three

The Library Ghost

Demetri

23 days ago

I think I fucked up pretty bad tonight. Looking back, I'm not even sure what I thought was gonna happen. I just saw Tom heading out of the barracks, and after talking to Monica the night before, I kinda just felt like giving the guy a hard time. I don't really know why. He's always been standoffish, which, whatever. Not my problem. But something about seeing him go fucking nuts over Nina out there... it was cool. Badass and intense, and cool.

After that, we were all just holding our breath a little because she's been in quarantine, and you never fucking know... but then Monica reassured us Nina was gonna be okay. We were relieved, obviously, which maybe made me a little reckless. It was like, I wanted to fill him in 'cause I knew he'd wanna know... but I also wanted to needle him. Just a little bit. Fuck if I know why. It sounded like fun for some reason. He's so damn uptight, and now that I know there's a person in there, I kinda wanted to poke him and see what happened. Fucking stupid.

My stomach's all messed up like when I fucked something up at school and knew I'd have to tell my parents about it. I don't wanna have to tell Tom this thing. He opened up to me—I mean, kind of—more than he ever did before. I don't want that to have been a mistake. I feel like shit. If I can fix it in time, no harm done maybe. No one needs to know.

The stupid fucking wink... I was just having fun. I wasn't thinking.

The consequences hit me after, leaning against the common room wall, looking around and deciding if I felt like getting laid and who with. That's when it came back to me—that shy face peeking out from behind the bookshelf, all wide-eyed, drinking it in, enjoying the show from what it looked like. And hell, it was over-the-top as fuck, and I was having fun putting it on. So I threw her a wink at the end, just to let her know I knew she was there, like hey, hope it was good for you. *Stupid*.

But she wasn't just staring, she was *listening*. I was talking a world of shit—that part's no big deal, of course, who cares—but it led to Tom spilling a secret that he and Nina have been trying to keep for months. Hell, not just trying but succeeding, considering it was a shock to me and Davy and even Monica, who knows her best.

Their secret could be out, and it would be all my fault. I saw someone sneaking around, clocked that it was a woman, and went full fucking showboat instead of using my goddamn head.

It's way too late to do anything about it tonight. I came back to the barracks and settled in, all set to have some fun until my brain caught up with my ego. I don't deserve to relax and enjoy my night. If she's a gossip, it's already too late. If she's hardcore about the rules, same thing.

On the other hand, does she *know* the rules? They're for us, not her kind. So maybe not? No, I couldn't be that lucky... I have to assume most, if not all, people know the stuff they should report outsiders like me for doing.

Maybe I can get her to blow it off, though. I'm pretty good at talking my way out of stuff, especially with women. If she hasn't said anything yet, I bet I can convince her not to.

That thought is finally enough to get me closer to sleep, which I need. Tomorrow's shift is gonna be brutal. I already have to work harder at focusing than the average Helmet, and now I'm all preoccupied with this bullshit.

I really fucked up. I don't want to be the reason Nina's life fucking implodes. Fuck.

22 *days ago*

I think I got lucky tonight. Not in my normal way; I was too worn out to bother, but I'll catch up on sleep tonight at least. I'm not really sure what's up with the librarian—*Stella*—but she wants no part of our drama, and that's good enough for me. I can't blame her. If I could sidestep the drama, I sure as fuck would.

Pretty sure I almost got a smile out of her toward the end there. Not sure why I care, since all that really matters is her silence. But it feels like a challenge or something. She was completely unmoved by my usual bullshit—the charm offensive, it's been called. I usually get by pretty easy—hey, at least I'm humble enough to know why and not just think I'm a fucking god or something, but Stella didn't fall for it. Maybe I should've known better than to try laying on the charm with a married woman, but I didn't spot the ring until I was right there in front of her, and it's hard to change direction mid-stride. She shut me down hard, though.

I can't remember the last time before tonight that I smiled at a woman and didn't get a smile—or at least a blush, in return. Nina was a blusher before she started getting laid regularly, which was the first clue for me. When she started smiling back instead of looking like she was fighting some kind of sexy devil sitting on her shoulder, I thought, *Good for her*. And I've done what I could to keep her secret safe.

Stella though...

Sadness is all over her. It's like she's not really a librarian, more like the ghost of one who refuses to move on. She's light on her feet—maybe to support her little eavesdropping habit, yeah, I'm on to you there, Stella—you didn't just happen to be in the right place at the right time to listen in on *my* conversation. That's a coincidence, and I'm skeptical as fuck about those. You snuck up, didn't you? On those light little feet, in that long, dark, flowing dress—so modest and classy... Except the way you leave the top buttons undone—there's a sexy devil on your shoulder, too, isn't there? Maybe you're being taken for granted. Maybe the rich pricks who built this place don't know how to treat a woman. I'd believe you're not getting what you deserve—that would explain a lot. Does he appreciate you? Does he even notice the way you let those soft breasts spill out just a little bit—not enough that anyone's gonna call you on it, just enough so a guy like me can't keep his eyes out of the trap, his mind out of the gutter, drawn in by that soft, warm, perfect tunnel between your breasts where I shove my dick and watch you lick the tip as I thrust—

Fuck. I haven't masturbated in... well, however many months since I've been living in the barracks, I guess. I clean up, blinking away the fantasy that came on so strong, so out of fucking nowhere. I did need to relax. It was a stressful 24 hours, but I can sleep easy. Everyone's gonna be all right.

15 days ago

"Walk with me, will you?" Tom said, and I just fucking did, I don't even know why. He's not my superior fucking officer or something, and we still barely know each other. There's just something about him that's hard to ignore, and it's funny, because that's not something I'd have said a couple of weeks ago. Nobody would've—okay, maybe Nina, but nobody else. His whole persona out there, it's been a big fucking joke for so long. It still would if I hadn't seen him in action that night.

It was dumb luck I was even there—four teams, four Helmets in close proximity like that isn't supposed to happen, but the danger was on the edge of two sectors and so bad both backup squads were deployed. Plus it went on so long winter's early sundown came and went... Everything was completely fucked, more than usual.

People have made fun of him plenty, rolling their eyes about "Alpha." I hear so much secondhand shit-talk about helmet heads, I let it go. And yeah, he seemed like kind of an uptight dick, but he was tough and capable, so who cares? But that night, he dropped his above-it-all act. He was, in Monica's words, "scared angry," like the thought of something happening to Nina made him rage against reality.

Not only wasn't he my commanding officer in any fucking sense, he was asking us to do something Command said *not* to, but I still went. I would've said it was because my friend was in danger, and that's true, but I can't swear I would've done what I did *just* for Nina, not with Command in my ear saying otherwise. But he would—he *did*, and I respect that. I actually really dig that.

And so tonight, when he wandered into the common room and made eye contact with me, I was more than intrigued, not gonna lie. He sought me out, and I wanted to know why. He made a little *this way* gesture, just standing still and jerking his head toward the door, and then he turned and walked out. I handed my pool cue to Marcus and told him to play the rest of my game, then followed.

He asked me to walk with him, and he hasn't said another goddamn word since. But every time I look at him, he still seems to know where he's going, so I just keep following. What the fuck is it about this guy that makes me wanna follow him?

Finally, he stops, and it's pretty clear what he was looking for, now that I see it. He's brought us to a corridor where there are no doors or other hallways in listening distance. Pretty smart. The kind of thing a smart guy thinks about before having sensitive conversations.

"I've been thinking about our chat. In the library," he says, and I tense up inside. Has he found out about sneaky Stella, the sexy library ghost? Why do I feel like a bratty kid brother who broke a vase? The sudden ache causes me to miss something—or mishear it, because there's no way he just said, "You told me you'd never fucked my Nina, but you wanted to."

"Listen, man, I don't—I would never—"

Tom raises his hand to say *Stop,* and he looks impatient or something.

"You seem to have inferred territorial intent, and nothing could be further from the truth. I'm not offended, Demetri. Or threatened, certainly."

I want to be offended by the insinuation I'm no threat, but it doesn't feel like he means it that way. It seems like he's just secure. That's cool.

"I am curious, though. Do you want to fuck her?"

My mouth opens, but I have no idea what words it thought it was about to spill, because I have no fucking clue how to handle the weirdest fucking conversation of all time.

He cringes, and I get the sense he's annoyed with *himself*, which somehow makes me less uncomfortable.

"My people skills were a bit lacking even before the apocalypse, I'm afraid, and I've had very little practice of late with anyone but Nina. I apologize."

Relieved, I say, "No worries, man. It's all good. Whatever's going on between you two, I totally respect that. I was talking a world of shit that night, and you know I didn't—"

"But you did," he says, confident and matter-of-fact as he cuts me off.

"Okay, right, lies rooted in truth and all that," I say, thinking of our cute, mousy eavesdropper. "But still, I would never—"

"For the last time, Demetri, I am in no way concerned about your intentions toward my Nina."

My Nina. That's twice he's called her that. It's cute. I can't help smiling.

"Good," he says, and I feel like he's misinterpreted my reaction, not that I have any idea what he thinks I should be reacting to.

"What the hell are we talking about, man?"

"Your reward, of course," he smiles.

Oh, shit. He's mad at me? No. Fucking with me? Maybe, but why? I feel my forehead wrinkling up in response to how this conversation has wrinkled my brain.

"Demetri, relax. I can see I've put you at odds. It's been some time since I interacted with anyone who didn't... well, do as I say. I suppose I'm a bit spoiled."

Warmth and affection spread across his face as he speaks, and I actually do relax. I relax enough to process what he said, and I blurt, "She does whatever you say?"

It's like we're having two different conversations, because I know my voice came out confused, a little weirded out by the whole idea, but he's not offended or defensive, and he doesn't try to explain anything.

"Very nearly," he says, like he's just remembered the times she didn't. "But I don't give her orders she doesn't want to follow."

He seems like he's somewhere else for a moment, thinking about Nina, I guess. Then he makes eye contact again, back to business, and he says, "So. I'll leave you to think this over. If you'd care to claim your reward, come find me at the library tomorrow evening. We'll discuss details."

I open my mouth, only to again realize I'm out of words to respond with. He turns and walks away. I lean back against the hallway wall and wonder what the hell I'm getting myself into if I show up at the library tomorrow... Aw, who am I kidding? *When* I show up at the library tomorrow. That was the weirdest interaction of my entire life, and what'm I supposed to do, just leave it there? Just go back and play some more pool and forget about it?

After a few minutes, I decide to head back to my quarters for the night instead of rejoining the crowd. I'm all in my head now, in no mood for company.

14 days ago

I look around the room for Stella when I arrive. The cleavage-y eavesdropper and I make eye contact, and she quickly drops her gaze. I was right; she won't be snooping on the one person who knows she's a snoop. So I guess the library just became safe for me, at least, which makes it safe for him as long as I'm the one he's talking to... *Dammit.* I could tell him about her... but I'd have to tell him how I know, and I really don't want to. I took care of it, the secret's safe, so what does it matter? Still, if we're friends, how can I not tell him... Are we friends?

Let's find out. I sit down across from him, and he smiles like he never doubted I'd show.

"Here's what I was thinking, Demetri: My girl's been away. I'd like to welcome her home properly. With a party. Of sorts. She'll be the guest of honor, receiving twice as much attention as she's used to."

I adjust myself slightly in my chair. He's really talking about letting me fuck his girlfriend, and it feels very, very wrong to find that hot, especially since it's Nina we're talking about.

"One problem," I point out, "she's not into me. I mean, I told you that before."

He looks amused. "You told me you enjoyed watching her get all hot and bothered; you were quite pleased with yourself."

Fuckin A, I really was talking a mile of shit that night. "Okay, yes, I said... that. And yeah, I mean, I could tell she needed to get laid, but not with me, apparently. So... get it?"

"Yes, and I understand your concern completely. But it's misplaced. Her lack of interest had far more to do with herself than you."

"Okay, but—"

"Furthermore, I assure you, when she wantonly invites you inside her under the circumstances we're discussing, that too will be entirely about her. And me, of course."

Is this guy for real?

"That's... not as comforting as you probably wanted it to sound," I tell him.

"All right," he agrees, and his ease in discussing this whole scenario is making me feel like the crazy one. "Think of it this way:

Nina will not be bothered by the identity of the additional man in the room. All that will matter to her is that I selected you."

I grit my teeth and try again to get the point across. "Dude, you're not... she's not gonna be into it."

"You don't know her like I do." His serene confidence shuts me up. "I'll give her time to anticipate the experience. She'll have decided how she feels about it in theory hours before she enjoys the temptation of it in fact."

The wrongness of this is still clear to my brain, so why is my dick not getting the message?

"Man, who are you, anyway? We barely—you don't hang out at all, and now you're inviting me to—hell, how did you and Nina even happen? Did you meet here?"

He cocks an eyebrow. "No. Why?"

They read the same books. But that's not something I would know, and I stammer, "I don't know, it's not like you hang out in the rec. When'd you even talk to her?"

Another of those big grins as he says fondly, "I didn't."

"What do you mean?"

He looks me straight in the eyes, smiling. I feel like he's about to confide that he knows the secrets of the universe and everything's gonna work out in the end. "She came to me. We'd never spoken. She's never seen me out of gear. She just chose me. Gave herself to me. And for months, she's been mine. Every night... every night she was mine." As he talks, he looks away, turns in on himself again before eventually trailing off.

Suddenly I get it, and I feel like an idiot. He's in pain, of course that's it, and I feel stupid I didn't figure it out sooner. This isn't real. This whole crazy "party" he's trying to sell me on, it's bullshit. He's lonely, missing his girl, and the first person who even kinda tried to be his friend was a fucking jackass about it, started off talking about how much I wanted to fuck her... I feel bad for arguing with him. If he's worried about her still—and why wouldn't he be?—I bet planning this insane, not-gonna-happen menage a trois for after she's safely home is just a coping mechanism or something.

"She still is. She'll be home soon." I make sure my voice sounds absolutely confident about this, like a foregone conclusion, which it's obviously not, but statistically speaking, if you're past the halfway point, you're gonna survive quarantine.

"Thank you, Demetri. And you'll help me welcome her home, then?"

"Sure, man, absolutely," I say, certain I will never be called on to fulfill that promise.

And then he starts walking me through his plans for the various stages of the event and contingencies for which things she might react to which ways... by the time he's done talking, my confidence in the whole *not-gonna-happen* theory has dropped to fifty-fifty.

"Have you done this kind of thing before?" I ask, a little amazed at how much thought he's clearly put into it.

"Never."

"Then how do you—"

"I don't, I suppose. I could never have done something of this nature with anyone else. But Nina... she tends to want what I offer her. This time, that will include you." He stands. "I'm going to head back."

Behind him, I catch another glimpse of our librarian friend in the distance, trapped behind her desk, no doubt wishing she could have gotten in on our juicy fucking discussion tonight. Without really knowing why, I answer his implied invitation to walk back together with, "I'm gonna hang out here a little longer."

This is the most pointless way I've ever chosen to waste my time. I could be heading back to the barracks right now. I could see who's up for helping me fuck off some of this nervous energy. Instead I'm apparently in the mood to annoy the married librarian.

As I approach, I feel a smirk coming on. Yeah, for some reason I want to bug her a little. Maybe it's the smile I almost got out of her that one time. I wanna see her break. Smile at me for real.

I lean on the counter at her and aim for sly.

"Sorry you had to miss the show. You'da loved it. Very salacious. We coulda had a podcast back in the day, him and me."

Why the fuck am I teasing her about this? My mouth is three steps ahead of my brain, and my mouth's got a running start. That's what Lenora would have said. My grin fades, and now I bet we look about the same level of morose. *Shit.*

"I'm sorry, Stella. That was uncalled for. I came over here to say hi or whatever, I wasn't planning to be an asshole, but sometimes it just pops out. I should leave the funny stuff to the comedians."

"Think there are any left?" she asks, and by the time I realize she's made a joke, we're both smiling.

"That's what I was hoping to see. And I'm taking partial credit for it," I inform her, feeling lighter.

She blinks in confusion and asks, "What?"

"You. Smiling." I give her a little wave and turn to go, suddenly in a hurry. Something about her eyes has me feeling this crazy impulse to offer to walk her home. As if we don't live in the safest place on the planet. And I'm sure her husband would appreciate it too, I remind myself.

Walking back in the cool winter air, I think I must have misheard Tom again tonight, because it sounded like he said, "She's never seen me out of gear," but that can't be right. He must've said *She'd,* like she hadn't seen him before making her first move. Fucking impressive though. Got a girl in bed without relying on his looks. That sexy little devil on her shoulder must've been his wingman.

This guy's fucking wild, and I dig it. He's kinda flailing about Nina being out of reach, and I get that. Went through some shit when Rachel first went off to college before we gave up on long distance. So sure, man. I'll sign on to this insanity. Why the fuck not? Nothing's gonna come of it.

And at least I finally saw some life in our library ghost. Too bad about the neckline tonight—was I really just trying to stare down a married woman's dress? After spending an hour humoring my new buddy about how I'm totally gonna fuck his girl in a coupla weeks... There is really no part of my life now that would have sounded real to me a year and a half ago.

9 days ago

Holy shit.

Ho. Lee. Shit.

I'd've sworn on a stack of whatever that this thing wasn't happening.

This morning, Tom shows up in the mess grinning like a madman, and he tells me to be there tonight. I'm like, yeah, okay, but I know there's no way it's actually happening. I'll show up, he'll make whatever pitch, she'll be amused at best—more likely offended or disgusted, and I'll slink away hoping he was legit about her knowing it was all his idea so she wouldn't wind up hating me.

But he pressed her up against me, and my dick reacted because of course, and she just pushed her ass back harder like she was suddenly craving it. I looked that crazy motherfucker in the eyes, and he just smirked like *toldja*.

From there he told us both what to do and we did it. I don't think it ever occurred to her to doubt him—I know I never doubted him again. It was an insane experience. I was like, on the periphery of their relationship, and it blew my fucking mind. I wasn't a full partner in it or anything, but not like an accessory either—it was more like being a guest star. Like, you get your moments, you get to shine, we appreciate you, but you're not the show. You're not why people keep coming back.

I never saw anything like that before. The way Nina trusts him. He wasn't bullshitting about the blindfold—she didn't even know who I was at first. She didn't need to know. He said she was safe, and she never doubted it. He said he wanted to make her happy, and she believed he would.

I've been in this place a pretty long time. I've fucked nearly every woman who's come through, most of them as often as I pleased.

I've never been kissed like Nina was kissing Tom tonight. I've never been so into a woman that I could tell someone else how to touch her just right the way Tom did.

I don't know if I could ever be the guy who *wanted* to tell someone how to do that, truthfully, but I do want to be the guy who *knows* it. Who cares that hard and catalogues every fucking detail and remembers every moment. I want to feel totally secure with someone, like they do. I didn't know I was missing anything until I saw it up close like that.

Fuck. I miss being in love.

I told Tom I needed to talk, so here we are again. The "safe" place... and that's just one more thing eating me tonight.

"I never saw anything like that," I tell him, and the words aren't right, aren't enough, but there's a lid I'm holding down. Enough could be too much.

He raises his eyebrows. "I was under the impression you were quite the resident Don Juan," he says, so I clarify.

"Not the sex, I mean... the way she trusts you. And the way you know her. It was... intense." The skin of my face is hot and tight. I feel like I'm confessing my sins.

And then suddenly, I am. I tell him about Stella. That I didn't stop talking the moment I noticed her listening, but she promised not to say anything, and if he's gonna talk to anyone else in here, he should keep an eye out—she only steers clear of me 'cause I know. And these big fat idiotic tears come spilling out of me, because it's hitting me all over again how I didn't do a goddamn thing right. I wasn't taking things seriously. And I love this guy—this crazy motherfucker—and I'm sorry.

I thought I'd fixed it so I wouldn't have to deal with the consequences—not just the consequences that would've hit my friends but the idea of having to tell them what I did, having to risk them not trusting me anymore, but I don't know if I knew what trust really felt like before. It all just hit me after last night. And not just the shame, not just the need to come clean. Something else.

I've barely spent a night alone in all the months I've been in here, so how the fuck did it just sneak up on me that I'm lonely?

"Thank you, Demetri," he says finally. "It's good of you to apologize. Fortunately, there's been no harm done that I can see. If she had any intention of turning us in, she would have done it already."

I wipe my face and sniffle, feeling like a loser kid brother again. Tom seems strangely chill. Lenora would've made me grovel. Since my eyes are already leaking, they spill over a little more at the thought of her. I almost always manage to avoid this kind of thing; it feels pointless. You start letting the pain get you, and where does it stop?

"You're lonely?" he asks, looking thoughtful. Sympathizing with me, maybe, because he must've been pretty goddamn lonely before he met Nina. And I was decent enough to him, far as it goes, but that mostly meant I was less of an asshole than the average non-Helmet.

"Yeah, man. I guess I am. I didn't even know what I was feeling, which means I was doing a really good job staying too busy to feel much of anything. Now... I don't even know where the fuck to start."

I look up and meet his eyes again. Mine are still kinda blurry; he looks like he's reflected in a puddle. But the puddle-Tom looks like he cares, and that adds a cushion under the weird, bruised feeling I've got.

"I'm hardly the one to advise you on finding what I have, Demetri. I'm a lucky bastard who was smart enough to grab hold of something special, and in truth, I nearly failed that test out of habit. A pernicious thing, inertia. I suppose what I mean to say is: If what you're doing fails to bring you closer to what you want, perhaps it's time to try something different."

The corner of my mouth curls, a twitch of silent laughter. "You're saying I should take a break from getting laid. Stop getting my rocks off with *everyone* and see if I feel something for *someone*."

There's fondness in his devilish smirk. "Who could have foreseen the transformative power of letting you fuck my girl?"

"Yeah... why did you?" I didn't know I was going to ask. Before it happened, the whole thing felt hypothetical, almost a joke. But more than that, deep down, it didn't compute that he could love her and share her. Now I know how much they love each other—I felt it from outside like a poor kid watching a banquet from the wrong side of the glass.

He takes a moment, like he's considering how to answer. Or *whether* to answer... but I don't really think he's gonna leave me hanging.

"I've never attempted an explanation before. It's funny. These escapades come to me in any number of ways. In this case, you inspired it right here when you sought to get under my skin that night. Once I was over the initial annoyance, I was amused by the idea of you wanting what I have—you're not the sort of man who hears 'no' all that often, are you? And your crack about a reward—she wouldn't have offered you that reward, because she's mine. But I could, if I chose. I could bestow her on you if it pleased me. Idle thoughts, you understand; it was a long month without her. But once an idea takes hold... The image was satisfying. Giving her a new way to surrender to me. Watching her accept and enjoy the touch of another man on my word, as if he were an extension of me."

Whoa. He's goddamn hypnotic. No wonder she does whatever he says—no wonder I have, too.

The smirk returns to break the spell. "Then I thought how I'd never fucked a woman while she was being fucked, and I wanted to try it. It was fun, wasn't it?"

I feel the release of tension in my laugh even as I think I'm fucking blushing or something—seriously, what the fuck is that? He's so open and blunt, and it's weirdly comforting.

"Yeah, man. It was a good time." *Life-changing, apparently.* "And you're a fucking madman."

"You're welcome, Demetri."

All the things he's saying with that phrase hit me all over again, and I'm choking back another surge of emotion, forcing it back down to avoid a second public outburst. *Jeez, get a grip.*

"I never had a friend like you before," I tell him.

"No," he agrees. "Nor have I."

Stella's back is turned, and that makes it as good a moment as any to bail. I don't know whether she noticed me all red-faced and weeping like a twerp, but if we get too close, she'll definitely see the evidence, and I just don't want her to know. Not like I think she'd tell anyone, so I don't know why it matters.

We make it outside without running into her, without making eye contact with her at all. And even though it's what I meant to happen, it feels like a letdown.

20 minutes ago

Tom's ranting about Nina, again. Danger, terror, out of his reach, out of his control, etc. It's not the first time I've heard this rant. It's not the fifth. It might not be the tenth.

"Well, I don't know what to tell you. I mean, you're obviously not gonna marry her."

There it is—the indignant look, eyebrows gathered into an angry ripple, eyes narrowed, nostrils flaring. I've successfully tripped him out of his loop.

"What the hell is that supposed to mean?" he demands, gearing up to defend her honor.

"It means you're the smartest guy I know, so if you're sitting here driving us both crazy over how to keep your girlfriend safe, you must've already rejected the obvious solution."

He slumps back, frustrated. "Marriage is a complicated topic for her."

"C'mon, man. Since when does she say no to you?"

He scowls at me as if I'm just willfully missing the point. "She has ideological objections. As do I, of course, as would anyone, but—"

"But you're gonna let her ideology herself to death? Get over it. Put your foot down or talk dirty to her or whatever the fuck you do that makes her go all gooey. She loves you. Do whatever it takes to make her shut up and say yes already."

I'm grouchier than I mean to be about it. He's studying me.

"Going on a week since you've been laid, yes? I'd think you'd bear up a bit better than this. I've half a mind to invite you over again before you piss off someone who isn't so fond of you."

"Oh, fuck off," I tell him, but at least he got me laughing. It's not just sexual frustration that's got me wound so tight, and I'm pretty sure he knows that—he's deadpan as fuck, but I have started picking up his sense of humor. Anyway, I don't wanna talk about my bullshit right now. It'd be spin-my-wheels boring, and I've got less patience for that than he does. I love the guy, but he thinks too much.

When he asks if I want to walk back with him, I again find myself looking beyond him, wondering what Stella's neckline might offer my increasingly necessary spank bank. Why the fuck a married librarian is the featured player in my fantasies instead of any of the women I've actually seen naked, I don't fucking know. Okay, maybe I do, a little. She's softer than they are, that's part of it. And it's not like the women in the corps have a choice about it—we're all out there tromping around for miles every day, there's no body fat left to burn on any of us at this point. But it's not what I like in a woman, if I'm being honest. I like Stella's soft, full breasts—what I've seen of 'em, which is not enough—fuck. I bet she's smooth and just a little bit soft all over. Thighs that cradle and caress you instead of gripping. This isn't like me. I've never been the type to hit on married women or even flirt with them. I saw enough friends with broken homes to know how wrong it is. But fuck it. I'm not flirting, I'm teasing her a little, right? And myself, but whatever. What she doesn't know, yada yada. Maybe she does know… maybe I'm just one of many guys who show up here with their pathetic and obvious hot librarian fantasies.

I reach the counter just as she turns to look. She jumps, her skin gets pink, and the little bit of cleavage she's showing tonight jiggles. And yeah, I already feel just a bit better.

I'm not sure what I even meant to say, but I wind up spilling my guts a little about Tom and Nina—why not, right? She's the one person it's completely safe to talk to; she already knows and clearly doesn't give a shit. Besides, she's a woman, so I don't feel like an idiot being out-loud happy for them.

"It's nice that you come in to visit your friend—"

"And you," I interrupt, looking for another of those shy, blushing smiles, which I get—*score*—but she asks why I didn't used to show up here before I started hanging around Tom. Fuck, I was busy getting laid, but I'm sure as fuck not gonna say that, so I just flip it around.

"Why are you always here?"

I was playing, and okay, deflecting, but I didn't mean to cause the look on her face right now. It's like something about her turns to crystal right in front of me. I've been trying to shake her out of the sadness and make her smile—for my own selfish, immature purposes maybe, but still. I didn't mean to make her sad all over again.

"I'm happy here, and I don't really have anywhere else to be," she says.

Fuckin A, if this is what happy looks like on her... I make another joke to try and rescue the mood.

"Ouch! Don't let your husband hear you say that."

And there's this crazy blank confused look, like, *Husband?* And I immediately know I've fucked up, so I just nod at her hand and the big fucking diamond, and then wait to see how big this shoe's gonna be when it drops.

She looks like I reminded her the stove was on. It's the weirdest thing. She looked sadder telling me her own damn name than she does explaining her fiancé died. I'm apologizing, and she reaches out just as I take my hand back, and we just barely touch, but it—I swear it sparks, like sure okay it's static electricity in the winter air, but is it also kinda maybe a sign? And I still feel like an ass—I was stupid levels of careless here, but deep down, there's this totally fucked up part of me going, *Not married?*

It must be okay for real, though, because she's in a better mood than I've seen before. It's cute as fuck, she's teasing me about how we never crossed paths. The smile's getting bigger, lighting her up more. But fuck, she's teasing me about *that* again, the stupid semi-bullshit she heard me talking to Tom and how it was the first time I ever set foot here... and okay, yeah, I wasn't exactly hard up for entertainment, I was getting laid. Not like I feel bad about it, but I don't wanna *talk* about it, not to her—

"Who has time?" I say, kinda blowing it off.

"Right. All the ladies. More than your fair share, that's what you said, right?"

"Whoa, I don't, I mean, I told you, I kinda hoped you didn't take that stuff too seriously—"

"And I told you, while it was clear you employed hyperbole to some extent, the most convincing lies are rooted in factual ground."

Damn, that's hot. I always did love a woman who could teach me something. *Shit.* I stopped talking too long. No walking this thing back, I'm gonna have to own it.

"Okay," I admit, "but... I mean, there's not much else to do but hook up."

There's this little quirk of a smile like she's kind of enjoying making me uncomfortable. It's a sexy, playful look that raises my body heat. What's it doing to hers? Is her skin as soft and warm as it looks? I wanna reach into that dress and feel how velvety warm and smooth she is all over.

My eyes dip down again and I drag them back up. Either she didn't notice or she's not offended. *And if you're not offended, are you interested?* Then she says she figures I'd've never come in here if not for Tom, which, okay, true, but it kinda sounds like she's saying a guy like me would have no use for a library, and okay, I guess I'm a little offended.

"Jeez, I feel like I need to defend my honor or something. I mean, it's not like I never read a book before. It's just not, you know, like, my personality or whatever."

She kinda shrugs. "I'm surprised he hasn't rubbed off on you."

I know she doesn't mean it *that way*, but my adolescent fucking brain takes it and runs with it, and I'm choking laughing—

And suddenly she's right in front of me, in my space. Her hand lands lightly on my collarbone. I get control of the laughter so I can enjoy this moment, looking down into her eyes, all big and dark and open with sweetness and concern. She's so close. I could pull her against me right now. Feel her all lush and warm.

Just as I'm imagining that feeling, she starts to pull away and I can't stand it. I wanna grab her hand and hold it, keep it on my body, move it to my back, get her arms around me. Let her feel me grow hard as I press into her belly. Watch her eyes as she realizes she's thinking about letting me fuck her. *Fuck, Demetri, that's not okay*—I kill the impulse, keep my grip from closing, let her fingers slide through with barely a graze.

This sly smile comes on all of a sudden. *Are you listening to that sexy devil, Stella?* I'm back to wanting to pull her onto me, and once again, I have to be mishearing things, because it sounds like she just said, "So, nothing to do but hook up?"

Is she asking me to hook up? I arch my eyebrow and say nothing, practically begging her to say it again if it's what she means, because I do not have it in me to ask.

And despite everything, I'm not a hundred percent sure I'd have it in me to say no if that is what she meant.

"But who has time to read?" she echoes, taunting me with my own half-assed, poorly thought-out responses.

I grimace, laughing at myself. I'm off in my hot librarian fantasy and she's teasing me about how I've never cracked a book since high school. Well, fuck. I'm off the party circuit anyway, right? What the hell else have I got to do besides listen to Tom bitch about his commitment-phobic girlfriend, tease the married librarian—the *unmarried* librarian, and read a goddamn book?

"Okay," I shrug. "What should I read?"

Chapter Four

Waking Up Is Hard to Do

Stella

My eyelids flutter rapidly. A startled somnambulist trying to wrest away the haze.

"What?"

"I'm serious," he says, clearly unaware of the existential crisis happening six inches in front of his face. "Recommend me something."

"Oh—I didn't—"

I'm stammering helplessly, feeling for all the world like a coma patient who just awakened to find that science had artificially animated her body to keep her from neglecting her duty to society.

"I've put you on the spot," he says decisively. "Take your time. I'll come back tomorrow."

Demetri and his dazzling smile disappear again, and I'm free to have a breakdown, to hyperventilate, to pinch myself. But I don't do any of these things.

I breathe in and out. I look around the library. *My* library. Not a coma, I think, a cocoon. I needed to hide, to hibernate. After Greg... I've been in a cocoon, and now I'm tearing away that veil, seeing the world without a hazy curtain over it. Awake.

The walk back to the mansion is one I've made hundreds of times, impossible though that seems now. I'm like a trolley car that's achieved sentience, trundling along the well-worn path I know I've taken so many times on autopilot. *Going home.* Now more than ever, the thought of that place as my home is crushing. Yet I have nowhere else to go. Will Celeste look at me and know? Will she see in my face the spark of rebirth? Will the set of my shoulders betray that some burden has been shed?

When I enter the dining room, she glances in my direction, then stands and leaves without acknowledging me in the slightest. Has she been waiting for me? Are my whereabouts a matter of concern to her? Or am I intruding on her evening, driving her from the common areas to escape my presence? Is she monitoring me or wishing I'd disappear once and for all?

I sit down to eat the meal that's been set aside for me this evening. The silence is perilous, untrustworthy. The library at its emptiest could never be this kind of quiet. This is the ominous hollow of echoing secrets and bone-deep resentments.

As soon as I've finished the meal and tidied up, I return to Greg's room. Less my room now than it was even this morning, now that I've shaken off the living death that hung over me all these months. I can barely breathe in here. It was so much easier being a sleepwalker. How will I survive this now?

I close my eyes. Feel the silence and stillness of this space. The air is stale and dusty. Have I just not noticed before?

My bedtime routine feels like a scene in a play. Though the door is shut, any sense of privacy is an illusion. It's only after I've turned off the light that I allow myself to relax and think about the moment when our hands touched. The loose, gentle slide of his fingers around my hand, like he didn't want me to pull away, yet wasn't about to hold me there against my will.

Tears slide silently down my cheeks in the darkness. It's not that I'd stopped believing men could be gentle. I'd just somehow forgotten they might be gentle with me.

If I've been a sleepwalker to myself, what have I been to the Genneros? A designated mourner, perhaps, with the closet they emptied of color without a word.

After Greg died, my wardrobe was selectively winnowed. I simply returned to our—*his* room that evening to find all the colors gone.

I understood, of course: I was in mourning. Perhaps someone without my background in literature might have been surprised by the antiquated tradition being imposed. But the Genneros were among the founding families of Illustris, and Illustris was never a traditional place by modern standards; it was traditional by the most classic standards.

They had never cared for me—well, Roger seemed to accept me for what little that was worth, even found me amusing at times like a horse who could tap a hoof to count on command. But Celeste... To Celeste, I could never have been a worthy daughter-in-law. The least I could do was grieve as expected.

Perhaps my colorful clothes are still here somewhere, packed away. Perhaps they were redistributed among the population of the Stronghold as community property, a sartorial reversal of fortune and a touch of karma after how much my library claimed from every home. I would hardly have dared to ask, had I been emotionally capable of wondering. The haze in which I existed for so long was a kind of protective cloak.

They clearly prefer to ignore me. *Why don't they let me go?* I've been dazed and wandering through life on autopilot for so long, not fully interrogating my situation, but now I can't avoid it any longer.

Their son died, leaving behind this woman he chose but they never bonded with, or in Celeste's case, even liked. *I'd* want to be rid of me, if I were them. I'd have long since found somewhere else for that woman to live. Reclaimed my home, my peace. Why haven't they?

The day passes more quickly than usual as my mind is full of strange, fluttery wanderings. It's not as if I envision some sort of potential for a future involving Demetri. He's a young man living life for the moment, doing whatever he pleases, not to mention facing great danger beyond the wall. I'm a widow, more or less, living a quiet life that revolves around the library he wandered into once on a lark. It's an accident of fate that we even met. He said he'd be back tonight; if he shows up, I'll give him something to read. And he probably will show up, because he felt challenged, and he doesn't seem the sort to shrink from a challenge.

I can't help thinking I may never see him again after this, though. He'll take whatever I give him, and he'll crack it open once or twice, but he'll be too embarrassed to admit he didn't finish it, maybe even hated it. Tonight could well be our final conversation. I consider a rotating list of titles, trying to determine if one or another makes it any likelier he'll ever return.

But not everyone comes into your life to stay. Some just pass through to teach you something or help you get where you need to be. Going from mourning to morning is scary, but it had to happen, and he made the moment beautiful. Perhaps that small taste of joy will be enough to sustain me, perhaps not, but I'll always remember it.

Demetri takes the book from me and scowls at the cover.

"That's a rabbit," he says skeptically.

"Yes. I've always loved this book. And I happen to know that one of your friends does too, which means they probably both do."

His brow wrinkles in offense. "I have more than two friends, Stella."

"Of course. I didn't mean—"

"I'm fucking with you," he interrupts, grinning widely.

"You do that a lot," I say, hoping I'm not blushing at the memory of his lewd monologue to Tom that first night.

He shrugs. "Sometimes I can't help myself."

Suddenly I know something about him. I've thought he seemed like Tom's brother, and now I understand why. "You strike me as someone who grew up with siblings," I say cautiously, wanting to learn more about him even as I know it's a potentially painful topic.

Fortunately, he looks more fond than saddened at the mention of her. "Older sister, yeah."

"And she's... not here, I take it."

He shakes his head regretfully. "She went off to college across the country and made a life there. Came back for holidays sometimes. But when the shit went down, she was far away. I don't know what happened to her after we lost phone signals and stuff. She might be okay," he finishes, and it's clear in his voice he knows how unlikely that is.

"I'm sorry."

"We've all lost a lot," he says calmly. A gentle, sad half-smile softens his handsome face. Leaning on the desk, he seems to suddenly remember what's in his hand. "Hey, tell me about this book."

"Right, well, it's quite a unique story. It's about rabbits, obviously... they've had to flee their home and start over, and they'll have to build their whole society from scratch. There's a whole rabbit mythology and even a language—look here in the front, there's a glossary! You get to see the world from the perspective of these gentle, soft creatures who are prey for basically everything. But that's why they have to be not just faster but cleverer than everything else they come up against. I'm sorry, I could go on and on," I say, suddenly self-conscious. I've probably said more words in the past sixty seconds than in the past six months.

"Don't apologize," he says. "In fact, don't stop talking. Tell me the story."

"But then you wouldn't even need to read it," I object, enjoying the physical sensation of smiling. It's still so unfamiliar.

"Well," he says slyly, "I don't really *need* to read anything, right? Did they ever make a movie of this?"

"Yes. A couple of times, actually."

"And if I'd seen one of them, would you say that meant I didn't *need* to read it?"

"No!" The idea is anathema. My appalled reaction is strangely invigorating, more pieces of me awakening bit by bit at his provocation. It feels good to care about something so small. I'd forgotten how.

"Well? There you go!" He grins, proud of the way he's argued his case, then puts on a faux-serious look and lays it on thick. "Stella, I'm a soldier. What if I start reading a book and never get to finish it? That'd be worse than never starting. Do me a solid here."

It's absurd. He's just casually mentioned the constant threat of death he lives under. It should be the darkest, direst of topics, but he's playing it like a joke. Or like a man trying to convince his girlfriend to sleep with him before he goes off to fight. He's invoking the specter of death to get me to tell him a story.

Because he saw it. He saw me animated, excited, alive.

He's encouraging me to waste his time here tonight because he likes making people happy. My heart pumps like it's trying to break loose from some brittle shell.

So I tell him the story of *Watership Down*. I let myself relax and enjoy it. I feel more like myself than I have since I met Greg, I realize. Not just since the world ended, or even since I came to Illustris. I changed so much to suit Greg, then even more to try to please his parents and to belong here. But don't all people change in relationships, I thought? I was inexperienced, and he made clear there was room for growth on my part. He would show me the world I'd never had access to before—not just in terms of money but sophistication. He would be indulgent and tolerant of my shortcomings.

Somewhere under his scrutiny and tutelage, I evaporated. Even crazier, I'd forgotten it happened. The person I used to be had just ceased to exist at some point, and in this place where no one had ever known her, she went completely unmissed.

Demetri sees me. Somehow, he sees me. And incredibly, he wants me to be here.

At times over the course of telling the story, my emotions get the better of me. When I feel myself choking up, I redirect it into the narrative. By the time Bigwig sets off for Efrafa, I've moved out from behind the desk. We face away from the counter and lean back against it side by side, inches apart, our arms at first grazing incidentally before settling into delicate, unmistakably deliberate contact.

When our heroes are digging in to fortify their home against the impending attack, I trail off.

"Well? What happens next?"

Looking at him, I feel certain he's no longer merely drawing me out for some charitable reason; he wants to know how the story ends. I turn to face him fully, still leaning on the counter.

"The good guys win, of course. But how it happens, the heroic exploits, the clever plans—that's what you'll love. You were right. Knowing the story isn't a deterrent to experiencing it, but there are some things I can't just tell you. Some things you'll want to feel all for yourself."

Even if he was in earnest about wanting to be spoiled lest he never get to finish reading, I've promised the comfort of a triumphant conclusion. That's a spoiler in the tradition of a good novel that follows the conventions of its genre. The mystery will be solved; the evil will be vanquished; the lovers will live happily ever after.

He looks down again at the book in his hand, then back up at me. This close to him, I feel almost dainty; I'm tall for a woman, but he's actually tall. If I leaned closer, I could rest my cheek comfortably on his shoulder.

"Thanks," he says quietly, and gives me a long look before retreating to his own life. As soon as he's on the other side of the big double doors, the library feels empty in a way it's never been. Earlier I decided to acknowledge the likelihood of never seeing Demetri again. That flimsy peace has been demolished. The entire construction of my life is unsteady since I blinked awake under the radiant glow of his smile.

Zorn, I think, recalling the language of the rabbits: the word for destruction, catastrophe.

Laughing at myself, I wipe away tears for the dozenth time tonight. I'm being so dramatic. He's a kind man. He saw a sad, lonely person and reached out to her. He noticed a spark of joy and fanned it to a flame. That's an act of kindness. Don't overreact. Don't make it anything more in your mind. Just accept a gift when it's offered.

And for your own good, don't look happy in front of your hosts. I'm not sure what I'm afraid of, exactly, but I am afraid. These people think so little of me, and my one saving grace thus far may be the perception that I loved—and miss—their son.

If I were suddenly happy... if I were a *woman* again, with all that entails... what would they intend for me? I am, after all, a human resource under the Genneros' purview.

They've kept me under their roof, sacrificing their own comfort and happiness to maintain dominion over me. Perhaps they simply don't trust me. They're right not to. I have no loyalty to them or their kind, and far too much knowledge. I was Greg's wife, for all intents and purposes, and my spirit was broken; they spoke openly in front of me. I was involved in the creation of this new world, privy to the strategy sessions as Illustris evolved into the Stronghold.

Hell. I helped name the damn place.

"What was Holland on about earlier?" Greg asked his father. He and Roger spent many an evening doing these little post-mortems,

filling each other in on their separate areas of focus and the gossip and goings-on in their individual spheres. They looked like they should be swirling snifters of brandy, but liquor was now a precious item to be hoarded, brought out only in moments of celebration or mourning. The breweries were dark with so many of the workers conscripted, and the stills being devised by the lower caste were unlikely to yield anything that would please the Genneros' palates.

Roger sniffed in derision. "Oh, that. Well, you know he married his company's PR director? I imagine you spend the rest of your life trying to prove that was a good decision." The two men chuckled, and Stella's shoulders drew inward slightly. She might as well be invisible... yet she was still there, and she couldn't help wondering how they might casually describe her if she weren't.

"She's been in his ear," Roger continued, "about the name. Illustris. Apparently, it's 'ghoulish' now."

More laughter from the men, and Celeste scoffed. "Ghoulish! Preposterous."

Stella quietly agreed with Holland's former PR director wife. It was ghoulish. The world was burning down around them, and they were still definitionally bragging about their wealth—wealth that was now wiped out.

But ghoulish was beside the point, wasn't it? The name had a much more glaring flaw that might be more compelling to the Genneros.

"Illustris conjures images of wealth and luxury. That conveyed power before, but it won't for long as a new order develops. Wealth and luxury are associated with soft, uncalloused hands. With muscles honed for esthetics rather than conquest. It sounds like the sort of place where, once the barbarians breach the gates, they'll meet no resistance to speak of."

Stella hadn't even known she was going to speak until the words spilled out, a murmured monologue that brought up painful echoes of the girl she'd been long ago—was it truly that long? It felt like *a different life. In school, among friends, among professors and colleagues, she had been prone to similarly lengthy and thoughtful outbursts, but with fire, the words bursting forth as if each chased the one before, desperate to be shared.*

Who was this shadow? Was there still a flicker of Stella herself hiding within? Would any oxygen ever be allowed to feed the guttering flame?

Greg's hand tightened on hers. She prepared herself for a punishing grind of her fine bones in his larger grip. Had she just implied he was weak? He would remind her how hard his soft hands could be.

But Roger considered her words and nodded thoughtfully. "It's a valid point. Illustris was a beacon and a badge. Might it now become a target we've painted on ourselves?"

Whether persuaded by her words or, more likely, his father's, Greg looked at her with something like encouragement. "That's a good insight, Stella. We may benefit from your outside perspective. And your facility with language. You've identified a potential problem. Might you be able to propose a solution?"

Her eyes flew to his in shock. Sudden hope ached in her chest. Was he looking at her as if he'd remembered he used to like her? Had this all been a dark interlude of sorts—was there a chance he could be good to her again? Could she love him again, after everything? The brutal answer came instantly: What choice did she have? She was trapped either way; the only question was whether she could find a way to be happy in the trap.

Her voice had a bit more color when she spoke again. "Illustris was an aspirational name. Everyone wanted in because of what it meant to be here, and everyone understood the barriers to entry. It was a fantasy for the average person to imagine they might someday amass sufficient wealth to be worthy of this place."

"Or receive an invitation," Greg reminded her coolly. Her heart thudded as hope and fear collided. She mustn't be ungrateful. She wasn't out of the woods. Remember your place.

"That was an even more powerful fantasy," she answered carefully, trying for a fond smile as she watched his gray eyes. He nodded slightly, and she let herself breathe again. "But to most people, Illustris was impenetrable, not just because of the walls but because of the power of wealth and influence. Why were middle-class houses burglarized so much more frequently than mansions? It's not because the thieves imagined the spoils would be comparable or even because the mansions were truly impregnable, it's because you don't bite the tail of a much bigger dog. Most humans are rational. They don't overextend their reach."

The words were beginning to flow now. Her lungs expanded to draw in the air it took to say more than three words in a row, to let her mind express itself after the long suppression and silence.

"The name projected the version of strength that was meaningful in our world. That world is gone, and the notion of strength must evolve accordingly. How does this place remain intimidating to the people outside, who have more reason than ever to covet what's yours?"

"And aspirational," Roger added ominously. "You said Illustris was aspirational. The new name has to capture that as well. We need to make it known that our doors are, in fact, open to worthy outsiders. Just like the old days. If there was no path to the good life, we were a monstrous hedonistic enclave and the example of everything wrong in America. But by offering a fair chance, giving people hope, we got them to compete with each other instead of fighting us. That's what we've got to do now. For a number of reasons."

"It's a fortress. But not—we can't let the name be a reminder of tangible rewards that lie within. It has to be..." Stella's voice trailed away, and then she gasped. "The equivalent of the old name... You want it to exude power—in the sense of a natural resource. This is not *just a place where people with strength want to be; it's the place they already are. The average person might think of Illustris as a place to be conquered. They would come to the Stronghold as supplicants."*

Greg smiled then. It wasn't the smile she remembered from their whirlwind courtship, but it wasn't the impatient scowl rife with buyer's remorse she'd spent these last weeks wilting under.

"Holland will be so pleased to hear his wife's idea has inspired real change," Roger said, his lips curling into a smirk.

Celeste adjusted the hem of her dress. The motion caught Stella's attention, and she glanced over automatically, making eye contact. It was a mistake—the older woman's glare was like a pin prick starting a slow but steady leak in Stella's good feeling. She may have reminded Greg of something about her he liked, and she may even have favorably impressed Roger, but Celeste was unmoved. The woman hated her, and if anything, Stella had just made things worse in that area.

In a burst of understanding, Roger's words flew back to her: We got them to compete with each other instead of fighting us. That same principle would apply to gender relations, of course. Celeste didn't like another woman under her roof, in her family. Would she have liked a different kind of woman, Stella wondered, one who knew the wine regions and could identify fashion designers without looking for a label? Or was the power women wielded so minimal, so illusory, that the rule of scarcity hampered their ability to relate to one another at all?

What a lonely place this was. Stella accepted that she had no hope for friendship within these walls. Greg was her only connection. She would love him, she decided with hollow resolve. She could probably live without being loved in return, but she needed someone or something to love, somewhere to pour her energy, a way to feel useful. He was all she had.

Chapter Five

Resistance

Demetri

T urns out I'm a hell of a wingman when it counts. I wore Nina down, revved Tom up, and hunkered down to watch the fireworks show from across the room with Monica. When he goes in for the kiss, Monica elbows me, and we exchange a grin. I think I'm about done here. I'll slip out and head back to my room to read some more about the goddamn rabbits. It's weird how much I wanna see what happens next even though I pretty much know. Stella did a good job giving me just enough to make me want more.

And now I'm thinking about her leaning there beside me, letting our sleeves touch, tickling the hairs on my arms into little conductors of the electricity I know she felt too. At the end, I almost kissed her cheek—the weirdest fucking impulse, and I stopped myself. You can't just kiss someone, even on the cheek, and what if she wanted me to touch her as bad as I wanted to? Would she lean in and give me her mouth?

Would I know where to stop, once I started? Do I remember the lines with a woman I'm not just trying to fuck? Hell, do I even know what I want? I meet a beautiful woman and don't get to fuck her right away, after months of fucking everyone in sight... how do I even know what I'm feeling? One thing's for sure: She's been through enough. I don't know how much, but I know how sad she was. I made her smile, and that's what I wanna keep doing. I don't need to take anything from her to do that.

What if she made a move? Yeah, right. Her whole wounded bird thing was in full effect till like ten minutes ago. Even if she threw herself at me, I couldn't take advantage.

What if she hadn't seemed married, though? If I hadn't gotten used to the idea of her as off-limits before I went on my fucking sabbatical. Forbidden fruit is hot and all, but if there was nothing keeping me from plucking her right away... Yeah. I'd've fucked her. It's not even a question. I wonder how deep she could take me at first. I always get there eventually, all the way, watching a woman's eyes roll back as her body learns to want more. But the first time isn't always easy. I've learned to hold back, go slow, resist the urge to bury myself all the way in no matter how bad I want to. Nina took it good. Tom told me she would, not that I believed him when I still thought it was just talk. He reminded me again when I took her ass for him. *She can take it. Harder, don't hold back.* Fuck. It's a hell of an adjustment, trying to go cold turkey on the number one leisure activity of the last year or so of my goddamn life.

But that's kinda the point, isn't it? I got used to seeing everyone as free game. I didn't have to think about it. Didn't want to. Now that I do, I'm grateful for that ring on her finger, even if she'd just as soon have it gone. I thought it was a red light, but it was a yellow, slowing me down just enough to avoid a wreck.

No harm in fucking Stella's soft tits and clever little mouth in my imagination though, right? Get some of this fever out of my veins, help me settle down and read. I wanna go back to her with something useful to say about this book, so I should finish it first.

It feels right to set limits. If I don't pace myself, keep my jets cool, I'm practically guaranteed to flame out.

"You haven't been around as much lately," Monica says, and the tone in her voice is like she's aiming for casual observation but knows she missed the mark.

I turn to meet her eyes, expecting she's hitting on me and I'll have to figure out how to decline, but that's not what I see. She's just curious, wondering if she's losing another friend to the dark side. Makes sense. This is how it started with Nina. She just stopped hanging out for so long in the evenings, claimed to be spending time alone. *Reading*, no less. I chuckle at how it's going to sound like an insulting lie when I say the same thing.

"Ah, you know, this fuckin' guy," I say with a vague gesture at our newly engaged friends. "He's a bad influence. I'm suddenly all absorbed in a book about rabbits. Who'da seen that coming."

It's not a lie, really. I left Stella out of the story, but it's because of Tom I even met her.

Monica's smile is a little too aware somehow, and I guess I shouldn't be surprised. We've known each other a long time, been friends from day one, and fucked plenty along the way. She can take it. She'd rather ride it though. *Stop it.*

"You ever think you're gonna get bored of all this?"

"Not enough to follow in her footsteps, if that's what you mean," she says, nodding in Nina's direction.

Nina looks all flushed and glowy, and I know why—I can see Tom leaning close to her ear. Hypnotic motherfucker.

"You don't wanna fall in love?" The question just tumbles out and we look at each other again. Somehow I know the entire fuckbuddy element of our friendship is behind us. No need for awkwardness about it, thank fuck, she's just Monica, and we're cool.

But there's a tightness in her expression when she answers, "Not here, I don't. For Nina it was a hurdle, but for me it's a non-starter. Living on the sidelines of the Stronghold is plenty, thanks. I won't be moving further in. Don't get me wrong, I'm happy for her. She really does want it all, she just wants it on her own terms."

Or at least on his.

When they stop dancing, and he pulls her out of the room, it's as good a time as any to make my own escape. Maybe I can catch them on the way out and give them a hug.

"I'm gonna go," I tell Monica. "I gotta see what's up with these rabbits."

She laughs and says good night.

Out in the hallway, I shake my head at the sight of him pressing her up against the wall right beyond the doors, her knee hooked over his elbow as he practically fucks her through their clothes. So much for that hug.

He makes a crack about starting a revolution, and my snicker gets their attention. I congratulate them and go on my way instead of sticking around to see whether he keeps mauling her right there in the open—wouldn't surprise me at this point. Feels like nothing Tom says or does will surprise me anymore. He's a fucking mad-man, but I've kinda got the hang of him now.

6 days later

I wasn't expecting to see Tom so soon. They had a whole four days of honeymoon, and he was back on patrol yesterday. He didn't show up here after, and why would he? More to the point, why is he coming my way now?

Without even glancing at the people around me, he says, "Demetri. Can you take a walk?"

"Hey," Monica interrupts. Tom turns, his face a mix of confusion, irritation, and awkward nerves. "You know that woman you just married is our friend. Are you ever going to bother introducing yourself?"

He mutters uncomfortably, "You... know who I am," clearly hoping to get out of this situation. But Monica crosses her arms in front of her chest and stares at him like *Really? That's how you wanna play this?* And he caves, looking like he's been called to the front of the classroom to explain himself.

"I'm Tom," he admits.

She smiles like *Was that so hard?*, then introduces herself, Manny, and Davy. Sure, they've "known" each other for months, but he was always hiding under the helmet before, and Monica has attitude about helmet heads. Having accomplished this minor victory over the poor guy, she stops holding us up, gives me a little smirk.

Walking away from the three of them, it strikes me they have a different dynamic than I'm used to seeing here. Maybe it's because of Monica's rule about not fucking teammates. Not to say Nina didn't fit or anything, but they seem just as complete without her. And the new guy is part of the team on patrol, not so much part of the club after hours.

Tom asks if we can talk in my quarters, and the implication is ominous: Whatever's up with him requires real privacy, not just a library or a long hallway. He's quiet the whole way up, and the sharp edges of his whole vibe are kinda freaking me out. Finally, the door to my room clicks shut.

"I need your help." Just when I thought I was done being surprised by this guy.

"Thought the honeymoon would last a little longer," I say, aiming for light and chill, but he's not having it. He inclines his head and stares at me hard from beneath the furrowed brow, and I burst out laughing. "Dude! Haven't we been through this? Like, last week? Do your thing, turn her on, shut her up."

A dark, troubled quiet follows. Shit, this is serious, isn't it?

"I'm afraid it's too late for that this time," he says quietly. He turns to stare at the wall, and it bugs me. On Tom, avoidance looks like defeat.

"What the fuck does that mean?"

His head swivels enough so our eyes meet again, and I was right. There is defeat all over him, and I can't stand seeing it.

"She had a choice to make," he says. "It had to be made quickly. Perhaps I could have talked her out of it... but I got home that evening, and it was already done. She's in this thing, whether I like it or not."

"What 'thing,' Captain Cryptic?"

He gives me a long, sobering look before he answers, and the moment he speaks, I realize I already knew what he was about to say.

"If I tell you, you'll be in it too."

Anyone else said something like that to me, I'm pretty sure I'd say *thanks but no thanks* and send them on their way, relieved not to have to deal with whatever fucking bullshit this is.

I put a hand on his shoulder. "I'm with you, man. Tell me what's up."

"Kinda your own fault, in a way," I say after he's given me the rundown. "You had to go and joke about starting a revolution."

He gives me a rueful smile. "She assures me her role is purely research and carries little to no risk." The frustration spills out again as he adds, "As if she could possibly know that!"

"What options have you considered in terms of shutting this whole thing down?"

His shoulders slump. "Fuck, Demetri. What options? Turn in the bastard who recruited her? Kill him with my bare hands? I can't do the former without jeopardizing her anyway. The latter is a fairly satisfying mental picture but that's all. And it's not just that there's nothing I *can* do to prevent this, there seems nothing I should do. Any action I take that's not supporting her is betraying her."

Laughter bursts out, and I explain, "It was just a few days ago I was thinking I had the hang of you—no more big surprises coming. Your girl's a dark horse."

"Is this a metaphor about the barn door she's already escaped through?"

I hadn't thought of that, but sure, let's roll with it. "Exactly. So what's the next step? You can't undo it, but what *can* you do?"

He takes a long breath and stares into space. The idea that this big brain motherfucker comes to me for counsel is a little bit ludicrous. I feel like my dad would've been proud to see me with a guy like Tom for a friend. He'd've thought it was a sign I was finally growing up.

"It's no different from before, is it?" he says, pondering the situation. "She was in danger, and I could see further ahead, know the threats she faced, and protect her. If she's put herself in a new kind of danger, my only option is to go deeper into it than she already is, learn the layout of the land, see what's coming. Keep her safe."

"I'm in."

He leans back a bit, making the face that says *Oh, I couldn't ask you to do that*, but it's a done deal.

"Dude," I remind him, "you came here tonight and the first thing outta your mouth was you needed my help. I don't know if that was a Freudian slip or what, but I'm not sitting on the sidelines while my best friend dives face-first into a shitstorm."

The look of hilarious disgust as he processes that mixed metaphor gets me cackling.

"Okay," I say, holding my hands up in apology, "I heard it as soon as I said it. But a shitstorm it is, and you're not going in without me. What's the plan?"

After Tom's gone home to his troublesome bride, I need to settle my mind before bed, and what the fuck is going on with me that I reach for the book instead of my dick. Bigwig—a badass rabbit, and who'd've thought that was a phrase—is undercover in the evil empire, trying to liberate these does who just wanna live free, choose their mates, and raise their young in a healthy, hopeful environment. And even though I'm a hundred percent on Tom's side in every conceivable way—bros before does, I guess—I feel like that's kind of what Nina's after too. She chose her mate, no question, but she's been outspoken from the start that having a family here feels wrong; safety isn't enough. I think about the doe that reabsorbed her litter because she didn't feel confident about the world they'd be born into.

Okay, I'm still on Tom's side. A hundred percent. But maybe I'm on her side too.

And it occurs to me how Stella said my friends loved this book, and maybe that's why I suddenly know that, for all his frustration and how bad he wants to protect her from everything, Tom is on her side in this. He hates it. But he's with her.

I should've seen this coming.

At the dumb party, Samantha was rubbing against me when I danced with her. I can't help getting hard, it's not like it's a conscious choice or something. She made it clear she'd like to get together, and I kinda brushed it off like a *hey, who knows* or some shit. I need to figure out the right way to deal with these encounters; I can't just keep disappearing and hiding out in my room, ignoring the occasional knock and hoping people stop wondering whatever happened to party-time fuckboy Demetri.

It doesn't help that I actually would love to get laid. So bad sometimes I can't believe it's been a few weeks and not fucking months. Ain't easy cooling off when you've been running so hot for so long.

Since the party, I have managed to steer clear of temptation and confrontation. Bully for me, right? Someone should bake me a congrats-on-keeping-it-in-your-pants cake. But Samantha's decided to push it today in the one place I can't get away from her.

Thank fuck it's a backup shift at least. I literally can't handle anyone distracting me when there's real danger to watch for.

She isn't subtle, sidling up and leaning her hip against my shoulder during my card game. Her squad leader, Anye, makes eye contact with her before giving me an awkward look and setting down his cards. I think he feels bad for me, but he still walks away. In case I needed proof my change in behavior was a topic of conversation among my fellow soldiers.

Now that she's got me alone, Samantha rotates to face me, maintaining unnaturally consistent contact as she leans back to perch on the edge of the table, letting her leg rest against mine.

"Hey," she says, and I'm not sure whether to read her manner as desire or challenge. Probably a little of both.

"Hey." It comes out miserable. I'd rather be anywhere but here, and there's no hiding that. I'd rather be activated to rush out the gate and fight off a horde of goddamn zombies than have to explain myself to this woman I, as recently as a few weeks ago, was down to fuck.

I don't know how to say I'm not. I don't know what explanation to give or how to make it make sense to someone who isn't me or who doesn't know me like Tom.

I feel kinda pissed that there's anything to explain, and then I feel like I deserve this discomfort; I used to basically torment Nina for fun. I knew she was horny just like the rest of us, and I didn't understand why she wasn't doing anything to relieve her tension. Now I fucking get it—maybe not the same reasons but the same outcome anyway, and I'm paying for how I treated her. That's how it feels. I have to be taunted. I have to know everyone looks at me as completely goddamn incomprehensible, withholding when there's a good time waiting to be had.

One hand still rests on the table, clutching my cards. Samantha's gaze drifts toward it, and I realize I'm gripping them so tight they're bent. Shit. I try to smooth them out with a gentle reversal, then stack them flat and apply a little pressure.

She adds her hand on top of mine. "Careful, Demetri, there won't be any new decks coming to replace this one."

I nod and grimace, feeling trapped. My skin is hot and almost itchy as tension floods my muscles. I could slide my free hand up that thigh she's got pressed against me. Find the heat between her legs and rub at her through the uniform. Get her wet. Leave her suffering.

See if I can resist the temptation to throw her down later and finish what I started.

Maybe I shouldn't have gone cold turkey. Maybe cutting back is enough. It's been long enough already, hasn't it? I deserve a break, to take the edge off? I could come in her instead of my own hand, just as a reward for being so good lately. She wants it. Give the people what they want, right? Why not?

The pads of her fingertips slide along the edge of my hand in a gentle, tantalizing graze.

"It would be a shame to mark these just because you're wound up."

My dick is too big, too hard. I have to shift in my seat for comfort. She knows what I'm doing and why, and she smiles.

"I haven't seen much of you lately. If you're feeling down, maybe I could help."

Through my fog of arousal and distress, I wonder just for a moment if she's trying to be my friend. I look up, meet her eyes, hold my breath.

"I miss riding that cock." Her voice is low enough to keep the conversation semi-private, but it suddenly feels appallingly public. It's a jarring feeling, because I sure wasn't shy about this stuff. I went to a public place to taunt a near-stranger about how many times I'd tried to fuck his girlfriend, how much I knew she needed to be fucked. I winked at the wide-eyed librarian I caught listening in. *Stella.*

I pull away and stand despite the discomfort, but the fog is clearing a bit.

"Thanks for helping with the cards. I think I'll lift some weights."

There's a look in her eyes, wounded or confused, as I turn away. Why do I feel like food that got taken off the menu, like I'm supposed to feel bad about being unavailable, like I owe anyone an explanation or a goddamn apology? It's hard enough resisting my own urges. I resent feeling like anyone else's are supposed to be my problem too.

This place fucks with you, and that's the truth. I work my lats and breathe a sigh of relief when my dick calms down after a dozen reps.

For our *let's start a revolution* get-together, we go see Tom and Nina's new place. Me, Monica, Manny, and Davy. Just the people she trusts most, because Tom's antsy as fuck, obviously; the only people he trusts are me and Nina, but he's gonna have to start somewhere.

We're barely through the front door when Monica hooks her arm through Tom's and asks for a tour. She's relentless. Nina and I share a silent laugh that's not entirely at Tom's expense; this is good for him.

While Tom reluctantly shows the others around, I grab Nina by the shoulder to hang back. She looks nervous, and it's easy to guess why. I'm sure Tom wouldn't deliberately make her feel bad or anything, but he is upset, and the fucker's not easy to read. Besides her, the person who knows him best is me. If he was angry with her, I'd kinda have to be.

"Poor guy just barely started to relax, and now you go and do this," I tease.

She looks up at me in surprise, grateful I'm playing when she probably thought I was about to give her a hard time. I put an arm around her shoulder and pull her into a side hug.

"This whole thing... you had to know he'd hate it."

"Yeah," she admits, with a half-shrug and a look that says *it had to happen, though*.

"I get it. Weird, right?" She giggles, a little sheepish about agreeing with me making fun of myself. "And if *I* get it? No chance he doesn't." I drop her a wink.

"Thanks, Demetri." She relaxes under my arm.

It is weird though. Weird I see it so clearly, all thanks to the damn rabbits. Or to Stella for making me read about the damn rabbits. It's hard not to smile even just thinking her name.

The others come back down the stairs, Monica still hanging on Tom's arm and being aggressively cheerful. It's more fun than it should be, watching her torture him. She'll befriend him whether he likes it or not.

"C'mon," I say, tugging on Nina, still tucked under my arm, "let's go corrupt our friends for the greater good."

"What exactly are you supposed to find in Archives?" Monica asks.

Tom huffs with annoyance as Nina explains that she doesn't actually know.

"From what he said, it seems like it's more about having someone in place, someone who can access information when the need arises? In the meantime, I get to know the system and fade into the background so no one suspects I'm anything but a newly married civilian counting the days till I can go on maternity leave... forever," she finishes glumly.

"So what do you need from us?"

Manny, asking the big questions.

"Nothing," Tom says quietly. "For now. Maxwell hasn't asked Nina to bring anyone into this, and I don't care what he might think of the decision to do so. For what it's worth, you can blame me and only me for placing you in this position. I insisted that she have real backup if she were to do this. Not just the civilians or *pfft*, a bloody Commander. People she trusts. People who care about her."

Monica's hand shoots across the table and grabs his. "Thank you," she says emphatically.

Before we head back to barracks, we have to plan how to stay connected. We can't just hang out here all the time. Tom's still military, so he can come and go from the barracks, but Nina would be out of place there now. Remembrance Hill would be a great option but not in wintertime.

"The library could work," Davy chimes in.

Monica scoffs. "Oh, hell no. Don't tell me I'm the only one who's noticed that librarian skulking around."

"Don't worry about Stella," I say, surprising myself. "I can keep her busy."

Tom and I exchange a look, and the son of a bitch is laughing at me, I can see it.

"But you wouldn't be in on the discussion—" Manny starts to point out.

I cut him off. "It's no big. Fill me in after. I'm not the number one brain on the team anyway, right? This can be my contribution."

"Then it's settled," Tom says, clearly still suppressing his knowing grin. "Demetri will secure our location for skullduggery. Really big of you, taking one for the team."

I glare at him, but I'm also fighting a smile. He fucking knows me, and he knows exactly what I just did. Bought myself a neat little excuse to hang out with a girl I like. Whatever, it's as above board as it can be. We'll be in public the whole damn time. My friends will be fifteen feet away, for fuck's sake. I can just get to know Stella better. I won't be able to do anything stupid. If this is just a case of misplaced desire, it'll pass, and in the meantime I'll have made myself useful.

And if she's under my skin for good reason? Even better.

Chapter Six

Masks

Stella

Stella had the loveliest of dreams. A lucid dream, it seems, that lasted marvelously long, carrying good feelings into the waking world for a time. She remembers her cheeks coming alive with sensation like a shot of novocaine wearing off. She remembers a handsome man. He was kind and gentle. He smiled just for her. But like any dream, its magic receded after too many hours in the waking world.

For a time, she buzzed with anticipation—the dreamer's manic belief that if they concentrate hard enough, they can return to the part of the dream that was so very beautiful, and this time stay in it longer. She turned corners hoping to walk right back into it. For a time.

Then she remembered the dreamer's truth: It is never the same dream twice. Even if you do trick your mind into reopening that door, you will be disappointed by what you find. You will wish you had not reached for seconds. The first taste was freely given, and gluttony will sour the palate. A dreamer who stays too long at the feast is sure to find the meal suddenly moldy, rank, and crawling with bugs.

Days have passed, and she is herself again, perhaps more sub-dued. The exhausted sleepwalker whose REM stage seemed to last so long it couldn't help but be disrupted. An Illustrian has entered her library, one of the ones she recalls seeing among the Genneros' crowd. They don't often come to the library, and usually it's to pester her about their emotional support first edition of *Catcher in the Rye* or some such banality.

She looks blandly into his face, expecting confrontation. It's a benefit of sleepwalking that she doesn't respond to such stimuli; they tend to go away in a bluster, doubly unsatisfied.

The man smiles, which seems strange to her. Remembering her place, she approximates the mask of civility with a soupçon of servitude appropriate to dealing with the Illustrian elite.

"Stella," he says as if greeting an acquaintance or perhaps a person with whom a date had been arranged online. She waits for more, but her name seems to have been a complete sentence in this context.

"Yes. How may I be of help? Are you looking for a particular book?"

He frowns slightly, and she wonders what she could have done wrong in such a simple interaction.

"I'm Dwight," he says as if it should mean something. Perhaps she's meant to be impressed? Is he important? She wouldn't know. Greg wasn't given to acknowledging others' contributions.

"Did you need me to look into something at Archives?"

That was generally the purpose of a visit to the library for his sort, after all. To demand that she check on the status of the books collected from his home, expedite the processing of a favorite so he could reclaim it as surely it would have been deemed too precious to fall into the hands of the general public; surely there were other, cheaper copies lying about.

His frown deepens. "I merely wanted to stop by and extend my sympathies. Long overdue, of course."

Oh. Greg. "Thank you," she says, her face falling again into desolation, the mask dropped.

"Well, I can see you're not... I'm sorry to disrupt your day with personal matters. Perhaps I'll see you again another time."

She nods vaguely, her eyes failing to properly focus on him as he backs away and turns to go.

Several more days and nights go by as she feels her dreamscape slipping further away.

When Tom and Nina walk in together, there is a pulse-pounding sense of déjà vu. They are unmistakably *together*, arms linked from bicep to fingertips; she leans into him as if deriving the strength to stand, to walk. They got married, Stella thinks, just as Demetri thought they would. Her reality doubles in déjà vu, déjà rêve perhaps, as she recalls the conversation that left her peculiarly invigorated, if only for a time. Her heart both swells and aches.

She collects a stack of books to return to the shelves, distracting herself with another wander. Several minutes later, a startling *ding!* from the center of the vast space alerts her to someone at the desk. Making her way back, she glimpses a tall, dark-haired man in casual clothing, and as she nears, her heart syncopates.

"Hello again," she says carefully, fearful of Morpheus' wrath.

He turns to face her fully, confronting her again with his impossible beauty. No one looks like that, she had decided as the dream faded. No real man has those cheekbones, that brow, that smile.

It was vaguely comforting in the hazy aftermath of her dream to acknowledge that he simply could not have been real. *And if such a man did exist, it's not you he'd be smiling at,* she could practically hear Celeste sniping.

"You're back," she observes inanely, moving behind the desk to place a true barrier between herself and this ill-advised fantasy about a sweet, handsome soldier.

He slides a book across the desk. *Watership Down.* Of course, that's from the dream too. She stares at the cover a moment too long, her brain reckoning with the tangible evidence of what she'd accepted as ephemeral. She closes her eyes.

"I finished it last night. Actually, I probably could've brought it back right away, but I was busy wiping away tears. Very manly tears."

The smile breaks my face open a moment before I dare to open my eyes and discover he's still there, smiling back at me. Still so beautiful I almost don't believe it. Perhaps my brain simply can't contain this much handsomeness and has to sand down the edges for storage.

He continues with a playful accusation, "You promised me a happy ending, you know. I don't think happy endings involve tears."

I somehow find my voice to clarify, "I promised you the good guys would win, and they did. Surely you're not saying the bittersweet denouement negated the triumphant climax."

My face heats again as I hear myself saying the word *climax.* I drop my gaze and reach for the book, but he doesn't let it go. The well-worn paperback between our hands provides gentle tension, and he lets his fingers brush mine before releasing.

"Are you... here to see your friends?" I ask steadily, so steadily, reaching for calmness.

He glances over and grins at the sight of Tom and Nina, then turns back to me. "Can't I be here to see you?"

I have to think a moment before answering. It's impossible to believe he is here just for me. I used to know my worth, didn't I? No, he's being kind. It's a joke. A friendly, good-natured joke you're treating as an overture. Pitiable.

My right thumb and forefinger find the soft meaty spot at the base of my left thumb and squeeze. It's the perfect way to cause a sharp, memorable pain without leaving a mark. *Ask me why I know that.*

"Stella?" Demetri says. I hear concern cloaked within an attempt at sounding calm and easygoing. He's seeing too much of the damage. How broken I am. It's not becoming. My worth. Was I really just thinking about that? Like a bad gambler, I bet it all on a wild gambit and went bust. I got stripped for parts. I have nothing to offer a decent man. That's a relief, I suppose. No wild expectations, no dizzy hopes. No pressure.

I look up again, and it's both easier and sadder. "So, what was your favorite part?"

He talks about Bigwig defending the tunnel. His fond smile is satisfying to behold. I've done it: converted him to a reader. He'll have to be willing to let the activity become a habit, but I've given him a viable gateway drug. He's describing a fictional rabbit's courage and cunning with the same emotional investment as he would talk about a beloved friend.

"What about you?" he adds after his speech.

"It's one of those questions that tends to change with time. Favorite moments, favorite characters, they reflect who you are and where you are in your life... you can read the same book a few years later and have entirely new thoughts about it. I think, right now, Hazel's act of self-sacrifice on the farm. He doesn't know he'll ever get to see the bright future himself, and all that matters is helping to secure it for his friends."

"But he does make it home," Demetri notes, refusing to let me think about the all-is-lost moment without acknowledging the good-news twist that follows.

His energy and positivity are soothing to the point of intoxication. I choose to gratefully soak it in. If he wants to be here, for whatever reason, I'll take it. Like an astronaut who's found a backup oxygen supply to extend their hope of survival, of rescue, I resolve to enjoy the blast of clean air for as long as it might last.

Behind Demetri, Tom and Nina approach. As my vision shifts to focus beyond his shoulder, he turns to greet his friends. Nina's holding onto Tom with both hands, leaning on him like she still can't believe her luck.

"Congratulations," I blurt, and she turns her grin my way.

"Thanks," she beams.

"We're off," Tom tells Demetri. He gives me a little nod, as if I'm becoming part of the welcome backdrop of their lives. No longer a ghost haunting the common spaces, not even just a quiet caretaker. Becoming something like a friend to Demetri makes me friend-adjacent to the others. It's such a normal, human thing to think about being.

"So what's my next assignment?" he says, pulling my emotional roller coaster back off track.

"Don't put it that way. You might start thinking of it as a task."

"Not every task is a chore, Stella."

As he speaks, a slow smile starts in his eyes and gradually fills his face, only landing on his lips with my name. It's as if a gust of wind blows only within my body, and all the dust is sent swirling.

"C'mon," he urges. "Send me to bed with something good."

He's succeeded in making me blush, and I take the excuse of turning my back to walk out from behind the desk while I try to recover.

"I—I have something for you. This way," I say, struggling with the fluttery sound in my voice.

I dared to ponder it briefly those first couple of days before the haze settled back in. As such, I ultimately failed to make a selection. Recalling his friends love the Narnia books, I considered something in that vein or perhaps by the same author.

Demetri wears a mask, though I've never seen him in it. His closest friend wears a mask which, until recently, few had seen him without.

I lead him to the right section and drop *Till We Have Faces* into his hands. "Another one I've always loved. I don't know if your friends have read it—I know, you have other friends—but they like this author, so it's possible."

"Are you going to tell me how the story goes?"

He's standing far too close. We're hidden from view back here between the shelves. It was hard enough to relax and enjoy these unfamiliar sensations out in the open.

"Not this time," I manage, barely above a whisper, before backing away and scurrying into the aisle to escape—what? Not him... myself. I bite down on the swelling regret. Running from myself. Again.

My flight disrupted, I stop just after we re-enter the atrium and turn to face him again. It was foolish to run. I betrayed my own intention to drink in this kindness and warmth before it goes away for good.

I feel the wistfulness in my gaze as our eyes meet once more. He studies me, perhaps trying to interpret my erratic moods.

"If I get back now, I should be able to make a dent in this before lights out."

I nod, suddenly regretting my selection. It's going to be another week or more, isn't it? If he returns at all this time? Have I given him too much? It's a shorter book, but denser. I thought perhaps in our strange little world where so many hide their faces every day, Demetri might find something that resonates, but what if he finds it impenetrable?

My voice suddenly erupts in a desperate babble.

"You know, there's a lot of mythology and—theology and—maybe you'd get more out of it if we talked about it along the way than if you waited until you finish—"

My face reddens. My breath goes shallow and feathery. I'm making a fool of myself over this man. Taking advantage of his kindness.

But he smiles, and the tense clench subsides from my lungs.

"That your way of saying you'd like to see me more often?"

"I didn't say that." My sheepish voice underlines how flimsy this deflection is.

"I'll take that excuse and run with it." His grin eases into something quiet and sensual. "I'm not sure I coulda stayed away as long this time."

Using the book to offer a little salute, he bids me goodbye. As soon as the door closes behind him, I slump against the nearest table, my muscles collapsing at the release of nervous energy.

The next morning, I'm eating breakfast in their stuffily appointed dining room when Celeste catches me staring into space. Thinking about his fingers brushing against mine as he handed back the book, our arms resting gently against each other the night I told him about it. Imagining it differently: He slides that arm around my waist, pulls me to him. Is he about to kiss me?

Celeste huffs. "Taking our time this morning? You typically shovel down food like you think it might come to life and run away."

It's been so long since I've stood or sat still long enough in her presence to provoke her. I think I had almost recovered from the constant barrage of cutting comments. Once again, I feel the sinking effect of her disparaging scrutiny. Not good enough. Never good enough. I could hardly retort that I eat quickly in the interest of escaping her presence. I've never been the sort to pick fights, and besides, Celeste doesn't just cow me, she genuinely frightens me. I can't let go of the strange certainty that she holds my fate in her clawlike grip.

I wish only that I could be unaffected by the barb. Celeste has had many words to spare for me, but never a kind one. I can't imagine what a cushion of self-confidence one would need to absorb the many blows.

Greg held Stella's arm in his as they walked up the front steps. His parents' mansion would be their home for the next few months; he'd generously offered to let Stella be part of the house-hunting process in Illustris rather than committing them to a home before she arrived in the city.

"I'm so nervous," she confided, a helpless titter coloring her words.

He gave her a smile and patted her hand where it rested on his forearm. The door opened, and there they were.

Stella burst out in the manner of taking a plunge, "Hello! Roger, Celeste, I've heard so much about you, and I'm so grateful to be here—thank you for welcoming me into your home—into your family!"

She heard herself rambling with edgy exuberance and she felt both embarrassed and sad on some deep, dim level of her mind. This wasn't her, was it? What had happened to the woman who belonged in important rooms with intelligent, accomplished people? Why was she suddenly desperate for approval?

Approval that would not be forthcoming, she could see from the polite, vague look on Celeste's face. What had Stella done wrong already? Should she not have addressed them by name until invited? Should she have waited quietly while Greg spoke first? That was probably it. Oh no.

Her eyes flew to his face in alarm. She'd messed up. Again. He was so patient with her. He kept telling her all the ways she could be better. She needed to try harder. She'd never been a poor student, but moving into a new social stratum was harder than anything she'd done before. She couldn't have done it on her own, certainly. Greg was not only her sponsor but her tutor. She hated the look of embarrassment and impatience he sometimes gave her—how many times could she fail before he would look upon her with regret? She'd given up too much to be here with him. She had to do better. She would do better, be *better.*

"Well," Celeste said finally, "come in before the neighbors wonder why my son is holding hands with the help."

After letting the insult sit just long enough that no one could take it for a joke, Celeste made a sound approximating laughter. Greg laughed. Roger smiled and patted Celeste's shoulder. Stella forced a nervous smile and token chuckle. And with that, she was admitted into the home. She watched herself walk in with the detachment of a helpless dreamer telling herself to stop—here there be tygers.

Chapter Seven

Novelty

Demetri

When I show up at the east gate, there's a new face on Rich's squad. Not new to me exactly, and the way she looks at me, all wide-eyed and unsubtle, tells my idiot dick she'd love to say hello. I close my eyes and breathe, telling it to stand down and not just because we're about to go out on patrol.

Astrid's just out of training, but it's not our first encounter. I was on the team that brought her in through the south gate a couple months back. The second we were inside the walls, I ditched the helmet as usual, raked my hand through my sweaty hair, and saw her staring. She might've wanted me under any circumstances, but the way things played out, I was like a knight in shining armor to her.

I wasn't all fucked up about anything back then, so my asshole brain flipped on and I gave her a grin. I thought, *See you around the barracks someday, I'll let you thank me properly.* I'm in a different place now, but the way she's staring, it seems like she didn't get the memo.

"You nervous?" Aaron says, distracting Astrid. At least his dumbass question gets her to look away from me.

"Yeah," she admits. "I keep hearing it's even more dangerous now than when I got here?"

Aaron puts a hand on her shoulder, and if he's trying to comfort her, it's not working. More squads should have adopted Monica's rule, now that I think of it.

"Good days and bad," he says in a half-assed attempt at calming her nerves. "No need to be scared. You got here all right, and now you're trained, and you got us with you." He gestures vaguely in my direction. "Plus a Helmet. It's gonna be fine."

Her eyes flicker my way again, and she shifts slightly like she wants his hand off her. Shit. I can't just ignore that. Sighing, I take a few steps and slap a hand on *his* opposite shoulder, surprising him into dropping his hand from hers.

"Hey. Astrid, right?" I hope pretending to be uncertain about her name discourages her crush a little.

"Hi, Demetri," she blushes, so I guess that was a bust.

Aaron doesn't bother smiling when he turns to face me. "Hey. Astrid was just feeling a little nervous about heading out."

"All the talk about Devil Runners..." her voice trails off, and the light in her eyes has dimmed. She's afraid. She's right to be.

"They don't come at us as hard lately," I offer, trying to give her something to hold onto.

"Maybe they've got their hands full," Aaron says. Fuck's sake. I cringe and bite back the impulse to dress him down hard, because I know what the fuck he's alluding to. Fortunately he doesn't elaborate; the last thing Astrid needs to hear is the Devil Runners might be a little overwhelmed with containing all the women they've supposedly captured. What pisses me off even more is the way he said it. It sounded like dark humor. I know, I know, humor's a coping mechanism. I should try to give him the benefit of the doubt, but it's hard, considering I already wanted to punch him a little.

Shoving down every instinct that tells me to put distance between myself and this pretty girl with her hero worship heart-eyes, I make an inviting kind of gesture, indicating I'll walk her to the gate. Just to give her an excuse to move away from him, nothing more, but she swivels her head and stares up at me like I've asked her to fucking prom.

I make a point of not making eye contact again as we reach the gate and I put on the helmet. I fucking hate the thing sometimes, sure, but right now... she's gone from being a pretty little blonde who looks like she's wondering what flavor of ice cream my dick might be to a grayscale representation, a little flattened, a lot less interesting. Not that I want her to be interesting anyway, but it's hot as hell being wanted. You don't really get used to it, even when you think you should.

Monica, for instance. I've fucked Monica I don't even know how many times. I never doubted I could fuck her again. But it never got old having her come at me in the rec with that look. Or Samantha, goddamn her. Practically begging for it in the middle of a shift. It's so good knowing a woman wants me. Every time. Every woman. *Fuck.* I need this out of my head. I need to concentrate. Another deep breath and I drag my mind out of the gutter just in time for the gate to swing open.

Poor fucking Astrid. Not gonna get a quiet first shift after all. I stop and raise an arm to alert the team, then quietly fill in the team leader, Rich, on the private channel. With an experienced squad, I'd lay it out straight, but a newbie in the mix complicates matters. I want Rich to have advance knowledge of what we might be coming up on.

"Movement beyond the tree line. And some that aren't moving. Could be captives, or fresh kills, and whoever or whatever did it."

"Can we just back away? They might not have spotted us."

Fucking coward. "We have to identify the threat. I already notified Command," I lie.

"Fine," he bitches, but once he flips to the general channel, he plays it tough. "We're moving toward an unknown threat. Just beyond the tree line. We have to get closer so our Helmet can positively identify it. Be prepared to shoot, run, or shoot and run."

As we move slowly closer, I laser focus on the shapes of whatever we're approaching. It's almost just a *shape* for a long time. Too big and misshapen to be mistaken for a single organism, too uneven in heat signature to be anything but a combination of death and life, closer than those two things should ever be. Closer than they can be for long.

If the cold spots are dead people and the warm spots are living people, that makes them Devil Runners, almost certainly, scavenging their victims. I'm not assuming Thrashers. They don't hang around long after a kill.

But it's the opposite, I can tell as we get close enough to differentiate a little better. My stomach drops, not with fear but sympathy and a deep sadness for the people just beyond the trees.

The warm spots are the victims. The cold spots are zombies.

My voice feels hollow and stony in my throat as I ping the general channel. "Human victims, maybe not yet dead. We're gonna have to put 'em out of their misery. Deal with the zombies first."

"On three," Rich agrees, then does the count.

We spent the rest of the shift dealing with the mess. I notified Command what our final position was, so they know which sector of the quadrant went completely unpatrolled on our watch. A pile of zombies and dead people dragged clear of the trees and torched, per protocol... that shit takes time.

"Fuck." The word rides my ragged exhale as I pull off the helmet at last and shake my hair loose. How the fuck Tom ever dealt with that constant pressure, or the other helmet heads who haven't outgrown the habit... I'm always grateful to get the gear off me, and never more than in moments like these. It's easy enough on quiet days, knowing that this is our lives, but a slaughterhouse scene like that reminds you: *Oh yeah, this is what life is going to be every day for the rest of it, until I'm old or injured or just plain dead.*

Astrid is shaken up, I can see from across the room. She's listening to Rich with kind of a glassy look in her eyes. He's probably lying to her about this getting easier over time. Or maybe it's not a lie, maybe he really thinks that. Maybe I'm the one who's weird because it only seems to keep getting harder.

Her gaze shifts and she catches me looking at her. *Shit.* I turn away, breaking eye contact as quickly as possible.

I hand off my weapon and get the hell out of the armory to head back to barracks, and I manage to get far enough ahead that no one bothers running to catch me up. Halfway there, I start to feel like an asshole. An egotistical fucking asshole who thinks every woman in the world is trying to fuck him.

Sure, she was giving me the eyes before we headed out, but after what just went down, she probably needs to be treated decent like a goddamn human being. Aaron'll be all over that... and it's not my problem, but I don't feel good about maybe helping him move in on her when she didn't seem too excited about it.

At some point, I'm gonna have to learn to be friendly again. It's nobody's fault but mine everyone thinks I'm chronically down to fuck. I was making myself pretty goddamn available till just recently. I probably need to calm the hell down and try being semi-social sometimes.

"Damn, you look fucking morose. Aren't you too pretty to be glum?"

Glancing up to greet Manny, I try for a smile but it fails. "Rough day, I guess."

"No kidding," he says, agreeing, letting it sit. He's a good guy. He doesn't miss much, but he doesn't pry. Just kinda lets you talk if you're inclined. And I guess I am.

"There were some bodies to clean up today. Pretty sure they used to be Ark Angels. I mean, there wasn't a lot left of 'em, but one of the faces looked familiar to me. And not in a way that made me wanna kill 'em all over again, you know?"

He huffs bitterly, and I figure he's also remembering the time Monica took his head off about his homicidal urges toward Devil Runners.

"Bet you're right," he says. "We haven't seen much of the Angels lately. The way they were getting hit, it was probably a matter of time."

We both pick at our food in silence for a few minutes. There's this wistful kind of nostalgia you get sometimes about the freedom to skip a meal. When the world is brutal and fucking disgusting, you should be allowed to lose your appetite. Like, out of respect for the dead or something. But we're working too hard to be able to pass up food even if sometimes we can barely taste it through the despair.

"What's been up with you lately, anyway? And feel free to tell me to shut the hell up, mind my own business, et cetera. It's just—in my old line of work, if someone's behavior changed, it was something to keep a close eye on, try to get 'em talking. Because our lives were in their hands and vice versa, and... well...."

"Yeah."

Manny would have more experience with literally putting his life in someone's hands every day, up there in the sky, pilot and copilot. Most people didn't do life-or-death type stuff in the old world, not like him. I did some climbing, but even that's about trusting ropes and gear as much or more than trusting your fellow climbers.

"Hey," I ask suddenly, wondering how I never wondered it before, "you'da been an easy fit for Helmets, what with your background and all."

He shrugs.

"Why didn't you go through training? Hard to imagine you failed out."

His mouth sets into a serious line. "Didn't want it. I might have made a different call later, but... it was too soon. I wasn't ready after... everything."

He's staring at something, and I follow his eyes—Monica, of course. Yeah. I bet he'd have made a different call looking back. If he'd've known he was gonna fall for someone who wouldn't cross lines with a teammate. She and I fucked plenty, sure, but Helmets don't stick with any one squad. Suddenly it occurs to me I fucked the woman he's pining over. But we've always gotten along fine. He probably compartmentalizes pretty good. Most of us do.

"C'mon, man, you haven't played pool in so long I might even be able to beat you. Give me a shot," he rags.

"I could use a beer," I admit, and he grins in triumph. We make our way to the rec. This is healthy, right? Social activity, normal shit.

"All right, show me what you can do. Kick my ass or humiliate yourself trying."

He makes a goofy scowl and goes to rack the balls. I take my first sip of beer in over a week and glance around the room at all the soldiers letting loose, living like there's no tomorrow because there may not be. I kinda wanna check in on Stella. I know it's not a good idea to spend every free minute at the damn library, and not just because of what my friends are up to. I've gotta let this thing breathe.

But I wonder if she's thinking about me. Hoping it's me every time the door opens. Picking out the next book she wants to give me. It's maybe a little unfair how I always know where she is, what she's doing, and she just waits to see if I show up. I gotta hold back, though. Let myself want something instead of just fucking having it just 'cause I can.

I could, though. Couldn't I? Get her alone in those aisles she uses to spy on people, make much better use of that semi-privacy. She wants me. It would be so easy to say fuck it and just have her. And who's to say that wouldn't be okay? It's not like no one ever fucked along the way to falling in love. What the fuck am I waiting for?

"Yo. Earth to Demetri."

Right. It's my shot. I reassess the layout of the table, which balls have moved or disappeared while my mind was elsewhere. I take so long about it that Manny offers to remind me whether I'm stripes or solids.

"Fuck off," I tell him and line up a shot. Just as I pull back the cue, a set of hips appears in view right above where I'm aiming. My eyes drift up to see Astrid, and I whiff the shot, not nearly enough oomph. The cue ball spins lazily off to the side, and Manny laughs.

Astrid smiles invitingly. Suddenly the last thing I want is to hang out and be social, let alone finish my beer.

"I'm gonna quit while I'm behind. Good game," I say, handing Manny my cue.

I make it around the pool table and a few feet closer to the door before—

"Hey." Astrid is in my space. Shit. She thought I was bailing on the game *for* her, not because of her.

I'm suddenly disoriented, like I just walked into a room but forgot what I came in for. My feet fail me, my words are nowhere. I don't have it in me to look at the girl, so I just stare inward, looking for answers when I can't remember the question.

If I move any part of the left side of my body, I'll run into her. I try not to breathe, in case expanding my lungs brings us into contact. *What do you want?*

But I know what she wants. I've done this a hundred times. Put myself in reach and wait for the woman to close the distance. It's so easy.

"Today was intense. I mean, for me."

"Yeah. I can imagine."

Her hand on my arm, just above my elbow. It's not quite a squeeze, definitely more than a pat. It's a caress, an invitation. I breathe slowly and tell my blood to stop moving south. I'm Pavlov's fucking pooch, and it's pathetic. It would be so easy.

She closes the gap, lets her breasts rest against my bicep. They're not full and warm like Stella's would be, but they're here. I've been good. I've been resisting urges left right and center for weeks. What's this bouncing alarm in my heart rate? Is it just novelty? I've never had this one. That's it, isn't it? I've been turning down women I've fucked before. I knew what I was missing. It's pathetic how hard it burns my balls, the idea of turning down something *new*.

Just once, just to know, just because I can.

Stella and I aren't together. We haven't even kissed. I don't know if we ever will.

Why am I doing this to myself? Depriving myself for no reason? Here I am, bird in hand—they call women birds in England, right? Tom. Would he laugh if I told him I went for the bird in hand?

No. He'd give me a sad kind of smile because I fucked up. Because this wasn't about Stella originally, it was about me.

"Listen, Astrid, thanks for… um, I don't know what, but I gotta go."

She's startled by my brusqueness and by the fact I'm not even looking at her. She lets go, backs off just an inch, and I beat feet back to my quarters before I can question how well I just talked myself out of adding her to my collection. I got so used to having everything I wanted the moment I wanted it.

Maybe some things aren't meant to be quite that easy.

I don't jerk off. I don't feel right about it, the semi being from someone else propositioning me and all. I ignore it and let it calm down enough to allow me to focus on this book.

And it's kind of karmic the way the book seems like it's designed to smack my hand away from the all-you-can-fuck buffet.

The narrator's thinking about how even the best of men is fundamentally unable to stay committed to any task, any feeling, because some physical urge will inevitably distract them. Thank fuck I held it together tonight. This character's kind of a bitch, actually. If I was living down to her ideas of what men are, that would be insult to self-inflicted injury.

But I did it. I got through another goddamn gauntlet of temptation without doing anything I'd regret.

Stella chose this book for me. Because she wanted to put its ideas in my head or just share something she loves, or have something to talk about next time we're together. She thinks about me. Wants more from me than my dick. But she wants that too. *Don't you, beautiful?*

The way her eyes light up at first every time she sees me. The way her pupils get so big because she's trying to take me in. *You wanna take me in.*

I'll come for you, Stella. Just you.

Chapter Eight

Privilege

Stella

True to his word, Demetri appears two days later. I feel myself light up at the sight of him, and I force myself to look away as from the sun.

"That's kind of an intense book you gave me. I mean, wordy or whatever, it's... I can totally handle it," he finishes with an air of vaguely macho defensiveness.

I find myself suppressing an urge to giggle, and it's both sad and beautiful. I haven't had giggles in me for so long, it seems a shame to fight them. I wouldn't want him to misunderstand my laughter and feel insulted, though. He's just terribly cute.

"I suppose it is rather advanced," I say apologetically. "I was thinking about masks and hidden identities. I suppose I thought it might strike a chord for you. Helmet and all," I add with a demonstrative flourish, making a circular gesture around my head.

He seems totally at ease now, leaning gently on the nearest shelf and grinning at me.

"Did you read this in college or something?"

"No. Well, yes. The second time I read it, I was in college."

He frowns. "And the first time?"

I blush and admit, "Fifth grade," again hoping I'm not insulting him.

Fortunately, he laughs, shaking his head. "Smart women," he mutters. "Something about 'em that's... like this chick, um, princess, I guess. The one who wrote the—I mean, the main character, fuck—"

He's adorably flustered and trying so hard. *To impress me?* My hand drifts out of its own accord to touch his briefly, and he calms down.

"The narrator? What about her?"

"Yeah. That. She's kind of terrible, isn't she?"

My cheeks ache a little. I wonder how long it might take me to get used to smiling again.

"Terrible how? I mean, yes, I suppose she is, but tell me what makes you say that."

"Well, she's just so selfish. Her love is selfish, you know? She's afraid of being left behind, not being good enough. She throws ultimatums around at the people who love her because like, that's the only power she has over people is that they love her, and she's terrified of losing it."

"Wow." My smile has fallen away in awe at his explanation.

When his expression falls as well, I realize he may have mistaken my silence for disapproval, and I rush to encourage him. "Demetri, that was a beautiful insight. You're entirely right. She's bitterly envious about the beauty she lacks, the shallow love she's missed out on. She's been rejected so much for the wrong reasons that she doesn't trust deeper love or even comprehend its relative worth."

His shy smile warms me further, and he adds, "It does get you thinking. About appearances and masks... and beauty."

The way he says *beauty* makes me want to believe he means me. I start to fall into his eyes, but movement behind him distracts me just enough before foolish notions can take hold too deeply.

"Oh," I say, recovering, "your friends are here. Are you going to—"

"Stella," he reminds me playfully, "I'm here to see you. I see those guys plenty."

"O—okay." *Keep talking, Stella.* "Beauty, right? Istra, the youngest sister, is supposed to be the most beautiful woman in the world. The book seems to treat her as a combination of several important figures from Greek myth, which is not that uncommon; there's a fair amount of overlap in the great stories. She's Psyche, fundamentally, but there are echoes of Helen, Pandora, even Hercules—but I said I wasn't going to tell you the plot this time, didn't I?" I pinch myself to stop my rambling.

His eyes quickly dart back up from my hands, and a dark frown clears with seeming effort.

"I hate to burst your bubble," he says, "but what you just told me was not a spoiler. I don't know what you're talking about. Do I need to?"

"No," I assure him, "you don't need to recognize any of the references to follow the story. In fact, I'm already enthralled by hearing your perspective without the distance of academia."

He chuckles. "I feel like you just called me stupid. Just a little."

My eyes fly open in horror, and my hands raise in a panicked gesture of *wait, I didn't mean it!* But he just laughs again.

"It's okay. I'm not offended. And it's not really—I mean, I know I work harder than the average Helmet."

My curiosity displaces my dismay. "How do you mean?"

He shrugs, looking a little embarrassed. "I've got a rep for being super serious and quiet on duty." Off my surprised smile, he admits, "Yeah, I know, hard to believe. But it's a lot. Staying on point in that gear takes major focus."

He leans across the desk as he reflects, "I used to think maybe the helmet heads were kinda nuts, but I got to know Tom, and there went that theory. So I figure maybe they're all just smart as hell like him. The effort it takes to live inside that thing on patrol is all I can handle. I can't wait to get out of it the moment I'm off duty. Walking around in it all the time? I'd be a wreck."

"I can only imagine," I say, recalling how difficult it clearly was for them to read while encumbered.

Demetri blushes, suddenly sheepish, as if he's remembered something he shouldn't admit.

"What?" I ask, a note of playful demand in the smile I'm still so grateful just to wear.

His lips purse in cheerful chagrin. "Okay, but—it's not my own thoughts, okay? It's not, I wouldn't—"

"Just say it!"

With a vocal exhale, he confesses, "Some people think the only reason I'm not a helmet head is I'm too damn vain about my looks. Like I said, it's not me, it's—"

This time I allow the giggle to burst free, and it feels good. "It's okay, it's hardly news that you're handsome. I'd hardly penalize you for being self-aware."

He tilts his head, smiling gratefully like I've done something of greater value than stating the powerfully obvious. "Truth is, I've always been super lazy. Being a Helmet's the most I've ever worked. At anything. My dad used to give me such a hard time about it. My sister was smart and ambitious and driven, and I was just... I dunno. I was always just kind of okay with how things were. I didn't have the motivation or something. Like, there was this gym rat a few years ago trying to sell me on his lifestyle. 'With relatively little effort, you could look this good!' And I was like, but the way I look now takes approximately zero effort, and I do all right!"

He suddenly looks flushed and serious, as if he's said something he regrets. He mentioned his father a moment ago, so perhaps he's drifted into the dark thoughts of those we lost.

"You're more than a pretty face, Demetri. Forget about why you're not a 'helmet head,' because you are, in fact, a Helmet. From what I understand, that's quite a big deal. You should be proud."

He shrugs again, and there's a sweet shyness to his smile. "I guess... but the helmets are also just really cool. It's like having superpowers. I mean, it's a matter of return on investment, right? Spend your time at the gym for muscles bigger than you need, or go to business school to get a job that makes you wanna jump out a window. But if I could have been Batman? There's no amount of effort it wouldn't've been worth to be Batman."

My smile falters. Here in Illustris, we're surrounded by people who could have chosen to be Batman, couldn't they? With all the money in the world at their disposal, they built a private enclave and populated it with workers for the farms and factories they'd deemed indispensable for their creature comforts and, indeed, to keep them self-sufficient just in case...

I mustn't be ungrateful.

My eyes lose focus, my face goes blank. I don't deserve to be here. What right do I have to be cheerful, to bask in the presence of a man like Demetri, after all I've stood by—

"Hey," he says urgently, "I'm sick of talking about me. Tell me about you."

I drag my eyes back to his face and feel the effort of refocusing like I'm looking through a phoropter at the optometrist. *One...or two?*

"Me?"

Looking relieved to recapture my attention, he nods. "Yes, you. I wanna know more about you."

"There's not much to me," I reply automatically, but no, that's Greg. That's Celeste. That's the damaged nub of my personality after being worn down with ruthless efficiency. It's not me. I want to be me again. Demetri seems to want that too, and it doesn't have to mean anything. He's got a kindness to him. That's all. He's reaching out to someone in need. If I let him pull me out of the ocean, maybe I'll remember how to swim by the time he gets bored and moves on.

"I was a professor. Of English." The words fall out with no energy behind them, but it's a start. "It was very early. In my career. I had so much to prove, I worked so hard, I—" *I gave it all up. Threw it away.*

Seeing me falter again, he hurries to keep the conversation on track. "Was that here? In Illustris?"

The question shocks a laugh out of me. "Oh, that's right, you're not from around here. Neither am I. Illustris considered higher education a literal waste of space. In their estimation, a university enriched the wider world, not its local community. They sent their children elsewhere to obtain an education and bring its value back with them to enrich Illustris."

Demetri's dark eyes are rich with sympathy. "You worked really hard and wound up in a place that called it a waste of time."

His insightful observation elicits a gasp. First the book, now this. He's smarter than he gives himself credit for.

"Waste of *space*, not time... but... yes. I met Greg at an alumni fundraiser. His family had donated one of the buildings on campus. I was there to try to schmooze and sweet-talk donors."

"You were there to be pretty," Demetri corrects matter-of-factly.

I'm not sure whether to be flattered or offended, but truthfully, I'm mostly confused. I just stare, waiting for him to explain the joke.

"And charming!" he adds as if he'd forgotten to say the most important part before.

"That's ridiculous. I was there to represent the university."

"By being pretty and charming," he says, continuing to make it sound like it should be self-evident. I frown, feeling increasingly like the butt of a joke he's failed to explain.

"Do you look way better now than when you were teaching? Was it like a super long time ago, so there's been like, a glow-up?"

I laugh bitterly at the idea, thinking what a meal Celeste would make of this humiliating moment, this handsome man making fun of me.

"Then you were there to be pretty, Stella. Sorry!"

"That's not how it works—*worked*. Academia isn't—*wasn't* a beauty pageant—"

My flustered, miserable stammering conveys my distress. He's shaking his head, giving a little wave of his hands, trying to calm me down—with a gush of relief, I realize he didn't mean to offend me, probably didn't realize I might take offense.

With an apologetic grimace, he says, "Everything was a beauty pageant. Sorry, but it's true. If you were up for the job and the other person was less attractive or charismatic, that's why you got picked, and it's not your fault—these things are outside your control, and it's not like you picked your parents or which genes you got from them. Pretty, charming people got stuff for being pretty and charming. Rich people wanted you around, so you were."

He's so matter of fact about it. So at ease. I don't think he even understands why I was upset; he's so comfortable with himself, and he's extending that to me. *He thinks I'm pretty.*

Rich people wanted you around, so you were. It feels like a small taste of absolution, and I don't deserve it, but I do need it.

"Thank you, Demetri," I whisper, unable to conjure real sound.

Behind him, a few people pass by and head for the door. He glances over his shoulder at them, then back to me. "I gotta ask Tom something. I'll be back in another chapter or two, and you can explain some more stuff."

I laugh and nod, feeling the tightness in my chest start to subside again. I don't know why he's here at all, but every visit from him eases my burdens a little more.

Knowing that Demetri is coming to the end of *Till We Have Faces*, and feeling only a touch remorseful for having thrown him into the deep end with my second, less careful selection, I allow my mind to pore over a number of options in all the quiet moments my days and nights tend to offer. It's a new dreaminess that has settled over me of late. A far better kind, to be sure.

This evening, he finds me back in Sci-Fi/Fantasy again, reshelving my rejects. I look up and again feel my mind has utterly failed to catalog him properly. He's just too beautiful to believe.

"I've been thinking about you," I say, then blush feverishly. "I mean to say, your next read."

"Okay," he agrees, looking gratified.

I glance down, attempting to recover, and pluck a book from the pile beside me. "I got you to read a book with a rabbit on the cover; let's see if I can get you to try one with a unicorn."

When he takes it, his face falls. Something tells me this isn't Demetri being playful; he's not about to tease me about this selection. He's affected by it somehow.

"Are you all right?" I venture delicately.

"Yeah. No, it's... it's cool. It was a movie. My sister—it was her favorite. She made me watch it about five thousand times. I pretended to hate it after the first thousand. It's kinda like an obligation, complaining about your big sister's favorite movie. But I didn't hate it. She knew that," he adds, and for a moment I see and hear a shade of the kid he was then. He might be seeking reassurance that the other kids were lying about Santa not being real.

Our eyes lock for a long moment, his quavering, mine steady. "Absolutely she did," I confirm quietly, and he looks down at the book again, blinking deliberately, clearing his eyes of emotion.

"Guess I don't need you to explain this one to me," he says, and I can't read the emotions in his voice; there are too many.

"Should I—" I reach to take the book back and offer an alternative, but he finally looks up again, clutching the book to his chest.

"No. It's good."

I try for a smile and am relieved when he responds with one of his own, albeit far from full wattage. A little *ding!* startles us both. Our heads swivel in unison toward the sound.

"I'd better—"

He nods and makes a little *you go ahead* gesture with the book, indicating he'll wait here for me.

As I approach the desk, I cringe. The man is facing away from me, but that is unmistakably the couture of an Illustrian. I start a preemptive apology. "I'm sorry, I hope you weren't waiting long—"

But he just smiles pleasantly and holds up a hand to cut me off. "No need for an apology. Good evening. Stella, isn't it?"

"Yes." I put on my dealing-with-an-Illustrian expression, though it feels different than it has before. *I'm* different, of course.

"My name is Benjamin Croft," he says as if that should mean something.

"Is there something I could help you find?"

He seems to be studying me, and I feel myself shrinking, trying to make my cardigan bigger so I could disappear inside voluminous sleeves that suddenly fold around me like a tesseract. Illustris people used to be an enticing species. One I wanted desperately to please—and not merely for self-preservation. I want to slap the younger version of myself. In the here and now, I settle for an unforgiving pinch.

"Perhaps you could recommend something," he says, and I can't guess why he sounds coolly disappointed. Disappointed in what? Me? Am I in trouble? No. No, get a grip. I've done nothing to endanger myself. There are no thought police.

"What sort of recommendation?" My words are bland, dusty, chalk on a board.

Once the door closes on Benjamin Croft and a bit of historical fiction set in Ancient Rome, I glance around the room to make sure I'm not leaving anything in need of immediate attention before returning to where I left Demetri. There's a sound getting louder as I near the spot, and I know just before I see him what that sound is. I can picture it so easily—that night he wept while I stood behind the desk, wishing I could go to him.

He's sitting on the floor, back against the wall, knees up. His handsome face is screwed up tight as if sufficient muscle control might allow him to capture the emotions trying to escape. When he senses my presence, he makes a clumsy gesture to shield his face from view. I catch his hand, hold it as I sink beside him. He lunges into a desperate hug, burying his wet face against my shoulder.

His breath hitches as he surrenders to the outburst. Warm, juddering exhales broken by gasps that steal back that warmth just long enough to miss it. Tears smoothing the slide of his cheek along the side of my neck. My arms close around his back, one hand daring to reach up and touch the dark silk of his hair.

This isn't merely the most physical contact we've had, it's the closest I've been to anyone in nearly a year, and for so long before that, no touch could be trusted.

Demetri's breathing slows, becomes less erratic. A moment later, his arms around me loosen slightly. I feel a pang of loss disengaging from this hug, but the somber embarrassment on his reddened face drags me out of my selfish concerns.

He's so beautiful. We're barely three inches apart. *Kissing distance.*

"Are you okay?" The words are a foolish necessity. Of course he's not, but I had to say something. To focus.

He leans back against the wall, unlocking his vulnerable eyes from mine, moving his still trembly lips out of reach before longing can lure bravery near enough to form temptation. I settle into a more natural position, my right hip and shoulder bearing my weight. With a bit of wonder, I realize I barely noticed the awkward clench of my thighs or pressure on my knees when all my attention was on the man weeping in my arms.

"You were just gonna be gone for a minute, right, so I thought I'd just check out the first page or two. I sorta even remembered the movie in my head, and it's been years. And I still woulda prob'ly been okay." His voice is thick, his diction almost defiantly lazy. "But there's this part—these guys are talking—one guy says girls all turn into silly old women eventually, right? But Lenora—she's not gonna do that." He wrestles with a fresh sob, dragging the emotionally loaded breath between clenched teeth, wringing it out.

"You don't know—"

But his eyes flash with bitter pain and he cuts me off in the midst of my well-meaning equivocation.

"We all know. No point pretending otherwise. Anyone who wasn't close enough to try for the Stronghold is a goner, even if they're not gone yet. It's kinda my fault she was gone. I coulda made different choices that maybe I'd've been gone and then maybe she'd be here."

"I don't understand," I prompt gently, because stating the obvious seems like the encouragement he needs to unlock the burden of these words.

"It was supposed to be me. Who went away. If our dad got his way about it? He had this idea about what a man's future should be and stuff. Not like he was a bad guy or anything, I don't mean... but like, he figured someday I was gonna have a family and be the man of the house, and when he looked at Lenora, it was like, she was never gonna be the man of the house, so she didn't need the same stuff along the way. He was putting aside money for one kid to go to a really good school, and he thought that should be me. Just, like, automatically.

"But Lenora was amazing. She was so smart, and she had real ideas about what she wanted to be. I didn't feel like I was half as clear about my life. She was only a year older but she was so far *ahead*... I wanted her to be the one. So I kinda bailed. Just, I mean, not totally; I still did fine. But I wasn't gonna be her competition, especially when I had an unfair advantage. I stepped back and watched her soar." He smiles fondly at the memory. "Dad was pissed. Rode me for a while before he gave up and started cheering her on. Like once he was finally on board, he'd never doubted her or something. And I just became the fuckup he didn't expect much of."

He pulls a handkerchief out of his pocket and swipes it across his nose quietly. "That's how my sister went away to a good school and started a new life on the other side of the country. It was supposed to've been me. And then maybe she'd've been here."

I place a hand on his, gentle comfort, nothing more. He widens the splay of his fingers and lightly squeezes mine when they fall naturally into the spaces between. Our eyes meet in the longest, deepest silence.

I'm glad you're here, I think, knowing it's not the proper response to offer.

"I think I gotta call it a night," he says apologetically.

"Of course."

He uncurls his long form and towers over me, then holds out his hand to help me up.

"You're such a gentleman," I say, blushing as I regain my normal stature beside him.

His eyes flicker with sudden decision, and he leans in to drop the softest, most gentlemanly kiss on my cheek. Before I have time to worry how I'm meant to react, he's already turned to go, so I remain, hoping no one else will ring the service bell before the fire has faded from my face.

Chapter Nine

Gray

Stella

To simply exist in the world is astounding after all that time in the murk. Wandering the stacks out of habit, I indulge in a propensity for reverie, replaying little moments. Demetri's smiles, his playful manner, his flirtatious glances. The times we just barely touched... the desperate way he clung to me as he wept... the kiss on my cheek. I'm like an Austen heroine, all a-flutter over the merest contact.

Scandalous. I quietly laugh at myself.

From my current vantage point in the first aisle off the central seating area, I see Tom and Nina take their usual table. Maybe that means Demetri will be here soon... funny he and his friends are typically here at the same time, yet he's never really with them. Glancing up again through the shelf gap, I see several others arrive.

"There you are." Demetri's sudden greeting makes me jump. My hand flies to my chest as if it could contain the leaping chaos of my heartbeat. He didn't mean to startle me. He probably doesn't know just how jumpy I am. That's good. If we are only as broken as we seem to those who know us best, perhaps I'm in better shape than I've dared to hope.

"Sorry about sneaking up. *Excuse me miss, is this guy bothering you?*" he adds playfully.

"Somehow I don't think anyone ever finds you a bother, Demetri."

"Oh, you'd be wrong. I've made my share of... I was gonna say enemies, but that's a lie. But people who weren't my biggest fans anyway."

"Like who?"

He thinks about it a moment. "The fathers of girls I dated in high school?"

"I bet. I also bet you won a few of them over."

"Yeah," he admits with an easy grin. "What about you?"

"No. I had one boyfriend in high school, and his parents loved me. Sorry."

"I meant, how am I doing on winning you over?"

I look away as if there were any chance of concealing my reaction to him, as if it mattered. He knows the effect he has on people. I have no idea why he's spending so much time with me, treating me to this outpouring of his undeniable charm.

Once again, I catch sight of his friends near the center of the atrium, speaking quietly. They look serious, and among their group I spot someone who doesn't fit. He's older, not the sort of person you usually see in the Stronghold defense corps.

"Hey," Demetri says, putting a hand on my shoulder to regain my full attention. "You know, I really like this book. It's almost like the movie, except kind of darker."

"Yes," I say, still a little distracted by a stray thought trying to form in the background. "Well, the movie had to be accessible to children, but the book is... universal." I can't stop my eyes from drifting again to the table where his friends are sitting with the out-of-place Illustrian, which I'm now sure he is.

"Stella," Demetri says, again adjusting his position, "is everything okay?"

And all the pieces fall into place. He's here because they're here. He's being nice to me to distract me. Because I get nosy, and they need privacy.

The flood of emotions takes her feet out from under her, and she sags against the shelf but somehow doesn't knock anything over—it's Demetri, of course, he's caught her. His instincts, whether as a soldier or a dastardly faux Prince Charming, were to rescue the damsel in distress. *Bastard.* She'd like to glare at him, snap at him, tell him to get his hands off her, but nothing works. She can't see, can't speak. His support may not be welcome, but it is necessary; his arms are the only tangible element in her immediate environment. Everything beyond a few inches of awareness around her head has gone gray.

"Stella?" He sounds far away. The effort of keeping her eyes open in the gray just keeps increasing, so she lets them slip shut.

"Stella," he says, his voice low and steady, "I'd like to get you to a chair, but I don't want anyone wondering what's wrong with you. So I'm going to take you to the desk and get you settled in there. Okay?"

The air is jagged. It pokes at her and feels like plasma on every inhalation.

"Stella?"

She'll never make it across the room in this state. It's impossible. He'd have to carry her if he wanted to move her. Let his friends see he's failed. *Serves him right.*

No.

I can't be weak. No one can see me like this. Letting him help me is the best thing for the library.

I think I nod. I'm not sure it's even enough motion to be visible, but it's more than enough to send my fragile equilibrium spinning even more. His arms tighten around me.

There's a sound like a baby crying in their sleep from the next room, and I realize it came from me.

"Okay, I'm going to do most of the work. Just trust me—"

Another inadvertent sound—this time, bitter laughter. He exhales in frustration, like I've hurt his feelings but it's not the time to argue.

"Stella, are you with me? I need you with me."

Hitching breaths, the onset of tears. He holds me tight, not just propping me up but embracing me. *And I can't even enjoy it. More's the pity.*

"It's okay, Demetri." I force the words out of my clenched throat past my parched lips. And it is... maybe not okay, but better. A relief in a way. To be unburdened of hope once again. "I understand. It..." *it hurts, but I understand.*

"Understand what?"

My eyes still closed, I jerk my head slightly in the direction I think his friends are. The little motion would be enough to send me to the floor if he weren't holding me so tight.

I'm so weak. My head finds the side of his neck and rests there, desperate to stop trying to hold itself up. Demetri's skin smooths the air for me. His scent is easier to breathe.

"We're going to walk now. You don't have to do much. Try to look as normal as you can manage, okay? I've got you."

He's stronger than I even imagined. I practically levitate, shuffling my feet a bit to approximate walking in case anyone looks over, but not bearing my own weight. *He's got me.* Pins and needles set in in my extremities, and the edges of my vision start to expand just a little, clearing away some of the gray.

When we reach the front, he starts to lead me all the way to the open end of the oval desk, but I smack his hand away.

"You're not allowed back there," I say as if old world etiquette carried weight now.

Even as hazy as my vision is, I can see he thinks I'm about to fall over. "Are you sure you can—"

"Yes," I hiss, pulling free of him, but the truth is, I'm still so unsteady that I use the edge of the desk to support me the whole way around until I reach the chair. It's a tall chair, and after I hop into it, a fresh wave of vertigo leaves me certain I'm about to pass out after all. *Breathe.*

The moment passes, and I open my eyes again to glare at him in resentful triumph. *See?*

He shakes his head like he's dealing with a petulant child. "You're gonna feel really silly about this," he mutters.

I lean forward tentatively, afraid to commit my weight to the motion until my forearms find the counter, then relax as much as I dare. Being upright isn't working for me right now, so leaning will have to do.

"You've been distracting me." I mean it to sound angry and accusatory, but it just comes out wounded. He takes my hands in his and caresses them. I pull away, and he only tries to hold on an extra moment before conceding.

My eyes open, and my vision is gray around the sides but clear enough at the immediate center. "I bet they laughed. When you told them all about... but I've never repeated a single thing I've heard in here. I wouldn't."

Surprise arches his dark eyebrows. "I didn't tell them all anything."

I give him a disdainful frown for lying to me.

"I'm serious," he protests. "Stella, you may not really understand how bad that story makes me look. You think I was eager to tell my friends I'm a dumbass who knowingly lets a sensitive conversation get listened in on as long as she's a *cute* spy."

The game is up, and he's still trying to deploy flattery. My eyes roll, an instantly regrettable impulse that brings the vertigo back on hard.

"Then why do they need you over here keeping me busy, if you didn't say anything?"

He actually laughs. "You think no one else has ever noticed you?" He shakes his head as if he can't believe how stupid and clueless I am. Then he tries to take my hands again as he says, "You don't exactly put the *Stel* in stealthy, okay?"

I stiffen and try to pull my hands away again, but this time he's not letting go. A chill invades my body. Is this how I learn he's not the good guy after all? Is this how I learn what a fool I've been? Again?

My vision threatens to close down, the gray returning and refilling, starting from the edges and working its way to overtake me.

"Where are you? Come back to me."

Stop making fun of me.

"Stella? I'm not joking around here. You don't want to be seen in this condition, do you?"

No. He's right about that. I can't afford to be seen in such a state. Or letting him hold my hands like this.

"I want you to open your eyes for me, okay?"

Go to hell, I think at him, and he laughs.

"You're really pissed at me, I can see that, and that's okay. But open your eyes and look at me."

Reluctantly complying, I scowl at his horribly handsome face. He has the nerve to smile. He squeezes my hands. *Jerk.*

"Stella, nothing has happened yet that changes anything. For anyone. You haven't made a scene. You're just sitting down in your normal space."

"I never sit." I can't help arguing with him. I can hear my own pout.

"Well, you do tonight," he says with irritating authority. "And we're gonna hang out here until my friends leave, and then you and I are gonna have a private conversation."

"It's unnecessary," I say through gritted teeth.

"That's where you're wrong. Actually, you're wrong about plenty. So sit tight, and just be as normal as you can manage for a little while longer in case anyone else comes in. Can you do that for me?"

"It's *my* library. I'll do it for me."

He chuckles, but it's a sad sound.

"Panic attacks, huh? You always have those, or just since—"

He means the apocalypse probably. I nod, knowing I've failed to answer; it wasn't a yes-or-no question.

"Yeah. Rachel had those. She was my girlfriend. In high school. Someone whose dad didn't think much of me at first. I was younger. Not like, by a lot, or anything, but at that age... She was my sister's friend."

Color has started to fill in around the edges. He's managed to get me listening, paying attention to him despite my best efforts. Because I'm weak, no doubt. Greg could influence me even after I knew better.

"She was a great girl, you know? Smart and pretty like you—"

My glare returns with a vengeance.

"She went away to school same year as my sister, of course, and I still had a year of high school left. We tried the long-distance thing for a coupla months, but it was doomed. I was relieved when she said we should give it up. It was driving me crazy, you know?"

I bet. You couldn't wait to be a free agent.

"I was sitting home nights thinking about her, wondering whether she was thinking about me. It was only about a week before she stopped having time to talk as much. The writing was on the wall, you know? If she was holding herself back, not doing stuff she wanted to do, resenting me for it... I didn't want that. I didn't wanna be a drag. So when she finally made the call about moving on, I was just glad to be done with the uncertainty."

He sounds sincere. I've lost a little of the edge I was holding onto. It's hard to hate him. I don't want him to be something so different from what he's seemed. *Your judgment is faulty, or you wouldn't be here,* I remind myself.

"But after we broke up, some bad stuff happened. It's stupid to feel like I could have prevented it—what was I gonna do, decline the breakup? If one person wants out, the relationship is over. But when I would see her after that, when she came home for vacations, she wasn't the same. A little bit fragile, and... the panic attacks. First time I saw her have one, I almost called 911."

He looks me deep in the eyes, and I want to cry. I want to tell him it's okay. Whatever his friends are doing, it must be important, or he wouldn't be doing so much to help them. I forgive him for the subterfuge, and I'll get over the pain of briefly believing he liked me. It was stupid of me really.

"Stella, the meeting's breaking up right now. My friends are going to walk by. Try and look as natural as you can, okay?"

I nod numbly. A couple of guys wander out, then the older man, then a female soldier, then Tom and Nina, leaving us alone. I feel so stupid.

"Is there likely to be anyone else here tonight?"

I blink at him in confusion.

"How late do you have to keep the library open?" He's patient about having to rephrase his question. That's nice of him.

"Have to... I don't... really have to. I just... don't like to leave."

"Well, I'd like to talk to you somewhere people won't walk in on us. Can we do that?"

He's not going to let it go, is he? This is his job. I'm his job. He won't just blow it off because I say I won't report on him or his friends. He might if he knew just how my life has been here... but no. As little as he trusts me, I'd be an even greater fool to trust him.

Varying my pattern is likely to raise questions if I'm caught. If the main lights are off but the door's technically open, I could claim I had a migraine and was waiting it out in the dark before heading home. Demetri's presence might raise an eyebrow, but he could just be a gallant soldier who didn't want to leave without making sure I was all right. It would sound convincing to anyone who saw him the way I'd gotten used to—

Fighting a resurgence of useless emotion, I tighten my throat, hold my breath, and flip the switch behind the desk, plunging us into near darkness. "With the lights out, no one is likely to try the door."

"Okay. We'll stay here. Can I join you behind the desk, though? It's dark, and I'd like us to be able to see each other a little better."

"No," I say stubbornly, not wanting to take back my earlier restriction so easily, even if it was just me being snippy in the moment. "I'll come out."

I hop down gently and tentatively make my way around the desk, still wobbly, afraid to trust my equilibrium. The only lights left on are around the perimeter, and they're low wattage, just meant to provide maneuverability on my way to the exit.

He's just a shape in the darkness as I approach. It's easier now that I don't have to see his face. I can let my memory sand him down a little, dull the torment of knowing I was foolish enough to think *this man* was attracted to me.

Just as I get near enough that his features start to take form in the gloom, I feel his hand cover mine on the counter. I don't pull away, though I am about to object, but then his other hand slides around my waist. Before I can even decide how to react, he's kissing me.

I'm stiff and helpless as his lips touch mine. It can't be real.

But it feels real. And after everything... I might as well enjoy it.

With the choice to surrender to sensation, I let myself melt just a little. Then a little more. Unsteady as I was, I'm now weakened in a new way. If he dropped me, I would shatter.

"That's why I volunteered to do this," he says, his lips still brushing mine with the words.

"I don't understand."

In the darkness, his eyes are nearly black but filled with heat. His hand plucks mine from the countertop and pulls to encourage me to wrap my arms around him, and I'm nowhere near strong enough to pretend I don't want that. He brushes my hair back and says, "Sure you do."

With no distance between our bodies, the second kiss is even more devastating. I feel as he grows stiff, pressed tight against me, and my body hums with reawakened longing.

When my hips start to wriggle against the delicious pressure and a little moan escapes me, I pull back. There are still questions.

"Demetri—"

"I know. It's too fast," he says, sounding regretful as he moves back, taking his body just out of reach.

As I play back the words he just spoke, I realize we're not having the same conversation.

"Too fast?"

He reaches out, traces a finger down my cheek, my jawline, across my lips. "I didn't mean to kiss you tonight. If you hadn't... we've been getting to know each other and... it feels good. Doesn't it?" he adds with a hint of sudden vulnerability.

"Yes," I agree hesitantly, because I'm not sure what I'm agreeing with, but *yes*, this has felt good.

"It was my idea to be here. I mean, someone else suggested the library, but it was vetoed because... well... but I saw my chance to spend more time with you, and I jumped. Because I like you, Stella."

"But you're so—and I'm—"

"I'm not sure which one of us you're about to insult, but maybe just don't," he says helpfully.

"Demetri, I don't know what's real. I'm sorry I took it so badly because the truth is it doesn't matter. Even if you're using me in some way, it's the best thing that's happened to me since I came here."

He pulls me into a fierce embrace. "That's unacceptable. You're gonna have to get used to expecting better things to happen to you. I'm gonna make sure of that."

He's so strong, so *hard*. It's intoxicating, the feeling of him pressed against me, the thought that I've aroused this desire in him. My exhale barely avoids being a moan, and he hears the helpless desire given voice. It compels another kiss, and I'm grateful.

"I'll make good things happen to you, count on it."

Another kiss, deeper, more savage. He pushes me against the counter, grabs my hip, pulls my leg up so he can rut against me. If he wants me now, I won't refuse. Even with some small doubt about his intentions, even knowing the risks of that unlocked library door, nothing could stop me from feeling him inside me if that's where he wants to be.

His grinding hips press hard and hold his erection against me, my leg at hip height, my center open to him, only clothing between us.

"We're not gonna do it like this," he says as if reminding himself of a commitment. He doesn't pull away, but he eases back just slightly, ceasing the wonderful pressure, triggering a barely suppressed instinct to pull him to me again.

"I think this could be something real," he tells me, and the simple sincerity takes my breath away. "Can I keep coming to see you?"

What? "Of course! I—I would like that." The words are too much and not enough. I don't care if it's real. I don't care if it's just a brief intermission between the devastation of the recent past and the emptiness of my uncertain future. I won't deprive myself of this taste of joy, no matter what may come after.

"And I'm serious. I'm gonna be so gentlemanly and chivalrous and all that shit. You're gonna be amazed how well I hold back, now that you know how bad I want you."

"Careful. If you keep saying that I might start believing it." It sounds like a joke, but we both know it's not.

He kisses me again, long and slow. When he starts rubbing himself against me, he pulls back with a frustrated little grunt like he's annoyed at himself.

"How careful do we need to be about this? From your perspective?"

"What?" The question comes out of nowhere, and my brain is sex-fogged.

"I know the rules for people like me, but I don't know your rules."

"Oh." I hope it's too dark for my discomfort to show. The question is too big, the answer amorphous, mostly fear and supposition on my part. In this place, newcomers are given the comforting certainty of restrictions, legacy citizens the quiet burden of freedom. Being neither, I remain in limbo, waiting for proof of my path. And I can say none of this. Not to him.

"I told you where I live. And who with."

"Your in-laws, or they would've been."

"Right." I blink at the wetness in my eyes and wrestle the frog in my throat into submission before speaking again. "I think if they knew I had... made a friend... I think they might resent that."

Demetri nods and pulls me close, this time in comfort, encouraging me to rest against his firm chest.

"Then we'll keep doing things just like we have been, all right? I'll come see you, we'll talk, we'll be so respectable and maintain a safe distance from each other. The only difference is now you know how much it hurts me to do that."

I want to believe that, and wanting makes me reluctant. I've believed in men before. I start to pull back just a little, and he takes my mouth again for another mind-bending kiss, powerful lips and confident motion.

Maybe wanting to believe is enough. For the life I have now, it's far more than I could have wished. I won't fight you, Demetri. And I will never betray your trust. The tangle of our lips and tongues renders this a silent vow, no less true for being unspoken.

"I should go before I stop caring about doing the right thing. Because I want you, Stella. But not tonight. You still don't know for sure if you can trust me."

It's on the tip of my tongue to say I trust him as much as I'm capable, but he's not done talking.

"I want you to love me."

He kisses me again, perhaps to prevent a reply, as if I could have formed one. I take the kiss, breathe in the taste of him, absorb every sensation. If he's lying, this could be the last moment like this... he's right. I don't really trust him.

But I want to.

Chapter Ten

Restraint

Demetri

I want you to love me. I didn't know I was going to say it until I opened my mouth, but I meant it. I kissed her before she could say a goddamn thing in response, and then I fucking fled. Made it as far as the nearest shadow under some trees halfway down the block and stopped to catch my breath, let my dick calm the hell down for the walk back to barracks.

She smelled so good in my arms. Every inch of her reaching for me, soft and warm and needy despite her fears. She would've let me have her tonight, right there, wouldn't she? I could be inside her right now.

This is the opposite direction my thoughts need to go in. I take a deep breath in and force it out slowly.

When I held her while she was freaking out, even as bad as things were right then, even as angry and confused as she was, she couldn't help leaning in close to my neck and breathing me in. She wants me.

I could go back. Say fuck it. Bury myself in her before either of us has time to remember why I just said I wasn't going to. I could kiss her so hard her mouth can't form words, fuck her so deep her brain stops working, so hard my brain goes offline entirely. Pour all of this into her until it goes away.

Shit. Knock it off.

Another slow, steady exhale. The cold air helps. A white plume of steam escapes my lungs, giving away my position. If she comes out right now, will she think I'm keeping an eye on her? Would that make her feel watched over? Or *watched*?

Just in case it's the latter, I force my feet into motion. She's got some damage, anyone could see that. It's up to me to make things easier for her, not worse.

I intended to head straight for my quarters, but looks like Monica's been waiting for me. I find her leaning against the wall near the front entrance, and she pops upright at the sight of me coming through the doors.

"What's up?" I mutter, annoyed. It's not like me, but fuck, I just don't wanna deal with her right now, whatever this is.

She smiles like this is a casual, friendly chat, but I can see in her eyes she's not playing. "I need to talk to you. Why don't you invite me up?"

I blow out a gust of irritation before pasting on an equally bullshit smile and gesturing to her to walk with me.

As soon as the door closes between us and the rest of the world, she drops the show and says flatly, "Demetri, what the hell happened tonight?"

Shit. "I thought I did a pretty good job covering."

She shrugs. "Pretty good. Not good enough. I was facing your direction. So was Nina. So was Tom for that matter, but he was busy. Another dick-measuring session with Maxwell."

"What was it this time?"

"What is it ever," she grins, momentarily sidelined by the opportunity to talk some shit.

"Something Tom thinks is too risky for Nina," I recite.

She smiles fondly. "I don't need anyone to take care of me, just so we're clear, but... I love the way he takes care of her."

You don't know the half of it, I think, covering a snort of laughter by pretending to cough.

"The Commander's pushing for speed, no explanation why. Nina's only seeing new files as they come in, and what he wants is older. He basically ordered her to go poking around, but opening files leaves traces. Tom's stance is one hundred percent go-fuck-yourself, which, I have to admit, is pretty fun to watch.

"But back to the point. What happened with Project Librarian this evening?"

I look away. "Nothing you need to be concerned about."

"Demetri?" She sounds like a teacher after I said I left my homework on the bus.

"She had a panic attack. It's nothing. I mean, not nothing, it fucking sucks. She's been through some stuff, okay? I wasn't sure how to deal with it, and I didn't want to cause a scene. I helped her to safety is all. Nothing to worry about."

Yes, it's a lie, but I trust Stella. She won't screw us over. If the others knew, maybe they'd think it was best to stop hanging out there, but screw it, let's say Stella theoretically *might* do something... that would be likelier to happen if I stopped coming around after this, right? I'm making the smart call. Monica doesn't need to know.

She's staring at me hard, looking for something I haven't admitted, waiting for me to crack. I'm not fooling anyone here, am I? I guess it comes down to whether Monica trusts me enough to let it go.

Her shoulders drop just a bit, and her frown goes from searching to accepting. I won this round.

"I've got some reading to do. I'll see you tomorrow."

After a pause, she nods, then adds, "You can talk to me, Demetri. If you need to."

I hold the door open for her and mutter thanks. It's probably true, but I don't want to talk about this.

After she's gone, I fall back against the door and yank open my pants. I close my eyes and take myself in hand, and it's no time at all before I'm right back to full strength at the memory of Stella's soft heat just begging me to push away our clothes and have her. She wanted it tonight. I wanted her, and I deserve a fucking medal for resisting. I grip the top half of my dick full force and wonder how deep she'd take me right away. Would I have to go so slow with you, Stella? Or would you be pulling me deeper, begging to feel it all? You've got a lot of need, don't you? I felt that tonight, just out of reach.

I have the presence of mind to cover the tip with my other hand as I start to spurt. The captured wetness in my palm is a kind of tease—nothing even close to where I want to be right now. But this former hotel doesn't have maid service like the old days. Can't have my spunk funking up the thick carpet—what am I, a teenager? That sort of mess wasn't a concern before. I never used to spill anywhere that didn't quiver or swallow.

This place made life too easy in just the right ways to keep us from thinking particularly hard. I guess that was the point. We were like the rabbits in that warren with the poet and the mosaics. The Stronghold wanted us totally sanguine about our likely deaths. I see it now that I'm not spending every night literally living like there's no tomorrow. This place wants us to serve our purpose and shut the fuck up about it. It wants me and Tom to fight. Monica too, until she succumbs to her biological clock. It wants Nina to make babies.

What does it want from Stella? If she knows, she doesn't trust me enough to say. She needs to believe I'll catch her, like I did tonight when she lost her shit. I want her to know I'll always catch her. And that'll take time.

There's no way to know how much time we have. Everything's stuck in this holding pattern. Tom and Maxwell locking horns, everyone waiting for news or orders. And me, I'm on Project Stella, which now includes pretending I haven't already failed at my one job. I'll get Tom alone and brief him on how bad I screwed up, but he's the only one I trust to not overreact. Monica would probably want to change locations. And someone like Maxwell would—

Fuck.

This isn't just about me screwing up, I realize, feeling like a fucking idiot. If someone didn't trust her to keep the secret she just figured out, they wouldn't just stop flaunting it under her nose and hope for the best, would they?

This is way too big. Their lives are in her hands, and I can't help thinking that means hers is in mine now. If someone thought she was a security risk... I can't bring myself to think it out loud.

I know her. I trust her. With time, she'll learn to trust me. I know she wants to. I'll earn it.

Forget reading a while before bed when I'm all scattered like this. I kill the lights early and close my eyes. But instead of nothingness taking over, Stella fills my mind again. Is she in bed? I can't picture what a bedroom in an Illustris mansion might look like. I've never been anywhere that nice in my life. Who cares about the surroundings, though? Do you sleep naked, Stella?

Are you frustrated, empty, wishing I'd sneak in and finish what we started tonight? Do you touch yourself? Can you make yourself come? I know it's harder for women. Harder for you to ask for what you need. You won't have to ask. I'll give it to you.

Fuck.

I really had to go and commit to this taking-it-slow thing, didn't I? It's probably healthy. When I'm finally inside her, she'll trust me.

She'll love me. And I'll have been fucking my hand in her honor for long enough I won't even remember what another woman feels like.

It's for the best.

Patrolling with Monica's squad today has been great except for how much it slows me down on the way back to barracks. I let being among friends keep me from zooming to change, eat, and rush off to see Stella, but damn if I don't almost resent them for it. I get caught up in laughing along with them for a moment, then rankle all over again at how I could be farther ahead if I just bailed on them. I force myself to chill, bite down my impatience over and over.

Once we separate to get cleaned up, I rush the process as much as possible, wolf down my food, bolt for the library before they can catch up and maybe make me wait to walk over together. I have to see her. I can't wait, not tonight.

The way she looks up when I walk through the door, I know she's been half afraid it was all a dream. She seems to be almost holding her breath for a moment, but as we stare at each other, her shoulders loosen, and she seems to trust me just a little bit more already, just because I'm here right now.

I cross the room, and it's fucking unnatural all of a sudden to be so close and not touching her. I barely got a taste and I'm ravenous.

"I'm such an asshole," I reflect. She looks confused, but I explain, "To me, I mean. I'm cursing myself for making noble idiot statements about being a goddamn gentleman. That's the last thing in the world I wanna be."

She blushes. It's sexy as fuck. I let my eyes dip down to her cleavage now that I'm not trying to hide anything. My gaze travels back up the smooth skin of her chest to her throat, up to her lips, finally back to her eyes.

"I've been trying to be subtle about staring at you all this time. How'd I do?"

"Perfect gentleman. Mostly."

Her sly smile is so fucking sexy it hurts. I want her smiling at me all the time, no matter how much it aches my balls not to be touching her. I just want to never see her go away again like she does. Make her world feel too good to wanna get away from.

When Tom and Nina show up, I say hey, hoping they'll pick up on how I want them to engage instead of heading straight to sit down. Fortunately, they seem to get it, making a beeline right for me and Stella.

"Hey!" Nina says too brightly and directly to Stella. My eyes narrow as I watch Nina's demeanor, which is not natural somehow, though I'm not sure what I'm seeing yet.

"You know, civvie life is such an adjustment," Nina says. "I haven't gotten to know too many people yet. Maybe we could eat lunch together sometime."

I already had things to discuss, but now I wanna ask Tom what the fuck his wife is up to. He discreetly motions me away, and as much as I don't like what's going on with Nina and Stella right now, I go with him.

Just as I open my mouth, he cuts me off. "Nina observed a situation last night. Care to disagree with her assessment that we need another set of eyes on Stella? Perhaps a more objective set? No offense, Demetri."

My lips press tightly in frustration. "I have it handled."

"Then what did you need to discuss?" His eyes are bright with quiet laughter. He knows I was about to cop to a huge fuckup and only got derailed by Nina stepping in like this.

"Stella's cool, man. She's not... she's not one of them."

"Explain how you can say that with such certainty." He's challenging me, and it's only because I know him that it doesn't feel like a dick move. Objective is kind of his default.

"She knows. Okay? That's what I wanted to say. She figured out you were having me run interference. But I handled it. She's not gonna say anything."

He stares at me, and I feel the pressure of words building up inside.

"I kissed her," I say, though the words feel too simple and small for what happened between us. My gaze drifts over to her. She looks so happy. She might not even question this sudden chance to make a new friend; she doesn't know Nina's real smile from a fake one.

"Tell your wife to be nice to her," I say in a rush of protective angst. And it's dumb. Nina's my friend, and I don't distrust her. But Stella... "She's been through a lot."

In the corner of my eye, I see his face change, and I turn to see a gentle smile aimed my way. "I trust your judgment, Demetri. I also trust Nina's. If she thinks a female perspective on our unwitting hostess—*formerly unwitting*, that is—would be valuable, I'm not going to talk her out of it. I won't tell her what you've shared with me, of course. Not only would I not betray your trust, I wouldn't corrupt our new source of intel."

This crazy motherfucker is always good for a laugh. I can't believe he just described his wife as a "source of intel." I mean, I can, but only because it's Tom.

"Listen, man... I am sorry. I screwed it up. I was supposed to keep her occupied, and I failed."

He puts a hand on my shoulder. "I wouldn't say so. It seems more a reflection on her intelligence and perceptiveness than your efforts to distract or dissuade her. If anything, you've been humbled by the discovery that even your looks and charm aren't enough to stun and disorient a good woman. I'd have thought you'd learned that when you failed at seducing my Nina, but some lessons require repetition to sink in."

"You don't have to enjoy it quite this much," I point out, though I can't help laughing.

"Feeling better, then?" He smiles knowingly.

"Yeah," I say, shaking my head, and we rejoin our women. Stella's hand is resting on the counter, and I reach for it. She blinks in surprise and looks from me to Tom and Nina, then back again.

I just hold on, gently but with purpose. I'm letting Nina see it. Letting her know. I might not have gone public like this with anyone yet if she hadn't come in tonight ready to study my girl under a goddamn microscope.

The *whoosh* of the door opening forces me to let go—my friends knowing is one thing, but whoever might be walking in is another. But I've made myself clear, I hope. I make eye contact with Nina, and yeah, she got the message. Stella's my girl.

I was expecting it to be our people, but it's some Illustris jackass. Shit. The only natural move is for me to join Tom and Nina in walking away from Stella. For once, I guess I actually have to sit through one of these goddamn meetings.

We don't have to wait long for the rest of the crew to filter in. When Manny sees me at the table, he does a double-take—I guess he didn't look directly at Stella and this fucking guy she's talking to, he just assumed it was me *because it fucking should be*.

The gang starts talking through stuff, and I can't focus at all. I can't take my eyes off Stella. The guy's not old, but he's older. Gray hair, slim build. Dressed like he's coming from lunch at the country club or some shit. He didn't come in carrying a book. He sure doesn't seem to be here for a book. What the fuck is his deal?

Finally, he leaves. I glance at Tom, and he gives me the slightest shake of his head: *No.* He's right, as much as I hate it. I can't just wander away in the middle of the meeting. It's too transparent. Only he and I know Stella's aware of the situation, but if I bail the second she's unattended, the others might pick up on the weird vibe.

I'm still barely paying attention, but something Nina says drags me back.

"—saw a Thrasher today."

My head whips around at the insane combination of words. I must have heard her wrong.

"It's easy to get into a zone at a job like mine. Just scan and file, scan and file, you know? And your mind wanders... Every so often I see a familiar face, but it's like, someone from the kitchens. This one, though, I dropped my papers, they went everywhere, I had to reorganize a whole pile—"

"Darling?" Tom gently nudges her back to the point, and from where I'm sitting, I can see him comforting her under the table, holding and stroking her hand. Secret fucking softie. I cover my grin with my fist.

"I mean, I know it wasn't really him. The man whose picture I saw today was older, for one thing, and not... you know, feral with mindless rage. But I swear he looked so much like one of those things I fought."

Nina's gone pale. Her eyes look haunted. I hadn't even thought about it, but she probably has nightmares. Most of us haven't been through a close encounter like that.

We're all quiet for a moment before Davy blurts, "Hey, I just had—what if you didn't have to open the files?"

Everyone stares back at him blankly, and he seems to realize he's completely failed to explain his idea. The words start tripping over themselves in the rush to get them out.

"What if it was enough to know a file existed? Like, if you ran really specific searches. If you were curious who in Illustris owned a pool table or something. You could just search on pool table and whosever records got pulled up, well, you know those are the files that have the words pool and table. See?"

Nina's face fills with hope and gratitude. "Davy, that's amazing. That could really be the answer—"

"If only we knew the question," Tom notes quietly.

She turns to him and nods, accepting the incomplete victory. "Okay, yeah. Then that's the goal. Figure out the question—or questions—specific enough that a file only has to exist to tell us something useful."

"No problem, sounds easy," mutters Manny glumly.

Silence hangs heavy, but then Stella crosses the room and disappears into the stacks.

"On that note," Monica says, standing to go. Her guys follow her out.

Nina leans into my line of sight to drag my attention her way before asking, "We still cool?"

I can't help rolling my eyes and don't bother suppressing a smile. "Yeah, get outta here."

They turn to go, and I don't wait another moment before going after Stella.

I find her immediately, which tells me I was right; she walked into the stacks so they'd break up the meeting, waited right here so I'd find her easily. I don't say a word. I cage her in, gripping the shelf behind her in both hands, pressing her body with my own. I kiss her long and deep until her little whimper reminds us both we're not paying attention to our surroundings.

"Put the book down," I tell her quietly. She looks down at her right hand like she'd forgotten she was holding anything, then sets it on the nearest shelf edge.

"Hands on my shoulders. Hold onto me."

Her eyes widen with uncertainty but she does it. *Good girl.* I've never been the type to order a woman around, but from what I know of Tom's dynamic with Nina, it's not entirely about that. He loves ordering her around, no question, but she loves it too, and it's not about servitude. The way he explained it, it's about permission. When he orders her to do what he wants, he's also giving her permission to have what she wants. Stella wonders if I'm real, needs to learn to trust my desire for her so she can enjoy it. If I let her pull away, she might. If I tell her to accept the way this feels, maybe she'll let herself want more.

My hands slide down to her waist, her hips. I grasp just below the swell of her ass and lift, her legs opening to clasp around me, surprised but obliging. It's not too far to the nearest wall, where I know we've got a bit more privacy—not enough, not for everything I wish I could do to her, but just enough for the small amount I'm allowing myself.

I lean her into the wall, her ass resting just above the little decorative ledge so she can't just set her feet down and reach the floor, she has to hold onto me with her arms and her thighs, keep herself open to me.

"Feel that, Stella? I thought about you so hard last night. Again. I've fucked you so many times in my mind, and we barely even touched till you turned off the lights for me. Did you know what would happen?"

A little shake of her head, and our faces are so close our lips brush together with the motion, so I take it further, giving her my tongue. She sucks on it like I'll take it back if she doesn't grab tight. I thrust against her, let myself enjoy building a rhythm, and a helpless, needy sound tells me I'm pressing her clit, so I hold the angle and rock a few times. Her arms tense around my shoulders, and her hips widen even more as her legs try to pull me harder against her.

"I want to get you alone so bad," I breathe. "Really alone. Hear the sounds you make when you're not trying to hide."

There's something painful and pleading in her eyes. I want to believe it's all about how bad she wants what I want, but I see darkness there too. She's doubting me, maybe, or afraid. There's something she wants to say—I can see it in her face, but she just pulls my mouth into another desperate kiss.

I've taken it too far tonight, and I know that, so I ease her sweet ass down the wall a few inches, gently rub the back of her upper thighs to signal she should try to stand again. As her legs slide away from me, I again fight the urge to throw her on the nearest table to see how hard I can give it to her.

Her belly is such a welcoming place, though, I hate to pull away. I would do anything to relieve this need for both of us right here, right now. I take her hand in mine, kiss the smooth inside of her wrist, resist the impulse to put her soft fingers around my dick and let her stroke me.

"I said I was going to be respectable, didn't I?"

"I'm not complaining," she says, breathless and wanting.

"Respectable starts tomorrow, then. I couldn't resist tonight. From now on, every moment I'm not touching you, I want you thinking about this. Suffering, same as I am. It pains me not having you."

She melts against me some more.

"The thing about this place—" I slam the brakes on a thought I didn't mean to express, but I probably had to say it at some point. Guess my subconscious decided to force the issue. "The things you heard me talk about that first night. The stuff you've teased me about a little. I didn't wanna hafta talk about it to you but I should. Just a little."

Stella's gaze opens fully, ready to absorb whatever this is. I pummel the urge to just kiss her again until she forgets I ever started speaking.

"This place was like Christmas, Stella. Coming from outside, where we took turns sleeping—and you never sleep well, you know? Terrified you'll wake too slowly to save yourself when shit goes down. There's no relaxing, no joy. Then you're here and it's not just peaceful and safe, it's a party. Life before wasn't ever a party like this is. It's just so easy.

"And certain stuff, when it gets easy, it becomes like a lifestyle. You stop thinking about it. So I thought maybe I should change it up. Give myself a reset, see if I could have something real instead of sticking around the party 'til I died and never.... But it's hard enough to stop your body, meanwhile your brain holds on to the habit you formed, so I look at you, and I want—"

Realizing my hands have taken over again, grasping and pressing her closer, I pause to breathe and force myself to let go.

"I don't trust my instincts. I don't wanna screw this up. I want inside your heart. And you can think about how to let me know when that comes true. 'Cause *fuck*. I want inside your body too."

Chapter Eleven

Spectrum

Stella

His confession ends on a kiss that weakens every sinew, loosens every tendon. I'm lost. I know I will fall in love with this man. I know it the way Dr. Manhattan knows what is because it will always have been. My fingers slide into his hair, relishing tangible warmth and softness on this man who can seem so cool and tough.

"That might be the most words I've ever said at a time in my life," he says with a shy little chuckle.

"They were good words," I promise him.

His gaze dips down to my chest like he can't help himself. His hands at my waist clench a little like he's actively resisting the urge to use them.

I tilt my head and look at him again—it's a funny thing we do, a way of literally trying to see things from a new angle.

This place takes from you. It makes you feel like you're being served, rewarded. All the while it takes. I know that in ways he only suspects. On the other hand, what *does* he know? What do his friends know, and how do they hope to alter our course?

"You held my hand tonight."

"I hope that's okay. I know it has to be a secret, but... well, Tom already knew."

"Nina and I are going to have lunch tomorrow." I can't help smiling at the thought, even as a confusing shadow of disapproval flits across his mouth. *Does he not want me to be friends with his friends? Or with anyone? Greg got me alone, isolated me—*

"Listen, I—" He frowns as if he resents the thought he's about to give voice to. I hold my breath. *Please don't be the man who tells me not to make a friend.*

"I hate that I have to say this, but I want you to be part of my life, Stella. So—*fuck*. Here goes. If I'm friends with a woman, I've probably had sex with her at some point along the way, and I need you to know it's no big deal and all in the past, and I hope it's not too weird."

That's all? My tear ducts swell in relief, and I almost laugh.

"I'm not going to hold anything against you, Demetri. Or your friends."

His grateful smile is accompanied by a heavy exhale and his shoulders visibly relaxing. This must have been weighing on him.

He asks almost shyly, "Can I kiss you for a while before I have to wait to kiss you again?"

I pull him close, and there are no more words tonight. Eventually, his kiss becomes rapacious, and his hands grip me harder just before he pushes away with regret.

His thumb brushes my cheek in a gesture of good night, and with one last searing look, he turns to go. As I watch him pass out of my view at the end of the row, it strikes me how reckless this was. An anxious rhythm skips across my heart, and I spin to check for prying eyes in a far-too-late gesture.

The truth is there's no way to know whether anyone saw. If the door opened and closed, we wouldn't have heard it. Not from back here against the wall and not while we were so absorbed in each other.

There's nothing to be done now, of course. It will just be one of those time bomb worries for a while, I suppose, like a trip to quarantine. I'll be edgy and watching for the other shoe to drop until I finally accept that we skirted danger this time. The odds are good; it's cold out, after all.

Still, I walk the whole library before shutting down. Not finding anyone isn't as much of a relief as I'd like it to be, as my mind insists on pointing out they could have come and gone quickly—that seeing our clinch would have been reason to flee.

It's for the best we've committed to holding off on further risky behavior. For him, for me, for us. *Us.* That restores my smile despite my nerves. Demetri's like no one I've known. I wouldn't have put us together on paper, certainly. But that can only be a good thing. I shut down my sanctuary and return to the illustrious home of the perfect-on-paper man.

They were only meant to have lived with Greg's parents for a short time, of course. In those early weeks, the prospect of choosing their own home was part of the flurry of activity that kept her occupied. More than that, it provided a rainbow of justification and hope, a willful delusion that Greg would be good to her again once they were out from under his parents' roof. Wasn't it perfectly reasonable, in fact, that he might be irritable and short-fused because of them, not her? Yes, he was taking it out on her, but if she wasn't the cause... she chose to believe that removing him from that environment would make all the difference.

Naturally, their wedding plans had been halted by the apocalypse. It would have been selfish to inquire about proceeding with their relocation plans in the immediate upheaval as well. But as the new normal began to settle in, Stella dared to ask.

"What you and Roger were saying earlier, about the Council taking inventory, allocating housing resources...."

Her voice trailed off. She was nervous to say it outright. Couldn't he just tell where she was going with this and make it easier on her?

Of course he couldn't. Wouldn't.

A fluttery, high-pitched tremor entered her voice as she forced the next words out, knowing if she stopped here, she'd be too scared to start again.

"I wondered—we were going to—have you asked, or considered, I don't mean you wouldn't have thought of because of course you would have thought but—"

His thumb on her upper lip, the knuckle of his index finger on the underside of her chin. The pinch extinguished her words like a candle.

"I have a lot of work to attend to, as you well know. As does my father. I think a new environment might be too great a shock to your system right now. And you wouldn't want anyone to think you preferred solitude over my mother's company."

She held his stern gaze as long as she could, then dropped her eyes and shook her head within the small range of motion available. His pinch grew firmer as if making a final statement on the matter, then fell away, his hand landing on her thigh.

"We'll talk about it once you're pregnant."

I eat dinner quickly and escape to my room—it almost feels like my room now, after all this time. It helps that I crack the window open a little every evening, bringing in air that's bracingly chilly but fresh and new, livening up the space breath by breath. The taller buildings and those closest to the walls no longer even have windows. It sounds so impossibly stifling. For all the mansion feels like a prison, it still at least looks like a home.

My eyes slip shut. I remember breathing in Demetri, tasting his lips and tongue, feeling him press into me, igniting feverish desire. The heat between us seemed like it could melt away the clothing that separated our flesh, leave him free to sink into me.

In the moments between kisses, staring and studying his face to identify truth from the potential for deception, I saw the slight imperfections that combine to make his improbable beauty truly perfect. A tiny, faded scar behind his left cheekbone, the weather-beaten cracks of mildly chapped lips, and wasn't that part of the powerfully masculine signature of his kiss? As he spoke, I imagined leaning up to pull that full, lower lip between my own, suck on it just for a heartbeat, just to let him feel me sucking on him, let him know I want to. I want him in my mouth and more. A chasm of want has opened inside me.

When I'm in the common areas of the house, I seek to portray myself as small and bleak as ever, but in my room, I can't contain the heat of the fire he's stoked in me. I can't relax enough to masturbate—afraid the scent of sex would fill this space, alert predators to the succulent prey cowering on the second floor of the Gennero mansion, trying to remain unnoticed. But I've awakened in the middle of the night several times lately, my hand firmly between my thighs, my hips working to move me close to orgasm in my sleep. The moment my conscious mind notices, the spell is broken, and I lie there uncomfortably, waiting it out until I can fall back asleep.

Flexing helplessly, my bottom presses against the wall and my thighs squeeze together, searching for some kind of relief in the tension of my muscles. I don't dare even sigh aloud, so I just exhale miserably with the frustrated need to be touched. And then a prickle on my arm sends a cooling message to all my heated nerve endings. The point of injection.

As the fire inside dies down, I can't prevent my worrisome mind from turning the recent strange events over and over, studying them.

Dwight. Benjamin Croft. Christopher, tonight. Three Illustrian men have paid me the strangest visits. As if rather than library guests, they were gentlemen callers.

Suitors.

Deep down, I think I've always known this was inevitable. If I never came back to life the way I have of late, I'm sure it would eventually have happened anyway. Perhaps later, once every other available woman had been claimed, I'd be handed over to someone as a consolation prize. I suppose my awakening has renewed my appeal. It's a vile, chilling thought.

I've often heard it said that falling in love makes you more attractive to the world at large. The radiant glow of desire and joy is better than cosmetics at approximating the flush of post-orgasmic bliss that inspires competition among men to witness the phenomenon firsthand.

It is the cruelest irony that my budding feelings for Demetri may have accelerated my doom. But if his friends can help... the thought is frustratingly foolish. They obviously have their own problems. Bigger problems, I know. Only Demetri even knows me at all, and the rest likely see me as Illustrian. Why should they care about my fate?

I'm meeting Nina for lunch tomorrow, though. If I can befriend her, maybe... I try to cut off that line of thought, not just because hope could kill me but because a perceived agenda could damn this friendship before it starts. And on more than one very selfish level, the idea of having a friend fills me with longing.

I'm like a desert traveler who's glimpsed an oasis. It could still be a mirage, yes, but it could also be what I so desperately need and hadn't thought to find again.

At midday, I arrive at the nearest kitchen a bundle of nerves. We go through the line together with occasional comments on the fare but no real conversation.

I feel pitifully shy, like I'm on a date or interviewing for a dream job. *Like the job I left for Greg.*

"What was that?" she asks, letting me know my change in mood was visible. I chuckle sadly.

"Teachers always loved me. They said I had an expressive face, so they knew I was engaged."

Engaged. The momentary peace of remembering something nice just brought me back to the bad place again.

Nina cocks her head and studies me. "I always assumed you were Illustris, but you're not quite. At first I thought it was just because you love books."

"A universal green flag, as they say. Don't you think? I never knew what to make of people who didn't read."

"You mean, like Demetri? You've done a number on him."

If she'd said it differently, it might have sounded like a compliment.

"Look, it's obvious he likes you, and I have good reason to respect his instincts about people. But I can't help being concerned about my friend developing feelings for someone who lived here before the fall. We may be in your city now, but we don't really live in the same world."

Her frankness is unexpected, refreshing. The edges of my mouth soften comfortably into something that could become a smile.

"Thank you. I really appreciate your being so straightforward with me. It's not how people are here, but I'm sure you know that."

She nods slightly, like a flower touched by a gentle breeze, her eyes on me hard. Her concern brings my ghost of a smile to life.

"Demetri is special, isn't he?" I feel the color bloom high on my cheeks. "If you care about him like this, I'm not wrong to like him. To... trust him." My voice dips down to a whisper, and I watch her eyes closely for any hesitation.

An edge of muscular tension drops away in her posture, and she smiles kindly. "Tom trusts him completely. I used to think he was kind of goofy to be honest, but maybe that's not such a bad thing either. I probably didn't give him enough credit. The world being what it is, someone keeps smiling and finding joy in life... yeah. Demetri's one of the good ones, no question."

I look down at my tray to conceal the heady rush of limerence.

"So you can understand why I'd be worried about him," she adds, bringing me back down to earth. "There's not much precedent as far as I'm aware. Outsiders like us mixing with the upper crusties. No offense."

"No," I confirm, my voice hollow. "That's true."

"Are you even single? You've got a rock on your hand, but I don't think Demetri would fuck around with an Illustrian's wife. I mean, he's not trying to die."

The bluntness of the question stuns me into meeting her gaze again.

"Demetri didn't tell you?"

"We're not close like that."

"And Tom—"

"Doesn't repeat everything his best friend tells him. I'm asking you."

But you're not close like that. My eyes narrow. She's coming at this with an *I'm worried about my friend* angle, but it's not ringing entirely true the more she talks.

This is about the other thing, isn't it? She's evaluating me. To see if I'd help? Or because she's worried I might interfere, even rat them out?

"You're right that I'm not quite Illustris." There's a cool edge to my voice, and that's how I discover my feelings are bruised by the false overture of friendship. The coolness fades as I continue, but the edge only sharpens. "I moved here a few weeks before the world started to fall apart. I was going to be married. He's dead now. They took every colorful item from my closet to render me a widow for all to see. Does that sufficiently address your concerns over whether I'm *single*?"

It's too big, my reaction. My chest is dense with raging, impotent emotions all at war. The realization that these people are coming to see me as single, that I'm likely on a clock, about to have everything taken from me... the thought of losing Demetri even as I've found him. Nina's not the person I'm truly angry with, of course. I squeeze my eyes shut against the intensity of my feelings, and a damning tear slips out.

"I'm sorry. You're right to take offense," she offers. Her tone is apologetic yet hesitant; she's not done, and she can't leave without what she came for, can she? "I was prying. I should trust Demetri's judgment as much as Tom does. But the way he looks at you... it's hard to trust someone when they're in their feelings like that. Are you gonna break his heart? Are you... using him?"

"As in, for information?" I whisper, giving her a resentful glare.

Her eyes widen almost imperceptibly. It's impressive she managed not to react in any way that would be obvious from the nearest possible prying eyes. I let the moment hang in the air.

The effort of staring her down combines with the emotions I'm wrestling, and my voice goes as soft and wet as my eyes.

"I would never hurt him," I vow quietly.

Hours later, my lashes feel brittle with the salt of intermittent tears. I fear I've compromised my desperate, grasping notion of being rescued by this apparent resistance. It was foolish of me anyway, of course. They can't know anything of value, can they? The way this place works... no one with real information or access would ever risk their own comfort, let alone their safety, to help the lower castes improve their lot.

Who was that man who joined them the other night? Illustrian, certainly. Not one of the Genneros' peers. Whatever he may know, can it possibly be enough to matter?

I could tell them plenty... but I can't. Perhaps that makes me a true Illustrian after all. A bitter, tragic thought. Those aren't my people. They never were.

Today was supposed to have been my chance at making a friend. It's a little odd how much I feel the loss of something I never truly had.

Turning it over and over in my mind, I dare to hope it's not a lost cause. I certainly recognize the precarity of her situation. So she engaged me under false pretenses. What of it? I've forgiven far worse and for far less valid reasons.

Wandering the labyrinth of shelves, I watch and listen, seeking distraction to carry me through what I expect to be a long, somber evening alone. Demetri was here the last two nights in a row, which means I shouldn't hope to see him tonight. I've failed to identify a pattern, probably because they're trying to avoid establishing one. At least I know he wants to be here. Still, every time the door opens on the darkness beyond, I can't resist a tiny glimmer of hope.

A chatty group of female soldiers a couple of aisles over reads excerpts from old potboilers aloud, mocking the melodrama. Their companionable laughter echoes in the large space, and I feel lonely again.

Christopher. Benjamin. Dwight. The creepy familiarity with which they approached me. As if we'd met before, which I don't recall. Of course, I spent so much time in survival mode, which throws memories in the blender after you come out. The last year of my life is like a TV series I know I watched but am now being forced to process as reality. *Of course that wasn't real life. That would be ridiculous.*

But then I started thinking and feeling and perceiving again. Demetri reached into the darkness and retrieved me, and now I have to relearn the world with the new awareness I've gained. It's funny; I wouldn't have called myself naïve or sheltered before I came to Illustris, but I didn't know darkness.

I knew indifference, that's all. I watched my father discard my mother when she became more burden than benefit to him, and I innocently imagined that was the worst thing a seemingly decent man might do. Yes, there were bad men in the world, bad women too, but they were *different.* You might run afoul of one if luck abandoned you, but that was an extraordinary circumstance. The people you encountered in polite society existed on a spectrum of decency. Selfish, callous behavior like my father's was on the harsh and ugly end of that spectrum, surely.

Greg's casual cruelty was something I never could have seen coming. It was too far beyond the edge of anything I'd envisioned.

Then I was here, immersed in it, and I turned to him for safety because he was all I had left. He may have been a monster, but he conferred protection from other, more literal monsters. I clung to him, made myself useful. Helped him.

Nina is deciding whether to trust me. Demetri does, but that's not enough to convince her, and she's right to doubt. I don't want to be a monster, but I have aligned myself with them and acted in their interest. I wish I could offer the resistance my support, beyond merely declining to betray them. I could tell them so much. But I'm a coward. If I gave voice to the dark truths I carry, they would take on life beyond my reach. There's no way to be certain they would do any good, and the disturbances caused could be devastating.

And in the meantime, Demetri would know the worst of me.

I can't bear that. After a hard pinch to castigate myself for the selfishness of this petty concern, I take refuge again in the objective truth that my secrets are almost certain to do more harm than good. The potential for effecting change is negligible. The potential for damage is obvious, and that damage would be catastrophic.

I can't hold Nina's doubts against her, I conclude. Too much is at stake not to doubt. Emotions and desires are unreliable masters. I may have been able to comprehend that as a concept before, but I know it now as truth.

Stella had fallen rapturously in love with Greg—it was a glorious discovery that made her ashamed to have ever questioned him. There was no more room for doubt; the sensual truth of it was inescapable. This was proof she'd made the right choice after all, was it not? How

could she feel such intense desire if he was anything but the perfect man for her?

Yes, they'd had their bumps along the way. But wasn't it all worth-while? Every moment they weren't in bed, it seemed she could think of nothing else. She'd never been so sexual, but then, she'd never felt this powerful ravaging need. How lucky she was to have taken that leap of faith—yes, she'd questioned it at times, certainly, but this intense chemical desire was her reward. Everything would be okay now, she was sure of it.

She fairly skipped home from the library that afternoon. Every day had been like this lately. They would still have to spend some time with Roger and Celeste, but even her mother-in-commonlaw's snippy attitude couldn't diminish her when she was quivery with anticipation about going to bed with her husband. Husband, yes, who cared whether a wedding had taken place?

At dinner, she scooted her chair indecently close to him, ignoring Celeste's disapproving glance. She stared at him, all soppy and ador-ing, not a hint of self-consciousness to her. He favored her with a smile that spoke of satisfaction and pride. Stella was so overcome, she might have missed the conversation entirely.

How much easier things might have been.

"...eat, drink, and be merry," Greg was saying, and when everyone laughed, Stella did too.

He was so powerful. How had she ever seen him as reserved? She was undoubtedly the luckiest woman on the planet.

"Of course, we need to be looking more long-term as well," Roger noted. "The social structure is part of the equation, but we've got to herd them effectively. We need them to drop their guards, lower their inhibitions."

"We need them to rut like animals," Greg said, putting it plainly and laughing—it was a sexy laugh, a little arch, yes, but he was bril-

liant. Was it wrong to feel superior when one actually was superior? "Don't worry about it. I'm on top of that."

Another laugh from the men, darker, and somehow exclusive.

A chill set in as Stella failed to ignore the terrifying whisper from her subconscious. He was on top of that, *was he? The choice of words. The laugh. The way his eyebrow tipped up as if in acknowledgment of some private joke.*

The recent overwhelming sexual heat she'd been revelling in and crediting him for.

Well, she supposed, he did deserve the credit either way. The implant she'd cheerfully accepted on arrival in Illustris was a multi-functional piece of tech. Greg was among those responsible for its design. It could turn fertility on and off like a switch. It could regulate blood sugar; no one in Illustris had ever needed insulin. It interfaced with the medical scanners, aiding in diagnosis of all manner of ailments.

He had never mentioned whether it could be used to inflame the mating instinct. Stella was suddenly, dreadfully certain it could.

She made it through the rest of dinner. She examined her reactions as carefully and quietly as possible. The fundamental facts were unchanged, of course. There was nothing to be done about her situation. She had been moony with hormonally charged infatuation a couple of hours before, and she should do her best to keep living in that state, if she could.

It wasn't that difficult, really. He'd engaged her body's responses in a way she couldn't deny. She didn't have to pretend anything, at least not in bed. But she stopped feeling that tether between her womb and her heart. The pleasure he caused her was expertise not on a physical level but a programmatic one. And either way, it didn't make him the perfect man, or even perfect for her. She was disgusted to realize how easily swayed her emotions and judgment had been. Mercifully, her body's responses were not affected by the observations of her mind; not only did it make it easier to hide her feelings from him, it provided her some consolation still. She was trapped, but it was a pleasurable captivity, if only physically.

After he died, someone clearly turned it off. It was a relief that she would be spared the endlessly surging sexual energy, but also mortifying, because it meant someone knew what he'd done to her. Of course someone knew, she thought ruefully, acrid tears raging. They'd have been monitoring and testing and discussing... At least she had never gotten pregnant. Thank goodness. She had been spared that.

The implants were tiny devices. The insertion had not left a scar. Yet sometimes she still felt a prickle at the spot. A reminder of the leash she'd been put on, the leash she still bore, helplessly aware some unseen master might pick it back up. It was chilling to think her awareness would prevent the full effect from ever taking hold again; perhaps the physical conditioning would remain powerful enough, if she was lucky, but the emotional aspect—the thrall—would never return to alleviate her captivity.

In another cruel irony, what I feel when Demetri kisses me is every bit as intense as the engineered sexual spark I experienced back then, but so much better. It's real.

When they yank me back into their world and turn on that tether again, I'll not only know how false the sensations are, I'll know the difference. I'll have to live with that.

Too smart for my own good. It's been said many times throughout my life, and it's true. If I hadn't figured it out, I might never have become immune to the emotional effect of it. I might have believed I loved Greg right up to the end.

Would that have been better? It's impossible to say.

As I go about my bedtime routine, my morose train of thought comes to a screeching halt. My closet door stands open, displaying the full spectrum of colors restored to my wardrobe.

Chapter Twelve

Nowhere to Go

Stella

The next time Demetri sees me, there's a skipped beat in between the smile and his eyes. My heart plummets. Whatever Nina said to him must have changed things. He's here to monitor me because his friends consider me a risk, but his feelings—if they were ever real—have soured. I brace myself for this lovely interlude in my life to end even sooner than I feared.

But his smile eases, and he says by way of hello, "You look so different. I had to stop and think about it. Like in the old days, your girlfriend gets a haircut or a new pair of glasses, you're an asshole if you don't notice. I've never seen you in this color."

Or any color, I think, feeling a woozy kind of reluctant relief; it's not fair to indulge this dream, is it? Not fair to either of us. I should end it, shouldn't I?

Yet my voice says, "Girlfriend?"

"Shit," he laughs. "I'm gonna let you walk me real slowly through whatever section of books feels most welcoming, so we can dig into that Freudian slip as deep as you feel like taking it."

Realizing he's only compounded the innuendo, Demetri blushes adorably. "I really just said that."

I reach my hand halfway across the desk, just in case he wants to
hold it, even for a moment before we might have to break apart.
Grateful comfort fills his eyes, and he rests his elbow on the edge
of the desk, lets his fingertips brush against mine.

"The way you looked at me just now was very *hot for teacher*,
which I never thought I'd be into when I actually was a teacher,
but...."

"Damn," he says, his tone colored with heat, the smile returning
to his lips. "You had to go there, didn't you. I'm trying to be good
here, you know."

"If you tease me, I'll tease back," I murmur, continuing to surprise myself.

"Promise?" he whispers, and his fingertips flex to pull mine into
the barest version of handholding, just one knuckle deep.

The word *promise* pains me anew, and I again think I should
end this. Before the words can try to form, the door swings open
behind him. Our hands return to a respectable distance.

"Read anything good lately?" I ask, grateful for the excuse to
shelve my dark thoughts and the sense of duty they inspire.

"I'm almost done, actually. You better give me something new
to tide me over."

"Well, maybe you should let me walk you, really slowly, through
a welcoming section of books," I smirk.

His eyes roll in a parody of embarrassment. "I said *real slowly*,
didn't I? You're gonna red-pen my seduction techniques. Probably
my dirty talk too. Shit. Maybe I am hot for teacher."

"One of our first conversations, I was kind of joking about not needing to read something if you've seen the movie. But now I actually get the difference." Demetri's sad, lopsided smile makes me ache to touch him, but we're not out of sight yet. "The prince is all noble and heartbroken. It's like the saddest happy ending. I remember that about the movie too, but...."

"But it hits harder," I agree. "Everything hits harder when it happens in your mind rather than on a screen, filtered through other people's interpretations, no matter how well they deliver it."

At the top of the stairs, we glance around the room to affirm no one seems to be looking our way, then vanish into an aisle between shelves.

Just as I'm on the verge of reaching for his hand, he asks, "Hey, how'd your lunch date go?"

I see in his eyes that he's afraid to know, which tells me he does know. If not the details, at least that her intentions were something beyond girl talk.

It takes me a moment to decide how to respond, and his face falls. Before he can voice the apology or explanation building in his throat, I try to reassure him.

"It was fine. She..." *meant well?* I don't know how to characterize it in a reassuring way after all. I should have prepared a lie for him. I was distracted.

"Stella, I want you to know I trust you completely. I would never—"

"I know. I didn't think you did. And it really was fine. More or less."

I watch him struggle for a moment before giving in and reaching out to cradle my cheek. The simple exploration of his fingertips on the side of my face feels powerfully charged now that I know he's restraining so much heat.

He reluctantly drops his hand again, and we settle in, barely leaning against the shelf, face to face, just far enough apart.

"It doesn't justify... whatever," he says, "but there's a lot going on. She's a good person though. I'm really closer with Tom, but I've known her a long time. She was just kind of uptight before he came along."

Failing to suppress a chuckle, I admit, "She said she used to think you were kind of goofy."

He laughs outright. "Yeah, that sounds like something she'd say. She and Tom are good for each other." His hand slides along the shelf between us and finds mine. "You've been good for me."

My stomach drops. My breath catches. I don't deserve this, do I? I'm a hypocrite. Raging at the notion he might have used me when all this time I have committed to harboring secrets and concocting lies. Resenting their intentions toward me when, if what I suspect is true, he would be better off not having real feelings for me. I open my mouth to confess something, anything, but my voice turns to smoke.

I can't do it.

Demetri's eyes, so rich with concern and caring, again see my dismay without understanding the cause. He slides a hand to the nape of my neck, lovingly massages the muscles. He's such a physical being. He can't use his whole body to make love to me, so he'll get the message across every other conceivable way.

"Maybe next time, you have lunch with me. Hm? I've never seen you outside the library, you know. You can reassure yourself I'm not just living out the sexy librarian fantasy."

"I don't—we shouldn't be seen together like that, I think—"

"I know," he says, a little glumly but undeterred. "We'll go somewhere private. It'll be okay. Trust me. I mean, only because I won't have enough time to make a proper move before you have to be back here, but still. Trust me."

I nod, feeling almost hypnotized. His eyes dart around the vicinity before he drops a quick kiss on my lips. His fingers slide down my arm and lace into my hand, and then he drops it and backs away a step, exhaling intently.

"Yeah. Lunch break is good. Just long enough, *not nearly* long enough."

Our theoretical lunch plan is set for Demetri's next day off, and he assured me he would take care of the details. As his friends started to filter out, he regretfully acknowledged that he should go too. I'm getting used to seeing the little signs of thwarted desire now that I know what I'm looking at: the gestures, glances, and vacant grasps as his hands resist reaching for some part of me that wants touching.

Would it be so wrong? What if Celeste would be grateful to be rid of me? What if they're just trying to shove me out the door after all this time? Ending my mourning period, trying to introduce me to eligible bachelors in their strange way? Would they be relieved to learn I'd found a lover without their intervention?

Wishful thinking, I know. *I know*, and that's the problem. I look down again at the deep burgundy dress they only just gave back. It was one I wore in my brief time as a new Illustrian, attending a cocktail party on Greg's arm at the gallery. The gallery is shuttered currently, new art being deemed temporarily a tasteless display of the relative leisure time enjoyed by the upper echelons. It will come back, the Council agreed, once things settle in a bit.

My dress fits just slightly more loosely than it did that long ago night. I was on the trembling edge of my mid-twenties heading into late, the last gasp of youthful extravagance in my curves before I reached my true adult form.

Celeste's gaze travelled critically from neckline to hemline and back again, landing briefly at Stella's eyes to convey the absence of approval. Her mother-in-law-to-be turned without a word and strode to the door of the mansion. Roger offered Stella a vaguely conciliatory half-smile as he held the door and gestured for her to follow.

They were meeting Greg at the gallery, and that left her in the already familiar and miserable position of trying to impress or at least get along with Celeste. She kept having to remind herself to stand up straight because the older woman's wearying attitude had deflated her like a leftover birthday balloon.

The artists and photographers whose work was on display were all wives or scions of Illustris. It was fine, thought Stella charitably; perhaps it just didn't speak to her. A less charitable assessment flitted across her mind—that these people were lucky not to have to compete with the hungrier, livelier artists of the real world, but she pressed it into a corner labelled unseemly ingratitude *to be discarded with prejudice.*

A tall blonde woman, striking in her sleek updo and elegant black dress, stopped to greet Roger and Celeste with cool civility before turning a curious eye toward Stella.

"I'd heard there was about to be a wedding. You must be the lucky lady," she said, her tone belying the words.

Stella blinked back the threat of emotionality—would she ever be enough for any of these people?—*and held out her hand in greeting. The blonde woman smiled thinly during the limp, perfunctory shake.*

"Stella Vernon. Soon to be Gennero. It's nice to meet you," she strained.

The other woman's eyes changed: a deep sadness flashed there, followed by something like sympathy before returning to steel.

"Good luck," she said, then turned and briskly walked away.

To my surprise, it's Nina who turns up at the library on the day of my supposed lunch with Demetri. I know I look both confused and disappointed, and I try to wipe my face of the emotions quickly, but she laughs.

"Don't worry, I'm just here to walk you over," she tells me, her smile amused and understanding.

It's a good idea. A civilian, a woman, one I've spent time with already in public. We walk the peaceful thoroughfare at a brisk pace as suited to the winter chill as to my eagerness to reach our destination.

"Why are you helping us?"

"Favor for Demetri. He reckons I owe him. And you, for being kind of a bitch to you."

"No—you don't—"

"I do," she says, then smiles, a self-deprecating twinkle in her eyes. "I *was*. It's cool, I own it. And I do owe Demetri. He's been there for me. For us."

We fall silent as an Illustrian passes by in the other direction. Both Nina and I instinctually paste a bland smile on our faces and nod at him. No one I know, fortunately.

"Demetri's a very forgiving person," she says confessionally. "I bet if you'd gone at me the way I did you the other day, Tom would hold it against you till the end of time. Well, at least until I convinced him I was okay," she adds with deep affection.

"I understood. You don't need to—"

"I'm not," she says matter-of-factly. "I mean, you say you understand, so I think we can be straight with each other, especially since you already know enough that if you really wanted to, you could have us all killed."

I choke on my gasp and cough, slowing our progress as I recover.

"It's true what I said: Demetri and I aren't as close as he and Tom, but Tom trusts him implicitly. So by transitive properties, I'm choosing to trust you. It's hard, and I'm sorry you've taken the brunt of our discomfort with your kind. We've been through battle together, you know? Civilians are just different from us anymore."

"You are a civilian now," I point out.

"Only because Tom wanted it that way. Not that I miss fighting, don't get me wrong. But it's complicated. It was only after the Thrashers I started to wonder why I was fighting so hard."

Flashes. A series of colors like the world is a photo being run through filters. Thudding inside. A man would think *heart attack* but Stella knows women don't have the same symptoms.

"Thrashers," she echoes numbly, very, very far away.

"Yeah. Sent me to quarantine. Tom saved me. Demetri too. Oh, do you even know what they are? It's what we call—"

"I know what they are." This winter day, so gray. At least the cold seems remote and beyond affecting her, though her feet must be a little numb, the way they *thunk* with every step.

"Here we are!" Nina says brightly, oblivious to the state of her walking companion as she holds open the door to a high rise.

On the eighth floor, they step off the elevator, and Nina says in the closest thing to a whisper, "Don't think of me as a chaperon or anything. I'll be upstairs the whole time, so you'll have your privacy. Just here for appearances."

Stella nods automatically, still just putting one foot in front of another, not sure she remembers what she's doing here until they move past the apartment's entranceway—

—and I see his face. The emotions pile up like cars in a collision.

Nina, true to her word, gives Demetri a little wave before scurrying up the stairs at the back of the unit. As soon as she's out of sight, he reaches for me, hands finding my shoulders and making as if to slide my coat off, but he gets distracted halfway, leaves my sleeves mid-shrug in favor of caressing my arms, massaging my biceps as if trying to warm me up, his eyes devouring me.

A pained hesitation crooks his brow before he discards it and kisses me anyway.

His mouth takes mine with none of the questioning I read in his eyes just now. Whatever his brain may be struggling with, his body is clear about what it wants. He presses me to the wall and slides his hands inside my coat, explores my body more aggressively than he's had a chance to do in our library encounters, roaming my sides, my back, my hips, alternately stroking and gripping, thrilling my every nerve ending with the alternating pressures, smooth and tempting, firm and invigorating. Just as I start to notice sweat gathering, he pushes my coat all the way off, creating a rush of relative cool to ease me back from overheating.

On the way back from sliding the coat the rest of the way down my arms and off, his hands find my breasts. He squeezes luxuriously and presses his pelvis into mine.

"No bra." He exhales, a sound of pained longing. "I wondered, wasn't sure. I've been thinking about getting close enough to find out for so long, Stella. Wrap your legs around me, please?"

He sounds almost desperate, and I think about the things he's said to me recently. He's giving in to urges he decided to deny. The desperation in his voice is because he needs me to hurry up and do this before he has time to take it back. I'm probably supposed to be strong for him, tell him no, aren't I?

A fluttering around the edges of my eyes affirms that the Stella who could be strong like that may have been the one Nina collected from the library ten minutes ago, but not the one who arrived in this apartment. My hands grip his shoulders. My right leg encircles his hips, then my left as he lifts me to cradle his hardness through our clothes.

I would do anything to have these clothes vanish like magic. He pins me hard as I whimper and squirm and wish to envelop him fully. He thrusts suddenly, perfectly pressing my clitoris at the apex of his rhythm.

"Demetri, I—I won't stop you. If I was supposed to stop you..." I shake my head as my voice trails off.

When he closes his eyes, I know I did stop him with my offer to continue. I know it was the right thing, and probably even what I intended on the level of my mind that shoved the words from my mouth. He pulls back. Lowering me to stand on my own two feet again, he adds a softer, concluding kiss that is still warm but tastes of regret.

"You're right," he says. I'm not, though. My hand flies forward helplessly to link with his.

Our eyes lock. His fiery intensity fades into wry self-mockery as a sheepish grin overtakes his flushed and handsome face.

"You might have to carry the conversation for a while till the blood flow redistributes to my brain, okay?"

If he had wanted to take me right there against the wall a moment ago, I would have relished him as my last meal. Instead we sit, close but not scandalously so, and share a literal meal that still feels like it could be my last.

Nina reappears at the stair landing as our hour comes to an end. I say goodbye to Demetri, fighting the certainty that I'll never see him again. Our final kiss is semi-private as Nina politely turns her head, and it's not enough. I hold my eyes open as wide as I can before the door steals him from my view.

We walk in silence nearly all the way to the library.

"Thank you," I say as we reach the building, aware that my tone conveys wretchedness, not gratitude.

"Are you okay?" Nina stops walking and looks at me. She seems genuinely concerned. That's nice of her.

"I'm sorry," I say, knowing how meaningless it would be even if she knew what I meant by it.

"For what?"

"I'm sorry I can't help." The slight prevarication stings my eyes.

Nina only hesitates a moment before resting a hand on my shoulder. "You're doing plenty. Just by continuing to do nothing at all, you're helping. You don't owe me anything."

But I do. You nearly died of my secrets. Not mine... not truly... but can you keep that kind of secret without accepting ownership for its fallout?

"Really, are you going to be okay?"

"Yes. Thanks. No—no need to—fine."

Stella lets her eyes close. A moment of relief. When she admits the daylight once more, it's a cool, wintry gray and so is her dress which she'd somehow thought was blue. Funny, that. She turns toward the library where she's meant to be this time of day. In the background, she detects the other woman turning to walk away.

When Stella reaches the door, she veers right and keeps walking. Her feet are numb, spurring her to run before the icy blocks below her ankles stop holding her up at all. She runs and runs and runs without thought, without direction until she hits the wall.

So high above, stretching in both directions as far as the eye can see—someone else's eyes, not hers, not with the world closing down again—a blessing this time as she lets her weakened frame lean, just lean against the wall before succumbing to gravity in a merciful slide.

Vertigo. Her head spins as if processing a poisonous amount of hard liquor. The unyielding presence of the wall at her back is the only proof of her orientation to reality now that her bottom is steadily going as numb as her feet. Her forehead inclines at an excruciating, glacierlike pace until it finds her knees.

On the other side of the wall might be something or someone that wants to kill her. A fascinating notion. The numbness of her feet backslides cruelly, transmuting to pain, tethering her to this moment. She can't even escape herself.

The warmth continues to leach out of her into the earth below. The heat transfer gradually exchanges her flesh's softness and the ground's rigidity. She might disappear after all, in time.

A dim crunching sound permeates Stella's awareness, against her will. It grows louder as if noticing the sound has granted it permission to invade her space.

"Stella?" It's not an immediately recognizable voice, though somehow familiar.

Crunch, crunch. Frozen ground, brittle blades of grass scattered between patches of frosty earth, breaking beneath someone's approaching feet.

"Hey. It's Monica. I'm a friend of Nina's?"

Stella tries to make some kind of sound in response. Her chest feels strangely thick, blocky, like an ice column has overtaken her windpipe.

"She was worried about you. Soon as my team was off shift, she had us looking for you. What's going on? I'm here to help. Just take it easy, all right? It's okay...."

I'm not a wild animal, Stella thinks.

I'm not. The cold is suddenly far too real, too present and painful. How long have I been here? As my eyes fly open and my forehead lifts from my knees, I gasp down what feels like my first breath of fresh air after emerging from a bunker. It's viciously cold in my nostrils.

Monica stands before me in the dim evening light, uncertain what she's dealing with. I doubt I could make sense of it for her if I wanted to. She offers me a hand.

"Think you can stand up?"

I let Monica lead me back to the city proper, moving slowly as the feeling returns fully to my feet in rolling waves of numbness, pain, and pins and needles. As my vision refills, I panic in a thought I can't believe is only just hitting.

"The library! I—"

"Shh," she says, still treating me like a wounded beast. "Don't worry about that now. It's taken care of. We put Maxwell on it. His wife's there, and... he's working out an explanation for why. You're gonna have to trust us on this one."

"No, no," I whimper, "they'll take it away—"

"Stella?"

Her stern manner turns my very name into a reprimand. It reminds me of my mom, and I want to weep for a new reason.

"Just keep putting one foot in front of the other for me, because we're going to get you into a safe place to deal with whatever this is, and the faster we get there, the better for all of us, right?"

"I'm sorry you have to spend your time dealing with this. I'm not your problem—"

"Fuck's sake, girl! Less maudlin, more motion. Let's go."

When it's clear we've reached our intended destination, I balk at the sight of Nina and Tom's apartment building, but she says, "He's not here. If that's what you're worried about. Why d'you think she sent me instead of him when he could've probably gotten to you sooner?"

She wants me to move, I know, but I just stare, because I still don't know what's happening. I need her to explain.

Monica grimaces impatiently. "Nina wouldn't throw you in front of your boyfriend when you're looking like this. Um, sorry, you look... well, it doesn't matter 'cause he's not here. We got you. C'mon."

I stifle a sniffle that's more emotion-driven than a reaction to the winter air. It really is almost like having friends.

Upstairs, she draws a bath and tells me to give her my clothes and get in. I follow instructions without a word. The water stings so sharply I have to force myself to continue submerging beyond the tips of my toes. When I'm all the way in, every inch of skin screaming in protest, I draw in a shuddering breath and try to master my emotions, proving I can exhale without descending into sobs. My eyes start to close out of habit just because I'm in a bath and there's nothing much to look at, but I wrench them open in an act of resistance.

I try to orient myself, take stock of my surroundings. Bathtub. Water, hot. I think. I was so cold, I don't really know. The ledge of the tub. To my right, the wall is within inches. Behind me—no, no, turning my head is a mistake. Take it slowly.

To my right, wall. To my left, several feet of open space, a shaggy bathmat, another wall. In front, a sink, a toilet, another wall.

Monica brought me here. Because Nina asked her to. Because I ran. I ran like a rat who's gained sentience only to realize it lives in a maze. Demetri deserves so much more. I should push him away.

I don't want to, is the problem.

And under that selfish truth, this ignoble awareness: What he and his friends are up to could get them exiled or killed, and Nina's assurance that by doing nothing, I do plenty, was based on incomplete information.

What I know... if I could share it... if I knew how to...

Flares of panic press in from around my eyes once again, and my vision is assailed as dark red floods in, filling my view until I can't take it. I press my hands to my face to shut out the light.

Gray for going away. Gray is a relief in a way. It means I'll shut down. Lose time, lose track.

Red is worse. Demetri was right to assess the gray as a panic attack, but red is pure panic. It's a mix of fight and flight and freeze and fawn all colliding in my limbic system. My heart jolts like it's trying to find an artery large enough to escape through. My mind is an echoing chaos of compulsions to run, defend, hide, plead for mercy. My ears burn and buzz, feeling encased in plastic, miles from the here and now, trying to somehow avoid more pain, more unwanted knowledge.

Breathe. Breathe. Breathe.

It finally feels safe to try opening my eyes again. Just as I decide to risk it, I notice the water's gone cool. How long have I been in here? The question provides me a useful initial focus point, so I unclench my fingers and let the light in just enough to see the pruney ridges of my toes through the clear water. I don't know how long I was out there, but I got very lucky. If Nina hadn't sent Monica after me, if Monica hadn't managed to find me in time... how long does it take for frostbite to set in?

The tepid water starts to make me shiver now that I've come back to my body, so I make a gingerly effort to stand and climb out. I only make it as far as the bathmat where I surrender to a powerful urge to crumple onto its soft pile and curl up.

But the cool air on my wet skin keeps me from settling into this potential cocoon, and I force myself to look around for the nearest towel. If it were in reach, I could just pull it over myself and stay here forever, I think. But it's not, and of course I couldn't. Accepting the necessity of facing the world beyond this room, I drag myself upright, wrap a towel around me, and open the door.

I know I'm at Nina's home, and I have the vaguest, otherworldly sort of recollection of being led up the stairs by Monica. Casting my gaze right to left, I spot the upper landing and move that way. Just before I start to descend, I hear the voices from the living area below. It sounds like Monica and Nina. They're not speaking loudly enough to make out the words from here, disappointing my inner snoop.

Halfway down the stairs, I think I'm almost close enough to start hearing them clearly, but of course that's when I'm spotted.

Nina stands and looks at me with something like apologetic understanding. Monica remains seated, her arm slung casually along the back of the sofa, uncertainty in her eyes.

"I caused so much trouble—"

The shaky words are still fluttering out when Nina moves toward me, puts an arm around my shoulders, and leads me to the couch. She's right. I might have fallen over.

"I've got some food, and you need to eat it," she says with authority. She glances over at Monica who briefly rolls her eyes at the silent request before going to retrieve the food.

"First thing's first, because I know you've got to be freaking out about it. Maxwell made kind of a big play and you're not going to love it, but you have to accept it. In fact, the amount of not-loving-it we've been expecting from you is going to be good for selling the overall story about your little marathon today."

Nina stops talking and looks me in the eyes, probably to make sure I'm following. Satisfied, she continues.

"The official story is you've been forced to accept some helping hands around the library because some of the older civilian wives wanted something to do. Truth is, so far it's just Sarah Maxwell and her friend Cindy, but they'll probably have to accommodate some requests once word gets around, and not everyone's going to be one of ours, so... it's not a perfect solution, but you kind of didn't leave us much to work with. We had to act fast, and this is what we came up with."

She's expecting anger, protest, but I don't have the energy to deliver on that. Besides, she's right. I fell apart, very publicly, and they picked up the pieces for me the best way they could think of under the circumstances. Plus rescued me before I froze to death or at least lost a few toes.

"Maxwell. That's... the older man who joined you once?"

"Yeah. Sorry. I guess I forget you don't all know each other or whatever."

"Thank you for sending Monica after me today." The words sound numb and toneless, but they come out clearly enough.

Encouraged, Nina nods and reaches for some stiff bread with what looks like blackberry preserves. I don't resist her effort to feed me, and after the first couple of thick, dry bites, my body awakens to the necessity and begins to welcome the nourishment.

Once the bread is gone, as well as most of a glass of water, Nina gives me another serious look.

"So, you gonna tell us what happened?"

My stomach falls. My eyes are wet with guilt.

"Let me go out on a limb here. The last thing you said was you were sorry you couldn't help. But you can. You were sorry you *wouldn't* help."

I'm running out of pretty lies and the will to deliver them. I just stare back at her, wordless, expressionless.

Chapter Thirteen

Girl Talk

Stella

This silence will crush me like a cartoon piano if it continues another moment. They're waiting for me to offer up something useful, or at least to acknowledge my lack of intent to do so. Monica looks resigned; she doesn't know me, has no expectations I could fail to meet. Nina still looks at me with anticipation, if not quite hope.

My head starts shaking *no* and even I couldn't say for sure if I'm trying to deny the truth of her words or merely reacting in uncontrollable horror. My eyes squeeze shut against the tears that continue to burst through and course down my quivering cheeks, and I know I don't deserve any pity, yet the cushion beside me sinks as one of them moves to join me. An arm around my shoulders pulls me in with gentle comfort. I lose my tenuous control and sob outright, sagging against this undeserved kindness.

She holds me close and strokes my arm from shoulder to elbow through the soft fabric of the bath towel wrapped around me. When was the last time someone treated me this way? When did I last let down my guard around a woman, or anyone until Demetri just recently?

Eventually my sobs begin to quiet. "Why are you being kind to me? Why did you send Monica to find me at all?"

Nina sighs a bit impatiently like I've insulted her honor. "C'mon, you didn't think I'd notice you taking off like that? Didn't think I could tell you were in a bad way?"

I lift my head to look at her.

"I'd have gone after you myself but I can't be screwing around too much, not being where I'm supposed to be. I had to get some help, and there aren't many people I could ask. Besides Demetri, obviously, and there was no way I was doing that."

My brow crinkles. "Why?"

She tilts her head like I'm asking an incomprehensible question, and I suppose I am. She's been clear they're not that close.

But what she says takes me by surprise.

"Look, you saw him and then you went all weird and fucking bolted. I didn't figure it was anything he did, but it still could be about him. Whatever you needed, I wasn't sure he was the right person to give it. Besides, he cares too much, and a guy in that state can be a total mess, you know? And then you wind up comforting him because it stresses him out seeing you in pain?"

Her words sink in, and more than the words themselves, the sense of sisterhood. It's the thing I was afraid to even long for when she initially reached out, and now that it's potentially within reach, I'm about to smack it away, aren't I?

"I had to put my life on pause for a while after high school. I fell out of sync with people. When I picked up my studies again, the other students were younger, and I didn't realize at first that we weren't on the same team. I was competition. Far more so than they were to each other. My age, my life experience, that slight edge of maturity that made me stand apart. I didn't see it at first—the jealousy. I felt lesser for the same reasons they considered me a threat. They were on schedule where I was catching up.

"It didn't take long, a handful of incidents of ostracism, scape-goating, outright viciousness, before I learned my lesson. My undergraduate years were a largely solitary time. In grad school, I dared to try again; surely now we were on the same level. But after a casual brainstorming session with someone, I'd see my ideas claimed as her own the next day in class. In group discussions, backhanded compliments, damning with faint praise, insinuations my work was derivative—my inspiration obviously taken from something or other.

"I'm not saying this was exclusively female behavior, but... almost exclusively. At the time I judged women as a whole, I admit. Later, I came to understand that when men refused to treat you as competition, it didn't mean they were more accepting, it was simply a subtle way to convey superiority; they didn't deign to consider you a threat.

"It seemed to me that women saw each other as competition first and foremost, and letting down your guard was apt to cost you. I certainly found that to be the case in Illustris. All this is simply to say thank you for what you did today. I haven't experienced grace from another woman in so long, I'd forgotten the feeling. And I truly am sorry I can't help you. I wish I could."

I finally dare to look up again, to meet their gazes. Nina beside me, understanding if disappointed. Monica across the coffee table, less understanding, but seemingly resigned.

"You're just going to let this place be what it is?" Monica prods. "All your listening in, all your snooping around, we've all seen it, you've got to have heard something—"

"Is that what you think? That I've collected world-changing library gossip?" I wish it were so small. I wish I knew less than I know. I wish it were hearsay.

Nina gently encourages, "If there's anything that you could tell us, any kind of direction to look, clues to follow up on, it could help you too, you know—"

A flare of anger straightens my spine as I pull away from her. "It could get me killed," I seethe.

I brace myself for the inevitable storm. Will it be rage and re-crimination? Wheedling and conniving? But Nina's just staring back at me thoughtfully. After a long moment, silently regarding each other, the steam within seems to dissipate, the pressure releasing slightly.

"I don't know what I know that would be of value," I admit finally. "What's certain is that I'm the only potential source for much of it. Bombshells that would hardly advantage your cause yet would spread like wildfire... It will gain you nothing and cost me everything. I'm sorry. I can't."

"You can trust us," Monica starts to argue, but Nina holds up a hand to tell her it's pointless, never taking her eyes from mine.

"The more people who know a secret, the shorter its shelf life," Nina says simply. "I understand."

In my peripheral vision, Monica flops back in frustration, but dead ahead, Nina and I are on the same page. She nods slightly as if to echo Monica's words: *You can trust us.* Not in hopes of changing my mind, just a reassurance she's done trying, at least for now. My shoulders droop as the tension eases.

"My clothes," I murmur by way of asking. Monica stands and says she'll check.

"Blue," Nina comments. "What happened to the mourning wear?"

A nervous, miserable laugh escapes my throat. "I didn't... have any colors in my closet for quite some time. And then suddenly, I did." The gloomy pronouncement is markedly at odds with what is, on its face, a casual topic.

Monica returns with my rumpled clothes in her arms. "They're not clean, exactly? But... cleaner?"

"My shoes?" I ask with unconcealed dread.

"They're not cherry," Monica admits, "but nothing broke off, and I don't see any serious gouges, just scuffs. It could be a lot worse."

I sniffle, fighting a feeling of loss that is disproportionate to the circumstances. "Before I came here, those shoes were the nicest things I owned. They were an investment in a sense. It's silly how emotional I'm getting over this—"

Monica interrupts with comfort. "No. We all go through our moments of loss in here, some big, some small, but they all count, and they're none of 'em silly. You go on and cry if that's what you need. I know lonely when I see it."

The kindness saps the storm of emotions. My tear ducts retract in relief, reabsorbing unshed tears as the gathered moisture slips past my lower lids, barely making it halfway down my face before thinning out to nothing.

"You're both being so nice to me," I say. The words *I don't deserve it* are implied.

"Why don't you go ahead and get dressed. We'll um, turn around. Tell us about what it was like here, before," Nina suggests. I suspect they're unwilling to leave me alone now that they've returned my clothing, lest I run away again.

Inspecting my things, I find only mild residual dampness but some concentric circles indicating water stains and seeped-in mud. The dress has been rinsed gently and hung dry, not washed. The stockings are miraculously intact, with minor drags but no pops. I secure the garter belt and start pulling them on, already feeling a bit more myself.

"Illustris before. I wasn't here long, I'm afraid. And I wasn't—well, I didn't quite fit in. I don't know what I thought it would be like, in retrospect. I wasn't one of them, but I'd been chosen, so...."

Both stockings in place, I give the underwear a glance before deciding I can go without. I slip them in the pocket of the blue dress and slide it over my head, shivering a little at the not-quite-dry clamminess of the fabric as it settles against my skin.

"Sometimes I wonder if it might have been different. If the world hadn't changed so much, so quickly. Would he have... but in truth, that's not when the problems started with Greg. I wasn't quite right. I seemed to constantly fail to meet expectations no one explained in advance, and it was clear that I was a disappointment, didn't fit in, didn't make him proud. Out there, I must have seemed more interesting or impressive, and then here, I just stood out in the opposite way. But he was a brilliant man, you know. I suppose I brought out the worst in him."

When I look up from buttoning the front of my dress, my hands shaking, both women have turned to look at me with sad comprehension, as if they've heard this story before.

"I guarantee you that's not true," Monica says flatly. "A man who's got *worst* in him in the first place doesn't need help bringing it out. Whatever happened, don't try and own that shit."

"He was so embarrassed by me. I didn't live up to—"

Nina's voice cuts confidently through my stammering, "Oh please. Stella, these people are such snobs. I'm sorry, but I bet you ten million of their now-worthless dollars that he went looking for a woman from outside just so he could always lord it over her, so she'd always be grateful and scrambling to meet his standards. Which would be a moving target, by the way."

Monica interjects, "I'll go you one further: I bet he *had* to find someone from outside to marry him because the women in here all knew he was a piece of shit."

The blonde at the gallery, so long ago. Greta, I eventually learned. I've seen her a few times since the world ended as well, and she looks just as severe, brittle and unhappy. When we spoke at the gallery, I was unsure how to read her demeanor; I took it the way I took most Illustrians' attitudes toward me. I was being judged and found wanting, over and over, by everyone I encountered in this petty, miserable place. But even then, there was a moment—a flash of pained recognition. Monica's wild guess strikes me as potentially insightful, not that I suppose it matters much now. After all, he's gone.

I sink into the couch again, hoping I don't look as weak as I feel. Yet I must, because they both come to sit beside me and Monica takes my hand. She starts to speak, then realizes she's taken hold of my left hand and pauses to give the ring a somber glare.

"He needed someone poor. Relative to him, that wouldn't have been hard. Someone who wouldn't have an easy time getting away once he had her trapped down. Sounds like you didn't have a lot of family support, even out there?" I nod. "Yeah. Figures. Icing on the cake, far as he was concerned. That's how these guys operate. Lure you in, lock you away, and break you down."

"How do you know that?" My words are hesitant, resentfully hope-tinged. I fear the potential forgiveness in her version of my story.

"I've seen it." She shrugs bitterly, then adds, "Not the super-uber-rich part," again glancing at the rock I wear like an anchor. "But the isolation. This girl in my circle got caught up in a goddamn whirlwind relationship and we were all, *Oh, so romantic!*" She rolls her eyes and shakes her head sadly at her long-ago naivete. "We were young. He whisked her off half a country away and she stopped answering texts or DMs... and we were bitchy about it, like oh, guess she fell into her bliss and forgot all about us. Like, good for her, but also the hell with her, kind of. Few years later, a friend ran into her. She'd moved back at some point but didn't know how to come back to her life. Didn't know how to tell her old friends how bad she fucked up—that's how she saw the whole thing, that she'd fucked up, ruined her own damn life."

"What happened to her?" I ask quietly.

But she turns it around with deadly seriousness.

"What happened to you?"

I breathe. Slowly. In, out, in, preparing to infuse words with oxygen. Yet what comes out is, "I need to get back. There's so much to address. You said Commander Maxwell would be—"

"Yeah. He'll have talked the situation calm or thereabouts. Don't even worry 'bout that. Just be normal, as much as possible. Far as anyone knows, you freaked out over feeling like you were being pushed out, that's all."

"It's believable. They know how much it matters to me. What you've all done, I appreciate it, but there may be consequences for me."

"What do you mean?" Nina asks, her tone and her gaze exhorting me to open up. My silence in response is like a door slamming between us.

A moment later, I'm alone again, the apartment door shutting quietly behind me. The vault of my secrets remains undisturbed in the face of their friendship.

It is a lonely kind of safety, and tenuous. I make my way back to the Gennero mansion as slowly as I dare, assessing my mounting threats. The visits. The clothing. The erosion of my time commitment—my excuse to be elsewhere. I've been dancing on the edge of the mountainside, aware the ground beneath me wouldn't hold indefinitely, yet stubbornly maintaining my position lest the acknowledgement of peril only imperil me further.

If there were a way to give Demetri's friends what they need... but I don't know what's useful information and what's just inflammatory gossip. I am right not to trust that the information would be as secure once it lives outside my own head. Once you set it free, it will take on a life of its own. It may do them no good at all while costing me my life. It may cost their lives as well, come to that.

It's volatile and of uncertain value. It must be contained. Even so, there's a tipping point coming. I can't keep living in denial about my own future—about the fact that it is not my own.

The wrenching anguish of kissing Demetri today, wondering if he could taste the lies and secrets poisoning my blood. Knowing I could never hope to deserve the happiness promised by his touch.

He's been so clear about what he wants. He seems genuinely to know what that is. I envy him a bit. And yes, yes, I want him too, of course I do. But I don't deserve him. I came so close to selfishly pulling him over the edge today before finding the fortitude to deny myself the indulgence at his expense.

Walking up the front steps I might as well be ascending the gallows. Celeste hears me coming through the front door and emerges from whatever adjacent room she's been stewing in to glare at me. We face each other down in the foyer. Her glare pins me like a butterfly. She's as perfectly appointed as the house she haunts, while I, on the other hand, look exactly like someone who ran a mile in pumps, sat on frozen mud for half an hour, then brushed off the excess muck before trudging home the worse for wear. At my best and most confident, I've never held my own against her, always crumpled like a wilted flower underfoot. There's no chance I can stand against her now. Dusty, shabby, broken.

Celeste shocks me with a smile, but it's barely a millisecond of hopeful comfort before I see triumph in her eyes. She's enjoying this, and what Celeste enjoys has never been good news for me.

"You've had quite the adventure, haven't you, little ragamuffin? Appalling display, but no less than I'd expect, given your upbringing." Her grin broadens as she relishes this perfect excuse to unleash her bile. "I've been after Roger to unchain you a bit from that dreary routine of yours, anyway. It's not healthy, that attachment to work. It's time to bring you back into the world."

I don't want to be in your world. Not that I fool myself into believing she would care what I wanted. My throat doesn't even twitch. There are no words trying to form. She doesn't need a response from me anyway: This isn't an invitation, it's an announcement.

Her nose wrinkles as if she's just now noticing a foul smell. If I smell of anything, it's the clean scent of the earth.

"Get yourself cleaned up. And no more theatrics. Today was undignified. Work on being presentable. If you can manage that."

Satisfied with the last word she's gotten in, Celeste turns and disappears into the darkened hallway. I trudge up the stairs to my room and peel off the slightly stiff dress. It might never be perfect again, and while that would still be good enough for me, I know Celeste would be appalled to see a stained garment on someone at our supposed level.

Foolish snob. Give it a generation, and a dress that is stained but well-made will be akin to treasure.

I sit down on the edge of the bed and look at the damage I've done to my shoes. *Not cherry,* Monica put it, and that's putting it mildly. But like the dress, they're well-made. Afraid to worsen the scuffs, yet compelled to torment myself by tangibly confirming the worst of it, I drag a light fingertip across the aggravated surface of the leather. I kept them so perfect for so long. They were the nicest things I'd ever owned.

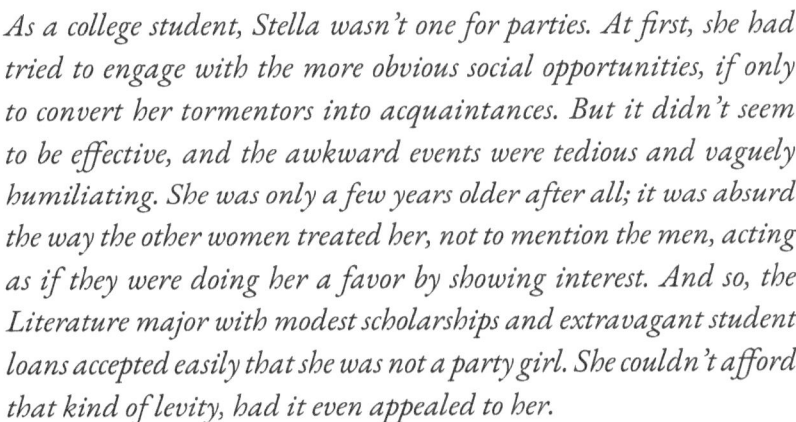

As a college student, Stella wasn't one for parties. At first, she had tried to engage with the more obvious social opportunities, if only to convert her tormentors into acquaintances. But it didn't seem to be effective, and the awkward events were tedious and vaguely humiliating. She was only a few years older after all; it was absurd the way the other women treated her, not to mention the men, acting as if they were doing her a favor by showing interest. And so, the Literature major with modest scholarships and extravagant student loans accepted easily that she was not a party girl. She couldn't afford that kind of levity, had it even appealed to her.

There was a different sort of party, however, that she absolutely loved. She would put on her nicest shabby dress and cheap heels, the scuffs camouflaged with a magic marker. Surrounded by women with professional updos, Stella wore a plastic barrette from which the gold paint had long since rubbed off. Yet it almost didn't matter that she didn't look like she belonged; she didn't feel inferior, because while some of those women were arm candy for the wealthy alumni and donors, Stella was there to be honored, celebrated. There was no significant measure of belonging besides academic excellence, and she was proud beyond measure regardless of her humble origins or meager closet. She was there to impress people with her intellect, opinions, and eloquence. In those rare evenings, she saw her future, and it was so bright, she shone.

She would never be the kind of alum the school valued—her path would never turn her into a wealthy donor. If she managed to climb out from under the student debt in time to start saving for retirement, it would be a minor miracle. She would surely never be anyone's benefactress. But that self-aware assessment never dimmed the moment for her.

As a budding professor, she gained greater responsibility at such events. No longer a star student—a shining example of what the school could produce, now she represented the university's future rather than her own. If she had once been a source of revenue via her crushing student loans, she was now a drain on resources via her pittance of a salary.

Her dresses were less shabby, but they made up for it by being out-dated. The old barrette might have passed as kitschy on a person who could obviously afford better; fortunately, it was now fashionable to wear one's hair loose and flowing. An absurd amount of Stella's mental energy was devoted to where she stepped, how she stood, how to cross her legs without bumping the table, because she truly couldn't afford to have to replace her stockings too often, and a scuff on her shoes would be disastrous—as a believer in Terry Pratchett's maxim, Stella had made one expensive purchase thus far in her adult life: comfortable, sturdy, attractive shoes.

Dressed up as much as she could manage, Stella dutifully attended stuffy alumni events, dialing up her energy output to five times the level of a lecture on Candide. She smiled endlessly, shook hands, and did her damnedest to charm donors. Her intellect and eloquence were still of value in these displays, though her opinions were generally to be suppressed or outright denied. This wasn't limited to politics or religion, topics understood to be verboten at any social gathering in a polite society. No, Stella was required to indulge absolute drivel within her own area of expertise. If an alum wanted to ramble for twenty minutes about how it takes a mature actor to properly portray Hamlet, she couldn't point out that the character was canonically a college student, she just had to nod along and praise their insight.

In fleeting moments, she thought she might love to spend an evening among people in jeans and t-shirts, playing drinking games.

But that stage in life was behind her, even if she never took advantage of it at the time.

After feigning enthusiasm for a predictably shallow viewpoint on the works of Ayn Rand (an author whose greatest devotees seemed never to have actually read), Stella felt she had earned the right to take a break and stand in line at the bar. Her attention was largely devoted to the drinks in the hands of people ahead of her as they turned to walk away; if they sloshed, she would have to be nimble. She pursed her lips, ruing the precious irreplaceability of her good shoes, and even more the tag inside her dress which read dry clean only. *Most of all, she resented the knowledge that almost no one else here calculated dry cleaning costs against groceries.*

"What department are you representing?" came a confident, intelligent male voice from behind her.

Suppressing her irritation at being forced to be on when she was trying to have a quiet moment, Stella turned halfway to acknowledge the man. When she got a look at him, she didn't mind as much.

"English. I'm a professor," she added superfluously. Was she trying to impress him? Or testing to make sure he wasn't the kind of creep who would be interested in a student—he was a bit older, after all.

He extended his hand. "Greg Gennero."

She recognized the name, of course. "Of the newly renovated medical science building, I presume."

He didn't respond. Had she said something wrong? But he gestured her forward; the line had advanced. She took a step to close the gap, then returned her attention to him.

"Are you an alumnus, then? Or someone else in your family?"

"Everyone in my family," he answered with that hint of sheepish self-deprecation cultivated by the ultra-rich. Stella hated that air of faux humility that seemed to express We really are just like you, but better.

She found herself pivoting to avoid the pitfall of disliking him.

"Alumnus is a very fun word when it comes up in class. One of those quirks of language that can spark real passion for the subject. The idea of a word with so many specific forms conveying nearly identical meanings—"

He gestured again, and she realized she'd started rambling, gushing about her work as if speaking to a real person rather than hobnobbing with a donor. She pressed her lips together and let her words die an awkward death.

A hand on her shoulder startled her, more so when it settled into a momentary caress. Surely a tap would have sufficed rather than this premature familiarity. She was on the verge of objecting or at least politely shrinking away when he smiled and said, "Please go on. I enjoy a good etymology discussion. What are you drinking?"

His proprietary touch still felt mildly unwelcome and off-putting, but he was handsome, not wearing a wedding ring, and seemingly interested in her. Stella's isolation pouted and begged her to let herself be charmed, if only for a little while.

She had barely gotten out the words "white wine" when the dawning smile on her lips twisted in surprise and dismay as cold liquid splashed the back of her calves and ran down to pool in her shoes.

"Oh, sorry," said a broad-shouldered man before he walked away without a glance—and without at least one good swallow's worth of the vodka-something soaking Stella's feet.

Greg Gennero's hand, still on her shoulder, slid down her bicep. It was as if he thought the spilled drink had bonded them, emboldening him to deepen the touch. Again her mind flashed discomfort and uncertainty, and again she quelled the response as not being anything she could deal with in a situationally appropriate manner even if she wanted to.

"Go get cleaned up. I'll be waiting for you on the balcony, and we'll have that drink."

He said it as if their having a drink together had been a settled matter, as if he didn't need to ask, but perhaps that was just what it was like being rich. A legacy alumnus and donor of buildings was used to being treated with deference. She mustn't overreact to the natural sense of entitlement informing his behavior.

She did her best to halt the progress of whatever damage the alcohol was doing to her shoes, dabbing first with damp paper towels, then dry. Accepting that her stockings would remain clammy against her skin for a while, she hoped the wine would divert her attention from the discomfort. Greg Gennero was waiting for her on the balcony with one glass of red, and one white, as promised. She took the white and thanked him.

With a raised eyebrow and a studiously apologetic tone, he advised her, "The red is considered a more sophisticated choice. I don't mean to be patronizing, of course, but I assume you'd like to send the right signals among a crowd like this."

She stiffened, and when she shifted her feet slightly, she swore she could almost hear the squelch of her sodden stockings. "I choose the white so I can continue smiling throughout the evening without wine stains mottling my teeth. But thank you for the advice."

His eyes shifted through a quick series of unreadable reactions before settling back on the sheepish rich boy smile.

"You're right. I didn't mean to be pompous. Let's forget this part and get back to when you were being charming, and I was, well, charmed?"

She wasn't sure she had been charming at all, certainly not in the deliberate way his tone seemed to imply. But it was nice to be seen that way, wasn't it? Nice to have a handsome, intelligent man of unimaginable means show such interest. Stella decided not to let the mild awkwardness of their introduction stand in the way of letting herself be charmed... and it was a long time before she remembered that she *had been instructed to charm* him; *he had merely reached out and taken what he wanted, pushing boundaries with subtle relentlessness until there were none left in his way.*

Chapter Fourteen

Displacement

Stella

Yesterday's tectonic shifts have left me simultaneously tender and brittle, like a rib that might be bruised or broken, and there's simply no way to know. I spend the morning in a haze, trying not to stare daggers at Cindy, the friend of Sarah Maxwell's who is supposedly shadowing me to learn the ropes.

When she finally leaves, I give myself permission to hide out in a corner of the mezzanine and cry for what I've already lost and what I fear I am about to lose.

A ring of the desk bell summons me back. I swipe at my eyes and cheeks. I paste on a bland smile. I make it through the day and remain present in my body.

I'm deep in thought and deep in a wander in the evening when Demetri arrives. He finds me, and I lean into his chest, inviting his arms to encircle me.

"I told you before that I met Greg at an alumni event. At the university where I was on a career path that I'd worked so hard for." Shaking my head breaks the embrace. Even now, my conscious mind grapples with understanding the choices I made before. "I threw it all away. I gave it up right when it was in reach. A man came along and told me none of it mattered and he wanted to take care of me, and I just put myself in his hands."

His fingers curl into mine gently to hold me in the here and now. "That was how long before the world ended?"

"Weeks before it started to end, months before there was no longer a question." My voice is dull and recriminatory. I am determined to indict myself for this terrible decision.

"You did the right thing, Stella."

Startled, on the verge of anger, I meet his eyes, silently demanding that he explain himself.

"You're here," he says simply. He lifts my hand and pulls it closer, letting my knuckles rest against his sternum. Gently trapped between his hand and his chest, my fingers pick up his pulse like a distant radio wave playing my favorite song.

"You can't regret the choice you made, I won't accept that. You've beat yourself up plenty, and that stops now, because you're here. I like you here."

"But he—he wasn't—I should have seen—"

"Shhh." He lifts my hand to his lips, then pulls it into his chest more firmly. "Don't feel bad about whatever brought you here. I can't think about you being anywhere else."

It's a comforting notion, nearly intoxicating, to imagine my bad choices being somehow redeemed by a fortuitous outcome. Not that I've earned redemption. He only knows I've been hurt, not the hurt I've helped bring about. Yet if I can believe my survival might be worth the price of my own pain, is there another price I might yet pay to earn a chance at happiness?

Both Demetri's hands close around mine on his chest, and he begins to massage my palm with his fingers and thumbs. It's nice, it's meant to be nice, he's good, not just decent but good, but my heart starts stuttering and my lungs clench. It's my left hand, of course, the one Greg held under the dinner table to communicate his displeasure if needed. Demetri's fingers wouldn't turn this caress into a pinching grip—he wouldn't, not ever, but I lose control over the impending panic attack and pull away.

I've offended him, hurt his feelings. It's not what I intended. I have to fix it. I regain my breath and fight away the gray. As I try to work out how to deal with any of this, I look up and see a somber truth in his eyes.

"He hurt you," he guesses. "No one should do that. I'm sorry anyone did."

He slowly reaches out again, making eye contact, checking in with me as he moves. My silence and stillness are the permission he needs to take my hand and raise it slowly to his lips. He drops the simplest, purest kiss against the hollow of my hand, never taking his eyes off mine.

"I wondered so many times. What about me brought that out of him. For a while, I tried to believe it wasn't me at all, that maybe it was his parents, then the stress of well, everything. He had a very important job, and—"

"No no no no no no." The word rushes softly from his lips. "You didn't... it was all him. If it wasn't you he was hurting, it would have been someone else. How you treat people, that's just who you are."

"How do you know?" It's a plea. I want this to be an answer I can hold onto. I want to be free of this one piece of my pattern of self-flagellation.

"Okay. My buddy Jordan was dating this chick who was fucking nuts. I shouldn't say that, right?"

"Which part? Chick or fucking nuts?"

He grins. "There it is. I'll make an ass of myself a thousand times to keep getting that smile. So Jordan's dating this nutty girl. And she's got issues, like, I don't even know. Keeps tryna provoke him, make him jealous, make him angry... it's really out-there behavior and we're all thinking the sex must be amazing if he hasn't dumped her yet—sorry."

But I'm breathing easier and a promise of laughter starts to tickle my chest.

"Anyway, finally she smacks him and stands there bracing herself for the reaction. Nothing, of course, 'cause he's not a fucking asshole, and she gets confused and she goes, 'It's okay, hit me, I know you want to.'"

My eyes wide, the incipient laughter forgotten. "What did he do?"

"He backed up a few feet, got out his phone, and ordered her a rideshare. Put her in it and said he hoped she had a good life. Because he was a good guy. And that's how you handle things when you're a good guy."

He makes it sound so simple. Is it?

Isn't it?

"You don't have a crazy ex-girlfriend story of your own?"

"Nah," he says with a shrug. "I didn't get into a lot of long-term serious stuff after Rachel. I kept things light. And I had good cray-dar."

The giggle returns and bubbles out of my chest. "Thank you, Demetri."

A serious look shadows his handsome face. "You're not the sort of woman who goes for guys like me."

I roll my eyes and prepare to point out that every woman on the planet goes for guys like him.

"Let me finish," he says with a hint of pain that shuts me right up. "I'm not talking about going *home* with me, okay? I mean the rest of it. There's no such thing as a trophy husband. No one wants a man who's not as good as her in the ways that count."

A knot in the center of my chest. He believes this. He's never looked more vulnerable, even when I've seen him in tears.

"The ways that count." Echoing his words, tasting them. They're bitter and brittle. "Greg was brilliant. A genius, successful, well-bred... I assumed a moral code and superimposed it on him in my mind, even in the face of evidence to the contrary. I tied myself in knots trying to continue believing in a man that existed in my imagination. He didn't even need to make excuses. I did that for him."

"You can't feel bad—"

"You told me to absolve myself of the bad choice I made. Because I'm here." I force the next words out through a sudden attack of nerves, "With you. You don't give yourself enough credit, and—"

"And you don't give yourself enough grace."

Silence breathes between us. There's a feeling almost like belonging. It's close. Could I bring it into reach?

"The truth is you're better than me. In the ways that count." My voice drops out at the end of each phrase as I shove the words into being. I have to say this or it won't be said. I have to do this, at least try. "You're brave." My eyes are burning, so I press them shut. "You care. I've been so afraid, so cautious."

But that won't save me.

"Stella?" he says in alarm. "Are you okay?" He must assume I'm freaking out again.

"Yes. I didn't mean to alarm you. Demetri..."

My rabbity nerves reassert themselves. Swirling, looking in every direction, terrified I'll spot someone nearby. Just as I accept there's no one visible at eye level, I become certain there's someone crouched down, listening. On the verge of beginning a search that would only escalate my panic and never satisfy my paranoia, I grab his hand and pull him to follow me.

Down the row, all the way to the wall. Look left, right—no one in sight, pick a direction, keep moving—surge to the right with him in tow, red flashes in the backs of my eyes—

He stops me short, pulls me close, whispers in my ear, "What's happening? Talk to me."

I surrender, and he soothes me into his chest. His scent revives me a way mere oxygen could never have done. The ragged goose-flesh on my arms starts to settle.

"We were too out in the open," I confess, barely above a breath.

"We were the same as we always are." He's not contradicting me, he's comforting me, or trying to. But he doesn't understand.

"I want to fix it. I want to help."

His muscles stiffen just for the briefest moment as he takes in the words and comprehends the full intent. "You can talk to me," he says softly.

But I shake my head against him. "If I knew what mattered... if I could whisper it all into a machine that would sort it... identify the details that could save the day and throw the rest into an incinerator... I wish I knew how to help, but I don't even know how to avoid causing more damage."

Demetri's solid strength surrounds me as he holds me close. He begins stroking my hair, and I let my eyes slip shut more naturally, not hiding from the world or myself but simply wishing to stay in the peace of this moment. Though we're still upright, closing my eyes allows me to imagine holding each other like this in the dark, somewhere peaceful, all alone.

"I suppose it was decent of you to pretend to need my help." My voice is dull, the words clipped. Sarah Maxwell seems like a perfectly nice woman, for what it's worth, but my rage is barely in check. I held it together a bit better on day one with her friend, but this is a Commander's wife, and he's the one who placed her here. I can't help perceiving this as a strategic incursion of my library.

And yet, I'm here. Still here. Fury seems to lend my heart a savage rhythm, binding me to my body.

"For what it's worth, I am sorry to intrude," she says softly. She sounds sincere, and that irritates me somehow. As if her apparent decency seeks to defang my rage.

Her mouth opens. Trouble shades her eyes. She seems to struggle with words on the tip of her tongue.

"Tell me." It comes out as emotionally flat as *pass the salt*. I can't compel her. She'll speak or she won't.

"This was coming no matter what. It just happened ahead of schedule." She's simultaneously sympathetic and matter of fact.

"Because there are plans for me, and at your husband's level, he would know that."

She grimaces confessionally. I suddenly know she isn't telling me this out of mere compassion.

"All right, out with it. Whatever you were instructed to ask me."

"It might not be too late to change things. Talk to me. Or Jim. We know you've seen things—we know who your fiancé was—you must have something that could be of use."

I forcibly unclench my teeth so I can answer her. "Your husband knew what was coming for me, and all he did was lay plans to take over my life once I was plucked out of it. Someone so resourceful doesn't need any help from me."

"You could make a difference."

"*Jim* was content to stand by and observe the game, knowing I was about to be taken off the board. Now he wants me to help him make a play before I go?"

Her expression hardens, and I feel a shiver. "He knows you're in the middle of a lot of things right now, Stella. Shifting loyalties."

Maxwell's afraid I'll try something stupid like trading information on him to improve my situation. Idiot. There is nothing that could win me favor with the Genneros. They would take the information, happily, but it wouldn't change the outcome for me. Maxwell still doesn't know how they operate, not really. He's still playing a different game than they are, and nowhere near the same league.

"I'm loyal to the library. I'll never endanger it." The longtime truth is easy enough to speak. "I don't give a damn about your husband. And neither does anyone at the Council level. That is what eats at him, right? He's got little to no chance of making a dent no matter what he does. Tell him that."

In the icy silence, the *whoosh* of the door draws our attention. *Leo.* I frown at the sight of one of my least welcome Illustrian visitors. The last time I saw him, he was sputtering at me over his first-edition Bukowskis.

Maybe that's why he's here now. Or maybe it's worse. If this man is about to try and gauge my potential as a wife... his blandly predatory smile indicates that may be the case, and I refuse to entertain the notion for the space of a single breath.

"If you'll excuse me," I say confidentially, "our pantomime that you somehow require my assistance seems a perfect opportunity for a last gasp of freedom."

I don't wait for any kind of response, and she flusters at my retreating back, "Where are you going? If anyone asks—"

"Archives," I say without a backwards glance. "Leo likes to know how his books are being treated."

Archives is a few streets over. The department is divided, keeping Illustris and Newcomer records separate. It's the only non-military cohort in which Illustrians are outnumbered currently; there are still many more legacy residents to keep track of. Illustrians maintain records for newcomers and vice versa. It's a flimsy sense of security but it hardly matters. Illustrians have nothing to hide from the newcomers except their own information. The division inhibits the discovery of their own intake forms, their medical charts, their psychological profiles. The records of those who were turned away, who might have been important to some of those who were admitted. Not important enough to stay outside with them, but perhaps enough to mourn or even to avenge.

When the library began absorbing private collections, it was agreed records should be maintained, detailing who donated what—whether in the interest of someday reclaiming them or because the belief in tax write-offs was simply in their blood at that point. Books and other physical media were boxed, labelled, and delivered to Archives to be carefully catalogued before they entered circulation.

Because my previous visits to Archives tended to be in response to petty demands from petty men like Leo, I have only ever needed to enter the side staffed by apocalypse refugees. It doesn't take long scanning the room to spot Nina's desk. She looks up in mild confusion at my approach.

"Hi. I seem to be free for lunch today. I thought perhaps... with a friend."

Nina's smile finds the fissures in my brittle state of mind and restores a hint of warmth. She nods, and we walk out of the building together, not exchanging another word until we're alone.

"I'm glad you came to see me. I've been thinking I should apologize to you. There's a whole us vs. them thing—us from outside vs. them who were here before. We lost so much. And they didn't. I'm sorry I ever thought of you as just some spoiled snob with barely a care in the world. That was wrong of me. I should know better, after everything I've seen."

Her earnest admission strikes a welcome contrast after Sarah Maxwell's attempt to wheedle me.

"Thank you."

At the kitchen, we fall silent again. Once we settle in at a table with our trays, I quietly give voice to the swirling confessional thoughts consuming me today.

"I may not have been a spoiled snob, but I was the next worst thing. A snob groupie. And it's ironic. I *was* proud to be successful on my merits all those years. The poorest kid in so many rooms, standing out among those whose parents could not only pay their way but assure their acceptance with a phone call. I bore the stereotypical chip on my shoulder: *I'm better than they are.*

"Yet the validation of someone from that world wanting me? The goalposts shifted instantly the moment there was a chance for an Illustrian man to whisk me away to his tower. If I could have a brilliant, wealthy man like Greg and live in a place like this, then I simply *had* to."

"How long did you know him before he proposed?"

Not long enough, I think, flagellating myself yet again that I didn't see any of the later troubles coming when I bound my life to him.

"Not long enough," I say, surprising myself with the truth. "I thought if I hesitated, he'd move on, and I'd always be dissatisfied with my life. The life that until I met him was a proud culmination of years of striving... I threw it away because if Greg Gennero wanted me, that was the real prize. I felt like a scullery maid being courted by a prince. I didn't want to risk losing the fairy tale by thinking about it too hard."

Nina gives me a sympathetic smile. "Fairy tales are fucking insidious, aren't they?"

"You've been so kind. Monica too. She was right, you know. I *was* alone when I met Greg. My mother had died a few years before, and I hadn't spoken to my father for some time before that. I didn't even let him know I was going to be married. I thought about it—a momentary spiteful desire to inform him of my new life. I imagined he would bitterly envy me, perhaps even kowtow to see if I'd bring him along... but I rose above that temptation, at least."

"He left you and your mom." The left side of her mouth twists into a knowing scowl. "Let me guess, younger woman?"

"No. Well, eventually there was a new wife, and she was a bit younger—not scandalously so, to be fair."

"Pfft," she interrupts, "don't be fair to him."

Warmth fills my chest. She defended me to myself. That's something a friend would do.

"I'm afraid my father's choice was more statistically common than just simply cliché. He left my mom when she was sick."

"That piece of shit," she breathes with vehemence, and I nod in agreement.

Despite everything weighing on me, I feel just a bit better. I suppose I've lived in my head too much. My vault of secrets that only grows, never purges. Speaking of these long-ago truths must be relieving some of the pressure.

"I've often wondered if there were signs I missed. That she missed too, perhaps. We were so focused on her—"

"Rightfully so," she adds.

"Yes. But still. We weren't paying attention to his behavior, his attitude. After he was gone, I realized I couldn't think of the last time we'd even spoken on any meaningful topic or spent time together. It made me angry all over again to think that he likely justified his abandonment of his family by saying he'd been ignored—under the circumstances, he was certainly wrong to take umbrage, but I expect it was a nice cushion to his self-opinion."

"Fuck that guy. Sorry. I know, he was still your father, and it's complicated. I just can't help that my instinct remains to call him a piece of shit and say fuck that guy."

A laugh loosens the habitual tightness in my chest and shoulders.

"I always did tend to hyperfocus on the priorities of the moment in lieu of the greater picture. Never traded the tangible for the possible. Until the day I just tossed my life in the air like a deck of cards and ran off before I had to see which way they landed... But Greg was a brilliant man. I thought that implied other positive traits somehow. Once again, I wasn't paying attention to the right things."

Nina's gaze remains locked on me, her eyes warm with growing friendship. She starts to smile, and I think she's about to speak, but then her eyes flit as if to observe her own mind as it waves at her for attention. Her head tilts, and I know I'm right. She's having a memory or an idea, and it's important.

I know this look. I've worn it. I know the helpless fury I feel when someone interrupts my thoughts right when they're flowing in a useful direction. I smile down at my tray and take a bite. I will sit in silence as long as she likes.

I've wished for a way to help. If something I said has been useful when I wasn't even trying, when I risked nothing, could such a small contribution to their effort win back a part of my soul?

There's so much I wish I could undo, unsay. All I gave to help build this place. What would it look like without my input?

"We're under pressure to grow our ranks quickly, of course, but we can't just let in everyone who shows up at the gates."

"Of course not," Greg said, his tone confirming the very idea was absurd.

"Regardless, we do need to move on this. Show some progress and buy a little time, if nothing else."

Greg pursed his lips in thought. "Straightforward enough. We can let in everyone who shows up at the gates—but only as far as Quarantine," he improvised with a flourish. "Shall we say: a month? Long enough to discover anything the scans could have missed."

"Missed?" Stella repeated with innocent alarm, and Greg patted her hand where it rested on his sleeve.

"Nothing to worry about. The tech is infallible in its ability to detect all known viruses. However, there's a minimum threshold for any infectious agent; if the exposure is too new, it could be below that threshold. Besides, new viruses are known to arise. Until they can be identified and added to the database, we won't be able to scan for them."

"How often does that—"

"Doesn't matter. It's mostly an excuse to establish the process. What do you think?" Greg turned to his father with a cool look that spoke to his pride in a quick, sensible solution to the problem Roger had posed.

The older man nodded. "It's good. I can sell this. The military can anticipate their new recruits while we continue to hone our criteria."

"*Being healthy and willing to fight isn't enough?*" Stella asked in guileless confusion. *The men chuckled indulgently, and Celeste huffed, apparently disgusted with Stella's foolishness. For a few minutes, Stella had all but forgotten the other woman was even in the room. The reminder knitted a clench into her shoulders.*

"*Illustris was exclusive,*" Roger said thinly. "*The Stronghold must be as well. If anything, more so.*"

"*I don't understand. Beyond our need for more people, surely there's a humanitarian—*"

Roger and Greg shared a belly laugh, clearly enjoying Stella's strange ideas.

"*We live in a meritocracy, dear,*" Celeste said witheringly from her position on the chaise in the corner. *She tended to remain on the edges of these interactions, rarely chiming in except to diminish her nominal daughter-in-law. Stella intuited that in the old days, Celeste was fine leaving the boys to their business and disappearing to another part of the house. Stella's presence had disrupted her life in any number of ways. When Stella didn't automatically adopt the gender-segregated social dynamic Celeste enjoyed, it created a new paradigm in which Celeste might be perceived as left out rather than opted out. That was clearly unacceptable, so she had to start opting in, much as she may have preferred to be elsewhere. Stella further intuited this wasn't entirely a question of boredom on Celeste's part: She thought Celeste might prefer to remain uninformed—blissfully ignorant of what failed to amuse or enrich her. That she was now compelled into these tableaux was just one more reason to resent Stella.*

"*Mother's right, of course. Now more than ever, we must maintain rigorous standards. There are humanitarian aspects to this decision, if not in the way you might be invoking.*"

"*Resources are not merely limited but, in many cases, irreplaceable,*" Roger noted soberly. "*To invite someone in to become another* active drain on any of those resources... well, they'd have to be a good investment, wouldn't they?"

Stella's panic flared. She had been one of the last to enter the city before the fall. Perhaps the last newcomer to be invited, as far as she knew. Had she been a good investment? Celeste wouldn't have said so. Greg had expressed his disappointment in her several times, though not lately.

He turned to look at her fully. "I am glad you're here for this," he said in an even, pondering tone. Stella mastered her emotions, swallowing her gasp of grateful surprise before it could be seen or heard. "Once again, I believe your outsider perspective will be of use to us."

Her heartbeat fluttered in anxious relief. *I'm of use*, she thought. To be of use was far better than the alternative, and while that was not a new thought for Stella, it had never been more factually accurate.

Chapter Fifteen

The Cooper Glitch

Demetri

It's important to polish off your human kills in a zombie apocalypse, but the fact of it never gets easier.

All those months, we thought we had it bad, letting our enemies walk away or at least limp away. We used to bitch about having our hands tied. We were downright eager to put these pricks down with extreme prejudice. Then Command altered the rules of engagement on us, set us loose. And it was effective; they did pull back and stop poking us once we turned from teddy bears to grizzlies.

But then the zombie swarms started coming harder and harder, more and more often, almost like they were being driven at us, herded somehow. It felt like a crazy thought, and I didn't say it out loud... but then I heard some of my fellow soldiers talking about it. Sure, it's probably impossible, everyone agreed, but on the other hand...

I thought back to that day we got hit so hard all at once, the day Cooper and a whole damn team got killed. The Devil Runner who was threatening Monica and Nina—well, threatening all of us with death, but them with worse. He said something about living out here with the zombies, getting used to them. We retreat within the walls of the Stronghold at the end of our shift. Their shifts don't end, though.

Is it possible they've adapted? I don't wanna think about how epically fucked we could be if that's true.

Nowadays, on the rare occasions we encounter Devil Runners, backup squads deploy immediately. Tom's leading the crew that joined us out here today. The hard stuff seemingly done, he and I scan the area on opposite sides of the clearing to make sure there's not another ambush incoming.

On our private channel, he mutters, "It's okay to retreat a bit on the inside when you can't do so physically."

"What?"

"I don't need to be able to see your face to know you're struggling. It's understandable. These people may be killers, but they're still people. You, on the other hand, didn't want to be a killer. It's been forced on you by circumstance."

I wanna tell him to shut up because I need to focus. Or maybe because he's right and I don't wanna hear it. Probably both.

"So what'm I supposed to do about it? I'm not goin' all helmet head if that's what you mean."

He chuckles. "I certainly hope not. No. I found a way to escape to an extent by portraying an alternate version of myself. It helps. It always did. In the beginning, it merely suppressed my fear enough to get me through alive, but now... I needn't be the same man who fights to the death against my own kind as the one who goes home to my wife."

I let his words sink in. I try to comprehend them. But I can't help pointing out, "It's a lie, though."

Another, shorter chuckle that sounds like he's agreeing with me. "When the truth is *this*, who could begrudge us a lie?"

We're nearly back in earshot of the others, so we knock it off with the chatter. Our teams are just about finished divesting the Devil Runners' corpses of weapons and ammo. We take positions nearby and continue to monitor the area for any signs of life. In my 360, all I'm picking up on is my own crew going over the bodies, making sure nothing of use has been left behind before we start the decomp. It's fucking horrific, but it's clean. Like a controlled burn at kiln temperatures with no sparks to fly, flames to leap, or embers to smolder.

I hate the HUD view, never more so than when I'm standing still while others are in motion. At least while we're walking, there's something steady about it. A cadence, them and me, moving consistently in our patrol formation.

When they're puttering around behind me like now, it's like being at a sports bar trying to ignore a TV right on the edge of my vision. You can't ignore it, not really. It's a flicker, constant motion, irritating the fuck out of you with its insistent *look at me!* I don't miss that bullshit, that's for sure. The way it looks to me on the HUD is even weirder, like it's right above my field of vision—above me, creating a sense of the sky falling, though I know it's displaying what's behind. I wish I could close my eyes longer than a blink, because it's giving me a fucking headache.

"Are we nearly done here?" Tom sounds as impatient as I feel, probably for different reasons.

In the cluster of motion at the upper range of my vision, one soldier's sudden furtive motion stands out. They look from side to side before slipping something into a pocket. I'm about to whirl around so I can figure out which one it was, but Tom must've seen it too, and he says on our private channel, just above a whisper, "Don't let on."

What? We're just gonna let this go, walk away knowing something just went down but not what or who!

But I trust Tom's instincts. And even just taking that extra moment between the impulse to react and the enforced reflection, I can intuit his reasoning. One of them is hiding something, sure, but what about the rest of them? If there's a chance we have a traitor, there's a chance we have more than one. We're outnumbered. This could go bad for us. That's assuming the worst, which I guess I am. And I'm sure he is.

"Right then, good enough. Anything you missed can burn with the rest of the rubbish. Move along."

Once the others have achieved minimum safe distance, Tom and I stand on opposite sides of the pile and pull out the burn cubes. Silvery and putty-like in texture, impermeable to direct blows or punctures, but give 'em a good twist, then toss 'em where you want something—or someone—very shortly not to be anymore.

A crackle, an eerie lick of unnatural, chemical flame. Confirmation our burn is commencing. Our helmets protect us from the danger of looking at it head on, like an eclipse, but it's still important to get clear before the fumes start up. We join the others at a brisk trot, then hold position until we can deliver visual confirmation to Command that the remains are cleared from our territory, leaving nothing behind to attract predators or terrify potential asylum seekers. Nothing but a patch of blackened, unnaturally shiny earth that will grow back greener and richer than its surroundings once it soaks up what we did to their bones.

As we finish out the shift, I have to work even harder than usual to maintain my focus. It's never been easy, but this time it's brutal. My mind keeps wanting to drift to the question of which squad has a potential traitor? Or maybe more than one... the shifty motion I saw was clearly meant to hide their action from others, but with two full squads present, it's impossible to know whether they only needed to hide from the second squad as opposed to their own. We could have as many as four disloyal, well trained, fully armed soldiers among us right now.

After everyone's cleared the med scanners and handed in the gear, Tom and I get out of the armory quickly to get some distance for a private conversation, but the moment we hit the open air in the Stronghold, there's Nina, waiting for Tom. She looks anxious, not scared or bearing bad news thankfully, but eager to speak to her husband.

"Hey, Nina. Do you guys need privacy? I can walk ahead or—"

"No, it's cool," she says in a rush, clearly eager to get to her news. When she leans in to kiss him, though, she doesn't seem in as much of a hurry to get on with anything else. I bet it still feels incredible to do that in public after all those months pretending not to know each other. My happiness for them isn't soured by my tinge of envy. Stella and I will get there. I know we will.

When they break apart, I say with a hint of apology, "Tom, do you mind?" I hold up my helmet, and he knows what I'm getting at. The best way to be sure we're not in range of any prying eyes is to use the gear, and he handles it a hell of a lot easier than I do.

"You don't think it'll look a little weird, my husband being all helmety?" Nina objects.

Tom gives her an apologetic half-smile and says, "Perhaps we'd best not hold hands, darling. We'll stand out slightly less."

She pouts playfully and gives him another quick kiss before he disappears under the gear for the walk.

As soon as we're in motion and he confirms we're clear, no one nearby to hear what she's got to say, Nina erupts with information.

"Tom, just before we met, my squad had been stuck in this weird glitch with the rotation. Same Helmet every day for weeks."

"Cooper. I recall," he says.

"Yes. And no one understood why it was happening. It made no sense. It was a glitch. But—what if it wasn't?"

"Go on." He's intrigued, and knowing him, probably already halfway to whatever conclusion she's building toward.

"What if it was more like misdirection? Create a big, obvious thing over here to hide something else happening over there?"

He stops walking and adds thoughtfully, "Or see what you might be able to get away with?"

She nods, encouraged by his response, and we start moving again.

"I think we need to ask Maxwell to look into it. I'm sure Command keeps records of the rotation. He asked us all about Cooper that time, because he knew we'd been stuck with her so long."

"How'd you come up with this?" I ask.

She bites her lip before answering. "Um, Stella, actually. She was talking about paying so much attention to a big problem that something unexpected blew up without her even noticing. It made me think about how we were all bitching nonstop about Creeper. Maxwell said he couldn't help noticing the anomaly in the rotation, but what if other anomalies were masked by that big, obvious one?"

I'm conflicted. I'd like to be proud and go, *that's my girl!* Stella helped, even if it wasn't intentional. I also haven't quite gotten over my resentment toward Nina for messing with her, no matter how good her intentions or how high the stakes. On top of all that, I'm weirdly jealous Nina's having conversations with Stella and learning things about her maybe I don't know. Fucking people was so much easier than caring about one is.

"She's okay?" I say, unable to resist the defensive impulse. "You got her talking about something heavy, sounds like."

Nina looks a little sad, like she's also wondering if we'll ever be exactly cool like we were before.

"Yeah," she says. "It was old stuff. Family. I promise I didn't wreck your girlfriend." *Again* is the unspoken end of that sentence, of course.

Tom brings us back to the pressing issues of the day with a segue back to what we were going to talk about before Nina's sudden appearance.

"If we can get a look into the rotation records, start with our teams today. I had Luther's, Demetri had Kelly's. There was a soldier behaving suspiciously. Unfortunately, we can't say which squad they belonged to."

She nods intently, a star pupil. "It's a place to start."

"You sat on this all afternoon? You could have tried talking to Maxwell earlier, already had some of the answers before we came in," I can't help pointing out.

Nina looks at me like I'm speaking another language. "I promised Tom I'd always talk to him first."

Smooth bastard. My mouth curls into an amused grin. He has her locked down hard, and I envy him a little. Almost as much as I did for them being able to kiss in the middle of the sidewalk. Stella holds back so much. Another bitter ping hits me at the thought of Nina knowing any of Stella's stories before I do, and my face falls again.

"She's crazy about you," she offers by way of conciliation, and yeah, it doesn't hurt to hear that.

"Nina, I'm sorry to ask, but I gotta talk to Tom. Do you mind?"

She blinks, then composes herself. "Of course not. I'll stop by the mansion, see if I can get started on an answer, and then I'll see you at home?" Her expression is pure devotion with a hint of wistful longing like she can't bear waiting an hour or so for her next kiss. *Lucky prick.*

After she's gone ahead, I lay it out, the thing that's been per-colating since Stella was trembling in my arms and talking about machines. If anyone was ever a machine....

"It's Stella. She's like a vault of secrets. She knows a ton. Not that she'll talk about it to me. Or Nina, so don't even—"

"Demetri," he protests gently, holding up his hands, "I wouldn't—"

"You would," I say matter-of-factly, "and I don't blame you, okay? But this is—it has to be you. Because you're like a vault too. That's what she needs. She's like a safe deposit box, okay? I don't know, did they have those where you're from?"

"Yes, Demetri, I'm familiar with the concept," he chuckles.

"Okay, so you know how it worked. You'd take little safes inside a bigger safe to open them. I know you can do that, because of who you are, and also... because I know you don't care about all this the same way Nina does."

"I'm not sure that's fair," he says, but his heart's not in it, which is exactly the point.

"Tom, we both know if you could've talked her out of this whole thing, you'd've done it. You'd do anything to keep her safe, and I know how you feel. Stella's ready to talk. She just needs the right person to talk to, and it's gotta be you. Someone who has no dog in the race. Someone who can sit on a secret for the rest of time if it's only scandalous and not earth-shattering."

"Of course, Demetri. Whatever you need." He's solemn, on board to do for me like I'd do for him. "All right if I take this off? I find it's not as comfortable as it used to be."

I confirm with a little nod that we're done with the heavy-duty. He pulls off the helmet and shakes his head to air out his hair again.

"Fuck, man, I forgot how much love sucks. It's so much harder," I admit, my voice shaky, on the verge of laughing at myself.

Tom smiles gently. "I'm happy for you."

Chapter Sixteen

Suitors and Society

Stella

C eleste eyes the bodice of my dress with a scowl. What have I done wrong this time? I tried to look as respectable as humanly possible. This would have been acceptable to her in the past, I'm sure of it. Feeling her disdain like a gust of winter chill across my flesh, I shiver and adjust, pulling the sides of my colorful scarf closer around my shoulders and chest. Her lips narrow further, as if I've deliberately irritated her.

The tightness in my shoulders feels new again and freshly tiresome. I lived with it so constantly in the past, I suppose my muscles simply adopted it as their natural set. Now, I feel the burn and pinch as my nerves knit me back into the clenched posture I associate with prolonged exposure to Celeste.

Roger slides up beside me and I gasp in alarm before trying to appear untroubled, apologetic, demure. *Grateful.*

"Sorry if I startled you. I expect you're nervous. Returning to society in a way, after being able to lose yourself in your work for so long."

Being able to lose myself in my work. Because I was in mourning, right. And I was, for the world and for myself. I've had more of a chance to feel than most, it now occurs to me, and I spent the time in a fog, attempting to avoid feeling anything at all.

"Fortuitous timing, really. With the bored wives club," he clarifies. "It was time to shake up your routine either way. We needed space to grieve, but life has to go on."

The newcomers are traumatized. We have to create a rigid structure to their lives; people like them need structure to be effective.

Stella has a point about grief, though. We mustn't be seen as unfeeling. Do you have any thoughts on how we might convey sympathy?

Life has to go on. It's a phrase I've heard from Roger's lips many times, but always in the context of the outsiders. Now it's applied to me, and I can't pretend I don't understand the implication. I'm a resource after all, granted a reprieve in honor of the Genneros' grief over their son.

Celeste's eyes flit again to my chest, as if she's wishing she had a higher-quality cow to take to market.

They were going to yet another cocktail evening at yet another acquaintance's mansion. The settings were beginning to blur for Stella. It didn't help that the exteriors looked very much the same; only the interiors were individualized down to the finest detail by exclusive designers who were no doubt giddy over the budgets they had to work with.

Most of the interior design work had been done by outsiders; it was ever true that the rich had to import hipness from places where one's finger could be kept on the pulse. Once someone settled into an

Illustrian lifestyle, they fell out of touch with the up-and-coming. Hip was knowing what was about to be cool, not what was cool already.

There was one interior designer in Illustris, a wife, about whose work Stella had heard snarky comments within the first week. She was inclined to side with the woman in solidarity toward a fellow target of Illustris snobbery, but actually seeing Vanessa Basher's home made it difficult. Gauche, *she thought uncharitably, then frowned in remorse, determined to be better.*

In the living room—did mansions have living rooms? Celeste had scoffed at Stella's attempt to describe the room where the Genneros kept the television as a living room ("That's the entertainment room, dear," she'd said, and Stella couldn't help wondering if it would have been a "living room" if she'd said "TV room," if Celeste simply couldn't resist correcting her).

The piano room, Stella thought, self-correcting just in case. For in this living room stood a white baby grand along a wall with in-built bookshelves, the books arranged by color. Noting the improbable symmetry of the display, Stella cringed at the sudden certainty that they'd been chosen not for their contents but as a rainbow backdrop to offset the radiant white of the piano. She wandered closer to scan the spines for any sign of personal taste she could discern, a hint that her instinct was incorrect. But there were cookbooks on contradictory diet needs (The Gluten-Free Life in the yellows, The Bread-Lover's Bible nearby in orange), a motorcycle repair manual tucked in among the blues (there were no motorcycles in Illustris, and if there had been, a man like Judah Basher would hardly do his own repairs), and nonfiction works on a baffling array of topics (was it possible that the same household would find Astrology for the Modern Housewife and Soapmaking in Colonial America equally fascinating? Perhaps. Likely? Stella didn't think so).

From across the room, Greg's laughter cut through Stella's thoughts and renewed the tension between her shoulder blades. Somehow it seemed to her that she had found his laugh charmingly arrogant in the outside world. Here, it had a clanging, aggressive tone, as if the architecture amplified a certain timbre, exaggerating its harshness.

Stella turned toward the piano. She hadn't played in ages. Could she even read music anymore? Would her fingers remember how to dance across the keys? Not that she'd ever been a truly gifted player, just good enough to enjoy it. She reached out, not intending to make any noise that would draw attention—she merely wanted to feel the keys bounce under her fingertips, to hear the whispery ripple as they depressed slightly, the soft bonks as they rose back to starting position.

The impulse was thwarted by a tacky sensation on the surface: the coating of dust that sits long enough to set up shop. Schmutz, *her long-ago piano teacher would have called it. This piano was not here to be played. It was like the books behind it: scenery. Unwelcoming furniture and useless decoration. The last of Stella's attempt at generosity toward Vanessa Basher evaporated.*

It's a chilly feeling returning to the Basher mansion. The previous party was such a normal Illustris affair. Normal is long since gone, but it hits me that they've settled into a new normal to which I must now acclimate again. While I sleepwalked through their city all those months, observing from the shadows when they entered my little realm, the Illustrians created a new way of life for themselves out of my view. I'm not merely out of practice at living in this world but more resistant than ever. *Resistant.* The word crinkles my brow.

My coat is taken by a woman who likes cozy mysteries. I smile awkwardly at her, wondering what new economy has been engineered to allow for the existence of servants. Reentering their society means exposing myself to their ways. It was such a luxury to be on the perimeter for a time.

Ignorance is perhaps the greatest of luxuries.

And yet there is undeniable allure to this environment, the siren song of affluence, offering to lull me into complacency if only I will let it. Demetri said the Stronghold was like Christmas; what is this but the elegant version of that phenomenon? The artifice of true civilization, created by a feint toward celebration.

Have we anything to celebrate? Perhaps not from my perspective, but these people have recreated the world in their image. They no longer have a steady influx of entertainment and indulgences, but neither must they fret over the performance of a stock portfolio or justify themselves to a board of directors. They're living less extravagant lives than before, but true scarcity has not hit and likely won't for at least a generation.

Celeste drags me around the room, not physically but on a kind of psychic tether; she intends to reintroduce me. I have become an asset in her portfolio.

"Lucinda, you remember my daughter-in-law, Stella."

"Of course, dear. Lovely to see you again. It's been so long."

As I shake her hand and politely thank her, Celeste shocks me by effusing, "Stella's been keeping busy, you know. Putting her doctorate to use in some small way and contributing to the Stronghold. I believe her presence in the library was quite valuable during a difficult transitional time. She created a sense of stability, and now she's free to step back."

The thin smile I wear doesn't feel convincing, but from the reactions, these people either can't tell I'm miserable or don't care either way.

I'm still here. I must be getting stronger. Just in time to lose everything. Again.

After Celeste has made a handful of similar speeches to various women around the room, she seems ready to be free of me for a while.

"You're supposed to be a bright young woman," she says caustically, "so smile and mingle. Be gracious to our host. I'm sure you know better than to embarrass me."

Mercifully, Celeste abandons me at last and joins several women gathered along the far end of the dining table. Thank goodness. Perhaps I can find a quiet spot out of the way and hide until it's time to leave.

"I was going to ask if you'd like your drink refreshed, but it seems you've barely touched it."

Judah Basher's sudden appearance makes sense of Celeste's vanishing act. She only left me alone once he was near enough to step in. *Be gracious to our host*, indeed.

They're done sending men to the library to evaluate me on my own turf; now I'm being presented to them in the comfort of their homes, as if to offer them the opportunity to judge whether I make a suitably decorative acquisition.

Choking on emotions too turbulent to enumerate, I aim for a polite smile.

"Thank you. No thank you, I mean. It's been a while."

His lips twitch in amusement. "Hadn't you best enjoy it while you can?"

Before I'm inevitably pregnant. By him, even. The thought slams into me, and I take a deep sip.

His smile deepens. "It's good to see you getting a break at last."

I swallow back a desperate twinge of loss before it can drag a sob from my chest. "I love the library."

"Of course," he agrees in a tone that implies it couldn't possibly matter less what I just said. His words are a social lubricant, nothing more. "I understand the appeal of losing oneself in work. We've got that in common, you and I."

Vanessa Basher was outside the city when the world fell apart. Some interior designer conference in Tokyo. Her status is unknown and unknowable, so she's presumed dead. Months ago, they had a kind of memorial service for all those who never made it back. He said a few words.

"Yes. I'm sorry for your loss."

The platitude evokes a thin, perfunctory half-smile, the look a person affects when they wish to convey *thanks, it's been hard, but I'm holding up.*

"Time heals, they say. I'm sure you're well aware."

I nod automatically, casting my gaze away in an instinctual need to conceal my lack of pain; a widow shouldn't look so unaffected, after all. As my eyes bounce back up to meet his, they fail to connect, because he's taken the opportunity to look at my chest. It doesn't make me feel sexy like it does when I see Demetri's eyes dip lustfully to my cleavage, it makes me feel evaluated. Celeste's disapproving glance at my bodice earlier makes sense now: I was meant to be more alluring, more desirable.

"I was pleased to hear you'd be joining us this evening. I don't know if you recall my stopping by the library a few times—"

"Yes," I interrupt thoughtlessly, my voice hollow, my face going numb. "I remember."

He smiles slyly as if I've confessed a crush. *I remember because I care about the library, not because I care about you.* What kind of person would I be if I could just say such a thing out loud?

"That's kind of you. I wasn't sure; you were in rough shape for a while there. But your color is back. You're feeling yourself again. I can tell."

My eyes widen and my skin flushes. It's not the sort of innuendo I would have taken note of before. Demetri's influence. That parallel universe moment when my accidental double entendre made him laugh. Thinking of him soothes me through this uncomfortable moment, in this ridiculous place.

"I'm not sure I ever had the chance to appreciate your smile," Judah says, his low flirtation disrupting my brief reverie.

My smile falls away, and I meet his eyes with mere civility. To his credit, he takes a half-step back.

"Thank you, Mr. Basher."

He nods politely, and I turn to seek a place of refuge.

Yet, somehow, I'm still here. Have I borrowed just enough strength lately? From Demetri, from his friends with the recent kindness they've shown?

There was once a version of me that was eager to belong in a place like this, among these kinds of people. She seems like a naïve stranger. I pity her. And yet, without that foolish girl and her tragic choices, I would likely be dead. I always abhorred the *everything happens for a reason* bromide, especially after my mother got sick, but perhaps Greg was the price I paid to survive.

And then there's Demetri. I'd never even have met him if I hadn't come here with Greg. Carrying the equation to its ultimate solution, the balance is off. He's more than I deserve. Can I change the equation? Balance it? Earn the chance at happiness?

A chance is still all it would be, of course. Nothing I could do would guarantee a favorable outcome for me. The safest, simplest choice would be to continue as I have. Let my fate be decided for me.

I have always been diligent and driven, never brave.

Or have I? Cutting my father out of my life cost me dearly in the years that followed. I must have known that it would, but I don't recall taking it into consideration. He hurt my mother. I reacted.

So perhaps I can be brave for others. Whether or not my own outcome would be favorable becomes irrelevant if my aim is merely to improve the future for Demetri and his friends. I helped create this place. If I could help them change it, that would be enough.

My eyes land on the piano bench just in time to avoid barking my shin against it. As my mind has wandered, so have my feet, and I find myself back beside the white baby grand. The bookshelves behind it stand empty, dusty outlines a couple of inches deep where the rainbow of random tomes once stood. At least in the library, some of them are occasionally appreciated.

I wonder where the piano might be of value to anyone. No doubt it was already tuneless before, unused as it was. Is there a piano tuner anywhere in the city? Would that be a skill they'd consider worthy in an intake interview? I doubt it.

The lid is down, concealing the keys and their layer of schmutz. Is an instrument still an instrument when no one plays it?

"Welcome back to the world." The woman's quiet voice startles me, and I whirl.

Her face is serious yet beautiful and teasingly familiar. Since she's very pregnant, I try to envision what she'd look like without the puffiness and stifle a gasp of recognition. *Greta.*

"We met once. A world ago," she says flatly.

"I remember. The gallery. You wished me luck." My voice is almost accusatory, though it's hardly fair. My bed had been well made by the time I met this woman who clearly knew what kind of man I was sharing it with. Even if she'd wanted to warn me, it was too late to matter. It's wrong of me to resent her. I will tell myself that as many times as it takes.

"To be fair, your luck could have been a lot worse," she notes, one side of her mouth twisting into something wry that's about 80 degrees too cool to be a smile.

"Fair indeed," I venture. Failing to shoot down even a vague allusion to my fiancé's death being a stroke of luck feels akin to confessing heresy in the Dark Ages.

"If you're not going to drink that, can we trade?"

For half a heartbeat, the social obligation to ask if she's sure she should be drinking rears up. It's absurd. Infantilizing. I gesture as if to clink glasses, then make the exchange.

She sighs and takes a rueful sip, then raises an eyebrow. "From across the room, no one'll know the difference, but do me a favor and drink that quickly before anyone gets close enough to notice."

I obediently taste the beverage, then take a longer sip to appease her. She relaxes slightly and confides, "You could do worse than Judah."

"I'm not sure what you—"

"Spare me. You're on a very short list of available bachelorettes from before the outsiders started flooding in. There's an order here. Hope you made the most of your little vacay."

She pauses to drain her glass as I blanch at her casual assessment of my situation.

"I can't decide if you're being kind or cruel."

A slight twitch between her nose and upper lip strikes me as bitter laughter. "Does it matter? Nothing I say matters. Or you. Nothing we say, and nothing we do. The illusion that it might? That's torture, and you're doing it to yourself."

No, you are. The revelation hits like concrete being poured into a foundation. Accepting her fate, the way I was inclined to surrender to my own. She's cosigned her own suffering. I don't have to. And even if it costs me my life, I don't have to be her. When we met at the gallery, I was a vision of her past. Now, she's the vision of my future. Unless I fight it.

She sets her glass down on the piano and walks away. I pick it back up and rub the spot with the heel of my hand lest any droplets be left to mar the poor forgotten instrument's surface.

You could do worse than Judah, she said. I know very little about Greta beyond our common experience with Greg. I can't imagine any of these men would qualify as good, but perhaps Judah is at least a different kind of bad.

Be gracious to our host, take two.

I spot him in the dining room, leaning against the little spot of wall between the kitchen doorway and an armoire. He's got an audience, and he must be finishing up an anecdote, because they're all laughing with him when I approach, empty glasses in both hands and what I hope is a bashful expression on my face. His gaze turns my way and sharpens. He stands up straight.

"When I saw you last, you had one full glass. Now two, and they're both empty? Trying to catch up, are we?"

"No, I spotted this one abandoned without a coaster, and I didn't want it to damage your furniture—I wasn't sure where to put it."

My flimsy excuse to approach him hangs in the air, causing a sly wolfishness to curl his lips. He pushes off the wall, abandoning his crowd to take advantage of my implied invitation.

When his hand closes gently just above my left elbow, I don't react. I school my features, aiming for bland receptivity, and overcome my impulse to pull away. I let him lead me into the kitchen which is mercifully not empty of guests, though he moves us as far from the others here as we can get, after a stop-off to set down one glass and refill the other.

"I'm not that scary, you know," he chides playfully as I take a big sip. "Not that I begrudge you the liquid courage. But there's no need to be nervous."

"Somehow that only makes me wonder whether I've been quite nervous enough."

He laughs. "I'm a teddy bear, ask anyone. Safe as houses. Let's get acquainted. No pressure."

"I can't help thinking there's nothing but pressure." The confession spills out from behind my crumbling façade.

Sympathy surprises me as it warms his eyes and displaces his grin. "I understand."

"You do?"

"Poor butterfly. You've only just emerged from your cocoon, and it's mating season."

It's not even a matter of control this time. Whatever level of effort I could possibly exert to react differently to this wouldn't matter, because there's no appropriate reaction to offer. He's stepped beyond the boundaries of pretense. I'm both horrified and relieved.

"Thank you for speaking plainly, Judah."

Incredibly, I'm still not going away. My vision is crisp and clear. If anything, the threatening pressure of my tear ducts adds a degree of amplification.

"I don't see what either of us has to gain from tiptoeing around it," he acknowledges, his smile gone, discarded along the way.

"Why am I here?"

"Because you're here," he almost laughs. "Because you *were* here. Before."

I'm legacy now. If only by comparison.

He continues, "I'm not the only apocalypse widower any more than you're the only widow. Though you are the youngest one left. That makes you something of a catch."

"I was a catch a long time ago. For better reasons."

He smiles and takes my hand. I fight my urge to pull free as his fingers stroke a soft line between my wrist and pinky.

"You are still," he murmurs. "This doesn't have to be a bad thing, you know. You're the center of attention. Enjoy it. Show off a little. See if you can't stir up some healthy competition over who gets to claim you. You might have fun."

Grateful for the abandonment of pretense between us, I don't bother concealing my scowl. No part of that sounds fun to me.

Judah leans close to my ear and adds in a low rumble, "I'm doing you a very big favor, Stella. You're surrounded by predators. If you play dead, you'll wind up with someone who likes that in a girl."

Breathe. Breathe. Don't go away. And not just because he's just made it sound like a death sentence.

"Of course, you might have a taste for a man like that. An acquired taste, perhaps. Unless it's what drew you to Greg in the first place?"

Pounding red as if my eyes have filled with blood. I blink and stare at him through my fury.

"You're what passes for a good man in here. Pity."

He laughs, surprised and seemingly delighted. "Oh, that's fantastic. You see?" He moves in to speak directly into my ear again, this time letting his lips graze with the words, "I knew you had fire in you."

When I pull away, he grips my waist, not pulling me against him, only keeping me close.

"Listen, Stella, you spent months wandering around like a zombie." He chuckles ironically and adds, "Not literally. I'm just saying that you're a beautiful young woman, but you're damaged goods and everyone knows it. You've got an opportunity here, but very little in the way of choice. Pick your poison. Make a move."

He's having way too much fun for me to credit him with a drop of sincerity, and yet I don't believe he's lying about anything in particular.

"If I'm damaged goods, a sometime zombie, why are you even playing this game, let alone talking to me so freely?"

He gives a bored kind of half-shrug. "Fuck the Genneros? For starters. They want to lead you around like a show pony and get credit for offering you up. It's crass. Beyond that? I don't hate the idea of an outsider, to be honest. The women who've been here too long, they get lazy. Cynical."

I frown. "It sounds like what you're really trying to do is trick me into competing for you."

He manages to look impressed while smirking at me. "Not bad. Put a little effort into this, maybe you'll get lucky. I am as good a guy as you're going to find. Certainly better than you're used to."

My eyes fly open wide—is he insulting Demetri? *Do people know about Demetri?*

"Greg Gennero was a menace." I remember to breathe—of course, he's talking about Greg. "People talk. I don't know everything, but I know enough."

A sudden exhaustion hits. I let my eyes close, hide from the world for a moment.

Yet I'm still here. Somehow.

"I laid out my cards. Are you in?"

I look up again to see the mocking challenge in his eyes as he says, "Seduce me."

I flinch and pull back at last, red flashing at the sides of my eyes. I don't know if I'm about to panic or pass out, but I have to get away. Now.

"Perhaps not tonight," he says dryly as I flee.

Before my vision can be overrun, I rush from the room and make for the hallway. In a minor miracle, the bathroom is in sight and unoccupied. I hurry inside, shut the door, and sit on the toilet lid, leaning over my legs and closing my eyes.

Has my propensity for disappearing simply worn out? That would be tragic timing as I'm seemingly on the verge of being wrenched from Demetri's arms and gifted to one of these walking balance sheets.

After I've recovered fully, I wash my hands and dab at my face with water, then pat it dry. Back into the fray.

Near an open door off the hallway, the furtive quality of a male voice triggers my eavesdropping instinct, and I freeze just out of view.

"—handle our Delia situation."

"Hmmph. Problem child Delia," another man replies dismissively. I can practically see his eyes rolling just from the tone of his voice.

"I don't think she's satisfied with the status quo," the first presses with quiet urgency.

"I don't think it's up to her."

"Jack, she's—oh, Benjamin, glad you're here. We're just debating: Will the Council make an official arrangement about household help, or do we have to keep playing this little game. What say you?"

A moment later, I emerge from the hallway, annoyed that Benjamin Croft's arrival put an end to what was sure to be juicy information. Something about Delia, whoever that is. It's a name I've heard before, long ago.

Stella was at her wit's end being trapped in that house. Trapped with Celeste. She was increasingly edgy, starting to play at the ends of her hair with her fingertips, an old nervous habit she'd managed to leave behind once she started getting her hair cut by professionals again late in her college career.

Celeste would host teatime at least once a week ("Dwindling variety in our treats hardly means we should abandon all civility," she said), bringing in several of her fellow Council wives ("Who else can possibly comprehend our particular burden? We must stick together," she told the gathered women with a warmth in her voice that mocked the deeply unserious burden *as Stella saw it).*

It was during a teatime get-together that Stella, sitting miserably in an adjacent room, grateful to be excluded from this group, heard of an edge case of sorts.

"Ought we to invite Delia?" a tentative voice ventured.

"I think that's perhaps a bit of a leap," Celeste replied, her voice just short of scoffing, but civil, no doubt uncertain how strong the pro-Delia sentiment might be.

"It's just, she's all alone now—"

"And," Celeste interrupted firmly, more confident now that this was seemingly about pity rather than devotion, "she was nearly on the Council herself, yet for some reason they opted against including her. We're Council wives. If she were to gain access to information they clearly preferred she not have, it would be assumed to come from these gatherings of ours. No, I'm afraid the only option is to keep this amongst us. We're privy to powerful secrets. This is rarefied air."

Chapter Seventeen

The Vault

Stella

I was a snob groupie, that's what I told Nina. I didn't know what was waiting for me beyond the ivory doors to the tower, I only knew it had to be better. And I hated the implication that I deserved less than that.

Whatever I said to her that helped, it wasn't enough. Of course it wasn't. And now I'm here.

Back in her home, this time with her husband. He watches me, his face unreadable. Impassiveness or impatience, perhaps. I would have to know him to hazard a guess. Demetri knows him, trusts him. That was good enough to get me here. It will have to be good enough to get me through this.

Still, as I try to call my voice forth to begin speaking, a cloud surrounds my head, gray and heavy, pressing at me. The feeling of humidity and torpor expands like an inflating balloon, extends steadily down, gripping my neck, my shoulders—

"Stella, please try to stay with me," Tom says from very far away. "I know you've been through a lot, but you're going to go through a lot more if there's any hope of changing our fate. Or yours."

I blink and fight my way back to the surface. That was a calculated risk. He could have stopped before that final thought. He didn't have to acknowledge an awareness of my predicament.

"How did you know—did Commander Maxwell tell—"

Tom cuts off my nascent spiral with a resentful tone. "Maxwell would never share information unless he saw an immediate advantage. No. I've spent a good many hours in the library."

He's seen the gentleman callers, intuited their purpose, likely before I was remotely able to see it.

"You're very perceptive. Does Demetri know?" I assume not, as he hasn't brought it up to me, and he's hardly taciturn.

"We haven't talked about it," he says evenly.

"He's your best friend. Right?"

A hint of a smile combines with warmth in his eyes, conveying genuine fondness. "That's right."

"And yet you haven't spoken of a situation you know will affect him." I aim for a tone of observation rather than indictment.

"Neither have you," he points out with a nod. "Yet here we are, taking this chance to seek a solution. For all our sakes."

"He was right. You're good at secrets."

That hint of a smile broadens. "I've largely kept my own counsel. Demetri knows that. He also knows I'll do whatever is within my power to make Nina's life worthy of her."

The controlled heat in his voice is moving. I feel a smile come on despite the gravity of the situation.

"I don't know what I know that has value," I admit in a halting, apologetic tone. "I don't even know for sure what's true. Some things I learned from Greg, some things I... intuited, I suppose. Other things I overheard, and you know how unreliable that sort of thing can be. To even know where to start, to pick out the truth from the rumors and hearsay and conjecture—"

"Let me worry about all that," he says calmly. "You can just talk. I'll listen. I'll sort through what you know, find ways to follow up on the relevant bits without disclosing where I got the ideas. No one need know what you tell me unless it has value to our cause, and even then, who says it came from you?"

My breath hitches as I fight a sudden temptation to break down. "Demetri would know. He sent me to talk to you, he knows I'm the source, he'll think so poorly of—"

"Never." Tom's certainty is unquestionable and somehow instantly reassuring. "His feelings for you will not change regardless of what you have to say to me. I know him. Don't you?" He lifts an eyebrow in challenge.

"Yes," I say, only realizing just now that it's true. I've been applying the past to the present in a way that is unfair to us both: expecting Demetri's feelings to be fickle and unreliable just because Greg's were. They're not remotely similar people. I have to trust Demetri as much as he trusts me.

"Very well, then. Let's get started."

He sits back and looks at me expectantly. I take a deep breath, waiting to see whether the cloud descends again. When my perceptions remain unencumbered, I start to speak. I tell Tom the whole story. Meeting Greg, choosing him, coming here. Celeste's disdain, Roger's amused indulgence of me at times that made me feel like a dog doing tricks.

"Some of the ugliest choices of the Stronghold's makeup... they're because of me. Because of questions I asked, objections I made... my 'outsider perspective' helped shape this place. And I'm sorry."

The words sound hollow as I force them out, but it's somehow easier to breathe having said them. They were lodged in my throat like an obstruction, and now there's nothing to hold back the words which must follow them.

"The entry criteria. We could have saved more people... I didn't understand what conclusions they would reach, didn't know where their thought processes would lead. I couldn't think like them, and that was the point. That's why they valued my input... and I thought I could help make things better, but I only made things simpler. Cleaner lines for their design."

He leans forward, studies me, waits for me to get where I'm going.

"If, for example, the corps represented the full spectrum of humanity. Well, you'd have to create a complicated array of rules to match, wouldn't you? By restricting it to heterosexual, cisgender men and women, they kept things tidier. The more rules you have to staple on, the more exceptions and outliers, the likelier you are to field questions, objections.

"If you tell lesbians they're free to retire as long as they agree to artificial insemination, let's say... and you couldn't just sit back and let nature take its course on that over and over, so you'd have to set a minimum number of offspring they'd be committing to... it all gets very complicated very quickly, and by defining it explicitly in the cases where circumstances forced you to do so, you would be implicitly defining it for the whole—and they were determined to avoid that wherever possible.

"The illusion of choice was very important. The illusion of equality as well. If you let in lesbians because you value their potential as mothers, how do you simply not let in gay men—but then you've got some men who never get the one supposed benefit available to male soldiers, because they'll never have a wife and kids they feel honored to protect; they just serve. All stick, no carrot.

"And yet I could have said nothing, could have let it all happen, but I said, 'People won't accept that. Even if the world is gone and our country is a memory, we're still Americans in our minds. We're wired to believe in equality and fairness.' The takeaway was that the illusion of equality was worth the sacrifice in potential numbers."

Tom huffs a sad, wry sound. "Somehow that's both more and less sinister than I imagined."

"There's a lot of that here. It's the most American thing we have left, come to think of it."

I bow my head in shame, preparing to talk about the implant. Greg's work.

"After you've been deemed worthy, once you're through quarantine and accepted into the Stronghold, they give you this incredible piece of technology, a medical miracle."

I still can't lift my head, can't face Tom while I explain the giddy flood of desire that briefly made everything stop mattering. I pause to struggle with my breathing and fight the cloud that threatens to return. Shoving my shame into its hiding place once more, I tell him about Greg's darkest achievement. I dare to look up then, and he's pale as a ghost.

"I'm sorry," I say. "I know Nina was... hurt. She's not the first, and she won't be the last."

He breathes slowly in and out, mastering a brief flare of emotions before asking, "Was Greg the first?"

I gasp, impressed with his perceptive leap. "He got what he deserved." Saying it out loud shocks me a little, as if I haven't thought it very, very quietly a hundred times. "But no, he wasn't the first hurt by the Thrasher Protocol. *They* were." The phantom itch at the spot of injection prickles again, and I rub at it through the sleeve of my dress. "The implants have been in use in Illustris for a long time and with numerous applications you might not be aware of. For newcomers like you, they've been birth control and a point of connectivity for the medical scanners to monitor your health. And, because you were brought in from outside, there's clearly nothing 'wrong' with you by Stronghold standards. They don't let people in with flaws. They hardly did before, but there were allowances made in some areas. For instance, the implants were found to control blood sugar fluctuations so effectively, diabetes was a non-issue for any Illustrian. Still is. That part works with the body's own tools, you might say, like the birth control. Like... lust.

"But there were other things that might go wrong with a person, things that weren't necessarily knowable until they happened. And you could hardly expel a family simply because one of those problems arose; it would be bad for morale and publicity. It would erode the promise of Illustris. So they found their own ways of dealing with these problems.

"Some psychiatric conditions are medicated for the benefit of the patient; others are treated for the benefit of society as well as the patient. In the case of the former, there was a degree of choice extended. You could opt in to having the implant compel you to maintain your dosage, or you could self-monitor. But when it came to people who might become dangerous if they went off their meds, control was automatically implemented. Schizophrenics, for example, lived peaceful, productive lives in Illustris."

"As long as they were citizens prior to developing schizophrenia," he says caustically. "So it was a lovely utopia for all right up until the drug shipments stopped arriving."

"Once again, good guess. They were rounded up and taken to quarantine. Their families were assured that every effort would be made to solve the problem. If no solution could be found, their loved ones would be humanely treated for as long as possible, I think, was the vague promise made. The idea that resources would not be wasted on keeping them in quarantine indefinitely was implied but not outright stated."

"And what other reaction might there have been, really? Not as though the families would have said, 'Forget it, the lot of us would rather take our chances outside.' Given everything, why not presume the effort to find a cure was in good faith, when the alternative was sacrificing all in lieu of handing over one?"

"So Greg got to work on what was initially the Placidity Protocol, playing with his new toys. He ran tests with hormonal triggers, brain chemistry suppression, automatic shutdowns if certain hormones surged... I don't know whether there was ever any real hope of solving the problem, to be honest. But he was having fun."

A chill echoes through my flesh. I can't help picturing how bright his eyes, how animated his speech, as he recounted the experiments he dreamt up and the results he saw.

"At the time, I was mostly grateful he was in a good mood." Shame casts my eyes down, and a splash on my right thigh darkens a dime-sized spot on my dress. I half-expect Tom to say something, to tell me I have no right to self-pity, but again I'm applying my well-formed expectations of the Genneros to people who have never been anything but kind to me.

"Most results were short-term, none especially effective. And then he found the combination that unlocked a new... life form, I suppose. A technician was killed in the effort to contain... it. The obvious response would have been to reverse the effect if possible, and if not, to eliminate the... test subject."

"Instead they named it and kept it to see what it might do next." His voice is leaden with condemnation, and though I know it's not aimed at me, I still feel the impact.

My eyes burn as I force myself to finish the story. "I can't swear they never tried to undo the change, but no, I don't think they did. They watched it long enough to be confident the condition wouldn't reverse itself over time. And then the Placidity Protocol officially became the Thrasher Protocol."

"They used their human resources."

"That's exactly what they did," I breathe, my chest throbbing anew at the inescapable knowledge that I too am just that to them.

"There's a vicious logic to it. These people were probably a lost cause, but now they could be repurposed. I am curious whether they knew prior to deploying them that Thrashers and zombies would take no interest in one another."

I shake my head. "They would have had to bring in a zombie to learn that. But I doubt it would have deterred them."

"No," he agrees soberly. "They would be happy to see the Thrashers clear the area of those they've rejected. How did your fiancé die?" he asks, pivoting back to the earlier unfinished thought.

"If they'd simply loosed the Thrashers straightaway, it wouldn't have happened. He'd still be here. We'd have had a child by now." The image of this parallel life sends a shiver of horror through me. Greg would have been as bad a father as he was a partner. I would have been unable to escape into a cocoon while caring for and worrying over our children. I would have been painfully present for every moment of that life.

"Stella?" He calls me back to the present again.

"Yes, I'm here." *Thank goodness.* "They delayed Thrasher deployment because the military ranks still included Illustrians. They had to replace the corps fully with outsiders before they could release these lost children of Illustris. They couldn't afford for someone to come face to face with their old friend or loved one. Find out the truth."

"We were all under orders to bring one back for study!" he explodes. Before I can respond, he starts to reason it out, thinking aloud. "No doubt they thought it would be impossible anyway. And if we weren't under such an order, we'd obviously kill them if we had the chance; knowing we were to avoid killing them in favor of capture, we simply sought to avoid them. Those living nightmares are our fellow soldiers in a very real sense, and we were given a seemingly contradictory protocol in the interest of preserving the resource."

The logical exercise seems to soothe him. Then he looks back up as a new thought occurs.

"The psychological evaluations at intake. We're under the impression that all who fail are ejected. But I imagine that might be a waste of potential resources."

I sigh in glum acknowledgment. "I don't know anything about that, but it fits. Why send someone out who was likely to become a Devil Runner when you could instead transform them into another weapon?"

"Yes. Something I've wondered about, and perhaps you can enlighten me: We've always been similarly instructed to avoid engaging the enemy when there was one of our own among them. Spies, we've been told. What kind of people would the Stronghold have trusted to act as spies... yet not considered too valuable to risk losing?"

My tear ducts and sinuses burn with pressure.

"It's a lie," he concludes. "Another one. Do you know the truth?"

I nod mournfully, again struggling against the wave of gray surrounding my head.

"It's a noble sacrifice. That's what the 'spies' themselves are told. Officially, they're declared dead. Or presumed dead, I suppose. Among the missing. These are Illustrians who were outside the city when the gates were shut for good. They made it home but got bounced at quarantine. For whatever reason."

"I'd have thought the restrictions would be somewhat more forgiving when it came to a returning citizen." Tom's brow is gently furrowed as he ponders the information with seemingly little emotion.

"I don't know if that's a safe assumption. I expect if there was someone with particular personal value to those involved in making the decisions, that may have weighed in their favor, but failing that... they're good at viewing us as disposable, interchangeable. And they're good at secrets."

He sits back and studies me. "Bearing in mind the Stronghold's concern with resources... when did it begin to strike you as odd that you've been allowed to lie fallow, as it were?"

I flinch at the crude comparison, but he's right. I'm a fertile field left unplanted.

"I suppose in retrospect there were signs I missed along the way. Men who came in to ask odd questions, as if the answers didn't matter. But I was in a haze for so long. It took Demetri to shake me awake. He's so... alive. He made me want to live again too. To believe I could deserve to be so happy. After all I've done."

Once again the darkness encroaches. I steady my breath and drag it thickly through numb nostrils into constricted lungs. *I'm so sorry. The things I know, the things I* contributed, *the times I sat beside Greg and held his hand and laughed at his smug superiority—*

"It was all theoretical, I know how that sounds, I know I sound so naïve, and I'm sorry—the way it was with him, with them—"

Sobs steal what words might have followed and crumple my torso onto my lap. Minutes pass in silence apart from my hitching, heaving breath.

"Stella, I sense you crave forgiveness. But I don't feel wronged by you."

I lift my head just enough to look at him. "Because you're happy? Because things worked out for you here?"

His gaze turns inward as he considers my perhaps unfairly combative words, and I realize what I'm doing: spoiling for a fight, seeking confrontation as he's chosen to deny me the condemnation I deserve.

"That may be so," he says evenly, and I understand fully how Demetri knew talking to him would be safe. "But it's not all about me and my happiness. You suffered here, and I am not inclined to hold against you the methods you adapted to survive it."

"I see why Demetri thinks so highly of you."

"He has excellent taste," Tom quips with a wry smile. "I'm fond of him as well. He has quite an ingenuous quality to him, doesn't he?"

"I've had that same thought." Our gaze locks, and we silently bond over our mutual fondness for that sweet, beautiful man who has no idea how dangerous it is to love me.

"All right," he says, seeming to reach a decision. "It's clear you're on borrowed time. There's going to be some kind of reckoning, and soon. Have you made any friends at all here?"

"Besides your friends? No. Before I met Demetri... I was barely even present in my life."

He looks grim. "Your situation is tenuous, to say the least. There's likely to come a time when you're not safe to return to the home of your host family. And there may be no way to know when that time comes until it's far too late."

"You think they'd just take me," I translate in horror.

A subtle incline of his head acknowledges the interpretation.

The desperate tone in my voice, the pleading helplessness in my eyes—if he had any doubt about his conclusion, he would backpedal it now just to be kind. Wouldn't he? But he stares back at me like stone.

"I think you're a resource, Stella. You've been given an interval of mourning out of respect for your fiancé and his family. Far longer, I'd wager, than if you'd lost someone of no significance to them. But your shelf life is not indefinite, and they'll want to recoup their investment."

"If I'd lost no one of value to them, I wouldn't be in this position at all," I point out miserably. "What they're going for here... it might make more sense to someone with your background, actually—"

"Blue blood," he guesses, leaning forward.

"That's right. I can't prove it, but it makes sense. The things people have said about this bizarre courtship process. That I'm one of the last of my kind, which I interpret to mean I was here before the world ended. Not just here, but officially welcomed into the upper echelons. They want to fill the open spots with people like me before having to mix with the commoners."

"You're right," he says ruefully. "My background does help me to comprehend this. Even in the modern era, the sheer number of people willing to give credence to the notion that royals were meaningfully different to the rest of us. By virtue of their blood. I suppose if one were trying to build a new world that largely functioned as the old one did, after the old ways of delineating worth have been stripped away by circumstance, this would be an appealing path. *Why are we better than you? Why do we have mansions when you have apartments, why do you toil to create what we idly consume? Well, you see, it's nature. We were born to it.*"

"I think the idea is to keep everyone living in the moment long enough to start to indoctrinate the first generation."

"We'll have settled in. We'd be unlikely to rock the boat. It would risk our children's safety, for whatever's wrong in here pales in comparison to what's wrong out there."

"I truly hope I've given you something you can use, Tom. For all our sakes."

"As do I," he says gravely.

I return to the library feeling desperately on edge. After what I've just done, the world continues apace? I'm not being snatched off the sidewalk? No, that's not their way. They would be likelier to invite me to tea, then simply never let me walk back out the door.

And, as Tom said, there's no way to know when that might happen. I'm on borrowed time. Even returning "home" is a terrible risk.

One I've taken every day without realizing.

One I'm set to take again, as a matter of course, at the end of this day.

My nerves are frayed and shaky as the afternoon wears into evening, but when Demetri arrives, I know what to do. Suddenly, finally.

In the big empty space, he's all I can see. I cross the room and take his hand.

"Take me home with you," I say, looking into his eyes. He nods, doesn't hesitate, doesn't ask questions. He leads me back out the door he just came through and toward the barracks.

"Um, you're not supposed to be here, I don't think," he says apologetically, ushering me in and moving me as quickly as he can through the halls to the stairwell. "Also, sorry about the stairs. They like to keep us moving, I guess."

They would. I squeeze his hand. "I'm not so delicate. How many flights to your room?"

He grimaces. "I'm on nine."

"Okay, I guess I'll get used to that," I say as I start climbing.

Five flights later, I'm slowing down, and he looks even more apologetic than he did at the start.

"I could carry you the rest of the way," he offers apologetically.

He's so sweet. I half-laugh through my shaky breaths and put a hand to his cheek. "Save your strength."

My words land just as I meant them. His eyes flare with desire. He leans me against the railing for a long, luxurious kiss. It occurs to me I won't have time for my stair-climbing sweat to dissipate before it's replaced with the sweat of heat and need.

"Stella," he says, then kisses me again. "Are you gonna give me all of you tonight? Do I get to touch you? Kiss you? All over?" Every phrase is punctuated with kisses.

"Not if we never make it to the room because you've weakened my knees with your lips," I tease, amazed at my own capacity for playfulness when I'm taking the biggest risk of my life. I suppose that's why I can be playful, actually. I've taken the biggest risk of my life just now. It's done. There's no going back. The decision is made. The die has been cast. I'm in a new place, literally and figuratively, and nothing is straightforward anymore.

With another squeeze of his hand, I start the climb again. When we reach the eighth landing, he scoops me up. Through my laughter I hear his words, "Don't worry, I'll have plenty in the tank."

Chapter Eighteen

Finally

Stella

He carries me all the way to his door, sets me down to open it, then picks me up again to whisk me inside. I hear the door click shut as he kisses me deeply, his hands travelling over my body in a way he has never been so free to attempt.

"Do I get to see you naked tonight, Stella? Do I finally get to feel these breasts against my chest? You have no idea how much I think about your breasts." Kiss. "Your thighs." Kiss. "Your hips."

I've never felt less shy. The way he wants me is so powerful, so immersive. Reaching between us, I undo the buttons down the front of my dress. His gaze follows my motion, and he looks like a starving man at a banquet.

The thought gives me a moment's pause. "Demetri, are you sure? Are you sure it's... me?"

"Baby," he says, shaking his head, "it's you. It's all you." He takes my hand and pulls it down to feel his hardness. "This is all for you. Do you want it?"

I close my hand in as strong a grip as I can manage through his pants, then look into his eyes.

"I'm gonna take this off now," he murmurs against my ear as he takes over the rest of my buttons and slides my dress down past my shoulders, following the fabric's path with soft, inviting kisses.

When he sees my stockings and garter belt, he groans. "God, I wanna leave this on. Probably shouldn't, though. Right?" He looks up wistfully.

"There are no new ones being made," I confirm.

Dropping to his knees, he says, "Then just give me a minute here. I need to appreciate this a little."

He presses his face to right above the garter belt, breathing in, dragging his lips across my stomach from one hip to the other. His fingers gather into fists against the fabric. He tongues the hollow of my hip, and I moan, my knees again threatening to go out from under me.

"Okay," he murmurs, his voice thrumming through me, "you can take it off. But I get to watch."

He stands and begins to undress, slowly, returning to eye contact with me as soon as his shirt is over his head.

"Stella, you're not using those hands for anything," he reminds me.

"Right. I was watching too," I say with a blush. "You're so beautiful, Demetri."

"If those stockings are still on you when I get my dick out, I make no promises," he warns playfully. Though I don't think he means it, it does get me in motion. I sit on the bed to attend to my stockings, unclasping the fasteners and rolling them down gently. Unlike the average Illustrian, I didn't have to learn to take better care of my fine things. I wasn't here long enough to settle into taking anything for granted.

When I look up again, he's watching me so hungrily. I maintain eye contact as I nudge the second stocking past my heel and beyond my toes, then stand to undo the hooks of the garter belt and set it aside.

The moment I'm fully naked for him, he closes the distance between us in a single large step and slides his arms around me.

"*You're* so beautiful," he whispers before sinking into another powerful kiss.

The promise of his stiff cock against my belly quickens my desire. My lips open wider, urging him to deepen our kiss. Our tongues collide and dance, and his hands go back to exploring my hips, grasping my ass to pull me harder into him.

A little humming sound like he's considering his next move, and then he starts walking me toward the wall.

"All those times we've made out against the wall. That's what I want. The first time," he clarifies, smiling sinfully. "I told you I'd have plenty in the tank. Can you take it?"

He lifts me slightly, balances my hips against the perch of wainscoting, then presses in again. The smooth, hard head of his cock is a torturous tease as he drags it up and down, just riding the edges of my labia, gathering wetness to glide against my clit. I wriggle helplessly, aching with need.

"Are you ready to let me inside you, baby? You feel ready, but I need you to say it. I'm dying to give it to you. Tell me you want to take it."

"Demetri." His name is a sigh. My hips twitch as if I can pull his iron hardness in like a magnet. "Make love to me."

His eyes go soft, and he stares into me for a long moment, absorbing the words. The feverish urgency seems to have dropped away, leaving behind only its heat. He leans in for a deep, tender kiss, and presses inside me slowly, deliciously aware of his pace, not rushing this first intimacy. As he fills me, I start trying to pull him tighter against me with my legs, my hips, and he murmurs against my lips, "Careful, baby, I don't want to hurt you."

Oh, that's sweet, he's worried about his size, and it is sizable, but I don't care. I moan and pull at him more, begging him to give me his whole body, now.

"Stella," he whispers nervously, but he surrenders to my pull, sinking in until his firm body is flush with mine from lips to core.

There's a mild discomfort I can't quite suppress in my moan as he hits deeper inside than I've ever felt touched, deeper than I knew was there to be touched, but I grip him tighter with my limbs to keep him from trying to pull away at the sound.

"Stay, stay, stay," I beg him as my body learns to take this feeling, to use it. A powerful intoxication builds as my internal muscles respond to the impulse to keep him like this.

"Oh, god, baby." Desperate surprise in his voice and sudden tension in his jaw tell me he feels an orgasm trying to escape, and he's trying to contain it.

"Give it to me, just like this, please. Don't hold back. Let me feel it. So deep. Let me feel it."

He stays deep, deep inside me, never pulls out an inch, just rocks his hips to give me all of that delicious pressure I never knew could feel so good. I feel myself holding on with everything in me, and the tension explodes into a chaotic hit of ecstasy that begins at the tip of his cock and rolls throughout my entire body—and his. He sucks at my lips and tongue as he spasms inside me.

"Stella, I didn't ask if I could come in you. Is it okay?" he murmurs a moment later, his breath still hitching.

I almost laugh. "I don't think I'd ever have forgiven you if you pulled away just then."

Our kiss resumes, deep and long, and I feel our combined wetness as his cock remains fully sheathed, slightly softened. The longer we kiss, the less softened it is, and he grows to fill me again.

"It's been a while," he says. "I don't want to hurt you, though."

"You won't. You aren't," I assure him.

He gives me one of his wicked half-smirks. "Are you saying you want more, Stella?"

In case my moan isn't answer enough, "Yes. Please."

The half-smirk expands to a gorgeous Demetri smile. He lifts me again. There's a tiny smacking sound as the sweat-slick skin of my back loses contact with the wall he's been holding me against. Still buried to the hilt, he lowers me carefully to the bed and says, "Good news. I've got more to give you."

His hips flex, emphatically demonstrating how hard he already is. It's tantalizing, almost a tickle deep inside me as my body strains for more of the rapture he's shown he can deliver. Another little whimper from my throat tells him as much as the way my hips incline to invite him. His mouth devours mine as he begins deliberate, steady thrusts. My hands at his shoulders grip and pull and push in conflicting impulses that gradually tell my brain this is somehow too much and not enough at the same time, and my greedy hips try to quicken his rhythm with short, needy upward thrusts.

His lips quiver as he almost laughs with delight, breaking our kiss. "Too slow? You want me to stop savoring you when I've waited this long? Say it. I'll give you anything you want. Say it."

My mind flails about for the right words to express something so new to my experience, words I've never said, never thought. In his eyes, I find them.

"Savor later. Be savage now."

His beautiful eyes darken. His hand slides appreciatively down the left side of my body, then grips my hip and tilts it up, opening me even further before settling in like a buttress to hold me in position.

"You'll tell me if it's too much," he murmurs against my lips, and I nod as we return to the deepest kiss just before he starts powering into me.

The angle has opened me to him enough that his deep thrusts also press his body against me in a way that teases my clitoris, leaves me reaching for him there too, which seems somehow to pull him deeper still, and that deep point inside me reaches more and more to have all of him because I need all of him, and the throbbing intensity of the orgasm rushes through me like an earthquake. I feel him come mere moments after. My body seems desperate for his orgasm too. My cheek drifts dreamily along the side of his throat. Sweat, smooth skin that gives way to light stubble in places, and the contrast makes me want to rub against him there too, like his hardness against my softness everywhere.

Suddenly giggling, I explain, "I'm high on you. I think this is the Doctor Manhattan moment."

He lifts his head just enough to look at me in cheerful confusion.

"There was a moment when I knew I was going to fall in love with you, before it happened. I felt like Doctor Manhattan, knowing what is because it will always have been. This feels like the moment I flashed forward to, being so high on you, feeling so safe. Giving myself this chance to be happy."

My voice falters on the last thought, my eyes heavy with emotion. He gazes into me so seriously, so determined to be my knight on every level, and perhaps at a loss for words, he gives me his lips again instead. Our kiss goes so deep and long, I half expect him to grow again inside me. I don't even know how I can want more, but I do. I want him utterly, rapturously. My hands grip at his sides, his hips.

This time it's his turn to laugh. "I might need a little while to catch up this time. Hey, when's the last time you ate? Don't you usually have dinner at, um, home?" His inflection on *home* conveys all the questions that are unfolding in his mind about the situation I leapt into tonight.

It's sobering, and the sex fog clears a bit. "I do," I confirm somberly, not sure how to start addressing the unspoken ramifications.

He fixes a reassuring *I-got-this* smile on his perfect face. "Lucky you, I'm a Helmet."

It all happens so quickly, I barely have time to mourn the sensation as he pulls out of me or appreciate the glorious flex of his biceps as he pushes himself off the bed and stands to dress.

"Helmet heads are a handy phenomenon, you know? This won't be the first time I've snuck an extra meal." He hesitates, seeming to regret the disclosure. "I mean, I get hungry, not—"

"It's okay, Demetri. I don't need an explanation. I told you before I'd never hold anything like that against you, and I meant it."

His grateful half-smile is the last thing I see before he slips on his helmet and leaves the room.

Chapter Nineteen

Two Nights and a Day

Demetri

With the helmet reassuring me there's no one in the hall directly outside my room, I slip out before I can shove any more of my foot into my mouth. Stella's sweet to say she's cool with all that, but I feel like a giant asshole bringing it up at all. The funny part is, it sounded worse than it even is. I mean, I needed snacks because I was fucking off a lot of energy, but she's the only girl I've ever worried about feeding... but maybe that doesn't sound that much better after all, so it's probably just as well I left it where I did.

When she said she wanted me, I didn't give it even half a second thought. I've been waiting to touch her, dreaming about her beneath me for so long. Just thinking about how much I've wanted her has me starting to feel ready to go all over again, even after coming twice in a very short time. I hope she can handle everything I'm eager to give her tonight. And I don't need sleep, not really, with tomorrow my day off and all. She couldn't have picked a better night to give herself to me.

But that's the question again, and I'm scared to even ask it.

What does this mean?

I asked about dinner, and she didn't say she should get home before she was missed. That's good. I wanted her to stay… but what does it mean if she stays?

Maybe I'll get back and she'll be dressed again, looking kinda sheepish about how she really needs to get home. That's probably the smart move, right? Stupid how my heart aches at the thought of the smart move. Stupid… but I want her to stay. I don't know all the consequences we're about to bring on ourselves, and I don't feel like caring about that shit right now.

Please be naked, Stella. Let me know you're staying. Let me know I get to keep you.

Opening the door to my quarters, I set down my tray on the table near the door, then pull off the helmet and dare to look and get my answer.

She's not naked. It's better. She's thrown on a shirt from my drawer. It hits her mid-hip, and I can see she's put back on her underwear but nothing else.

I just stand there and stare, and the smile that forms on my face feels hungry for every inch of her and none of the meal I just carried up nine flights of stairs.

"Turn around. I need to see you."

A shy, delighted smile. She's not used to being adored. Damn her shitty ex. She's gonna get used to it.

Stella's ass peeking out below my shirt as she turns around is enough to make me want to forget about dinner entirely.

I enjoy the view another long moment as she faces me again with that shy, hopeful look, like she doesn't know how to believe she's everything I ever wanted. I cross the room and pull her against me, grab her ass with both hands and press into her for a hard, hungry kiss.

"Get used to it," I tell her, our lips still brushing together. "Get used to how much I want you. I'm already ready for you again. Feel that?"

She's ready too, it's clear in her hungry little whimper and the way her body wriggles to bring every inch of us tighter. I dive into another kiss, and this is it—I remember thinking no woman here ever kissed me the way Nina kissed Tom, and this is it.

"I've got you now," I whisper, breaking the kiss to share the revelation. "You're not going back to that house, are you? You're all mine now."

Stella's eyes do that thing where she looks off to the left, like she's setting something aside, and I think she's about to lie to me. It hurts for just a moment before she drags her gaze back to meet mine again.

"I don't have a plan. I should have. I just—after I talked to Tom earlier, I felt like I'd let go of this terrible burden, and—and I didn't want to go back. I decided when I saw you that I was going to be happy, and I didn't stop to make a plan or think about how this would all work. And there are such risks—to you as well, and—"

"Shh." I stroke her hair, her cheek, kiss her again gently to punctuate my effort to calm her. "We'll figure it out." I don't know how, I don't know what we're dealing with, but it doesn't matter. I need her to feel safe.

"Demetri... Yes. You've got me. I don't know what they'll do when they realize I'm gone, but... I can't go back to that house.

I want to be with you." A determined little nod emphasizes this final statement, and she looks desperately into my eyes.

"Then let's get comfortable and get some food into you before lights out. I can't have you wasting away on me."

We settle in on the couch, facing each other, with the tray in between us.

"Lights out," she muses. "You probably have to be on duty in the morning, don't you?"

I spear some noodles on the fork and hold it up to her. There's this sweet smile, surprised and grateful, and she takes the bite.

"Stella, as it happens, you're in luck. Tomorrow is my day off." I rush to get another bite of food into her mouth to delay her response, force her to think about my next words. "I know there's a lot I don't know. It's gonna be complicated. But maybe we could just... hide out here? Just ignore it all, for a little while? Let the world end without us for a coupla nights?"

"I'm all yours," she whispers, and I know she's scared, but I also see hope in her eyes.

When lights-out is getting close, it hits me I need to get her settled in comfortably first. Unlike me or any previous bedfellows, she's not used to the layout, much less the pitch-black conditions.

I hold out my hand to her, then lead her back to bed.

"You look so good in this," I say, taking hold of the shirt. "Hope you don't mind if I take it back. I need another look at you before we go dark."

Her eyes are so huge, drinking me in like she still can't believe I'm real. There's this vulnerability to her now, not like the way she was before. She was brittle and broken before, but that was with everyone. This thing, it's exclusive. This softness and warmth, it's just for me. She trusts me. After what she's been through, it's a miracle she could find it in herself to trust anyone.

"If he wasn't dead, I'd kill him myself," I mutter. Her eyes flash with surprise, and I add, "Sorry. That's probably not... I just think about someone hurting you...."

She kisses me softly. "He never would have stood a chance against you."

"Yeah, I figure. Science dweeb vs. soldier? I'd've had him out cold—"

"No, I mean—I would always have fallen in love with you."

It's hard to believe. Maybe impossible. She's brilliant and totally out of my league, and I'd have nothing to offer her in the old world. Our paths would never even cross in that life, and she'd think I'm a go-nowhere loser.

But she reaches up to touch my cheek, and I suddenly get it. We're the same. Both awestruck and counting our blessings because we can't believe our luck. Because neither one of us knows how we got here, and we just want to stay.

I pull the shirt over her head and kiss her. A long slow kiss that carries us all the way into the darkness as the lights click off for everyone like me. I missed my plan to stand back and enjoy the sight of her, but that's okay. I'll have plenty of time to stare. Now's for touching.

My hands explore her in the dark, gripping, caressing, gliding along the curves and planes of her body. Full hips, the plush dip of her waist. The gentle cushion of her soft skin feels like velvet under my weathered hands.

"Do you know how much I've thought about your breasts," I say softly, cupping them gently and thumbing her nipples. I leave my left hand where it is and slide my right hand down to slip between her thighs. She's still slick from earlier, or maybe she's already getting wet for me again, but I'm taking nothing for granted. I want to feel this woman at her most desperate. I want to make her that way.

My fingertip swirls around and around her clit in a lazy rhythm, teasing her with *almost*. I kiss her neck and work my way down to find her nipple with my lips and tongue while my left hand continues to play at the other. A soft pinch there rewards me with a little gasp and a tiny jolt of her hips, so a moment later I let my teeth graze before sucking harder, and her arms fly up to grip my shoulders as she moans, because she wants more but she also isn't ready for this to stop.

Oh, I've got you now, Stella.

I abandon the circling of her clit and let my fingertip start tracing the edges of her slit, right at the opening, just along the line, never dipping in. Her hips flex and her hands grip. I lick and nip and lick and suck and she keeps reaching for me with her whole body. Maybe the darkness helps her feel all this want.

Her hips' desperate rhythm is trying to pull my finger inside, isn't it, but that's not what you want, is it, Stella? I stop everything and whirl her to face the bed. Reaching around her, I stroke around her clit in a more consistent rhythm as I slide my stiff cock between her thighs to glide along her lips. When the head hits her clit, she cries out and clenches her thighs hard, and I know it's for her, I know she's trying to hold my dick where she wants it so she can rub herself against me, but fuck, it feels so good—my hips pump, and these tight, shallow thrusts pressed against her wetness and gripped tight by her eager thighs are going to take me down if I let them. I kind of wanna let them. It's so new, it's all her, all us.

"Is this how you want to come, Stella? You want to use my dick to get yourself off? It's all yours. Use it. Come for me. Come all over me."

The rhythmic squeezing and rocking speeds up, and her upper thighs grab hold even tighter around me. "Fuck, I'm gonna come so hard, Stella, keep that up, yes—"

I can't hold back another moment, and my hands find her breasts and pull her flush against me. I pinch and tweak her nipples with my fingers and thumbs as my hips piston to bring the climax I'm now desperate to have. The head of my cock hits hard and fast against her clit as she practically sobs the orgasm I feel gasping and weeping out of her onto me as I spasm and spurt. My come shoots out and she moans again, so I let my fingertip find her clit and give her direct contact this time, the teasing long past. As she comes again, squeezing around me, I feel the thick texture of semen around the hood of her clit, and I know that moan was my come hitting her, touching her, giving her pleasure. I sacrifice the afterglow of sensation to disengage so I can turn her to face me again.

"Stella, I love you." The words barely make it all the way out of my mouth before I'm kissing her again. Within moments, my limbs start to feel heavy, and I fumble to pull back the covers without breaking the kiss, then maneuver us into bed.

Gradually, kissing becomes just kiss-distance proximity, and we hold onto each other as we fade, as if neither of us wants to admit we're afraid someone will come to take the other away if we let go.

My dick is a divining rod pointed straight at her, pressing deliciously into her lower belly. I can't help it. I press harder. It feels so good. A breathy little moan of desire tells me she's at least awake enough to agree.

"Stella?"

"Hmm." She moves against me. Still unclear how awake she is. I roll her onto her back and hold myself on my elbows above her. I'm achingly stiff as I let the tip of my dick drag past her clit and come to rest right at her entrance. I won't move another muscle if she doesn't invite me, but even if I'm just torturing myself right now, it feels good to suffer wanting her.

I kiss the spot where her jawline becomes her neck. She moans and writhes in a way that catches the tip of my dick for a luscious tease.

"Can I have you?" I whisper against her throat.

Her hands slide up my arms in the dark and find my face. She guides me into a kiss, and a moment later, I sink into her.

Fully inside, I hold still and enjoy the sensations for a long moment before starting to thrust. Her first moan interrupts our lips and tongues, but she doesn't want to let go, sucking my tongue to keep it from getting away.

I've been wanted. I've never been wanted like this.

Her breathing and moaning get more intense, and she loses focus on kissing me as her hips move higher, faster. She comes then, fluttering and tensing around me and under me and I keep fucking her, selfishly, wanting it to happen again before I fill her. Just when I think I won't get her there, she says my name, sounding surprised by the second crash of pleasure, and I let myself pour into her, her body pulling my orgasm like it's the other half of her own.

I collapse onto her, and I mean to roll off, but she wraps around me, arms and legs clutching to keep me.

"Don't go. Stay just like this. Just let me feel you," she murmurs.

I nod against her lips and kiss her again, expecting she'll loosen her grip as she falls asleep, and I'll slide off to avoid crushing her. But her limbs keep pinning me to her, and I feel sleep starting to come on again. Isn't it a little silly, I think on the edge of consciousness, trying to save her from something she wants....

Chapter Twenty

Playing House

Stella

When I wake up, our bodies have shifted slightly. We're both on our sides, and he's no longer inside me, but I'm still essentially wrapped around him.

The lights have come up again, and I enjoy a good stare at my sleeping lover's beautiful face. I don't know how a person could ever get used to a sight like this up close. *Such a man as all the world—why, he's a man of wax!* The rhapsodic Shakespearean musing makes me quake with suppressed laughter, and his lips curl in a smile before his eyelids start fluttering.

"Always leave 'em laughing," he says, nuzzling my neck. "What's so funny?"

Stroking his hair, I search for an answer that makes sense. "I don't remember the last time I woke up happy," I say finally, mildly regretting that I didn't come up with a more light-hearted response.

He leans back and gazes into my eyes. "Me either. Let's make a habit of it."

A tender, lingering kiss seems to be arguing both sides in a debate over whether to turn into more or ease off before there's no going back. Just as I'm about to grip him tighter against me and pull for the former, he stops.

"I'm gonna need to eat something. You too." Snorting with boyish laughter, he adds, "I swear that was unintentional. But also true." He follows up with a kiss that's both shorter and deeper, leaving both of us more reluctant to stop, but he's right about breakfast; merely mentioning food has alerted my stomach to its emptiness, and it's suddenly fierce on the subject.

"I'm gonna take the world's quickest shower, and you can have one while I grab us breakfast. I have a feeling if we get cleaned up together, we'll get distracted."

My gaze dips from his radiantly sinful smile to his thickening erection, and yes, we would be faint from hunger if we lingered another moment in arm's reach of each other's naked body. A giddy, almost light-headed feeling hits me, swirling my vision and flooding it with tears. I know this emotionality is likely enhanced by my need for sustenance, but the practical awareness does little to mitigate the visceral response. Sitting on the bed, I wrap my arms around my bent legs and rest my forehead on my knees.

It's a carousel of emotions and thoughts assailing my freshly awakened mind—all the things I managed to keep at bay when he went to get me dinner last night. I was high on his love and a little in awe of my own spontaneous, life-altering choice, feeling brave and reckless. Some self-preservation instinct prevented me from dwelling on the consequences immediately so I wouldn't be overcome with terror and try to take it all back. In an alternate universe, there's a version of me that was dressed and apologetic by the time Demetri returned with that tray of food, determined to slip back into the Gennero mansion and hope no one noticed I'd been out of sight for a while.

In the universe we actually inhabit, I stayed. We made love again. I slept in his arms and woke up happy. And now I have to deal with all of it. All the ramifications of last night's rash decisions.

I wouldn't take it back. That's the first thing I know, and it's soothing, like looking down in a dream to find you're on solid ground when you were certain you'd stepped into a chasm. I want to be with him. I love him.

My cheeks form a smile just in time for the first, bulbous tear to glide down, and it transforms into something like a cleansing.

When he emerges from the bathroom, I probably still look a little like I've shed a tear or two, but I don't feel fragile or shaky. He gives me another dazzling smile and drops a quick kiss on my lips before throwing on some clothes. In the moment before he slides his dresser drawer shut, he stops and grabs a couple of things, tossing them onto the bed.

"For you. I like you in my clothes."

Tilting his head slightly, he stares at me for a long moment, his smile faded to something softer, warm with the kind of longing that never doubts it will be fulfilled.

"I'll be back soon," he promises.

"I hope it's okay," he says of the single tray of food he's brought back. "I got Manny to fork over half his biscuit. If you're still hungry, I can try the helmet trick again—it's just I try not to do that too often, just in case—"

"It's fine," I assure him. And it is. The food tastes better to me than any breakfast I've had in ages. Choking down food in that stodgy dining room, under Celeste's withering glare.

He probably hopes I don't notice he's taking small bites and nudging more than half the food on the tray in my direction. A peaceful grin takes over my face.

"You're such a gentleman."

He looks up shyly at being caught in his quiet act of chivalry. I let my fingers rest on the back of his hand and add, "Don't forget; you'll need your strength."

His hand rotates under mine to let our fingers entwine. "Let's hurry up and eat, then."

"What if I just wear your helmet and get us a second tray? There's probably a female helmet head I could pass for at a glance," I venture playfully.

Demetri's lips purse appreciatively as he looks me up and down and says, "Not a chance. No one in the corps looks like you, Stella." He pulls me against him for another deep kiss, one hand plunging into my hair, the other kneading my lower back before gliding down to grip me tight.

"Besides," he adds, stroking my hair between softer, smaller kisses, "you can't just pick up a helmet and use it. There is *some* skill involved." With my eyes closed, I hear his teasing grin and feel it in the thin tilt of his lips.

"I know. I was kidding," I assure him. After another few light kisses, I add, "Not to mention the retinal scan thing."

He pulls back, startled. "You know about that?"

Awkward about having to acknowledge the source of my inside information, I grimace slightly. "Greg was a neuroscientist. He was part of the design... I know whatever he felt like bragging or rambling about any given day after work."

Demetri's gaze turns inward as if he's troubled, and my stomach roils; is he upset I mentioned Greg? Is this going to be an issue? My brow crinkles as the anxious feeling blooms.

"There's a thing we're dealing with right now," he says finally, still looking off like he's searching a card catalog in his mind's eye. "My friends... there's a question about who would or wouldn't know in-depth stuff about the helmets and how they work."

His mouth sets into a reluctant frown as he meets my eyes again. Of course. He's afraid to involve me even this way, afraid telling me what he knows will tread ground that causes me pain. But I've purged my secrets. I don't have to fear anything I might say; the worst of it is Tom's problem to sort through now.

"If I can help you, I want to. What's happening?"

"We're kind of on a clock, is the thing. We weren't before. When this whole thing started, it was kind of like, let's change the world but we're not sure exactly how or when. You know?"

"As resistance movements go, that sounds almost relaxing." I smile, thinking of his friends gathering for what may often have been more social than strategic meetings at the library as all the while, Demetri was winning my heart.

"Kinda," he admits fondly, no doubt thinking something very similar. "But then Maxwell hit us with a game-changer. About the helmets.... Know what? I'm gonna get our lunch first and then get into all this, 'cause... it's a lot."

I almost object to the cliffhanger, but who am I to say what schedule anyone should be on when it comes to sharing sensitive information?

When he returns, we sit again on the couch with the tray between us, and despite my hunger, I have to remind myself to keep eating as I listen to his story.

Commander Maxwell has people who are loyal to him in all walks of life below the elite realm he nominally inhabits. One of his informants is on the cleaning staff in one of the labs, and they were sent in to tidy up the office of a scientist who recently had a close encounter with the captive Thrasher and is recuperating in quarantine.

Knowing the scientist would not walk in on them, the cleaner decided to poke around, and they found a curious collection of what appeared to be colored contact lenses, each set labelled with initials.

"There's a set for each of us. All the Helmets. DS, Demetri Sandeaux. TE, Tom Everly. Only one missing is JC, Jennifer Cooper, the one who was killed a while back."

My breath is stuck in my chest, and I mentally force it free so I can respond. "Someone replicated all your retinal scans. They knew one of you would be killed, but not which." I grasp his hand desperately, as if he were at risk of being wrenched away from me even now by the shadow of this months-old peril.

"Yeah, that's the working theory. They prepped the whole set and then smuggled out the right one after they saw which Helmet's gear was taken. Every team that day got hit, could've been any one of us." At the pleading look in my eyes, he nods. "Yeah, I was out there. Luck of the draw which quadrant the bad guys were throwing all their big guns. The rest were decoys."

Drawing his hand closer, I kiss his palm and lean into it. I'm not even sure which of us I'm comforting, practically caressing my own cheek with his strong fingers, but they begin to flex, cradling my jawline as his thumb drifts across my lips, and I feel soothed for real.

"Thing is, there are two levels of need-to-know here, and if we can figure out who's right in the middle of 'em, we can maybe narrow down our search and figure out who's helping the Devil Runners. 'Cause not everyone knows about the retinal scan activation in the first place, but there's more to it than that, and whoever we're looking for, they don't know the next bit—"

"That the helmets aren't keyed to the individual," I fill in automatically. "That they only needed to make one set of lenses, because any valid scan would call back to the database and activate any helmet."

"Right," he breathes, looking unsettled.

"It was part of the initial development. They intended that the gear would be checked back in at the armory like your weapons. Greg had... strong opinions about it. He thought it would keep egos in check, not letting you keep your helmets off duty." Demetri barely suppresses a snort of laughter, and I know he's begrudgingly thinking Greg may have had a point. "When further testing proved the helmet's efficacy was highly dependent on how comfortably the gear fit, it was determined that using them interchangeably was impracticable. The notion was abandoned. But the system had already been put in place to support it. I doubt anyone would know about the database who wasn't involved in the developmental stages."

He nods thoughtfully and presses his lips together in an apologetic grimace. "I've got an idea for getting us both a full dinner without any extra trips; that's the good news. Bad news is I need to burst our bubble a little bit to update Tom on this. You mind?"

I almost laugh. He's concerned with my feelings in the middle of a civilization-defining resistance effort. It strikes me suddenly that he really has been focused almost entirely on me this whole time. How much does he truly comprehend about what he's involved in?

"Demetri, of course, yes. Whatever needs to be done, do it. More than ever, you're fighting for us too. You know that, right? What I did, coming here... oh god, I've changed your time frame, haven't I? I've made everything more complicated and—"

"Shh." He kisses me softly. "Stop. I already knew there was some kind of pressure on you, something you didn't wanna talk about. The walls were closing in, and you had a time frame of your own to worry about. I knew all that. You didn't need to tell me about it then, and you don't now."

As he stands, he trails kisses from my lips to the bridge of my nose to my forehead to my hair. I open my eyes and watch him in wonder as he returns to the table by the door where he left his helmet. This man is so strong, so good, and he loves me. My heart thrums. Impossibly, everything feels as if it will work out—it must. It's a fleeting feeling, I know, not the kind of peace my fretful mind will let me dwell in for more than a moment. But I make note of it. When the more familiar panic and distress return, perhaps I will find comfort in knowing I ever felt that kind of hopeful calm.

Under the helmet, Demetri is speaking, but it's muffled. When he takes it off, his hair is adorably mussed, and somehow the re-emergence of his face from behind the black plating makes me realize all over again how beautiful he is.

We stare at each other for a long moment, mirroring a radiant smile of discovery. He crosses to me, stands behind the couch, and takes my hand, tugging me to my knees. In this position, I'm staring up at him, my head at the level of his pectorals. He strokes my hair and cradles my jaw, leaning down to kiss me. I slide my hands around his hips and enjoy the feel of his muscular backside. Gripping tighter, I pull him against me. His stiffness prods my sternum and collides with the underside of my breasts, and he groans.

I pull back and look up at him. His eyes are rich with lust.

"The first time we spoke. I came back here after and I fantasized about your breasts. About fucking them. I wanted you right from the start, so bad."

The way he looks at me is so powerful. I've never been wanted like this. Emboldened, I pull off my shirt and unbutton his pants.

"Yeah?" He sounds almost afraid to hope, and again I feel that surge of power that this beautiful man has thought about me so hard, wanted me so much.

I look up and meet his eyes. "Yeah."

Gratitude, desire, and urgency collide in the feverish kiss he goes in for just before he stands straight and presses his erection hard against my chest. He takes hold of my breasts and pushes them tight to surround himself. His eyes slip shut, and his breath strains.

"Grab my ass again, pull me close," he asks, and he groans again when I comply. "Stella, I'm gonna fuck your beautiful tits now."

He starts to thrust, kneading my breasts in a way that isn't for me but turns me on just the same. Feeling him use me this way, knowing he's dreamed of doing this to me, transcends mere sensation. My eyes bounce between the smooth, glistening head of his cock as it slides up and down, trapped tight in the channel he's made for it, and the expression of pure ecstasy on his tilted back face.

When he looks down at me, he meets my gaze for a moment, hungry and happy, then stares down at the image he's been thinking about for so long. His thrusts speed up as precum drips to lubricate my flesh.

"Will you lick it, Stella? Lick the head of my dick? Let me see you do that for me, baby."

"Like this?" I say coquettishly and extend my tongue to meet his next thrust.

"Oh, fuck yes," he moans, pumping feverishly.

I lick my lips and lean in to alternately kiss and lap at the head of his cock as it comes into reach.

"I'm gonna come," he says, always the gentleman, warning me in case I don't want it in my mouth or on my face or on my breasts, but I want it everywhere.

"Do it. How did you come in your fantasies? Do it," I urge him quickly between licking and kissing his crown.

In a rush, one hand leaves my breasts to grip the back of my neck and grind me harder against him as he spurts heat up my chest and the underside of my chin. Letting go of my breasts entirely, he presses a thumb into my mouth, and I obediently suck for just a moment before he pulls it back out and wraps both arms around me. As his breathing settles, the stickiness congeals between us and starts to drip.

He laughs shakily and gently presses the tops of my shoulders, nudging me to sit back. Grabbing the shirt I threw off, he wipes me first, then himself. I'm amused to see him spare a glance for the couch cushions, seeming pleased he managed to avoid befouling them.

After he tosses the shirt into a pile, he leans down and kisses me rapturously, moving from behind the couch and turning me as he goes, keeping us connected at the lips. When we're fully turned, my back to the cushions, facing each other, he drops to his knees and tugs my hips toward the edge of the couch.

"Demetri—"

"Shh. Don't say a word unless it's to tell me where you want my tongue, or when you're ready to come for me. You hear me, Stella?"

He's right. My impulse was to assure him he didn't have to do what he was clearly about to do. Did he hear that in the way I said his name, or did he just know it was coming based on everything he knows about me?

I blink and answer the question, or perhaps the challenge. "Yes, Demetri."

A half-smile forms on his gorgeous face and then disappears from view as he sinks into position, his lips brushing my mons, his breath tickling me in a wonderful, tantalizing sensation. I feel the gentle pressure of his mouth as it opens directly against my flesh, his lips encircling the apex of my labia as his tongue expertly seeks my clitoris.

I'm so turned on from the heady experience of giving him his fantasy, the first stroke of his tongue makes me whimper and cant my hips up to beg for more. More pressure, more pleasure, more everything. Was I on the verge of shyness just a moment ago? One touch from him, and I want it all.

His hands grip my hips tightly, holding me open as he alternately licks and circles my clit, bringing me close, then pulling back, then building me back to the edge over and over. I start to whine in frustration, my hands opening and closing in repetition as if they can reach out and grab the orgasm he seems to be taunting me with.

Not taunting. Waiting. For my word.

As his tongue returns to direct contact, I moan, "Demetri, right there. Don't stop. You're going to make me come."

His fingers flex against my hips and his mouth settles firmly into position to take me to the finish, and I realize that's what he was waiting for—he wanted me to ask for it, to let him know I was ready to take it. The quaking feeling deep inside me seems to roll forward toward his tongue, answering his call. My whole body shakes and tenses, but he holds me tight and never stops urging me forward, licking until it feels like a compound orgasm, one-two-three in quick succession, and his lips close around my clit to suck forth one last quivering wave of pleasure, wringing me out, leaving me spent and breathless.

My eyes are still closed when he moves in to kiss me. I feel limp and weak all over, meeting his mouth with energy that the rest of my body can't begin to conjure. There's a low chuckle as he realizes how thoroughly he's wrung me out. His arms slide behind my back and under my knees, and I almost object to this effort on his part, but objecting feels like too great an effort on my part, and it would be an insult too, wouldn't it? He knows what he can handle. He'd want me to accept his strength and enjoy it. As I float into the air on his powerful arms, I drift into blissful unconsciousness.

Chapter Twenty-One

Bedtime Stories

Demetri

I've never enjoyed a woman's orgasm more. I've made a lot of women come, and I've always loved doing it. It's rewarding on so many levels. The selfish ones are obvious: The more you make a woman come, the more she wants you to do to her, the more she'll give you in return. You can get a woman to follow you anywhere you want to go, take you deep in her throat or tight in her ass, and she'll be eager and grateful to do it if she's panting with ecstasy from how hard you just made her come. That's a truth I stumbled on in high school after my fumbling around worked surprisingly well one night, and next thing I knew, Rachel was trying to see how much of me she could fit in her mouth.

For the next year or so, I studied her body and the way it responded to me way harder than I studied in any of my classes. I became an expert on her. After she broke it off, it was a while before I went there with anyone new, but when I tried, it was exciting to discover how women were alike and unique at the same time. How each one required a little bit of a learning curve and improvisation, no matter how well you knew the layout and understood the moving parts.

In the Stronghold, I spent a year perfecting my technique on dozens of women, and I enjoyed every moment of it.

But it's never been better than this afternoon with Stella, coaxing her closer and closer to the peak until she couldn't take it anymore, then pulling her down the slope all at once and sucking every ounce of pleasure she could feel right out through her firm little clit. When I gently placed my top teeth above it and pressed up with my tongue, she even squirted, hot liquid splattering my collarbone. I'm not sure she even knew it happened, but it was so fucking sexy, her body just surrendering to me like that, giving me everything.

I carried her to bed and wiped my chest dry before climbing in beside her, but I'm nowhere near sleep. Watching her, smelling her all over me—and me all over her, I'm ready for her to wake up and take me deep again. I need to watch her eyes slip shut as she feels me balls deep and her body tells her to tell me, more-more-more.

My dick, stiff and full, prods her hip. A drop of precum cools quickly between our flesh. I'm deciding how to wake her when I see her lips curl into a smile.

"Good. You're awake."

I slide my arm across her front and urge her onto her side, facing away from me. My fingers dip between her smooth, lush thighs, and she makes a little whimpery sound as her hips tilt to enjoy the rub right where she wants it.

"Even better. You're still wet," I say, low against her ear. "But are you still hungry for me?" I bend her knee up gently to open her legs so I can guide my dick like a paintbrush along her slick labia and eager clit. "You came so hard. Came all over me. It was the hottest thing I've ever seen. Do you think you can take more, Stella? I want to give you so much more, but I need to know you can take it. Are you ready for me?"

Her hips jolt as if searching for the head of my dick and she moans, "Yes, Demetri. I need you inside me. Please."

My arms close around her and I bury myself deep in one slow, deliberate thrust. She wriggles in my embrace, trying to make me fuck her again. It feels so good, I just hold her tighter and let it happen, my fingers drifting back down to her clit.

"Yes, baby, keep doing that. Let me feel you suck me with your pussy, that's so hot. Keep going, I want to feel you come like this."

Stella's gripping me tighter with every desperate little thrust as she swivels in my clutches, helplessly chasing her orgasm on the length of my dick and the gentle press of my fingers, slick with her own wetness. When she finds her pleasure, she quakes and convulses all around me, and she says my name again, soft and high. It could just be the sound of breathing out. I'm so deep inside her, I'm part of her.

"You're incredible," she says, already moving again, grinding to see if there's more where that came from. "You feel so good."

"Stella, I'm going to fuck you now. Keep giving me everything you've got. Keep sucking me in the way you do. I love it. That's what I want. You hear me? I want to feel you come again and again. Come until you can't take anymore and then surprise yourself with how much you still want. I don't want to come until you've soaked me. Keep using my dick like that, I love the way you love it."

Her back arches until she's straining against my arms, pulling me deeper, grinding against me with all she's got. There's no doubt when she finds the perfect angle, holding desperately firm and rolling in tight little circles.

This is going to be harder than I thought, I realize as my eyes slip shut. I wrench them open again and focus on delivering what I just promised her: a long, glorious ride that makes her fall in love with my cock so hard she'll never stop needing it.

Is that what I'm doing? The thought pulls me back from the edge, hard. Am I trying to addict her in case she doesn't feel as much for me after all? Using my skills to trick her into loving me, or at least believing she does?

"Baby, I need to know—" the words just spill out while she's still quaking around me, "did you come here to love me or to fuck me? It's okay if it's just—but I need to know, because I'm in love with you, Stella."

Her back straightens again to bring our bodies back into full contact. Her right hand slides up and finds my shoulder in a sensual grasp mirrored by what's probably an unconscious pulse of possession around my cock still buried deep inside her.

"I came here to give myself to you. At the risk of my life. I don't know what will happen, but it's worth the chance I'm taking. I want to be with you, Demetri. For real. Forever. It's not... *just sex*? Why would you even think—"

Kissing behind her ear, gripping her against me, I shush her. "I'm sorry. I think I got in my own way a little. I keep trying to believe you're really mine, and then I thought maybe I was trying too hard to prove it." My fingertip circles her clit again, and she writhes. "But it's true. Isn't it? I get to have you like this forever." I massage and lightly pinch and tweak, not taking my time, just trying to get her next orgasm to shudder and squeeze around me. "I'm sorry about changing the program on you, but I'm gonna need to fuck you pretty hard now, Stella. You're gonna come for me one more time like this before you take it all, okay?"

"Yes, Demetri, please don't stop—"

"So ready for more, I love it. I love the way you take me. You're gonna take me deep and hard, Stella. Tell me you're ready. Tell me you want it. Tell me with your sweet pussy, yes, just like that."

Her muscles are still quivering around me as I roll her onto her stomach. Her hips squiggle to open and tilt for me until I'm flat against her, buried so deep she must be seeing god. But that's not the same as feeling it pound her like I'm about to do.

"If it gets to be too much, you tell me."

She swivels again, relishing the depth I've found inside her. Oh baby, you like it deep, you are in luck. I plant my hands for leverage and start driving with more force than I've let myself give her so far. There's a surprised tone in her whimpers, and they start coming faster, lighter, and a tension in her upper thighs tells me she's adjusting. I should hold back, just a little, but I don't want to, and she hasn't asked.

I feel it when my strokes stop confusing her with sensation, when her body finds the right way to enjoy them completely. Her moans get lower and fuller again, and her thighs soften again. I doubt she knew they were clenching. I stay in this moment, letting her love this. Get used to it, Stella. Crave it. 'Cause I'm gonna be deep in you like this a lot, so I'm gonna need you to want it as bad as I do.

"Fuck, baby, you're so good for me."

She tries to answer, fumbles to shove her hair out of the way, and tries again. "I love what you do to me."

"I'm not done," I promise as I deliver another few deep strokes, enjoying the way she reaches for me inside, knowing she's really reaching for her next orgasm, trusting my dick to deliver it to her.

Sure enough, she gasps in dismay when I stop short as she's getting closer. I can't help chuckling quietly at the frustrated flex of her back muscles.

Taking her hips in my hands, I urge her back until she's kneeling in front of me, and I start thrusting up into her, holding tight. "Hmm, scoot forward with me, I want your hands on the wall." She obeys the way I knew she would, ready for more of everything

I want to do to her. When she's braced firmly, I grip her hipbones tight to hold her in place and take every inch.

A helpless sound that could be weeping enters her moans, but it's accompanied by a deep, rhythmic clench at the head of my dick, and I know my girl needs to ride this feeling all the way with me.

"Oh, Demetri, you can't know how good this feels—"

"How'd it feel when I came on you? Tell me."

She moans. "Explosive. Viscous. Hot and wet and thick, all over me."

Thinking about it has her gripping me tighter, good girl. I settle into the steady rhythm that's going to bring us both home.

"Are you gonna feel it just like that inside you? Now that you know how it feels on your gorgeous tits, I want you to feel it just like that when I come right now, right now—take it, baby—"

She convulses with ecstasy as I explode, letting her milk every drop. Her orgasm seems to surge again just as it's fading, like she really is trying to suck me dry and pull it deep, keep it all.

This woman is gonna have my babies. It's wild what a sexy thought that is. I'm suddenly reluctant to pull out even though I'm definitely spent for now and going soft.

I pull her gently into my arms and lay us back down to let our heart rates settle. Spoons in a drawer, we both drift off this time.

When I wake up, she's in the shower. It's a good idea. I almost join her except for the whole defeating-the-purpose thing. Glancing down at the bed, I laugh. I've been sleeping alone for a while, but even before, this kind of fuckfest was not the norm. I got plenty laid, here or elsewhere, but I've never seen my sheets this wrecked.

This is worse than the couple of group sessions I got into. *Better*. Way better than those. This mess is all us.

She exits the bathroom, and I give her a big kiss and maybe even bigger smile on my way in. I've never been this happy in my whole goddamn life.

Stella's helped herself to another of my shirts and settled in on the couch with the latest library book she sent me home with. Short stories this time. She said I could read them in any order. I tried a couple, but I couldn't even tell if I liked them for some reason.

I'm frowning over the thought when she looks up. "You haven't said anything about our good friend, Mr. Bradbury, yet. Did you read any?"

Cringing, I admit the truth. "Well... I looked at the titles, and I thought *The Town Where No One Got Off* sounded like it might be kind of funny... but it wasn't."

She laughs. "No, it's not a funny one at all."

The fact that she doesn't seem offended makes it easier to go on. "Then there's the one about an Ice Cream Suit, and that's not what you think it's gonna be about either. It wasn't a bummer, but it was kind of weird?"

"Yes, I can see that," she says, and her smile is so warm and encouraging, I forget why I was ever nervous as I sit down beside her. "Just those two so far, then?"

I nod, and she glances back down at the book, looking thoughtful.

"It was my whole life for so long, you know? I could see they were going to try to take it from me, or me from it, and on one level I just flailed and raged against the entire idea, but on another level, I had to consider what alternatives lay ahead and whether any of them could be acceptable, even worthwhile."

I wait to see whether she'll continue on her own or I need to give her a sign I'm listening. It's one of the big things Rachel taught me: Sometimes a woman is pausing because she wants your input, but sometimes she's just collecting her thoughts, and if you jump in, you'll never hear what she was building up to.

"They had plans for me, Demetri. I don't know whether anything I've done here could possibly change that. It's not as if they..." She trails off again, looking troubled.

I take her hand, wishing I knew how to comfort her, but I don't even know what's happening, let alone if there's anything I could do or say. Her fingers squeeze mine suddenly as she looks into my eyes, and I know she's thinking something similar, that I can't help her if she doesn't open up.

"It's because I was supposed to marry Greg. They've got it in mind to keep me in their world, because—it sounds insane, I'm not even sure how to explain it, but it's to do with maintaining social strata and defining where people belong and—"

"It's like in the book with all the mythology stuff, isn't it? Kings had to marry princesses, because royalty was supposed to be the bloodline of the gods."

She looks a little shocked, and yeah, I guess I'm impressed with myself too.

"I hadn't thought about that," she muses. "When I gave you that one, I was mostly thinking about masks, you see. How many people in our little world wear them, and how you live on the line between the masked and unmasked just as I lived on the line between Illustris and outsider... or thought I did. I hadn't given the royal bloodline concept a thought, but yes. That is what I think they're going for. A long game where within a few generations, no one remembers these people were ever the descendants of corporate titans; they'll just be innately superior in a way no one fully understands but that cannot be argued with. If only they had enough women to go around," she finishes bitterly.

"Well they can't have you." My words come out fierce and determined, though I know I have no idea what we're up against, not really. No idea what they're capable of. Maybe I should have been paying a little more attention to what my friends are up to... but maybe that's the answer anyway.

"Stella, I know you're scared, and you're right to be. But there's been a resistance movement going on under these rich pricks' noses, and we're close to something big. Closer than ever, thanks to you. We've all been flirting with disaster a little bit. It's a huge fucking risk what we're doing. But if we get it the fuck done... it's not just us that gets a better life. It's you too. You're with us now. You're with me. What we're doing, it's gonna be the answer to all this. Trust me."

Her hand drifts up and along my brow, down my cheek and the side of my neck until it comes to rest over my heart.

"That's the one thing I'm sure of," she says without a hint of hesitation.

Tom should be headed our way by now unless things went sideways on his patrol, so I check in via the helmet.

"Bro, you close?"

He hmphs at me, and I figure he's giving me shit. "Yes, Demetri, I'm nearly there. We've a lot to discuss."

"Cool. I'll head down to the mess."

I give Stella a quick kiss and slip out, but it pains me knowing we're almost at the end of our little hideout period. Tomorrow

I go back out on patrol, and she... what? One more awkward conversation waiting to happen, I guess.

And Tom's got one of those teed up as well, apparently.

"You've made a tidy little mess, haven't you?" he says, looking vaguely amused by the situation. "Maxwell's given us quite an earful. He was rather put out I wasn't inclined to bang on your door last night and convince your guest to hurry home before it was too late."

"She'd never have gone," I say, not entirely sure it's true but wanting to believe it.

He studies me for a moment, a fond smirk taking over his face. "Do you have any idea what you're doing? Not that I don't enjoy watching our Commander friend sputter in abject futility, but he's got a point: You've made a very big play that could well push us into an endgame we're not prepared for."

My gut fills with lead at the thought I've completely failed to think about how this could affect my friends. But knowing what I know, I'm not sure what I could have done differently.

"You don't seem pissed at me," I say cautiously, hoping he's not just winding me up before the beatdown.

"I know things Maxwell doesn't." Tom's voice is quiet and cool, and he seems utterly chill. He's talking about Stella's secrets. Whatever she told him, it's enough to make him feel like we'll get out of this intact, even after she went AWOL on the Genneros.

I clap a hand on his shoulder and say with a smile, "Good news: You're about to know even more. Let's get some food, okay? My girl's waiting."

Tom barely blinks at the sight of Stella all rumpled and casual. He hands her the tray he carried up and sits on the coffee table in front of the couch.

"I suppose congratulations are in order? Or would that be premature?"

She hesitates before answering. "A bit of both, I think."

He nods thoughtfully, and I swear it's like they had a whole extra conversation I just couldn't hear.

"I'm glad you came. I realized there was something more I should have told you the other day."

"Should I be here for this?" I interrupt, already making to stand, but she reaches for my hand.

"Stay. It's nothing... troubling. The thing is, I was mostly thinking about ancient history when we spoke, and it occurred to me I'd failed to mention something quite recent. I overheard a snatch of conversation between two Illustrian men. I don't know them, but one was named Jack. They were arguing about a problem with someone called Delia, that she wasn't satisfied with the current situation, and the other one was far more concerned about it than Jack was. Then they clammed up because Benjamin Croft was approaching, pretended they'd been talking about something else entirely. In fact, they made out that they'd been debating some rumors about the Council, so they're definitely not Council. Delia is also not Council, but she very nearly was, based on something I overheard Celeste say a while back. I don't know how helpful this is, or what it means, but—"

"No," Tom says firmly, "it's good information. All information is good at this point. We've got a major situation on our hands. More than one, really."

"You mean me," she says, and he nods. "Well, the Delia tip may or may not pan out, obviously, but I do have more for you."

As Stella explains our conversation about the retinal scan database, Tom's expression moves from curious to intrigued to something like hopeful.

"This is good," he says finally. "There are a lot of moving pieces here, but... I believe I'm starting to detect some of the underlying pattern. Nina has been following up on some things in Archives, and this may help narrow down her findings, so thanks for that. I've got to get home. Unless there's anything else?"

She shakes her head, and he stands, then hesitates as if he's remembered some unpleasant business he would rather not deal with.

"Listen, Stella, this move you've made to take back your life. I applaud it, truly. But you can't hide here indefinitely. What do you intend to do?"

"I thought I might go to work tomorrow," she answers carefully.

"What?!"

They both look at me, and it's this vaguely pitying look like they knew I wasn't going to understand something they both already knew, and it pisses me off in a way I wouldn't have expected.

"No. Fuck this. You're staying here. You can hide out. I'll have... look, I'll figure out getting you food when I'm not here. Someone'll help. And—"

"And what? She's to live out her life in your quarters? Even if it were plausible for her to be safely stowed here indefinitely, it's hardly a long-term plan in terms of a lifestyle."

My eyes are bugging out. He's being so matter of fact, and I usually find that comforting, but not this time.

"Tom, we're not talking about the rest of anyone's life, just—"

"Just what? Until they give up and say, oh well, fair play, you kept her out of sight and out of mind long enough, so you win."

"If you're trying to piss me off, it's working. I'm not an idiot, I know it's not that simple, but—"

"He's right, Demetri." Her voice is quiet but firm. When I shut up and meet her eyes, I see an apology where I thought I was seeing pity before. She hates telling me something she knows I won't like, that's all. Might be about the same way Nina looked right before she told Tom she'd joined a revolution. Stella's not feeling sorry for me that I have to catch up to their conclusions; that's my own insecure bullshit. I feel bad I ever read it that way from her. From either of them, really.

"You figure if you don't try to take charge now, you'll miss your window. That about it?" My voice comes out dull, but I do my best to unclench my teeth, my hands, my shoulders. Trying to look like I respect the choice even as it's scaring the shit out of me to watch her make it.

She nods. "I disappeared just long enough to make a statement, but if I stay gone, it's like I'm admitting defeat. I have to assert my place. My right to it."

I want to be strong and supportive, but it's killing me, and I can't help sounding weak with my challenge. "You think they're just gonna watch you defy them? *Yeah, all right, you stood up to us and we respect that.*' Stella," I almost beg, shaking my head as I stare into her eyes.

"The longer I hide, the worse it will be. And you can't protect me forever, no matter how much you want to."

"Well, wait another day at least! Tom, you're backup tomorrow, yeah? So stay here one more day. Then you can have Tom as an escort when you go back."

"Yes, happy to volunteer," he says wryly.

"Then what? I'm only allowed to leave your sight if your friends are available to keep an eye on me?"

Shit. This is starting to get out of control. Control being the operative word—she's on the verge of feeling like I'm trying to control her like her ex. And the comparison slams into my chest with the compound realization that I'm terrified letting her assert her independence from them will get her hurt like Rachel got hurt after she wanted her independence from me.

"No, he's right," Tom cuts in, and I've never been more grateful for his analytical tone. He doesn't sound like a friend sticking up for me, just a smart motherfucker who's about to tell us the best move and we better goddamn pay attention. "You're poking a very big bear. Flouting their authority and flaunting it. You're right to do it, but you should have someone to watch over you, at least in the beginning." He turns from her to me and says decisively, "Monica's team had backup today. They'll handle tomorrow. Nina and I will take the following day. It's a start. Yes?"

I give him a small, grateful nod, then make eye contact with Stella again. She nods back at me, and my chest finally unclenches a bit.

Tom stands to go. "I'll go find whichever of our friends is still hanging about the rec or the mess and pass along their assignment. Good luck, Stella. It's a brave thing you're doing."

He nods to me again on his way out, and the slight furrow of his brow tells me he knows I'm right to be terrified for her. That's the scariest thing of all. He knows she's in danger, and he can't see a way to avoid it.

I'm still staring at the door he just walked out, waiting for my heart rate to come down, when Stella steps close behind me and wraps her arms around me, resting her head against my back between my shoulder blades.

I want to say something useful. I reach for a way to sound confident, reassuring, but I come up empty. I feel like I should turn around and kiss her and take her to bed. If I'm short on words, use what always works for me, right? But my dick's feeling pretty quiet right now too. I don't know how to make this moment easier.

"What do you do in 'the rec' anyway?" she asks tentatively. It's funny, because if I could see her face, I'd know exactly what's up. With her behind me like this, she might be desperately trying to change the subject to calm me down, or she might be fishing for reassurance I'm not wishing I was elsewhere right now. Or worse, doubting me about the whole celibacy trip I've been on, doubting my feelings for her.

I want to spin around and see her face so I can be sure it's not a question of her trusting me, but that impulse feels like me not trusting her. So I hold still and force myself to make a steadier, stronger choice.

"Used to play a lot of pool. Have a beer or two. Up to a few months ago I was down there every night, pretty much. Lately, if I wasn't at the library with you, I'd be holed up in here with whatever the hell book you gave me."

Saying it makes the weirdest answer the obvious one. Probably the thing that would help me unwind right now is to read for a while like I've been doing at night for months. If we had more than one book handy, I might say let's sit and read together like an old married couple.

"Hey," I blurt, "why don't you read me a story? You pick."

Stella's arms tighten around me even more, a firm hug before she lets go. She picks up the book and sits down on the couch at an angle, propping her legs up and spreading them. The sight makes my dick regret its stubborn act a few minutes ago.

"Come sit," she says, patting the space on the couch between her legs.

Down, boy, I tell myself as I settle in, leaning my head back against her chest. But with the perfect swell of her breasts cradling me like this, it's gonna be damn near impossible to focus on a story. Damn, I hope she picks a nice, short one.

Chapter Twenty-Two

A Medicine for Melancholy

Stella

The moment he settles in between my legs and nestles his head between my breasts, I want to change the plan. I could set the book aside and reach down his chest to that hint of a bulge and massage it to full strength. What would he do? Slide his hands inside this loose shirt of his and tweak my nipples, turn his face as he moves the shirt out of the way so he can take one between his lips and his gentle, playful teeth?

Forcing myself to breathe normally, willing my pulse to remain steady as my body strives to skip ahead, I can't help wiggling my hips just a bit to enjoy the pressure as he rests firmly against me, nothing but a pair of his own boxers over my sensitive center.

"*A Medicine for Melancholy*," I announce, and I sense him settling in just a bit further as well. It seems we both spent the last moments wondering whether the other might throw aside the bedtime story in favor of going straight to bed.

As I read, in between needing to turn the page, I hold the book in my left hand and allow my right to stroke the glossy blackness of his hair, glide intermittently down his cheek, his jawline. At times, the act of reading becomes automatic, my eyes delivering the text to my brain and letting it provide the performance as my consciousness is diverted by the aching need inside. When the father in the story derides a doctor and shoos him away like vermin, Demetri laughs, the rumbling sensation between my legs a wonderful tease.

This tale is scandalously suggestive by the standards of yesteryear, yet obtusely tame to the modern eye—or ear. A young woman's undiagnosable affliction has brought her so near death that her desperate family carries her, bed and all, to the street outside their front door in the hope some passerby will recognize her symptoms and offer a better solution than leeches and laudanum.

Just as all seems lost at the end of a fruitless day, they are approached by a man who swears his own sister was saved from this same illness years ago. He exhorts them to leave the girl where she is all night long and let the full moon cure her, for it is Saint Bosco's night, an auspicious time for a full moon's healing effects. No one is quite sure they've heard of a Saint Bosco before, but, well, who can keep track of all these holy figures and their festivals?

At the climax of the story, the tantalizing mystery of Saint Bosco's arrival, I let my hand drift down to Demetri's chest. A gentle clasp of my open palm atop his sternum, a slow journey up the muscular slope to rest over his heart, the edge of my pinky grazing his nipple as it peaks.

In the wee hours, as the city sleeps around her, the girl waits for her miracle, and Bosco himself appears. The mysterious stranger climbs into bed with the story's ailing damsel. As their dialogue proceeds largely unadorned, I wonder whether Demetri is following the strange course of the tale. At sunrise, the girl's family rejoices to discover her health is indeed restored. The end.

Setting the book aside, I rest my left hand against his cheek and allow the fingertips of my right hand to coast along the very tip of his nipple. Does it tickle him somewhere much lower as I graze the tip, the same as it does me when his tongue flicks at mine as he pulls it between his lips? I want to know everything about his body, every reaction and sensation. I want to memorize him with my fingers and my mouth.

The muscles of his cheek form a smile that I feel in the palm of my hand before he tilts up to look back at me in wonder.

"Did he just sex her back to life?" His delight in the discovery is beautiful to behold.

"I thought you'd like that one," I say, grinning slyly back at him.

He turns to face me fully and tugs my hips to slide me down on my back before lying between my legs again. My thighs clasp him tight, and my ankles close around his hips to pull his hardness into my cleft.

"Dammit, we should have gotten naked before I let you read a sexy bedtime story." He kisses my neck. "You didn't tell me there were secret sexy times in that book." He chuckles as if something's just occurred to him, then nips my throat playfully and licks the spot. "Bad girl. You were gonna let me read that all by myself. I'd be all alone here," he pumps his hips twice, firmly taunting me with the pressure while still separated by all this clothing, "not even knowing when I'd get to fuck you." He grinds against me long and slow, and my breath comes out on a moan, but he swallows the needy sound in a demanding kiss.

"I've always liked that story, but I never related to it before." Grasping the back of his neck to make sure he can't pull his eyes from mine, I confess, "I think I'll die if you don't fuck me now."

Another kiss brings our torsos into full, heated contact as he slides his arms around me and I arch my back to aid him. Reveling in his strength again, I suck his tongue in eager appreciation as he lifts us both, my legs still wrapped around his waist.

When he stops, I know we're at the bed, and I want whatever's next, but I don't know how to stop kissing him either until his fingers playfully pinch and tickle my ass, signaling me to unfurl and let him set me down. I come to rest on my knees on the bed, and we both reach for his waistband. I look up with fever behind my eyes, and he lets me take over.

Working his cock free of his pants, I get my closest look at it yet. It's long and fiercely stiff. I give the head a long, circular lick as my hands wrestle with getting his pants off further, but his hands cover mine with a gentle squeeze that lets me know he can handle the clothes; he'd like my focus elsewhere.

With my hands free to explore, I let them dance up his firm glutes and forward to the crest of his hipbones. As my fingertips gently drift down, tickling the smooth skin, I take him into my mouth with a powerful suck. He drags in a desperate breath and loses focus on getting his pants all the way off in favor of grabbing my hair with both hands.

I know I won't be able to take him all the way, so I lick and suck lavishly, hoping to make up with enthusiasm what I lack in pornographic prowess. With one hand, I brace against his hip while the other slides down to graze his testicles. Another audible inhale and a new flex of his fingers in my hair encourages the exploration, so I softly stroke and cup the pebbled flesh there, alternately tickling and caressing.

"Stella." His voice strains, and his hands work my hair like he's making every effort to resist some intense urge. If it's to try to pull me in further and feel my mouth around him all the way to the base, I'm very grateful he can withstand that desire. "Stella, if you wanted me to come in your mouth, you have no idea how lucky that'd make me feel. Don't *let* me do it. Tell me if you want it. It feels like you do. Like you need it. God. Tell me sometime if you need it, and then suck me like this, like you're sick and my come is the cure. But for now, stop. Stop so I can fuck you."

He's just made swallowing him sound like the sexiest thing I can think of, and then told me to stop? In the heady confusion of arousal, I feel like retaliating somehow, so I dive in to take another half-inch or so of depth and suck with fervor for one heated moment before pulling away. I scramble backward to make room on the bed, throwing off my shirt and shoving the boxers down my hips in a mad rush to give him access to everything.

Demetri's perfect face is flushed, his dark eyes thrillingly preda-tory with lust. He's on the bed and kneeling before me in a rush of movement, gripping his cock at the base like he's telling it to be patient. He lets go and kisses me, guiding me onto my back and encouraging my legs into the air until my ankles are at his shoulders. Thus compressed, his bulk holding my legs tight against my chest, I feel his steady, powerful invasion inch by inch.

He leans back then, still on his knees, holding my legs to keep them in place, and begins slowly, pulling out in a steady drag, then tilting gently for a smoother, faster return to full depth.

"I wanted to fuck you in the library. Behind the desk. You wouldn't let me come back there with you, but that was before we kissed. Before you knew you had me. You'd let me back there now, wouldn't you?"

"I'll give you everything," I say pleadingly, arching my back and reaching for his hips. I want more. I want him to speed up, to go harder.

He traps my hands in his own, braces them beside my hips, and keeps taunting me with long, deliberate strokes and silken, decadent plunges at that steady pace.

"I was thinking about you on that chair. It's a good height. It's got those little wheels. I'd put you up on that chair, slide you back and forth, pull you onto my dick and push you off over and over again. Just like this."

Now that I see what he's doing, it's not a tease, it's a fantasy. *I'm his fantasy.* My inner muscles grasp at him as the image forms in my mind, being rolled on and off of him and trying not to let go.

"Yes, that's it, Stella. You want me to stay deep. You love it deep. Your pussy grabs at me so hard. Keep sucking me with your pussy, Stella. Fuck." His breath goes ragged. His eyes slip shut. This beautiful man is on his knees before me. He put us in these positions, but I suddenly feel like I'm the one with the power.

I give him what he wants, but the pulsing clench of my muscles around him is pushing me steadily to my own orgasm in a way that feels conscious and controlled. I'm pulling him in, holding him tight, compelling him to stay, longer, deeper, fuller.

The feeling of active muscular control soon becomes helpless, glorious quaking deep within me, grasping at him for all he can give.

"Demetri, I'm so ready to come for you. Keep doing this. Don't stop, don't you dare stop—"

"I'll never stop. You want it, you got it, baby."

"Yes, just like this—"

The orgasm overtakes me, and a long, gasping *ahh* rides the tremors of my body up and out along my vocal cords. My hips, thighs, clutched hands tremble and shake, and I clench rhythmically around him, realizing just as the pleasure wave ebbs that he's not even deep inside me. I came on just a few inches of his length.

As I notice that, he shifts forward, pressing my legs against my chest again.

"Now we're going deep, Stella. You want me deep?"

"Yes," I barely voice through my ecstatic haze, giddy for more. "Deep, and so hard, Demetri, give me all of you."

He slides in smoothly, and I feel that powerful twinge of recognition deep inside me, the sensation of *yes, this is the perfect fit, the place no one has ever touched, the need I couldn't know until it was filled.*

His strokes are shorter and stronger now, pulling out only enough to push deep again and again.

"That's it, baby. Take that dick. Keep it—it's yours, don't let it go—"

Demetri lunges into me and fucks harder and faster, seeming only to go deeper now, not out and in but in-in-in, and I strain at him with every part of me, pulling his orgasm from him, deep inside me where I need it, grasping at him for all he can give.

"I want it, I want it all." I'm still trembling all over, pulsing around him, when I breathe the words against his ear, loving the arch of his back and the steady, deep press of his cock as he's pouring into me.

I do want it. I feel him as he gives it to me, like a flower opening to a bee. In this moment, filled with his strength, pinned under the power of his lust and devotion, I truly do feel this is all going to be all right. Somehow.

The hopeful bliss doesn't fade as we settle into a drowsy cuddle. After all, this isn't a situation where *love* must conquer *all.* Right? There's a whole resistance movement hard at work on the real challenges. All I have to do is stay out of trouble. Go to work as usual tomorrow, under guard no less, and sneak back in here tomorrow night for more of this. If we can get through a couple of days on that routine, Celeste will have no choice but to accept defeat.

It's almost a surprising thought, instinctually identifying her as my primary oppressor in this. But the moment it comes to me, I know it's true. It may or may not have been her idea to use me the way they've determined, but it's important to her that they do so.

The men want a flower to pollinate, certainly, but she's the one who will be most outraged by my escape from the garden.

The uneasy thought follows me into the darkness. I slide a hand across Demetri's warm chest and let my arm settle around him. A sleepy, satisfied hmph rumbles out of his chest as he turns toward me, and, facing each other, we drift off in comfort.

Chapter Twenty-Three

Situation Normal

Stella

"I can't believe you're going to make me argue with you about this," I protest with a laugh.

It almost feels like we're willfully, mutually choosing a different disagreement than the real one looming over us this morning. That disagreement already played out, after all, and he knows he can't talk me out of my decision, so instead he's trying to make me eat half his breakfast.

"I'm not making you argue," he says with stubborn cheer, "you could end the argument right now."

"Demetri. You're going on military duty. I'm going to the library. Your caloric needs are undeniably greater, not to mention the potential downsides of leaving them unmet. I might feel a little cranky between now and lunch; you might—well, let's not talk about that, because I'd rather not even think about anything happening to you."

The playful tone of the dispute has faded completely, and he takes my hand.

"You win," he says softly, and takes a bite.

I'm wearing the same clothes as I was the day before yesterday, having no other options here, but it's all relatively clean, at least. I washed the underwear and stockings in the bathroom sink, then let them hang dry for a day, and the dress hung in the bathroom continuously to get the benefit of several showers' worth of steam.

His schedule is tight enough that we can't linger, and that's a good thing under the circumstances. No time to waste on rehashing anything that can't be changed. After he downs his breakfast, it's time to meet one of his friends out front so they can chaperone me.

It's one of the men, and since they weren't frequent visitors prior to their meetings, I haven't gotten a handle on which name matches which face.

"Davy," Demetri greets him, sparing me any awkwardness. "Thanks for keeping an eye on my girl." He's clearly trying to be his normal, easygoing self, but his mouth keeps settling back into a worried frown. I squeeze his hand in an attempt to be reassuring.

"It's no problem, man. I was probably going to hang around here all day. Might as well hang around there instead. Break up the monotony a little." He gives Demetri's shoulder a nudge, and I already like him, seeing how he's trying to ease my lover's troubled mind a bit.

I turn to Demetri with a smile that I hope conveys all my affection, plus far more peace of mind than I actually feel. He kisses me gently, holding the back of my neck and pressing his forehead to mine as our lips part.

"Stay safe today," he says, and again the absurdity of it is striking: He's going outside the wall, and he seems to think I'm the one in real danger.

"You just come home safe to me tonight," I tell him firmly.

Before we head in our separate directions, I wish I could see him smile—that beautiful, heart-winning smile, but it isn't to be. His fretful look follows me as I walk away with Davy at my side.

"It's good of you to do this for him. Thank you."

Davy shrugs, looking a little sheepish, as if he's uncomfortable with gratitude or recognition. Perhaps my being a near-stranger amplifies any awkwardness he may feel in that regard.

"Demetri's a great guy. We'd all do anything for him."

The slight flush in his cheeks combined with the vaguely defensive emphasis on *all* tells a story quite clearly, and I smile. Davy's clearly not a Kinsey 6, or he wouldn't be here, but judging by the quiet crush he has on Demetri, he's not a Kinsey 1. I'm glad the psych evals aren't catching simple things like a person self-reporting as hetero when that's not the full picture.

On the heels of that thought, the less comforting flipside: If they missed that, what else might they miss? Greg was quite high on his own genius. I don't need to know the specific Illustrians in charge of the different disciplines to imagine some would have shared that character flaw. He didn't believe he could be wrong, didn't see the possibility for anyone to fool him or slip something by him. That's a dangerous weakness to have when designing or administering the personality tests to admit desperate outsiders to your delicate little civilization.

When we walk through the library door, Sarah Maxwell's head whips around as if in alarm, reminding me of my old, rabbity ways, early in my somnambulist fog. I nod to Davy and go to join her behind the desk as he heads into the stacks to choose a book for his long morning on library stakeout duty.

"Who were you afraid was coming through the door just now?" I ask without preamble, my tone low and furtive.

"There have been people looking for you," she confirms in a library-appropriate voice. "After you rushed out two nights ago and never returned home, there was even a knock at my door."

Her lips purse in distress, bringing a halo of tiny wrinkles briefly into formation around her mouth. A sudden reminder that she's not my enemy. She's caught up in the same storm as I am, and she's got children to protect.

"I'm sorry," I tell her sincerely, my eyes dropping to the floor, my indignation deflated in an instant.

She surprises me with a gentle touch on my right hand. "It could have been worse. I pretended to be a little disorganized is all. *Thought it was just my turn to close up, wasn't expecting her back,* et cetera. Played it off that if I'd noticed you weren't where you were supposed to be, *of course* I would have reported it immediately."

"Why didn't you?" I ask, honestly curious. "You don't owe me anything."

Her eyes harden, and she lets go of my hand. "You're a danger to all of us." Her icy tone carries a strong undercurrent of disdain, implying the unspoken *you idiot* at the end. She turns her back on me as I accept the rebuke. I would never endanger the people she's terrified I could be coerced into betraying, but there's no point trying to convince her of that. She's a mother. My love for Demetri might be something she could relate to as a wife, but I have no doubt she would place her children above her husband if it came down to it. The power of romantic love is dwarfed by maternal devotion, a truth I only know in the abstract but have no reason to doubt. I've read enough stories that conveyed it powerfully, but I also heard it from my own mother. Long ago, as I raged at my father's betrayal, she reassured me in the oddest way, or so it seemed at the time. She said it hardly mattered, because the love she'd felt for him was the vehicle that brought her the only true love of her life. *Don't worry about my heart being broken,* she told me. *He could have done that before you came along, but never after.*

In the corner of my eye, I see Davy make his way to a table in the center of the room to settle in with his book. I turn and squint at the cover, but there's no making it out from here.

Glancing down at the counter, I see a pile of returns and gather them up, automatically sorting them in the proper order to match the best path through the shelves. I know this space completely. The library is mine, and I can't let them take it from me. Demetri's mine now, too, I think with a little shiver, goosebumps perking my flesh, making my breasts suddenly sensitive against the fabric of my dress. I can't help smiling, despite everything. There's no fear or stress powerful enough to dissuade my soul from this joyful response to the very thought of him. He loves me. He's kind and strong, and he will do anything to make our future happen. I believe in him. It's going to be okay, isn't it? Somehow.

Reaching the Classic Literature section, I pluck *The Yellow Wallpaper* from the stack in my arms—

Chapter Twenty-Four

Panic

Demetri

S tella made me choke down every bite of my breakfast, and now it's sitting in my gut like lead. This is sure to be the longest shift of my life. I can't afford to be anything less than perfectly focused, no matter how impossible it seems to think about myself instead of worrying about her. But she was right that my danger is clear and present while hers is probably more theoretical... and I need to come home safe to her, which means fucking focus, Demetri. Focus.

I can't help that I'm having flashbacks to my senior year. Rachel breaking it off and wandering into danger she didn't see coming. But fuck, that's not really fair to Stella, is it? Not just associating her with Rachel in the first place, though I know it's no fun being compared to the ex. But no, the whole point is how Rachel didn't know what she was getting herself into. Stella knows this place better than I do. She's not helpless. I have to trust her judgment. I do. I do trust her. It's just goddamn hard letting go, knowing I can't protect her from everything and everyone when that's all I want to fucking do.

Right now, I can protect her from whatever's beyond the wall and hoping to get in. That's gonna have to be enough to keep me sane until I can get back to her later, hold her, pull her into my arms and start learning to trust that every time we say goodbye won't be the last.

I think maybe I was almost hoping for a nice, big, distracting battle to pull my mind into focus and make the day go faster, but it looks like we're getting an uneventful shift. There's been nothing on my HUD, no chatter on the comms from other sectors, no updates from Command.

Anye says something to Jeremy about Snake, which means Jake, of course. I'm generally good at not listening to the squad's idle chatter so I don't get too distracted on duty, but it's funny how my ears always seem to perk up at the mention of a fellow Helmet. But before I can even get a sense of what they're saying about him, there's another voice, so close it might as well be coming from inside my head.

"Demetri."

Tom's voice buzzes low on our secure channel. Helmet-to-Helmet pings weren't part of the design specs, apparently, but just like Tom figured out tagging a target on his HUD and taught it to me so I could help him watch over Nina, one of the earliest Helmets figured out how to make a voice channel to communicate privately amongst ourselves. Either Command doesn't know we do it, doesn't care enough to stop us, or can't stop us. Or they're listening in and we're a bunch of naïve idiots. There's always that possibility, too.

"Yeah, buddy, what's up," I mumble back, struggling with distractions, impatience, and worry. My attention has never been this fractured on duty.

"I'm backup on East. Assuming no delays in either of our schedule, meet me at the corner where Brewery Row begins, and we'll walk together from there."

"Why?" I think there's something off about the request, but my mind is all over the place. Am I suspicious? Of what? Of who? Not Tom... I was gonna run to her, and that's what he's trying to keep me from doing, isn't it? Forcing me to slow down, move at a normal pace. Dammit.

"I thought you might appreciate the company," he says, and there's this gentleness to his tone that makes me feel like shit for being annoyed. He's being a good friend, maybe protecting me from myself a little, and I should calm the fuck down and let him.

"Yeah. All right. Thanks."

He exhales like he's on the verge of saying more, then closes the channel.

In the renewed silence, I notice the crunch of my boots on a patch of dirt. It was cleared of grass and whatever dead things had come to rest there so recently that it's still crispy. There's a heaviness in my heart. In the beginning, it was almost entirely zombies we were killing, and that's not too rough, really. You try not to think about the fact they used to be people, because they stopped being that before you ever saw them. Some people I knew got bit, yeah, but that was early days, before I came to the Stronghold. At the time, you didn't even have time to think about the fact you were killing your third-grade teacher or the barista you flirted with that morning. Even the worst of them, the friends, the loved ones, you were in such hardcore survival mode it was like it practically happened to someone else. Just hurry to do what needs doing and stay alive another minute, another hour. Mourn later.

And we did. We reached safety and got trained up and came back out here to fight with weapons and backup and strategy, and between that tactical upgrade and the fact we were all far enough from home the zombies were probably no one we should recognize, it got easier for a good long while. But the more people the city rejected, the more the outcast camps in the area grew, and the stronger and angrier they got.

I hate killing. I want out so goddamn bad sometimes. But there is no out. Just more and more until they're all dead or I am. There's this chilly, brittle piece of me that crunches like the ground where some poor fucker got melted down. It says, *Fuck it, then, let's go kill them all. Let's go as hard as we need to go to end this fucking thing. If we kill them, maybe we can rest. Kill them all at once and settle in to see what healing feels like when you can just do it and trust that it's the end of adding to the pain.*

A rustling beyond the tree line off to our left. In my HUD, I can see the whole squad freeze in response, waiting for me to identify the source of the noise. They're probably worried I missed something, let someone sneak up on us. Hell, under the circumstances, I'm a little worried myself, but no. It's not humanoid.

"No stress," I tell the team in a quiet voice that carries just fine on the still winter air. "Just a deer."

Samantha takes a few steps toward the tree line. She's still behind me as far as it goes, but on my HUD, I can see she's raising her weapon to 45 degrees.

"What the fuck are you doing?" The words come out in a commanding tone that says, *don't you move another inch*. It doesn't even feel like my voice. I may not have much to say on duty as a rule, but I rarely lose my chill under any circumstances.

"What? Venison sounds like a nice change of pace."

"No. Weapons down, stay in formation."

I turn toward her. I can see her no matter what, and she still can't actually see me, but I want her to feel like she's being glared at. I want her to back the fuck off this notion.

She cocks her hip and looks sullen. "Why not?"

I take a breath to put my thoughts in order. Truth is, there are several reasons I can give, and none of them's the truth of why it bugs me so goddamn much, but here goes.

"You gonna to try to drag that thing back? Hope no one *and nothing* comes at us while your hands are full—you and whichever teammate you talk into helping you, that is. While we're on the subject of things coming at us, just because I don't see anything in range this second doesn't mean there's nothing close enough to rush at us once you start making a racket. But most of all, *why fucking not* is I'm in command here and I told you not to."

She looks like she's itching to be insubordinate and see what happens. Finally, she settles for a resentful snipe, "You used to be fun, Demetri."

Just because I stopped being fun for you doesn't mean I stopped having fun. But that wouldn't help anything—not even my mood.

We hold position and I stare her down until she moves back to formation where she belongs. If I wanted to be petty, I'd call her a good girl and let her wonder whether she'd successfully goaded me into proving I remembered how to have fun.

But I don't want any part of her or her nonsense. I just want to get back to Stella safe and sound.

Anye clicks into the private channel for squad leader-Helmet chatter. "We cool? I almost chimed in, but I wasn't 100 percent if it would read as supporting or undermining, so I let it ride."

"Yeah, man, forget it."

"No, really, I—"

"I said forget it. I need to concentrate."

It's true. I always do. Today more than ever. Worrying about Stella is fucking me up just like Tom was over Nina. How many days like this will there be? How long can we keep her safe before they give up on her, and how will we know for sure when that time comes?

Tom probably booked it over from the east gate to be waiting for me at the top of Brewery Row like this. It's around shift change for those jobs too, so it's downright crowded here, which you don't see much anymore. As I approach, I slow down a tick. Much as I'm in a hurry, I'm also distracted by a question, a wistful idea, really.

"What do you think it would take to do a job like that instead? How injured is enough to retire but not too much to... you know, live."

"Demetri," Tom says hesitantly, like he thinks I'm on a ledge and need talking down, "did something happen today? Out there," he adds, in case I'm about to bite his head off when he knows the primary issue I'm sweating.

"Let's go," I say shortly, and we start walking. With so many people nearby, we maintain a reasonable stroll instead of the run I'd like to break into, so there's no real reason not to talk.

"We saw a deer out there. I had to stop someone on the squad from firing like a jackass."

"Hm. Yes, that could have been dangerous for you. But that's not the story, is it?"

Perceptive motherfucker. "No. It's not. I didn't want to watch something die if it didn't have to."

We walk in silence until I notice we're fully beyond the crowd, and I pick up my pace, not jogging, but as close to it as walking gets before it's conspicuous.

Tom gives me a smile and keeps up the pace without comment.

It's not quite full dark as we turn down the street the library's on. There's someone up ahead, leaning on a light post in the fading daylight, and when the light sputters on above, I see it's Monica.

Even before she turns and spots me, before that look forms on her face that's all sympathy and apology and regret, I know I was right. Stella underestimated her opponents. She got taken.

I run the last ten yards, Tom right on my heels, and Monica holds her hands up as if to try to slow me down, calm me down, as if that's even a possibility.

"Here's what I know," she says cautiously, then hesitates just long enough to be sure I'm going to let her talk. "Davy was right there watching, like we agreed. He said she was carrying some books from the desk to the stacks and the next thing, she hit the floor—"

"What!"

"He ran to her, but she was unconscious, no response. Still breathing, pulse seemed fine—"

"Oh, Davy's a goddamn doctor now?"

"Sarah Maxwell was there, and she summoned the medic—"

"Where is she? Where'd they take her?"

Monica hesitates, looking into my eyes, wishing she had a different answer to offer.

"Home."

Chapter Twenty-Five

War Room

Demetri

Home.

The word hangs in the chilly air longer than it takes the white puff of Monica's breath to fade. It's still ringing in my ears as I take off after Stella.

Monica's hand swipes at me as I go by, and then she and Tom both catch up beside me, trying to get in front of me, teaming up to slow me down.

"You cannot do this," she says, deadly serious. I'm not looking at her, but her eyes are so wide I can see the whites gleaming in my peripheral vision.

Tom's hand braces against my shoulder and he tries slowing down his pace while walking backwards in front of me. For a second I think about knocking him down.

That thought stops me dead, and he stumbles a little as his feet adjust to the unexpected change.

"Come back to the apartment. We've a lot to sort through. For now, we should at least get off the street."

I nod stiffly and let him lead me in the opposite direction of Old Illustris.

"Old Illustris," I mutter. "Fucking douchebags. The whole god-damn city's younger than we are. They call the richest part of rich-prick city 'Old Illustris' because it sounds classy or some shit."

"Just keep walking," Monica says. She sounds worried, like she thinks I'm on the verge of making a scene, or maybe turning and running for the snooty side of town after all, pounding on the door, demanding they give me back my girl.

We all take our boots off at the door. Tom and I set our helmets down, out of habit making sure to keep them separated so we don't mix them up, and then we make eye contact. His mouth curls up at one side as we both think about what we know from Stella: These things are basically interchangeable. A little extra padding in them to sit right on an individual's head maybe.

"She gave us a great deal of information," he says, clearly trying to help, and I wrestle with my impulse to snarl at him because I know he doesn't mean to sound like he's fucking eulogizing her.

My jaw clenches so hard I can hear the little squeak of my molars grinding, and I turn away.

Nina's gone off to see Maxwell, so we're just waiting to see what she comes back with. It's kind of a surprise when she comes back with the man himself. I've been leaning on the wall, too frenzied to sit, and when they walk through the door, I push off hard, propelling myself into a confrontation I'm not even sure is healthy. Nina's eyes flare, and one hand rises to waist level, not quite warning me off, more begging me not to make her wish she had.

"What the hell's happening to Stella? Everything you know, now. Did your wife sound the alarm so they could come get her the moment she showed her face?"

Nina's face withers in a look of *There he goes*. And yeah, there I go, try and stop me.

Maxwell, though, he just sets his jaw and stares me down. "Sandeaux, I don't know much more than you in this situation, but I can assure you Sarah knows far less. She's got fuck all to do with what happened today, and just this once, I'll ignore the dumbass implication to the contrary. Now have a seat and shut the hell up."

I don't know whether the look on my face is glaring or pouting, but I sit. That seems to give everyone else permission to sit, too. Maxwell grabs a chair and sets it dead in front of me so we're facing off. He's still staring me down like he's waiting for me to start up again. Tom sits to my right on the couch. Nina can't stand to be any farther from him than necessary but doesn't want to squeeze between us; she settles on the floor and wraps an arm around his calf, rests her cheek on his knee. My heart twinges. I'll get Stella back. We'll have our time.

Monica sits to my left, and her boys take the other dining chairs, not bothering to drag them closer like Maxwell did. I realize Davy probably feels like shit. Thinks I'm blaming him. I look over, make eye contact, try for something halfway to a smile. It's not even possible to smile, but I hope whatever I'm doing is enough to let him see we're okay. I don't know what happened, but I know it's not his fault.

"Stella's been in an awkward position for some time," Maxwell says, and it seems like he thinks he's telling me stuff I don't know about my own girl, so I interrupt.

"You mean because those uptight assholes are trying to fix her up with one of their kind. Yeah, I got that part."

"How long have you been aware of it?" Tom asks, and I almost bite his head off for what sounds like an insult to my intelligence, but when I turn, he's staring dead at Maxwell. Oh.

Intense silence as they stare each other down. And yeah, I agree this is a big fucking deal, Maxwell keeping this to himself if he's known what was closing in on her this whole time. But the tension is rising, and we need this fucker, however little we can maybe trust him.

"Doesn't matter now." The words are bitter as I choke them out. "Skip ahead to how we save Stella."

Davy's voice, plaintive and sorrowful, interjects, "I still don't understand what happened to her."

"I'm sure our friend from Command could explain it," Tom says acidly, "but I assume he's playing dumb because we're not meant to know what these implants they've given us can do."

Maxwell's tough; he barely twitches, but his glare at Tom is confirmation.

"So they what, they just... turned her off?" Monica asks, sounding like she'd give anything to unlearn this is a thing our leaders can do to any of us.

"Easy way to take her," Tom confirms. "It would have looked like a medical emergency. Their carrying her off would have been for her own good, nothing a person could have sensibly objected to." He nods to Davy in sympathy.

"Okay, that's how they got her, and we know why, because she's property as far as they're concerned and she wasn't cooperating. And we pretty much know where, the fucking Genneros'... but what do we do? How do we get her out?"

"We don't," Maxwell says.

Tom's hand shoots out to contain me in case I'm about to react, and I burn with rage, but I keep my mouth shut, for now. If Tom has something to say, I'll listen.

He sounds more hopeful than confident, though, which does nothing for my blood pressure.

"Nina? Was it a good day?"

"Yeah," Nina says uncomfortably, looking around at everyone who's now looking at her. "I know we were all getting impatient about how little useful info I could come up with. I was looking for answers without really knowing the question, and—"

"The question is 'who betrayed the Stronghold,'" Maxwell interrupts.

"No, that's the answer," Nina says. "The question is why." She pauses, wrinkles her brow, then plunges into her explanation. "I was overwhelmed with the big picture. I think we all were. We're so used to thinking of this in terms of survival. It's so terrifying to think of being stuck out there, or letting what's out there get in here. We're all equally motivated to preserve our sanctuary, right? How could anyone feel otherwise?"

"Exactly," Monica pipes up beside me. "It's madness."

"It is," Nina says softly. "Love is madness."

"You think an Illustrian somehow fell in love with a Devil Runner?" Manny's face is screwed up in the effort to take this idea at face value.

"No," Tom says darkly. "We think someone who is loved by an Illustrian became a Devil Runner. Theoretically, of course, he was encouraged to see himself as a spy."

He may have been responding to Manny, but Tom stares directly at Maxwell as he speaks. Maxwell's poker face is impressive, but he shifts a little in his chair.

"Was he the one who was lost not long ago?" Tom asks, still staring relentlessly at the Commander. "Do you suppose they killed him because they'd got enough use out of him and couldn't tolerate him any longer? I imagine Illustrians become tiresome when you're stuck interacting with them much. You would know what that's like."

Maxwell's eyes narrow slightly, but he keeps quiet.

Manny breaks the silence. "Sorry, I'm gonna need some of these gaps filled in. You're saying the so-called spies are, what, exactly?"

"Not sources of information, that's for sure," Tom replies. "At least, not in the city's favor. When they were rejected, these returning citizens who didn't quite pass muster, did you truly believe their loyalty to this place would be inexhaustible?"

Maxwell's lip curls, and he finally answers, "Not me. I had nothing to do with that decision. It was made above my head, and—"

"You just have to live with these things like a good soldier," Tom fills in smoothly. "I expect the change to the Rules of Engagement was the beginning of the end for our friend, the spy. When his captors—or comrades, as the case may have been, realized we were playing for keeps, they may have demanded he do something to address the situation. When he didn't, or couldn't affect the Stronghold's military in any way, they considered his usefulness at an end."

It's on the tip of my tongue to ask how he knows all this, but of course he doesn't. Some he knows, some he's just guessing, and it's just because Tom's so good at talking that I forget for a moment there's a difference.

Maxwell dials down the glare as he turns from Tom to Nina and asks, "So you were able to use this theory to narrow down our suspects, then?"

She purses her lips. "Davy's idea was good. I tested it on goofy shit at first, just to see if it set off any alarms. I figured if they caught me running random searches on how many people in Illustris had pool tables, worst they'd do is fire me. Nothing happened. So I had a good tactic, but I still needed a strategy."

"You needed the question," I say, proud again to think of Stella being the reason Nina made a breakthrough.

"The question: What Illustris citizens have been to quarantine? It was a longer list than you might think—"

"Because of people like me," Maxwell snarls. "People who fought for this place in the early days."

"Right," she nods. "So we needed a way to narrow it down. And the other day, Tom came home with some names."

"What, that Amelia or whoever?" I look at Tom for confirmation.

"Delia. Delia Morton."

There's a little *humph* from Maxwell. We all turn to see him looking thoughtful, maybe impressed.

"Good work. My people will take it from here." He starts to stand, but Tom is on his feet in an instant and blocks his path.

"Like hell. This clearly isn't the whole story. One woman hasn't done all this. Don't you even want to know how I got the name? Her co-conspirators were heard discussing her. You've got a much bigger problem on your hands than one bitter woman whose husband was refused readmittance to the city. And before you can take any action against her, we all deserve action on certain other fronts. Stella, for one. But more specifically under your purview, there is the matter of treachery among the corps. We brought you evidence of suspicious activities on at least one squad, and you've allowed us all to continue serving alongside them."

"Allowed," Maxwell repeats ominously. "That's right. Because I'm in charge. You don't make demands of me, and you damn sure don't issue orders. I'm the Commander here."

"You're no safer than any of us if the higher-ups decide you've lost your usefulness. Or if the ranks of your resistance break," Tom answers just as low and dark. He's a few inches shorter and way less broad than Maxwell, and it's taking all my restraint not to leap off the couch like I'm backing him up, but somehow I know that would undermine him. He doesn't need reinforcements right now.

Was it really just hours ago Anye was semi-apologizing for not jumping in to support my authority? I didn't understand at the time, but it was the right call.

They just stand there locked in, staring each other down like alley cats before a scuffle.

Without breaking the staring contest, Maxwell addresses us all. "Your instincts were good about looking for secondary anomalies in the rotation. The problem is trying to narrow anything to Kelly's or Luther's teams, because they didn't *have* teams."

Davy sighs, "That's what I said."

"They were teammates, and they got split up and promoted since. Maybe as a reward, maybe to make the patterns harder to catch moving forward, maybe to recruit more turncoats and double their opportunities. During the Cooper glitch, there were several unusually frequent pairings that failed to stand out in comparison, and some have continued after without drawing attention. And if the goal of breaking up the team was to make it harder to catch onto a pattern, it worked. We've narrowed it down to two Helmets whose patrol assignments fall outside the statistically likely patterns a random rotation algorithm should result in."

"Who?" Monica demands.

He gives her a look like *nice try*. "No thanks. Think I'll give up the entire operation because you can't control your suspicious attitude around 'em?"

"Well, what's being done about it?" Davy asks.

"Nothing, so far. We were in a holding pattern until we had something bigger. Nina, you've just given us something bigger."

"So what's *going* to be done about it?" Davy clarifies, and Maxwell finally turns to look in his direction.

"*Nothing*," he says again, more fiercely. "We start with the big problem. There's no safe way to deal with the minor players until we've got the major ones where we want them."

"Which you won't be doing without us," Tom insists.

"What's your problem, anyway," Maxwell spits. "I thought you wanted Nina's involvement to be minimal. I'm offering to take what she's given me and go."

"Things have changed. I know how at risk we are in ways I was rather blissfully unaware of before. And you haven't addressed the other situation at hand."

"Stella," I clarify in case he's forgotten, getting to my feet at last. I'm less broad than Tom, so nowhere near as broad as Maxwell, but I make sure to stand every inch of my 6'2" so I can enjoy that tiny height advantage at least. All glower, no slouch. My dad used to bitch about the slouching, which probably made me slouch a little harder, I admit. *Your boy growed up.*

When Maxwell looks me in the eye, though, he seems vaguely apologetic. "I can't help you, son. It's nothing to do with the military. Far outside my reach."

"You knew it was coming," Tom says again.

"That's a hell of a lot different from knowing how to stop it. Much less reverse it now that it's done."

"It's not done," I interrupt. "She just disappeared. Whatever they're planning, this is just the first step. We can still get her out of it."

"Maybe you could," he says sadly. "But you won't."

"What—"

He cuts me off before I can even get started. "You have no leverage, no ammunition. You can show up at their door begging for mercy, but they'll never show it. All you know that could possibly be of value to them is what we're doing here, and you can't use that for anything, not without getting every one of us killed. Your friends all winding up dead for just the chance at living happily ever after with your girl?"

"But if we make our move," I say, desperately clinging to hope, "we bring down the bad guy, we—we make our demands—"

"Yeah, kid," he agrees, and he looks sad but not unsympathetic. "If we can get this thing done right and avoid getting ourselves killed in the process, maybe that gains you some kind of edge. But for now, I need to know you're standing down."

I nod in resignation, and he glares again at Tom.

"I'll be sure to keep you informed of your next moves," he says, the edge back in his voice, determined to make clear to everyone present that this is a Commander we're dealing with, and he's the only one giving orders. As if that'll make us forget how Tom just forced his hand.

After the door clicks shut behind him, there's a long, awkward silence, broken by Nina.

"It's hard not to kind of empathize with the traitor... a little."

I turn in confusion, and Tom takes her hand. "I know," he says. "But it doesn't matter."

Monica says, "But if they're powerful enough to have done all this, they're part of the Stronghold power structure. Fighting it successfully and not getting caught—till now—maybe we should be trying to make them our allies instead of bringing them down? The enemy of our enemy?"

Tom shakes his head briskly. "That we can understand why they have been desperate enough to do as they've done is irrelevant. This is an incredibly small splinter faction off the powers of the Stronghold—it would be foolish to hope they could be enough to bring down the rest. The safer course of action is to use this knowledge to align ourselves with the true power and improve our position."

"Obviously, you're right," says Nina. "I just can't help thinking, you'd choose me if it came to that."

"I did. I would. I would let an entire army stand alone, fend for themselves without my assistance or cooperation, in favor of protecting you. But I wouldn't cold-bloodedly send a team into a slaughter. That's what we're talking about, remember. And while we're at it, remember that it was not targeted. It might have been your team that day. Or mine."

She makes a strangled kind of sob and buries her face in his chest, clutching his shoulders, and when he closes his arms around her, I swear the whole room relaxes with her.

Monica, Manny, and Davy are getting ready to head back to the barracks, but Tom asks me to stick around. If he's willing to put off taking his wife to bed after the scene they just made, it must be pretty big stuff. Not that I mind. What the fuck was I going to do with all this impotent fucking rage anyway? Might as well see what he's got on his mind.

On their way out the door, Davy turns to me again with the angsty eyes.

"Forget it, man. Nothing you coulda done." I give him a pat on the shoulder, the best I can do at the moment for comfort.

Nina's headed upstairs so we can talk alone, but I call after her, "Hey, um, good job. I feel like no one gave you props or whatever. That was pretty clutch, though."

Her eyes shine as she looks back at me from the landing, grateful for the olive branch. "Thanks, Demetri. Stella's brilliant, you know. She may not be a fighter the same way we are, but she's not helpless."

When she's been out of sight long enough to probably be out of earshot too, I turn back toward Tom.

He looks like he's got indigestion or his drawers got shrunk in the wash. I don't even wanna know how I look. Worrying about Stella feels like it's aged me ten years overnight.

"What is it, man?"

He grimaces, looking like he's hesitating before a jump.

"Something Stella said. About the implants."

"You know something more about what they did to her?"

"No. Well, yes, but not... not today. I'd never have brought it up, I'd have lived with it forever, but now that I've had to acknowledge the fact of the implants at all—"

"You said you'd keep her secrets. That was the whole point."

"Yes," he agrees miserably. I watch him chew on it, whatever bitter secret he's having a hard time swallowing, and I feel bad.

"Okay. Say what you gotta say." I can't even muster the energy to make it sound like I care. I mean, I do care, but also, this better be good.

So we sit back, and he tells me there's a chance, based on some of the stuff Stella's ex was working on, that the implants we've all got are juicing our hormones to make us extra horny or some shit.

"Okay, so?" I interrupt. Even if it's true, does it matter?

His eyes cloud over. He's feeling alone and in pain, and I'm his best friend. Shit. My head clears a little bit, and I want to be here for him like he's been here for me. I look at him straight, shove the angst down just enough to really focus.

"Sorry, man. I'm listening."

"I can't help feeling this... not doubt, I don't mean to say that—"

I've never seen him uncertain like this. It's unsettling. He's supposed to be so solid. Maybe it's not fair of me, expecting that of him.

"—but what if it explains the way Nina pursued me? Was this the true cause of the best thing that ever happened to me? Artificial stimulants?"

"Oh man, fuck yourself."

"Excuse me?" His upper lip twitches.

"Yeah, excuse you. You're sitting here feeling sorry for yourself when you should be fucking grateful."

Now I've offended him. Good. What I want to do is smack him upside his stupid, too-smart-for-his-own-good, can't-get-out-of-his-own-goddamn-way head.

"Grateful—" he starts winding up, but I won't let him.

"Yes, goddamn it, grateful. How many times have you razzed me about how I didn't nail your girl? You already knew she was living like a damn nun in here until you showed up and she went apeshit. So now you think there's a chance she wasn't resisting basic urges but biological goddamn warfare designed to make her wanna get fucked! Do you even hear yourself? If—*if* it's true, it's just more impressive she managed not to be all girls-gone-wild until you came along and flipped her switch. So shut the fuck up and enjoy being a lucky fucking asshole."

He looks half grateful, half embarrassed to have bugged me with this bullshit, so my little speech landed as intended. Of course, that makes me feel like a little bit of an asshole myself.

"Thank you for putting me in my place, Demetri. I was being selfish, asking you to entertain my petty feelings at a time like this."

"Feelings are feelings. Petty doesn't stop us from feeling 'em. Actually, thanks for bringing this up, because I need you focused."

"We'll get her back," he says simply, but he can't act for shit, so I know he doesn't have a clue how we're supposed to accomplish that. I miss the distraction of my brief anger when the hopelessness hits again, deep in my gut.

"How? We don't know what happened to her. We don't even know how to prevent the shitbirds who run this place from flipping some kinda switch to shut us all down the moment they realize we're not following orders. We don't know who to trust except Maxwell and whoever Maxwell says, and that would be something if you fucking trusted Maxwell!"

"I almost do," he says apologetically. "It's hard for me. There's something false about him, and I'm never quite sure I've got my finger on it. But I've often had that reaction to people throughout my life, particularly those in power or seeking to be. And that's the problem, isn't it? Anyone who wants to lead is not entirely to be trusted, because that drive seems to require one to engage in duplicity. He has to swallow his pride among the Illustrians who deigned to elevate him to his current position, let them believe he still respects the order they wish to maintain, still appreciates his place and wouldn't take action against them. Meanwhile, he clearly enjoys the status he's acquired, and I know he's got no intention of sacrificing his gains in the name of egalitarianism."

Tom goes quiet and stares at the wall a moment. He's either about to reassure me or scare the shit out of me, isn't he? Whatever epiphany his big brain is reaching, I almost don't wanna know.

"That's why I can't trust him. Not ever. He must have a kill switch of sorts in place. A way to end our endeavors without implicating himself if he senses failure is imminent. Perhaps he plays it as a private investigation he's been running to root out dissidents among the populace, turns us all in. For that matter, how can we know that hasn't been his true plan from the start?"

My head falls into my hands. My eyes slip shut. I wish I could wake up and be holding Stella. I'd make love to her and maybe I could forget about this shitty dream by the time I made her come.

"I've always known he would call the whole thing off if there were the slightest chance it would bring harm to his family, but it's worse than that. He's a Commander deploying resources toward a strategic goal, yes, but his starting position isn't unacceptable to him. He'd wipe the board to preserve what he has. Therefore, he has a means to do so."

"Tom, I can't deal with more questions right now. You're telling me we're a false step or a sudden betrayal away from being exiled into the wasteland to die. I can't take it, man. I just want Stella back."

He puts a hand on mine and says gravely, "Then trust that she wants the same, and that she's likely in a better position to affect her fate than we are right now. She's proven herself resourceful in the past, and she knows this place. It's not all up to you to rescue her."

Another of Stella's books comes to me, and I say with quiet resignation, "But that's what heroes do."

Chapter Twenty-Six

Justifications

Stella

For a moment, it seems that Stella wakes into the world of her dream. Has it all been a dream, then? How much? The dark times with Greg—could she be awakening on her first morning in Illustris from a vivid and terrible nightmare? It would make more sense, wouldn't it, than the world being overrun by zombies... but it wasn't all nightmare. Even in the haze as her consciousness knocks at the door of her mind, Stella would mourn a mere dream of Demetri more than she ever mourned her false image of Greg.

But how had she come to be here again... she blinks, swallows, tests a gentle clearing of her throat, looks around. Sitting up carefully, she notes a tenderness in her left hip and lower back, as if she'd taken a fall and landed badly. She gently stretches her limbs in front of her, one at a time, wiggles her fingers, flexes her toes. There's a bit of pain in a few places, but everything still works.

And this is undeniably real. My mind clears, somewhat reluctantly. Why am I here?

It was foolish to hope they'd accept defeat. Yet in my wishful longing, I had just about convinced myself they'd see the choice as killing me or letting me go; they would see that they couldn't force me to live their way, and they'd decide either to be rid of me altogether or let me fulfill my basic function as they see it, but with the man of my choosing rather than one of their kind. It almost made mathematical sense to me, trying to see it from their perspective and imagining they would rather have another woman having babies within their city walls than throw me away as a failed experiment.

Yet here I am, back under the Genneros' thumb. For whatever reason, they can't bring themselves to let me go.

I slide to the edge of the bed and test my equilibrium, gently lowering my feet to the floor and leaning upright just enough to know my legs will hold me before committing. The twinge in my left hip feels deeper than a bruise. Could be nerve pain or a joint thrown out of alignment. The price of defiance.

Though I know the door will be locked, I still make the effort to cross the room and test the handle. Having confirmed my imprisonment, I survey the space in a kind of wonder, marveling at how a place I lived for so many months can feel this foreign after two nights with Demetri.

My lungs feel heavy, flooded, like the tears building up inside have raised the humidity.

I don't know if I'll see him again. I don't know what kind of danger I'm in, exactly. But if they know about him, then he's in danger. Not just because of me but because paying attention to him could lead the Council directly to the resistance building under their noses.

Having an affair with me is a sin that could be forgiven, I'm sure. He's just a man who slept with a willing woman. That's not worth discarding a soldier, let alone a Helmet. But if they look too closely at him, at his friends... a lot of good people could lose their lives, including Demetri.

An interminable day drags out as I wait for any hint of what might become of me. I contemplate showering but can't bear to make myself quite so vulnerable, so I settle for simply changing into clean clothes. By sundown, I begin to suspect they intend to weaken my will with hunger. They may not even realize how little I've eaten in the last two days already, let alone that I expected lunch to be my first meal today. The rumbling of my stomach becomes a spiteful roil as my body declines to acknowledge my mind's continued belief that everything I've done was the right choice. Our bodies are masters of betrayal in so many ways, I reflect, staring at the bed where Greg used my procreative instinct to control me for a time. I'm certain I could no longer be affected emotionally, but physically... The idea of being compelled to accept the ersatz version of what I've now felt for real, with Demetri, is crushing.

Would they even try? Or might someone feel I deserved to suffer in perpetuity for the sin of trying to escape my fate? I think of the parade of suitors, the blatant staring at my chest, Judah Basher's indecent proposal, *seduce me*....

My thoughts are interrupted by the rattle and clink of a key at last. I whirl to face my captors, wishing I looked strong and confident, knowing I look merely what I am: trapped.

Roger steps in carrying a plate, looking vaguely awkward. Not apologetic, exactly, nor concerned, more as if he would rather not have to be dealing with this unpleasantness. It's being imposed on him, and I'm struck with the fascinating certainty that he doesn't entirely blame me for it.

He sets the plate down on the dresser and clears his throat. "I'm sorry it came to this."

"Came to what, exactly?" I say carefully, quietly, avoiding any impulse to be confrontational.

A slight grimace. He shifts his feet as if quashing an urge to flee this conversation altogether.

"You need to eat. I'm sure Celeste can explain—"

"And you can't?" I demand, dropping the attempt at demureness.

The implied insult rankles him as much as I would have predicted, but it doesn't inspire him to prove me wrong, it just makes him more comfortable abandoning me to my fate.

"Eat. She'll be in after a bit."

I carry the plate back to the bed, no longer feeling as desperate to soothe my undeniable, aching hunger. Celeste's in charge here. She's been in charge all along when it came to me, hasn't she? I'm her primary sphere of influence, perhaps. Does controlling my fate make her feel better about not controlling her own? Am I the indulgence bestowed on her by Roger, the toy that keeps her occupied? Is Celeste no more than a vicious Siamese who tolerates her bipedal overlords while amusing herself with a catnip mouse?

It's perfectly fine food, of course, but they've served it to me cold. Congealed noodles in a pasty white sauce that would have been palatable, perhaps delicious, twenty minutes ago. Insult to injury, I suppose. *This is what your little escapade has earned you.*

Will Celeste's voice ever be gone from my head? No matter what happens here, will she always haunt me?

I again fill the little cup in the bathroom with water from the tap and wash down the last bite of cold pasta as the door clicks open once more. It's almost impressive how Celeste managed to come in at just the right time to catch me in the bathroom—even just to get a drink, but still, it's forced me into a feeling of being caught off guard; there's a strange aura of embarrassment to being found in your bathroom with the door open.

She fixes me with her cold, assessing glare and speaks without emotion.

"At long last, you'll be out of my house by tomorrow. One way or another."

I was! Rage pierces my fear and confusion, putting steel behind my words. "If you wanted me out of your house, dragging me back here and locking me in was a strange choice, Celeste."

"Choice?" she hisses. "I tried to give you a choice. I gave you every opportunity to make the smart choice. And instead, you left me *no* choice. You'll need to be married immediately in case your little alley-cat adventure left you with child."

Demetri asked if it was okay to come inside me, and I didn't even think of it that way. I assumed my implant was set to some kind of a default after Greg's death, and why would that not include birth control? For an unmarried woman, just in case?

My heart thuds as I process the information. She's successfully unbalanced me again, damn her. "I thought... I assumed I was on a default—"

"Illustris default. Not military default. Women on active duty can't get pregnant. You very much can."

"I'm surprised you trusted me that much," I mumble bitterly.

"Until quite recently, you were predictable enough that trust didn't enter into the equation. I knew where you were, and I received frequent confirmation that you were the furthest thing from a merry widow it was possible to be. Far too broken to surprise anyone."

Too broken. Something dances at the back of my mind.

"When you started perking up a bit, I tried to move you quickly into your next phase of life. Not quickly enough, I suppose. Well, you met a handsome young man, and you gave in to temptation. May the memory sustain you. And may any child you conceive favor you strongly enough to keep rumors at bay."

"No," I say, helpless, blinking in disbelief as the weight threatens to crush me from all sides, the flashes of red around my eyes as if my field of vision is filling with my pounding pulse. "No, I—"

Crack. The harsh sound of her slap offends my ears before the prickling pain response begins in my cheek. My vision clears as my eyes widen in shock, staring hard at this awful woman who has been given dominion over me.

Why? Why is she my jailor? Why did she care about my disposition or giving me a choice at all... "Far too broken," *she said....*

"When Greg brought me here, you hated me from the start. It seemed like you didn't think I was good enough for him, but that's not it. People talk, you know." Judah's words come back to me. "Your son was cruel. He hurt women. He would never have married at his level in this place, this closed environment where everyone knew what he was. No amount of wealth or breeding would have been enough for a woman with forewarning and a choice. Were you relieved, in a way? Did you think you'd never have to watch the way he treated a wife? Or children?"

Her hand moves as if to strike me again, but I grab her wrist mid-swing.

"If he'd just gone out in the world and had dalliances, you'd never have had to think about it. He wasn't supposed to bring home a wife. Move into your home. Give you a front row seat to be confronted every day with the fact that you'd raised a man like him. Your failure. Right?"

She's white with rage, and her bony wrist wrenches free of my grip as I realize I can't hold on without hurting her. But instead of trying to hit me again, she takes a step back, quaking.

"All this time, I thought this whole mourning period was out of respect for your son. You just couldn't let anyone get close while I was *far too broken,* because you feared it would be obvious why. I expect you spent years characterizing his misdeeds as youthful, hormonally driven transgressions, and declaring that he'd grown into a wonderful man. You needed me healthy and strong before you whored me out so no one would see what a pathetic liar you are."

"Enough!" she seethes, her jaw trembling, her eyes fierce with unshed tears I don't for a moment dare to hope presage any degree of mercy.

"Judah Basher," I say suddenly. "I know I've lost. I know you'd rather see me dead than free... I'll fight anyone else you try to give me to. Tell Judah I'll... do what he asked."

Her lip curls vengefully as she delivers her parting blow. "Whatever he asked for, you deserve it."

I let her see me crumple as she leaves the room. As soon as the door clicks shut, I stand, smooth my dress, and go to splash cool water on my face to soothe the sting of her slap.

This gamble I've just made might be the end of me. But if I'm right, if the burst of intuition I had about Judah pays off, it's my only shot at freedom.

I'm unsurprised by Judah's arrival not long after. He's curious. Intrigued. And if I'm right, perhaps a little unsettled.

He walks in looking smooth, confident, ready to let me show him what I've got.

"I hear you asked for me. What a flattering invitation. Not to mention scandalous. Your late fiancé's bed is quite a location for a seduction."

He plants himself in front of me. Sitting on the bed, I'm positioned perfectly to unbuckle his pants if I were so inclined, and I suspect that's what he's testing to see if I'll do. I'm almost curious how far he'd let me go. Not nearly curious enough to try it, of course.

"I have a theory about you. That invitation to seduce you, you weren't just toying with me, though I admit that was my initial assumption. You certainly didn't think I would follow through, or even want me to." Swallowing hard, I press ahead with my big gamble. "You don't like the idea of a woman who's unwilling, un-wanting. It's not merely that you wouldn't want that in your own bed, either; you're uncomfortable with this whole arrangement. You didn't expect me to seduce you... you were letting yourself off the hook for whatever might happen next, giving yourself a way to believe that whoever I wound up with, it was someone I'd followed your advice to make a play for. But that's not true. It's not going to be true. I'm telling you that so you'll know absolutely that I'm not willing and nowhere near wanting. I don't think you can live with standing by and letting that happen when you can't pretend not to know."

Truly, I'm nowhere near as confident as I'm trying to seem about this interpretation. But there is another factor I hope will work in my favor: Men who perceive themselves as decent tend to want to live up to noble ideals when confronted with them directly, as long as it doesn't cost them too much. He called Greg a menace. He thinks of himself as a good guy, if only by comparison. Now to convince him there's an upside here.

"I can help you. I have information on a movement happening right under the Council's noses, undermining the Stronghold's security, endangering its future. If you let me get offered up, I'll never speak a word of this to anyone. I'll bite my own tongue bloody if you try to question me. If this place is my prison, I won't care if it's overrun. I'll let it fall."

Judah's eyes blaze with anger. In a flash, he's shoving me against the wall, one hand pinning me there by the roots of my hair, the other cradling my collarbone as if in preparation to grasp me by the throat.

His voice is low and brittle. "You still think I care if you're willing? Wanting?"

Forcing myself to remain calm, wishing I could control the speed of my heartbeat so he wouldn't see it fluttering like this, I refuse to wilt.

"Yes, actually. I do. I can see I've made you angry, but that doesn't change who you are," I lie optimistically.

His head inclines as if he might be about to ram me, and I can't help tensing up, but no, he's just looking down to look away. His fingers in my hair flex, pulling harder, and I hold my posture stiff in an effort to mitigate the pain.

"You're coming out of here with me," he says finally. "They'll start drawing up the marriage papers, but you're going to tell me everything you know. If your information is as good as you seem to think it is, maybe those papers never get signed and processed." He lifts his head and looks me in the eyes, his expression icy, his hand at my collarbone gliding down my chest. "If you've overplayed your hand, I guess we'll find out whether I care what you want."

When he releases me, relief floods my muscles now that my hair is no longer in danger of being torn out at the root. He's trying to scare me, that's all. I don't know it, but I do have cause to hope it, because his hand just now may have danced from my throat to the top of my dress, but it didn't go farther. He wanted to intimidate me, maybe punish me for manipulating him, but he could have chosen to hurt me, and he didn't.

Chapter Twenty-Seven

Maneuvers

Stella

My heart flutters as I walk into Judah's home once again. It's strangely reminiscent of walking into the Gennero mansion for the first time: the flutter of a bride, nervous yet excited. That girl is long gone. The woman I am now is both sadder and stronger, and far more reckless.

It probably seemed like I knew what I was doing last night in Greg's old bedroom. I played a weak hand, but I played it with an air of strength. I got Judah to cosign my wild swing, and then I spent the rest of the night wrestling with it in my mind, knowing he'd be back to collect me in the morning and I'd have to make good on my promise... or accept the consequences.

I'm led into a little room Celeste might describe as a study (unless I described it that way first, in which case it would no doubt become a sitting room or a parlor). The door closes behind me as I stand there assessing the space, so I guess this is my new prison for the time being.

It's just starting to look light outside when the door opens. I whirl to see cozy-mysteries Marie. She's brought me breakfast, not that she looks happy about it. I wonder if she's discontented enough to have sullied my food.

"Thank you," I say quietly. Then, as she turns to go, an idea strikes. "Marie, I wonder if you would deliver a message for me? To someone at the library."

She looks back at me resentfully, yet resigned, accepting that I have come to replace her. Likely she expected as much, but it hardly motivates her to do me favors.

"I get the feeling you'd rather I weren't here," I say carefully, staring hard, watching for any microexpression of confirmation. One corner of her mouth twitches in what I read as *If only*. "I don't want to be here either. I'd rather be there. My library. If they take it away from me like this because they've decided it's time for me to be a wife and mother... I don't mean to disparage those pursuits, certainly, but you must have seen how much I loved being there every day."

"You never seemed to be anywhere else," she murmurs, coming around. "Until recently."

"Exactly. They were pushing me out, and this must be why. If you would just tell Sarah Maxwell—you've seen her there lately, haven't you? Do you know which one I mean—graying red hair, seems to look worried all the time, likes flower print dresses—"

"Yeah. I know who you mean."

The sullen edge to her voice might be about me, the request I've made, some opinion of Sarah Maxwell, none of the above, or all three. It gives me pause, but I've come this far, and I don't have much choice but to plow ahead.

"Tell her... her husband needs to answer for his actions. Directly to your boss. Tonight, here—shit, she might not be there—I don't—"

"It's okay, I know where they live."

She looks more intrigued than irritated now. If nothing else, I've aroused her curiosity. Well, I knew this about Marie: She loves a mystery.

Staring openly at me, her expression unreadable, she repeats as if tasting the words, "Her husband needs to answer for his actions."

My heart pounds in an unsteady rhythm.

"Obviously, I mean pushing me out of the library," I say unconvincingly.

She nods, unconvinced.

"But let's leave it vague to light a fire under him," I add.

Her jaw sets firmly, and she nods once more before departing, closing the door again behind her.

I collapse into the nearest chair and let my panicked, heaving breaths take over, grateful I was able to hold myself steady for so long. Of course, Marie was practice. Before long, I'll have to face Judah.

He's not that bad, I reassure myself once more. Marie's feelings for him are evidence of that. I haven't walked into a lion's den... or if I have, at least I know this lion isn't starved for a meal. He might play with his food a little, but I have to believe he'll still let me go in the end.

The move happened early in the morning, likely to avoid unnecessary attention. Other than Marie bringing me breakfast and giving me the chance to coax her, I hope, into assisting me with this desperate play, I've been left to stew.

Never before have I had a reason to regret liberating all the books from these houses. There is truly nothing to do here but think, and I'm already wrung out and exhausted from thinking. I'd like to try to sleep, but the situation being what it is, I'm buzzing as if coffee were still a seemingly inexhaustible resource. I find myself trying to fidget with Greg's ring out of habit, but it's gone. Finally. Celeste sent someone in with a bit of grease to help reclaim it before handing me off.

As the hours drag out, I grow more and more irritated that Judah's leaving me shut in like this the same way Celeste did yesterday. By the time the door opens again, I'm worn down to my last nerve.

"Is this the kind of life I'd have if I did marry you? Locked up and left to go mad in an empty room?"

Judah blinks in confusion. It's the first time in our limited acquaintance that he's ever looked like he wasn't in control, planning out every move. Even yesterday in my old room, as surprised as I know he was by my proposition, he seemed ready to use that surprise as fuel.

He quickly regains his smugness as he assesses my outburst and demonstrates the cause of his momentary confusion: He pushes the door open further, holds his hands like a magician saying *nothing up my sleeve, folks!*, then ostentatiously turns the doorknob.

Oh. He didn't have to use a key to enter. The door was merely closed, never locked. I've remained shut in here only because I never tried to leave.

"Point taken," I say, my shoulders slumping as my indignation whooshes out like a stopper's been pulled.

He saunters in and takes a seat, gesturing to me to do the same. "Since you're so at home here, this is as good a place as any for you to show me what you've got. I considered making you come to my bedroom, but there'll be plenty of time for that after I call your bluff. And that was a good idea; maybe I will lock you in."

My eyes narrow. I stiffly move toward the other chair, but he clicks his tongue against the roof of his mouth as if correcting a dog. When my head swivels automatically toward the sound, he's gesturing to his lap. Gritting my teeth, I perch on his left knee. In a flash, his arm encircles my hips and drags me close.

"I've had all night to ponder it," he continues, staring at me like a meal. "Maybe you underestimate my interest in something new." His arms pulse to pull me more snugly to him for a moment as if testing the way my flesh gives under pressure. "Your curves have been taunting us all for some time, you know. There are some men out there feeling bitterly jealous of me, no doubt, now that the rumor is spreading that I've claimed you. Should I even consider throwing you back before I've had a chance to sample the goods?" His left arm continues to hold me possessively as his right hand glides up my outer thigh, one fingertip slipping into the top of my stocking.

I swallow against the thudding of my heart and try to resist the rising panic. I can't have miscalculated this badly. He's not a good man, but I truly don't think he's this bad. He's fucking with me, as Demetri might say. Albeit in a much less enjoyable way, from my perspective, not that Tom appeared to be enjoying it much that night. Yet they turned out the best of friends. I have to believe there's a good outcome here as well.

"You're playing with me. Or testing me. That's okay." I aim for unruffled in my tone, knowing the stiffness of my posture belies the façade.

"Is that so? You offered yourself up to me, walked right in my front door of your own accord. I don't have to let you go, no matter what happens."

The implication hits just the way he had to know it would, and I can't control my reaction: a sudden inhale, a look of alarm as I meet his eyes again.

"You're saying you might enforce this marriage agreement no matter what I tell you," I say breathlessly, my blood going cold.

"I haven't decided," he says coolly. "You're not wrong that I like a willing woman. But I don't mind a challenge. It's far more satisfying to bring your prey to ground than to shoot a sitting target in a gallery."

"You think you could make me want you?"

His hand on my thigh splays into an open-palmed grasp.

"I hope you're not relying on Greg's programming for that," I say coolly, daring to hope I've regained solid ground in this confrontation.

And there it is—the flash in his eyes: He didn't know I knew about that.

"I know a lot more than you might imagine, Judah. I was right there at Greg's side for so much of it. I'm not merely a bystander. I'm complicit. Ask Roger sometime. Ask why he came back the morning after a big debate with a useful compromise or a decisive plan. Ask whose *helpful* feedback shaped so many of the decisions in the making of this place. Ask him who named the Stronghold."

His comfortable smirk has faded, but he curls his lip to deliver a skeptical response. "You're saying Greg told you what he was testing out on you?"

I suddenly feel calmer and more confident than ever, hissing, "No, I'm saying *I figured it out*. I'm saying I'm smarter than they are. Am I significantly smarter than you as well, or are you paying attention now?"

Judah's expression flares, and he grabs my hips to turn me away from him, then pulls me back onto his lap hard. He's hard too, pressing against my bottom. His arms encircle me, adding continuous pressure to ensure I'm feeling the threat of it. Or the arousal, perhaps, if that really were his aim, and I've accepted that my read of him is questionable at best. I really don't know what I've gotten myself into, or whether I'll get out of it.

"A smart woman is even sexier, Stella. You feel me? Maybe I should have already flipped your switch so you'd be nice and wet for me. Still, I bet you're wet *enough*."

"It wouldn't work."

"I've read the reports. Hell, we all *heard* the report from your ex-fiancé's mouth. Bragging about how eager you were for him all the time, all day, all night, any time he was nearby, ready to be fucked."

My throat quakes, unable to form words even if my mind could provide them. My breath goes fast and shallow as I struggle to hold myself above the surge of panic.

He slides a hand between my knees and starts inching up my leg. "It's not just your pretty face or your big tits that had so many of us interested in such a difficult woman. From outside, not bred for this life. Still, I'm sure you're trainable."

Red at the corners of my vision. Lactic acid floods my muscles as I wrench to get free, surprising him enough to succeed. Regaining my feet, I face him and hurl the words angrily, "*Okay*, you've made your point. You want me off-balance. You want control of the situation. You're not afraid to play dirty. Most of all, you don't want me feeling like I've got one over on you. You've made your point," I say again, my steam fading after the pressure was released.

I step back, out of reach of a sudden lunge should he make one.

"It's good, actually, that you've let me know what the Council thinks of me. It's important you know I'm not deluding myself when I tell you what I want in exchange for my assistance."

"The exchange is your walking out of here a free woman," he sneers.

"No. A *Council* woman," I correct, hoping my face continues to cooperate with my ruse of calm confidence.

He starts to laugh at the ridiculousness of the notion.

"I'm serious, Judah. Your Council can't last as it stands now. It's already suffering challenges you didn't see coming. You're outnumbered by other factions, and even your own kind aren't fully behind you. It's going to have to evolve to survive. I'm a move in the right direction. Neither Illustris nor outsider, a woman young enough to be affected by the rules I'll be part of influencing—don't think no one's noticed the token female Council members are older. And I've been a huge part of building this place. I earned the right to be a part of its future. And to atone for my role in what it already is."

He leans back, regards me thoughtfully for a long moment, then stands. I fight my instinctive flinch and the desire to retreat as he moves within inches of me and grabs my hand.

"All right," he says easily, "if your revelations are so impressive... enough to destabilize the Council... I'll push to get you a seat at the table."

He pulls the back of my hand against himself, and I can feel the dampness of precum through his pants. My breath catches again as I fight for mastery over my instincts *fight-flee-seduce-weep.*

"But if your information doesn't get the results you want, you'll learn to deliver the results I want. I imagine you'll be begging me to turn Greg's programming back on before long."

"It won't work," I tell him again numbly.

"Bullshit," he dismisses assertively.

Tears flutter in my eyes, and I want to tell him it's not because he's beaten me or brought me down.

"After I figured out what Greg had done to me," I explain in a strained, wretched voice, "it lost its full effect. I still felt physical desire, still experienced the heightened sense of pleasure. That part, I expect, might still work again, even on someone who knows, even on someone who fights it. But the rest—the heady conflation of sex and love? That doesn't survive the illusion. You could make me enjoy being taken to your bed, but you could never make me happy about it."

He doesn't relinquish my hand, but he loosens the position so it's no longer pressing against him.

I feel emboldened to add, "Marie seems like she's happy about it. Do you really need the exertion of a hunt? The burden of a captive?"

He finally lets go and steps back. His eyes flare in suspicion.

"She didn't tell me," I say in answer to his unspoken question. "I've been to your home, remember? The night you challenged me to seduce you, supposedly lay your cards out? I saw her here serving you. I've seen the women in other homes lately, and Marie's different. She looks at you with affection, longing. The other women... they look businesslike and bored, if not outright hostile. Do you even know what you've allowed to happen here? Does the Council care?"

His lip curls in something like disdain. "Ask them yourself. Once you've dazzled me with your world-shattering intel, that is."

I choke back the emotions I hadn't intended to evoke, at least not in myself. It's frightening to see I've only made him angry in my attempt to make him feel concern, regret, or shame. How much about this man have I miscalculated? Is he merely adept at compartmentalization, or is he far colder than I dared to hope?

"Well?" he demands, a new chill in his affect. "Let's hear it then. The big secret that'll bring this place to its knees and get you everything you've ever wanted."

"I can't tell you."

The icy rage that instantly fills his eyes makes me take a quick step back.

"You think I trust you that much? After what I went through with Greg?" I improvise, my pulse erratic, my eyes wide with fear. "You think I'd do this without a witness, someone to hold you to your promises, make sure you didn't just sweep this treachery under the rug? I'm not a fool, Judah. I sent for someone."

"How, exactly, did you accomplish that, when you believed you were locked in this room all day?" His voice is low, his words deliberate, a restrained sound barely distinguishable from a growl.

"I asked Marie to do me a favor."

Judah closes the distance between us again and grips the back of my neck. "You're playing a dangerous game, Stella. If I have to break you in half to punish you for playing me, I will. And I'll make sure you can't help but enjoy being broken."

When he lets go and walks out, my limbic system floods again, and I can't hold myself upright any longer. I stagger backwards and find the wall so I can at least not hit the floor twice in a row.

The skin at the back of my neck burns as my nerves rebound from the punishing grip.

He's not a bad man. Just not a good one. He's flirting with cruelty. It's a game to him. Just an empty threat.

I don't know if I believe it, but I'm determined to keep lying to myself as long as it takes.

Chapter Twenty-Eight

Power Play

Stella

After leaning against the wall long enough for my panic attack to recede, I venture out of the room at last, daring to explore a little. It might be hours before anything comes of Marie's excursion on my behalf. Though I'm not at all sure I want to see Judah again so soon, it was claustrophobic in that room, not to mention crushingly dull. I poke around in the kitchen to find some rags, fill a small dish with water, and head to the piano room.

Very, very carefully, I dip the rags, squeeze them nearly dry again, and gently clean the piano keys. Each one takes several deliberate passes with a freshly rinsed and wrung cloth. The repetitive, simple task soothes me until I begin to feel like I can face Judah again when the time comes.

Marie appears in the open doorway from the hall. Looking flushed and agitated, jittery. My eyes widen in alarm—has something gone wrong? But as I stand, she steps into better light, revealing her condition in greater detail. She's not just flushed, she's rumpled. Her clothing, which looked fine this morning, is wrinkled. The skin around her mouth is red. He's taken out some of his aggression on her. My heart plummets, knowing I'm responsible for his bad mood and that I may have erred by bringing her up the way I did—by telling him I'd enlisted her to my cause.

"Are you all right?" I ask wretchedly.

She glares, takes a deep breath as if about to unload on me, then turns and storms back out of the room. I choke on my meaningless impulse toward apology and return to the piano. Dip, wring, dab, repeat.

A few keys later, Judah saunters in and comes to lean on the piano.

"What a waste of time," he observes. "No one plays the thing, and it's got to be out of tune."

"No reason not to care for it. In case someone, someday, sees its worth again."

We stare each other down for a long moment. His arch amusement cools until he's left just studying me.

"You're intriguing, Stella. I would have enjoyed being seduced by you."

"I'm sorry I involved Marie. I didn't think you would... punish her."

His voice darkens. "Is that what you think happened?"

My fist clenches, dripping a little gray water on my thigh and colliding with the keys to elicit a pathetic, dull note.

A knock on the front door breaks the excruciating silence, making us both flinch.

"The mystery guest. Oh, no, wait, no mystery at all. Marie coughed up the message before she choked on my cock," he brags.

My eyes fly open in terror; does that mean he preempted the message? Have I been outmaneuvered? Who's coming through the door, and to what end?

But Judah chuckles. "That's what you get for using her against me. Lucky for you, I'm still interested in what you've got planned."

Blinking back tears, I struggle to compose myself in time to face Maxwell and play this out.

The Commander steps in, looking murderous. When I sent Marie to deliver the implicit threat, I trusted the rumors of my engagement to convince him he had no choice but to show up. He knows I could destroy him, but we don't know each other at all. His wife and I have failed to bond, to say the least. He probably spent most of the afternoon trying to figure out if he could have me killed, and whether I'd already done irreversible damage to his cause. He might wonder if he's been summoned here to die.

"Maxwell," Judah says casually, "thanks for stopping by on such short notice." His playful smile implies full awareness of what's to come, yet somehow leaves equal room for friendly or fatal outcomes. I really have been playing on an amateur level against a master gamesman, haven't I?

Let's hope I have a strong enough hand.

"Commander," I say formally, "it's nice to meet you. I'm sorry about the circumstances, and I truly hope your wife wasn't alarmed by the mysterious nature of the invitation. She seems like a lovely woman, and I would hate to have upset her. Please sit down."

Glaring, he sits, his spine stiff. I take a seat across from him, and Judah irritates me by leaning against the side of my chair, his hand on my shoulder in a casually possessive gesture that makes me both rage and despair, thinking of Maxwell reporting it to Demetri as evidence that this betrothal is legitimate.

I take a deep breath and plunge in. "Certain people are often in a position to overhear private conversations. Invisible people, like librarians. And women. I'm sure you remember what it was like to be one of the little people."

He seethes but doesn't interrupt.

"There are those who consider the newly elevated Commanders unworthy of their place in the Stronghold. The way I see it, that makes us allies."

Suddenly less certain what I'm getting at, his eyes narrow.

"The enemy of my enemy, I mean to say. I don't know you, but as I said, your wife has made a favorable impression, so I chose you to reach out to with this opportunity to solidify your position. And to improve a lot of other people's."

Something in his eyes shifts as he begins to hope I haven't lured him into a trap.

"What 'chance' might that be, Mrs. Basher?"

I try not to react too fiercely but can't resist correcting him. "It's still *Ms. Vernon*, actually."

Judah squeezes my shoulders and teases, "Just pending the paperwork."

"Commander," I say, trying to infuse my expression with a plea to trust me and to convey to Demetri that there's some question regarding my intention to marry Judah Basher, "between what I've heard and what I've gathered from other little mice in front of whom important people seem to speak freely, there's an effort to weaken the Stronghold and strengthen the enemies beyond the walls. As a military leader, I'm confident you would never be a part of that, but even still, it wasn't until I heard how little these perpetrators think of you that I could be totally sure. Here are some of the details I've gathered: There's at least one scientist or tech involved in this conspiracy. I don't know a name, but it shouldn't be difficult to narrow down; he or she was injured and sent to quarantine, and they're concerned what could happen if their pet never returns or worse, is overcome with remorse and turns informant on them. Additionally, I'm sorry to tell you, they have at least one of your Helmets on their side and possibly some foot soldiers, conveying messages and smuggling supplies to the enemy."

Maxwell has settled a bit, understanding what I've done, and hopefully inferring the correct intent. I've presented the information as if it came from elsewhere, absolving him of knowing it without having reported on any of it. *Or depriving him of the achievement*, I realize with hollow dread.

"I expect you can act quickly on these tips and help us identify everyone involved," Judah says smoothly, happy to imply he was always in the know. "Naturally, we need to keep this ugliness quiet and avoid alerting anyone to the investigation before you have something to show for it. At that point, we'll bring you before the Council to report on which of our supposed peers is responsible for compromising our security."

Judah leans down and kisses me on the cheek. "Well done, sweetheart," he coos, clearly enjoying my quiet dismay.

Congratulations on the marriage. Maxwell's parting words robbed me of any hope he would reassure Demetri. I'm not sure if he believes I'm truly with Judah or he just sees a petty bit of revenge he can take on me for the position I've put him in today.

It's an enviable position, objectively speaking, I think, but he clearly had a plan, and I've derailed it for my own purposes.

"Coming to bed?" Judah's invitation is facetious, an ugly taunt. "I could have Marie change the sheets first, if that's what you're worried about," he stage-whispers.

As I whirl around, horrified that she could have heard his cruelty, he laughs.

"She goes home at night, Stella. I'm all yours." His mocking smirk brings out a fresh wave of anger on Marie's behalf.

"If you haven't learned anything today, perhaps you're a lost cause, and I've hitched my wagon to a dying horse."

"What should I have learned today, please enlighten me," he snarks.

"That we're always listening, always watching. Always looking for an opportunity to bring down those who mistreat us. That poor girl has been unfortunate enough to develop feelings for you, but a woman's affection is like an alchemical reaction. Falling for you turned some secret piece of her heart into gold, and that's a beautiful thing. But gold is malleable. The more you pound on it, the more dents and damage it takes, and there's only so much she can withstand before the gold reverts to lead. It's simple self-preservation. Trust me. I know."

I stare at him over burgeoning tears, willing them not to fall while he's watching.

His expression blank, robbed of playfulness, fury, even artifice, he enters his bedroom at last and closes the door between us. As I walk away to look for a suitable spare bedroom, my tears flow silently at last.

Chapter Twenty-Nine

Trust

Demetri

M onica looks at me with sympathy. Davy's hand twitches on his knee like he's fighting an impulse to reach out and offer me some kind of comfort. Manny's mouth is curled into a grimace of condolence.

"Oh, shit," I blurt in sudden realization. "You all think I'm sitting here all heartbroken or something."

"Well... yeah," Monica says, looking at me like she's not sure if I've been following the conversation, which, to be fair, I'm not always.

"No," I say, calmly shaking my head. When they just stare back at me like I'm delusional, I add, "I'm serious. It's all good. Stella's clearly got some kind of a plan."

"She's marrying an Illustrian," Monica gently corrects me, as if I must have missed that part.

"Yeah. Sure she is," I say dismissively.

"But—"

"No, I'm with Demetri," Nina interrupts. "There's no need for lengthy engagements in the Stronghold. Weddings are paperwork.

Done in an instant. There's something else going on here." She turns to lock eyes with me. "And I know how she feels about you."

I nod, grateful for the affirmation as much as the support.

Maxwell clears his throat. "Back to the matter at hand, then? Your ex put us in a difficult position."

"She's not my—"

"Sorry," he snarls, "your once-and-future girlfriend, whatever she is, and in case you hadn't noticed, your love life is pretty fucking far beneath my concern right now. She's put us on the Council's radar and forced our hand."

Tom turns an evaluating gaze on Maxwell. "I thought we were already feeling the time pressure thanks to our *friend* in quarantine. If anything, Stella's aided us greatly by providing plausible sources for the information, allowing your network to remain hidden."

Maxwell seethes in Tom's general direction, and Tom chuckles.

"Oh, I get it. She stole your thunder. You were looking forward to being the whistleblower whose horn brought down the walls, metaphorically speaking, of course. I suggest you nurse your wounded pride on your own time, *Commander*. It may not be the move you'd have chosen, but it's still a path to a win. For all of us."

"Including Stella," I add, in case anyone doubts for a second she's still my girl.

"We've got one name so far. It's not enough," Maxwell complains.

"How many do there need to be?" Davy objects. "We're acting like it has to be a big conspiracy, but what if it is just this one lady with her grudges and her heartbreak?"

"No," Tom says smoothly, "Stella was able to confirm at least two others, though not by name."

Manny pipes up, "Hey, how'd you know to start looking for a traitor in the first place?"

Maxwell doesn't even have time to answer before Tom fills in the blanks.

"Because the outsiders aren't dying off at the rate he expected they would. Twice in the time I've been here, he's assured Nina there was little cause for concern regarding the Devil Runners and indeed no hope for the Ark Angels or any other contingents that may arise. You were certain, were you not, that they would all be dead and gone by now."

"They should have been," the commander reluctantly agrees. "And yes, that's why I knew there was someone working against us. I had my suspicions, but then we lost an entire team... I never wanted to be sending people out to their deaths, dammit. We were supposed to have a clear advantage, and they were supposed to be doomed. They should have been struggling for basic goddamn survival! How the fuck did these people so much as get the lights on?"

Manny laughs, then explains, "It's hilarious you thought your *spies* would just accept being exiled to live in the wasteland."

"We thought," Maxwell booms, "they'd fucking die!"

"Because none of us would know them to take pity on them, right?" Monica reasons. "You must have had to hold them in quarantine longer than the norm, depending when they showed back up. Waiting until you had a fully staffed military of outsiders."

"But that would have given them plenty of time to realize something was wrong," Nina chimes in. "In quarantine, they're pretty straightforward about how this is going to work. Right from the beginning. Unless that wasn't always the case—"

"No, it was," Monica confirms.

"I've been here longer than any of you," I add, "and it was true when I came in as well."

"Okay," Nina continues, "so these former Illustrians were almost certainly assured at the gate they'd just have to wait a month in quarantine while the tests came back clearing them to enter the city. And then they fucking languished there for who knows how long—what do you want to bet some of them made contact with their loved ones during that time?"

"Some sympathetic tech or orderly," Davy suggests.

"Sympathetic or ambitious," Nina adds.

"It's entirely possible one or more of your spies was armed with valuable information or even laden with supplies from the moment they walked back out into the world," Tom concludes with mild amusement.

Maxwell nods, looking disheartened, and I suddenly know we haven't told him anything he hadn't already figured out. Maybe he's surprised we got there too.

Tom's gaze turns to scrutiny. "I expect that once you reasoned this out, you prioritized expanding your network into quarantine, just as you placed Nina deliberately in Archives once you had the chance. The ticking clock we've all been under of late, the scientist, you were going to have him killed."

"If it came to that, sure." Maxwell's matter-of-fact tone is almost shocking. "What's the difference, in the end? A quick death in quarantine would be better for him than any number of fates he'll meet out there, and better for us than if he managed to hook up with the other side."

"You think the traitors will be exiled, then."

"The Council doesn't have the stomach to do much more than that. It was an effort just getting them to alter the rules of engagement. Bunch of pussies. They sent us out to fight and die so they could go on like the world never even ended. Thought they could lure people like me to their side with a nice house and a promise our kids would be better off than the average. And I'd do anything for my kids. If I trusted these sons of bitches... but they're already excluding us. We're second-class citizens in better digs, that's all.

I've been trying to do what's right. To protect everyone under me, and most of all to keep everyone in here safe."

"So what's the problem?" I demand. "What's your beef with Stella giving you an opening? She invited you to be a hero and prove yourself to the Council and save the damn day."

Tom speaks up before Maxwell can build up the steam he's clearly gathering. "It's not the moment you'd have chosen. Rise to meet it. Keep everyone safe, yes? That *is* the goal."

The subtle emphasis makes his words a challenge. Who's the commander here after all? Of the two, there's only one I'd follow without hesitation.

"I agree with Nina, of course. I've spent less time with Stella, but our conversations have been... intimate is a fair word. I trust her intentions, certainly. Still, the possibility exists, and I would be remiss not to point it out: She could be using her new position to help us as a final act of love for you, rather than with any expectation that she could return to be with you. I hope my concerns are misplaced, but, well, I suppose I wanted to make certain you're prepared for the potential blow."

I put my hand on his shoulder. "I get it. And thanks, for what it's worth. It's not like it didn't occur to me too, you know. Jeez, you don't have to look so surprised. She could be pulling a *self-sacrifice for the greater good* routine. But even if... those turn out okay sometimes."

Maybe it's delusional to trust she knows what she's doing, but it's also necessary. It's keeping me together right now.

"I'd like you with me, if you're able," he says. "I don't mind doing the talking, but—"

"Of course I'm with you."

Our mission is to identify the Helmet—or Helmets—who turned traitor. There are two possibilities Maxwell flagged from the rotation logs: Grace and Jake. Then Monica had to go and ask how we could possibly be certain there weren't others whose involvement was less obvious or maybe got deployed in different ways. Fuckin' A. The focus is still on Grace and Jake, because we can't trail everyone, not when we're the only two Helmets we know we can trust.

The idea is to piss the traitor off and send them running to confront their Illustrian sponsor. Now, maybe that's Delia, in which case we're not gaining a whole lot of intel here. But if it leads us to one of the people we haven't identified yet, we strengthen our position. And either way, we need to know who the dirty Helmet is before they can do any more damage.

Stella, meanwhile, is handling her piece of this alone. All initiative and fire, no one giving her commands or permission. She's a badass. I'm proud of her. Hell, I'd be impressed no matter who did something like this, but Stella's come so far. I like to think I'll be of help here tomorrow, but I know I helped my girl find her fire again. That son of a bitch buried it, but it was always smoldering under the surface, and I'm so goddamn proud of her. Proud, grateful, and yeah, I trust her to come back to me. If there's any way out, she'll find it.

Chapter Thirty

Protégé

Stella

J udah studies me with a serious, and surprisingly sincere, expression.

"If we're going to pull this off, I need to know you can handle what you'll be walking into."

"*We*? Are we a team now?"

Wearily, I let down my hair and tilt my head from side to side to stretch the muscles that have been holding so much tension. Hearing little pops, I reach a hand up to massage the base of my skull and—

And he's not being grotesque about any of this. Not trying to touch me or offering to or even joking about it.

The realization stops me short, and I look back at him more seriously, suddenly willing to credit the notion of his investment, even if I don't necessarily trust it.

"Why would you care whether my gambit pays off?"

"Maybe I just don't want you making me look bad when I'm the one bringing you to the party," he says, but there's no heat, nor even mockery in his voice, and a twitching muscle below the right side of his mouth hints at a smile.

I lean forward, resting my crossed arms on the table. The posture puts my chest on display, but he doesn't react.

"I thought of that," I admit. "I imagined you might simply make sport of me. Invite everyone to have a good laugh, because you never intended that they should take the idea seriously."

He looks vaguely impressed. "You envisioned my betraying you? I'm shocked. Hardly sounds like me," he says wryly. "Down to business. Let's get you ready for battle."

An hour later, I've absorbed the background details, Council chamber layout, etiquette, and relevant gossip about the men—and three women—I'll be taking on tomorrow, and yet I still don't trust the man who's armed me for this conflict.

"Thank you, Judah. You've done more for me than I could ever have hoped. I'm grateful. I need to know why."

"What's that old saying about where not to look a gift horse?"

"The Trojans would have been better off looking. Tell me."

"You said it yourself during our first private conversation, right over there in my kitchen. I called you a catch. You were offended. At the time, I read your reaction as nothing more complex than prideful feminism. But I was wrong. You're not a catch. You're a resource. A man like me doesn't get to where I am by ignoring resources."

"You get there by exploiting them." My voice is dull as the truth begins to dawn.

His head tilts in a mild shrug, and he smiles, untroubled by the accusation. To him, it's just the truth, I suppose. Like any successful capitalist, he regards moral judgments as a luxury for those with far less to gain or lose.

"Any resource will be exploited by *someone*. The smart move is to lock the resource down, keep it out of the hands of the competition. Your ex? He was a genius... didn't make him smart. Greg Gennero would always rather be the only big brain in the room than share the spotlight. Roger's the same. But that's not good business. That kind of thinking leads to an ego-driven, top-down organization. And that's fine if you're the only game in town. The moment a hungrier competitor comes along, game over."

"It's not a game," I object, my heart thick with impotent dread.

He looks at me with something akin to sympathy which is almost worse than condescension, because he's not a psychopath. He understands right and wrong, even comprehends the distinction, but he can set ethics and morals aside.

"The Council suffers from a deadly mix of short-term thinking and delusional egotism. The structure we've got will hold, for a time, but to build something lasting takes fresh ideas and productive debate. I've made this argument before and been outvoted by weak-minded, wishful-thinking, fairy-tale optimists with their heads in the sand.

"And then you invited me into Greg Gennero's old bedroom on that seduction pretext. To think I almost declined outright. But I was curious. I thought I was walking in for a desperate, half-hearted blowjob just because you'd decided I was the lesser evil. Instead, you gave me exactly what I wanted. What I needed. You're going to hand me control of the Council, simply by proving I was right all along."

Laughing at the evident dismay on my face, he adds, "Stella, a little perspective, please! Am I not giving you everything you want? You tried to parlay your information into a very long shot of earning a seat at the table. I've decided you'll get it."

"Because you think you can control me?"

Judah laughs, seeming surprised I'd see it that way. "No! I wouldn't presume to, and I don't have to. Just be yourself. You can't help contributing to the solution, you've proven that in the past. Your involvement actually explains a lot. Roger was remarkably useful in the early days. The prevailing theory was he lost his mojo after his son died."

I frown. "Not that Greg had been the source of Roger's ideas?"

A sardonic snicker followed by a shake of his head. "No one who knew your fiancé would have made that assumption, no."

It's not news, of course, it's the same thing I threw in Celeste's face just two days ago. Her son was reviled among his peers, and that's why he had to seek out a woman like me, lock me down quickly, and break my spirit. Still, it stings. It hits me in my pride. I misjudged Greg so terribly. I'm not sure I misjudged Judah, per se, but I certainly failed to anticipate him. My heart pangs with longing for Demetri. The truly good man. The man with whom a conversation never turns into a cage match.

"So you don't expect me to agree with you or—"

He waves a hand to cut me off. "I don't want to feed you lines, I want to watch you work. Disagree all you like. Argue your perspective. It's not as if you could persuade a Council majority," he reminds me with something like pity, "but healthy debate can yield great results."

It has before, I recall bitterly. I said as much to Tom when I explained how my questions and objections had helped to form certain rules at the beginning of the Stronghold. My intentions are immaterial in the face of the outcome.

"Besides, whether or not you like what the Stronghold is, does it matter when it comes to protecting it? After all, you're part of it. I know you want to stay alive. Stay strong. Protect your loved ones. Your soldier boy."

My eyes widen, and he smirks. "Of course I know." He leans in to deliver the next words in a viciously lascivious taunt. "Once you pulled your little disappearing act, the whole Council knew. There was a debate how to handle it, when to act. The moment you were flagged as missing, we had someone start monitoring your implant. The Council was updated on your location... and your vitals." Laughing, he straightens up again as my face flames. "Don't worry, I'll support you there too. If you want to keep him, I mean. No judgment, of course, if he was just a snack."

My lungs burn as I snarl, "I want to keep him, yes."

He smiles down at me. "Follow my lead, Stella. I'll get you your seat. I'll get you your soldier. And you'll help me keep this place from falling like Ancient Rome."

"What if it deserves to?"

His eyes cool, and his smirk goes stale; he's getting bored. "I guess you've got some little moral quandary you'd like to play out. Have fun with that." He stands to go, then pauses and sets a hand on the back of my chair. "Seems pretty straightforward, though. Work with me and live a peaceful, happy life. And in case it enters your mind to cross me down the line, let's just get this part out of the way: The cards you're holding now are the strongest hand you'll ever have again. Try me, Stella, and see how that goes for you. As it happens, you were right that I have no use for an unwilling woman." He leans down and delivers his concluding threat in a dark voice right behind my ear, "But I don't have to fuck you to fuck you over."

I close my eyes and listen as his footsteps carry him out of the room and down the hall. It's true, what he said. Every word of it. I have little chance of changing anything in this place, certainly not the minds of anyone on the Council. I'm no cockeyed optimist ready to remake the world through sheer courage and pluck.

I'll be a Council token, a paean to progress. Symbolizing equality for outsiders and young women. It will buy them time to maneuver a little, to shut down their dissident faction and get things back on track.

But it gets me Demetri, and he's worth any devil's bargain.

Chapter Thirty-One

Helmet Locker Room Talk

Demetri

No backup shift has ever been longer.

All day, knowing what's supposed to go down at the shift change, waiting to see if I get activated for battle, wondering if Stella's okay, what's happening with her right now. This sick feeling in my gut because I can't do anything until I'm off this gate.

Too tense to pretend otherwise, too fucking edgy to engage in games or banter or even lift weights. Crazy to think yesterday on active duty was easier in a way. The desperate, single-minded focus required to function in the helmet kept me from obsessing over Stella, only because every time my dumbass brain started trying to go there, I got straight by thinking how getting myself killed out there sure as fuck wouldn't help her.

There are books in every backup shift holding area. I remember Stella telling me how they were chosen: titles the Stronghold library had at least three of, and the most battered ones got set aside for secondary collections like these. I lean on the wall by the little shelf and think about her sorting through the books, choosing them for us if not specifically me. There's a slim paperback with white creases down the spine that make it hard to read the title, so I pick it up to look at the cover. Some kind of astronaut adventure. It looks like the sort of thing she'd have said Tom likes.

A much older memory pings, Rachel and Lenora in the living room, their sophomore year of high school. Talking about the scent of old books vs. new ones. And me in the hallway, stopping just out of sight to listen, because I'd started crushing on my big sister's friend. I take a whiff of this old book and stuff down a feeling like I'm gonna cry.

I'm so sick of loss. Some miserable piece of my brain sneaks in a thought like maybe I just want to believe Stella's got a brilliant plan to come home to me because I can't stand to accept reality. And yeah, maybe. But Nina seemed confident too. And that helps. A little.

Maybe.

Shit.

Six hours to go.

The day ends at last, but the waiting isn't over. If anyone was caught up in a fight, their shift might have run long; the plan isn't set to go into action until all day shift Helmets are accounted for. I walk back to barracks, my gear in the crook of my arm. Every few steps, I lift it closer, frantic not to miss the ping of an incoming message. *Come on, come on.*

Finally, there it is. The little beep I've been waiting for. I put my helmet on for the first time all day and listen as my best friend announces on the general channel that we're all needed in the Helmet locker room immediately.

It's on.

Tom stands by the door, facing the crowd. I asked if I should join them and pretend not to be in on whatever was going down, but he said there wasn't much point when people might have picked up on us being friends. So I lean against the wall behind him and a little off to the side, which puts me in a good position to watch the faces of our fellow Helmets as he lays out the facts. This being the one room where we all know each other, it's rare enough to see anyone being all helmety in here, as Nina put it, but we actually can't afford to let anyone get out of showing their faces this time, so Tom makes that announcement first.

"What I've called you here for is a matter of life and death, and though I'm loath to say it, impostors. I'll explain presently, of course, but I must insist we all go bare-faced for this discussion to proceed."

The few helmets come off, and everyone is accounted for.

"We're not friends," he says. "In the last 48 hours, I've had occasion to reflect on that. Perhaps that's made it easier for you to work against us and endanger our lives."

I watch as his words land and people start to react. Some are merely shocked. At least one is afraid they've been caught. Fuck if I can tell the difference, though. Wide eyes, alarm, is it fear, confusion, suspicion, rage?

"A harrowing discovery has been made that sheds light on a particularly dark day we all lived through. All but one, of course. The late Jennifer Cooper, whose helmet was taken, it was said, as a trophy. For as we know, our helmets cannot simply be picked up and used by just anyone. Well, as it happens, there's a workaround for that. As someone in this room well knows. Because someone in this room smuggled out of the Stronghold and delivered into the hands of our enemies a set of contact lenses replicating Cooper's retinal scan."

Some of these faces are more scared than others, that much I'm sure of. And it's the fear of death, not the fear of punishment. I start paying more attention to the handful that don't seem like a ghost just walked over their graves.

Graves. That's what our friends call Grace.

"I wish I'd got to know more of you. I found comfort in isolation, as did many of us. Fueled by pain, anger, perhaps reluctance to bond with comrades only to lose them. The death of Cooper and that entire squad seemed to prove I was indeed better off with limited connections. But my error was the assumption we were in this together. That we all agreed the survival of this place and the people in it was our responsibility, if only because we enjoyed its safety for ourselves.

"If I'd allowed myself to form connections with you, to form opinions of you, perhaps I would have some inkling whom to trust and whom to doubt. Perhaps if we'd ever laughed together, your faces would be less vague and unreadable. I stand here now with no idea who among you would have happily delivered *my* eyes to the Devil Runners."

He pauses, and I watch as the words start to sink in, at least for a few of them.

"It was a random attack. Cooper was not targeted. She was not selected to die. It could indeed have been any one of us who was on patrol or backup that day. The reason we know this, the reason we know all of this: A full set of contacts, replicating the retinal scans of every soldier in this room, was found stashed away. Cooper's were the only ones missing."

Bruno turns to glare at everyone around him and surprises me by snarling, "Well? Suspicions, observations, bad vibes? Any of you want to give me an idea who to punch?"

Jake sneers at him. "Oh, that's a good idea. Be the first one to express outrage and deflect suspicion off yourself. Jackass."

Grace's eyelashes flutter, and she glances around nervously, moving her head as little as possible as if trying to avoid notice.

Carly says hesitantly, "Why is anyone taking this at face value?" Her gaze turns our way, blazing with accusation. "You don't know us? I don't know you, either! This could be complete bullshit meant to—I don't know, drive a wedge, sow disorder—"

"Make it easier for the real traitors to bring us all down!" Vance adds, getting to his feet and pointing directly at Tom.

I take a step closer to my friend, suddenly afraid this could go a very bad direction I sure didn't see coming. Have we just united a room full of lethal fighters against us?

"Hey!" I shout on an impulse to defuse the situation by getting everyone's attention, and it works. All eyes are on me now. Shit. Now I have to say something. "Some of you are pissed at us, don't know who to trust, scared if what Tom said is true. I get that. It's been hanging over me lately how we supposedly trust each other with our lives, meanwhile I wouldn't place bets on any of you not being a traitor. Here's a bet I will make. Someone in here is ganging up just to change the subject. Maybe a coupla someones. You think you've got friends in high places, but whoever's yanking your chain, you really think they put all their eggs in your basket? You think you're the only one, think you're special? Think again. They had lenses made to match *all* our eyes, including yours. They didn't give a shit which of us got got. So take a look around. Who else here might be working your same angle?"

A silent storm follows as everyone does look around at each other. Tom takes advantage of the lull to open the door, and we get the fuck out before the mood can shift again.

"That was well done, Demetri," he says softly as we hurry down the hall.

"You too."

"Any guesses? At all?" he asks, not expecting much.

"I got nothin'," I confirm.

"Then it's down to reconnaissance."

Monica, Davy, and Manny are trying to keep tabs on as much of Luther and Kelly's crews as they can, just in case. But none of us really think the traitor or traitors is gonna head for support among the rank and file. We just riled them up about the people giving them orders. Hopefully Grace or Jake heads straight for Delia Morton—or better yet, one of her partners in treachery.

Using Tom's old trick for watching over Nina, I tagged Grace on my HUD, and he tagged Jake. We'll be able to follow from a safe distance wherever they go next.

When Grace comes out of the locker room, she's back to helmet head, but damn if something about her body language doesn't strike me as furtive. Could be projection because I'm actively looking for reasons to be suspicious of her. Doesn't matter. I'm on. I nod to Tom, wait until she's out of sight but not off radar, and start moving that way slowly, maintaining a casual pace.

This is going to be a bear of a job. She can see me same as I can see her, as long as we're near each other. If I stay too steadily in range, she might twig I'm following. She could take off running, or decide to pick a fight. I've got to play this just right.

We talked this through, Tom and me. I just have to do it like we agreed. Randomize my moves a little. Stop to look at something so I fall behind. Jog to talk to someone so I gain some ground, then let it slip a little while I'm chatting away. I've got her tagged, so I know exactly which dot she is, but I'm just one of the dots in her vicinity, and I'm not obviously tailing her. I hope.

But yeah, sure enough, we're heading into the nicer part of town. It's not Mansion Row or anything, which kinda throws me, but it's the edge of Old Illustris. You'd think someone big enough to make this kind of mess would live in one of the mansions. Maybe Grace just has a friend or a lover or something? Maybe she's just shook up and heading to see a friendly face.

When her dot stops moving on the lateral and starts moving on the vertical, I close my eyes a second because it's making me dizzy. Shit. I won't have any way to guess what floor she's going to.

"Grace is on an elevator. High rise in the suite sector. Not sure how to follow, unless you can give me something to go on?"

"Sit tight, son," Maxwell responds. "We'll come to you."

I look up at the building as I wait for Maxwell and whoever "we" might turn out to be. The answers are on the other side of all that brick and glass. Somewhere inside that overhyped apartment complex is at least one major pl—

Chapter Thirty-Two

Negotiations

Stella

The Council chamber is old-school elegance, high-backed leather chairs, warm lighting, a large half-circle of a table behind which all eight men and three women will sit and stare at me. They'll be here any moment. So much depends on my performance here today. My entire life—Demetri's too, in a very real way. And our chance to be together. A fluttering at the edges of my vision forces me to close my eyes a moment.

But Roger's voice breaks through the terror and restores the rage that will get me through this.

"What is this, Judah? She has no business being here."

I can't let Judah speak for me, that much I know.

"Roger, you of all people know the Council's business has always been mine." I fix Roger with a cool glare of disdain and stand my full height. I think he's been so accustomed to seeing me faded, withered, broken down, he's forgotten I'm nearly as tall as Greg was, which makes me an inch taller than Roger in shoes.

Two more Council members were right behind him entering the room, and I catch a brief look of schadenfreude on the man's face. Roger is not as powerful as he'd like to be, certainly not as well-liked as he would need to be to stand in my way if I do this right. Judah saying this was one thing, but I needed to see it for myself.

Roger tries for a derisive laugh, glancing over his shoulder as if to say, *Can you believe the lunacy Judah's foisting on us?* Then he steps closer and pitches his voice to address me confidentially.

"Leave. Now. Whatever this is will not end well for you."

Satisfaction settles my blood at the thought of punishing Roger. I've given him too much subservience, and far too much credit. He enjoyed playing the good cop, letting himself shine in contrast with Greg's viciousness and Celeste's vituperation.

"You're a snake," I reply in the same private manner. "I've spent far too long feeding you smaller mice in the hopes you wouldn't eat me. Now I've caught a plump, juicy rat, and I'm going to choke you with it."

He's just starting to snarl when I step back and widen my gaze to move beyond him. Cutting him off before he can begin, I address the full group, some of whom are still taking their seats.

"My name is Stella Vernon. You may not know me, but you know my work. I have been an uncredited contributor. Roger's girl Friday in a manner of speaking. Some of my greatest hits include: 'They'll come to the Stronghold as supplicants.' 'They're all still Americans in their minds.' That was a big one. When you opted to sacrifice sheer numbers in the interest of surface-level equality among the corps? That was me. I did that. I have to carry it."

"All right," Roger interrupts officiously, "this has gone on long enough. Judah, take your bride home and keep her there. Then you can come back and apologize for—"

"Roger? Sit. Down."

He turns red and opens his mouth to sputter at me, but a man across the table interjects, "Fuck's sake, Roger, don't embarrass yourself. Take it like a man."

"Holland. How d—"

"Holland!" I repeat the name with delight. Roger swivels his glare my way, clearly wishing looks could kill. I give him a vengeful smile and turn to address his antagonist. "Holland who married his PR director. I understand it was she who first raised the idea of renaming the city. I know this because, unlike Roger, you credit your contributors. Good man," I add approvingly, not because I think any of these men qualify as good but because I need some of them on my side.

Judah's seat is beside Holland's, so I can see the gentle sneer of amused approval curling his lip. He leans forward and takes this opportunity to steer the conversation.

"Believe it or not, I was going to introduce my guest properly before she took the initiative. Stella's not my bride, Roger. Sorry for the false pretenses. I took her out of your house because you were determined to waste her potential, and it's frankly inexcusable. The Stronghold has benefited from her intelligence and creativity in the past, and you wanted to shelve her. If you'd succeeded in doing so, I'm not sure we would have learned of the brewing danger until it was far too late."

"What danger?" a woman asks sharply from across the table. Maureen, I think; Judah said she often wore her hair in a bun.

"You have traitors among you," I announce, recapturing the attention of the room. "Perhaps even in this room. Our guest will present evidence. Shall I invite him in?"

I look over at Judah for confirmation, and he's smiling proudly. I took his advice and went one step further, asserting my place among the Council in words as well as actions. Commander Maxwell is *our* guest, and *I* will invite him in.

Judah nods, and I open the door to welcome the scowling Commander. He stalks in with the energy of a private storm cloud that swirls around him alone. When he takes his seat and I remain standing, his eyes flare with awareness and distrust.

"Commander Maxwell," another woman says. Enid, I think. Judah said she would be the one nearest the center. "We're told you have evidence of treachery, perhaps at the Council level?" She raises a skeptical eyebrow. "Suffice to say, this better be good."

Maxwell glances at me in irritation and adjusts his position in the chair.

"No, Councilor. Not *at* the Council level. At least, not so far. But yes, there is a conspiracy against the Stronghold, and it reaches very high in your... social circle."

As he speaks, laying out the facts of the case, I watch every face in the room, one by one, always bouncing back to Roger, enjoying the quiet diminishment as he realizes his era is ending. He stood on my shoulders and gained greater authority here by presenting my ideas as his own. Just as young women used to do in college classes. I didn't understand it at the time. I thought women were doomed to compete with one another, but now I know: We competed with each other because we were encouraged to, because it kept us too busy and distracted to aim upward. Because the entrenched powers resented having to make a seat for anyone that wasn't just like them, so they called such inclusion a matter of enforced diversity and forced us all to fight amongst ourselves for those few spots, then to work harder than they did in perpetuity to overcome the ongoing assumption that we owed our success to society's magnanimity.

Roger has enjoyed the cachet of my reflected glory, and I've come to steal it back from him. He won't be ejected from the Council, but the power is shifting right below his feet. Not to me, of course. I'm still an outsider and always will be. But there has been a seismic struggle here for some time, and I'm the shakeup Judah needed. I don't necessarily feel good about helping Judah; I have no idea how dangerous a snake he might be in the grand scheme. But if feeding him means I get to watch Roger starve, that will do.

"Delia Morton," harrumphs a middle-aged man with a pocket square—Judah said Charles liked pocket squares. "Almost seems like we should've seen that one coming. There's a reason we decided against offering her a seat, after all."

At his wording, I catch bristling postural adjustments from the two women nearest him, Enid and the third, Lorelei. They don't love the reminder that it was always a case of the men selectively *offering* a few women places here.

Lorelei speaks up. "It was the height of hubris to think you could exile her husband and he would simply accept it. If I'd been present for those discussions, I would have argued against it, but, as Charles notes, you had yet to *offer* me a seat." Her acid tone matches her briefly venomous glance before she settles back into the depth of her chair.

Maxwell dares to ask, "Why was he exiled? A man at his level?"

Charles huffs derisively at the idea that Thaddeus Morton was ever properly on their level, and answers quietly, "Delia's husband was not well liked."

A few seats to his left, another man speaks up as if needing to correct a massive understatement. "He couldn't be trusted. If he'd been inside the city when the trouble started, I suppose we'd have been stuck with him and had to find a way to live with the chaos he introduced. It was a stroke of luck that he was among the missing."

"The son of a bitch should have had the grace to stay gone. Better people than him never made it back." Judah's interjection touches my heart somewhat against my will as I realize he is referring to his wife. He portrayed a certain callousness when we spoke of her before, but of course, we were strangers to each other.

"Delia was a brilliant businesswoman but her taste in men was...." Charles trails off, shrugging as if to say this was a common and predictable failing that barely bore further detail.

"What reason was given to *him* when he was rejected as a returning citizen and supposedly recruited as a spy?" I can't help asking.

"You don't know?" Lorelei raises her eyebrow, amused. "Roger, does that mean this idea actually came from you?"

Roger frowns and visibly swallows. "I, ah, thought to use the implant to alter certain biorhythms or cause alarming results on various bloodwork—"

"Oh," I interrupt in a burst of understanding. "It was Greg's idea."

Judah steers the discussion back to its purpose, asking Maxwell if today's Helmet subterfuge has yielded any additional names.

My eyes flicker to Judah in alarm that I dare not show, and his lip twitches slightly. Not that I should be surprised by the reminder we're hardly equals in his eyes, but this involves Demetri, and I can't help taking it as a subtle threat.

Maxwell grunts. "Confirmed what we knew, mostly. Jake and Grace were the primary suspects based on rotation anomalies, and what a shock, Grace went straight to Delia."

I stifle a dismayed gasp. Grace, who sat in my library weeping over poetry. I would have assumed the best of her.

"My people moved in quietly and took them both into custody. So far, Delia isn't saying much. But we searched her home and found a collection of truly fascinating messages *from the husband*." His use of finger quotes catches everyone's full attention, no matter how little they like to acknowledge him.

"Go on," Judah prompts with a barely detectable note of impatience.

Maxwell reveals a stacked handful of unfolded notes from his pocket. "The oldest ones are actually from him, I guess. Those aren't too interesting. Bullshit about his undying love and how he'd do anything to be with her again, raging anger at the Stronghold for exiling him, of course, and as you might imagine, requests for supplies and such. Instructions on communications, drop points, et cetera.

"Then something changes. And your *brilliant businesswoman* Delia was just a girl in love, I guess, deluding herself that her man was still alive and kicking."

"What do you mean?" Maureen demands.

"I mean," Maxwell says sternly, "the messages continue beyond his death, and I don't know who wrote them, but it damn sure isn't the same guy. The handwriting looks about the same, and the messages even kind of sound similar, same kind of information in 'em, but something's off. We need more time to analyze them—"

"Give them to me," I say urgently, holding out my hand. When he hesitates, I say, "I don't know who you plan to have analyze these or in what way, but if there's a linguistic expert in the Stronghold, it's me."

"You'll need a spot at the table to lay those out." Judah then addresses the man at the end of the table on the opposite side. "Clayton, slide in to make room for another chair."

His words are calm and decisive. The instruction makes sense in the current context. If anyone realizes what he's doing, they don't object, at least out loud.

I start placing the notes on the table. By the time I've laid them all out neatly, there's a chair ready behind me. I glance across at Judah. He gives me the slightest, nearly imperceptible nod, and I sit.

"We may be here a while," Judah says, continuing to assert control of the room. "I'll send for dinner. Maxwell, is your family expecting you? We could send word."

"It's fine," he growls quietly.

I set down my fork and clear my throat. Judah cuts across the background noise, "What do you have for us?"

The idle chatter dies off. Into the expectant silence, I read from the notes I've been making, "Lady, sorry about your husband but these guys are gonna bust up your shit and I can't pretend forever are you even reading these?"

"It does not say that," Maxwell objects.

"It does, actually. If you only read every third word. That's the latest. Whoever is writing these, they've employed a variety of encryption techniques, but they're not terribly complex or opaque. He wants these messages to be understood, just not to be obvious at a glance. I suspect he somewhat relied on saccharine sentimentality to bore anyone but Delia who might even look. And he's getting increasingly desperate."

"Have you read enough to form any kind of theory about the threat?" Judah asks soberly.

"I think the author of these notes is the Devil Runners' IT guy, for want of a better word. But he doesn't like them, so he might be a captive who proved useful, or just with them because it's better than dying alone. They gave him some kind of project, and he's been stalling. Some way to infiltrate the Stronghold, by the sound of it. Probably with the helmet they took off our dead soldier."

"And the contact lenses that let him use it," Maxwell adds gravely. "We need to identify all the conspirators and deal with them immediately."

"No," Judah corrects him, "*you* need to focus on the external threat. We'll handle the internal matter from here."

Maxwell almost leaps to his feet but marshals his emotions in time, gripping the arm of his chair and gritting his teeth. "You wouldn't even know about this if it weren't for—"

"Stella," Judah finishes coolly. "Don't mistake me, Commander, your contributions have been indispensable and are thoroughly appreciated. It's serendipitous that Stella chose you to reach out to with the information. You've done laudable work today, and it won't be forgotten. But this is a Council matter."

Maxwell is white with rage. He drops his gaze in acceptance. I stare fearfully, waiting for that gaze to turn upon me. Surely he will need to convey his resentment with a murderous glance...

When he just stands and leaves without any further acknowledgment or interaction, I realize that is so much worse.

Chapter Thirty-Three

Endgame

Stella

After Maxwell's departure, Judah calls the room back to order for one last bit of business.

"As I'm sure many of you recall, I argued for less restrictive guidelines on Council eligibility from the start. I was outvoted, but I hope we can now agree that additional viewpoints and skill sets occasionally prove invaluable. We got lucky this time, but we've been blind to internal threats. It would be foolish to assume this will be the last of them."

"You can't be serious, Judah. The librarian brings you one bit of useful information, and you want to keep her around just in case lightning strikes twice?" Roger's attempt at scoffing is laced with notes of desperation and fury. He's trying to make this sound absurd because he's afraid it will happen.

"No, Roger, I don't foresee this exact set of circumstances repeating itself. I see new and exciting problems arising. Possibilities which you've been dogmatic about refusing to consider. We are, after all, greatly outnumbered on numerous fronts. So far, we've had forces such as fear, complacency, and social inertia on our side.

You brought us some good ideas in the beginning, by which I mean you carried them like a messenger pigeon."

I wish I could bottle the feeling of watching Roger's impotent rage.

Judah continues, "We've got a room full of people who all fundamentally agree with each other on most points and who all come from similar places. That's the governmental equivalent of inbreeding. We brought in the best and brightest from outside to grow our population. We've got to apply that same strategy to expanding the Council. Stella has proven her value to the Stronghold. And don't underestimate the optics. Right, Holland?"

Holland perks up. "That's right. If this were a corporate scandal in the old days, Emilia would put Stella front and center for image rehabilitation. 'We've learned from our mistakes and promoted a scrappy up-and-comer to keep us honest.'"

"And it's not merely apologetic, it's aspirational," Judah says with a flourish, "gives the people hope. 'Not only does she speak for us, she's proof of our potential. There's room at the top for one who strives.'"

He grins and throws a cheerful glance my way. I smile as my blood runs cold.

It's a done deal. Even Roger can see it. He casts a token dissenting vote, but he knows he's stuck with me in the Council, which clearly enrages him just as much as being stuck with me in their home infuriated Celeste.

"Last thing," Judah says in the manner of an afterthought, "Stella's got a boyfriend in the military. I think it's clear she'll be more effective if she's not worrying about him out there. Not to mention," he glances at Holland again, "the optics."

"That's true," Holland says agreeably. "Conflict of interest, possible ah, military bias?" He seems to be spitballing ideas, and the dynamic is clear: He likes his role as the useful sidekick to the obvious new power in the room. He would have happily filled in the blanks for Judah on any number of topics.

Judah nods his approval. "So we retire the young man, find something else for him to do? Until you start having kids, of course," he adds in my direction.

I raise my eyebrow, and he explains as if it were perfectly obvious, "Stella, I'm sure you understand your work on the Council is far too important to take the kind of long-term maternity leave that's become the standard among women of the Stronghold. Yet, someone will have to care for your children. Emilia would love this, wouldn't she?"

Holland looks positively gleeful. "Oh, absolutely. Upending stereotypes, gender roles, a show of true equality—the exception that justifies the rule."

My head is spinning. I continue to nod, saying yes and thank you at appropriate moments. Mercifully, the meeting is winding down.

"Good work with those notes. You can continue your analysis later. Enid, would you help Stella lock them away for the night?"

The older woman approaches, eyeing me as if she's wondering what species I am. "I won't presume to help you gather them up, sure you've got some kind of order there."

"Yes, thanks."

"You jumped right into the deep end, didn't you? Or were you pushed?"

"I don't know what you—"

She shakes her head. "Doesn't matter. You're in it though. It's a lot to live up to. You just became the face of progress and possibility."

"I'm still a woman. Still destined to be a wife and a mother—"

"But not like the others," she stage-whispers. "You've secured a truly enviable position. And you will be envied. Envied, and resented, the more you fail to deliver on the promise of your very existence."

"You sound almost happy about that," I say, barely attempting to restrain a note of disgust, but she laughs, not unkindly.

"Oh dear, no. I sympathize. I don't want you to be shocked, I suppose. Most of all, I can't afford you to be vulnerable." She pauses as our eyes lock. "It's going to be difficult for you to set the kind of boundaries you must set. Whatever friendships you have are about to be strained in a way you've never known. The men of the Council don't have this same awareness. They can't. They've lived insular, relatively simple lives as the kings of their little worlds. Women who reach great heights do so in a wholly different arena. Of necessity, along the way, we form alliances and rivalries that these men would consider insignificant, even petty. Easily discarded or forgotten. But you and I know that's not the truth of it. You're going to struggle to leave people behind, but you can't bring them with you. You'll feel the pain of failing them and the indignation at their anger for it, because they can't understand the forces at play, the limits on your power. The fact that at the end of the day, trying to help others will only cost you everything."

Astonishingly, it feels more like commiseration than a threat. Enid is genuinely sorry for her impotence, even as she chooses to maintain it. She's inviting me into her pity party. Offering me the balm that soothes her occasional attacks of conscience just as she might offer me a leaf off an aloe plant.

I thank her and place the stack of notes neatly in the safe.

Judah tsks as I start to turn onto his street. I stop, only now noticing he is facing a slightly different direction.

"I know you've treasured our time together. As have I," he says with a theatrical hand over his heart, "but two Council members shacking up—there could be accusations of impropriety."

A laugh ripples my reply. "Impropriety? You? Perish the thought."

"I had someone move you in a couple blocks over."

I follow him, the words sinking in fully, and I point out, "That happened awfully quickly. Allocating the housing resource at a Council member's level, having my possessions transferred, all while we were in the meeting where I was approved very late in the evening."

"Are you saying you doubted me?"

"No... I suppose I'm impressed at how little you seem to have doubted me."

"You performed beautifully. From the moment Gennero walked in the room, I knew you had it. Rage turned on like a tap. There was hardly a question you could get the job done."

"Hardly?"

He studies me a moment before answering. "Maxwell threw you at the end. Made you sweat. Care to tell me why?"

Judah is too smart. Too perceptive, and far too calculating. If I am going to be ahead of him on anything, ever, I have a lot of work to do.

"You seem to have inferred my concerns readily enough," I prevaricate. "You secured Demetri's retirement, after all. So Maxwell can't use him against me."

His lip curls. "Fine, don't tell me. I'll always figure it out."

We start walking again, and I change the subject.

"I can see why Delia might have been desperate to believe the contents of the later notes and to ignore the clues. The increasingly flowery and emotional messages would have sung to that part of her soul that needed the bad man to be a good one, needed him to love her after all."

Judah cackles, and my anger flares again.

"You would know all about that," he says with dark amusement.

Not trusting any response I might form, I seethe in silence as our footsteps provide the only noise for several steps.

Then he says, "But you're wrong. She knew. Not a chance she was fooled. With the amount of access she clearly had—the amount of access we're about to have to root out among our people, among the structures that run our little world here, Stella, she clearly knew he'd been out there the whole time we were claiming he was missing and presumed dead. I think we can assume she learned of his actual death through her network as well. Then the messages just kept coming? *And* they were different, weird, *coded*? Please. She knew."

"You think she would have sat back and watched the city be overrun? As a final act of revenge for her husband?"

He chuckles. "Nah. No one ever thinks the worst will really happen, do they? Probably thought the military would keep the wolves from the door. And let's say she's been sitting there working up an ulcer over the impending attack, wishing she could do something, anything to prevent it, she wouldn't. Because she'd have to come clean first. Admit what she'd done. Accept the consequences. Never happen."

"Do you know her particularly well?"

"Not really. But I know the type. I don't like these women. I told you that before, not sure if you believed me, but it's true. When I thought you were just a climber, I thought maybe there was some potential there, because at least you know what it's like to want things and not have them. You can't trust women who've never had to want anything."

"What about men?" I counter in an acid tone.

"I don't trust them either," he answers with a sardonic smirk, "but there's a very big difference between a woman who's always had a platinum card and a man of means." He stops walking again and we turn to face each other. "I loved Vanessa. We met before I made my first billion. I trusted her in a way I could never have trusted a woman I met after that."

"Poor little rich boy." The words surprise me, bursting out from behind my reflexive scowl. "You don't know how to trust that anyone really likes you for you? You think everyone's trying to exploit you for money that, may I remind you, no longer exists. Marie, on the other hand, knows she's evaluated based on sex organs and little else—whether in a prurient way like you or a practical way like the Council."

He steps closer and hisses, "What the hell do you know about M—"

"I don't know anything about Marie. I know what it's like to be a woman. So spare me the egocentric, self-pitying—"

In a whiplash transition, Judah's face goes from seething to laughing again. My words die off as I wait to understand.

"I wondered if I'd gone too far," he confides ironically, placing a hand on my shoulder like we're old friends. "But now, well, I guess we're probably about even."

"What did you do?"

He gestures to the mansion right behind me. "Let's see."

I run up the front steps and turn to him expectantly as he makes a show of trying to find the key.

"Judah—"

"Patience—oh, here it is."

He starts to unlock the door, then pulls the key back out and leisurely waves it about as he says, "That's so rude, right? Opening your own door for you the very first time—I should really let you—"

It takes a couple of tries before I aim accurately and grab quickly enough to snatch the key away from him. As I fumble it into the lock, he grabs the handle just before I can turn it and says in a very low voice right beside my ear, "This has been fun. And I do enjoy the occasional challenge. But remember who gave you everything you're about to find beyond that door. Don't make me take any of it back."

When he doesn't let go right away, I know he's waiting for some kind of confirmation. I turn my head slightly, meet his eyes, and nod my understanding.

As soon as he removes his hand, I finish opening the door and rush in to find pretty much exactly what I expected: Demetri, unconscious, draped across a couch.

I fly to his side, kneel on the floor, and take his hand, then glare back at Judah.

"Like I said, even. Not sure how long he'll be out. You might have a better sense of it than I do."

"Why—"

But before I can demand an explanation, Judah jerks his head to the right, and I see we're not alone. Judah gives me a sarcastic little wave and closes the door behind him.

"Tom," I say miserably by way of a greeting. I truly can't remember the last time I was this exhausted.

"He went down just like you did, and obviously, unlike poor Davy that day at the library, I knew what had happened. I simply refused to leave his side, and the medics stopped arguing with me after a time."

I smile at him gratefully, then chuckle at the image and have to ask, "Did they even try to explain why he was delivered to an empty mansion rather than a medical facility?"

He smiles in gentle amusement. "Not even a word."

"He was part of whatever plan there was to identify the suspects?"

Tom nods. "He was following Grace, in point of fact. Made his report, and I abandoned my fruitless surveillance mission to join him. Maxwell and some of his people were there as well."

That son of a bitch.

"What?" Tom asks, seeing the revelation and accompanying anger forming on my face.

"Maxwell. He... well, I shouldn't be surprised that he didn't care to mention anything about Demetri to me. But Tom, I should probably warn you that I have burned that bridge quite conclusively. He will never trust me, and Judah's taken this step—complete with the *hilarious* incapacitation—to prevent Maxwell from being able to use Demetri against me. But you're still under his command. It might not be very safe to be our friend. I'm truly sorry."

He stares at me for a long moment, then looks at Demetri and smiles fondly.

"I'm not so easily scared off. It's good he's getting out of combat. He wasn't built for it, you know. And I don't mean he lacked in skill, certainly. He was very good." He looks me in the eyes and concludes somberly, "It was killing him. He's too good a man. You're not just saving his life, you're saving *him*. Thank you."

My eyes flood, and I manage to say the words back in a choked whisper, thanking Tom for this gift he can't possibly know he's giving me. It might be the only true absolution I can find for all the damage I may fail to prevent, may even do, in my new role. I may have sold my soul, but perhaps I really traded it for Demetri's.

"Tom," I whisper, and he crouches beside me to listen to my confession.

When I've finished pouring it out, he places a hand on my shoulder in an unconscious echo of Judah out on the sidewalk.

"One fire at a time," he says simply.

"What?"

"This place wasn't built overnight, but it could burn that quickly. We've got imminent, very real danger to face."

"But what about—"

"It wasn't built overnight," he says again, more firmly. "It won't be dismantled or even changed overnight. No invisible structure is as easily toppled as the physical kind. You can end lives in an instant, but to change hearts and minds is real work. The surest way to lose the war is to surrender."

"I might need to hear that speech again from time to time." I hope he can tell from the tears in my eyes and the sorrow in my voice that I'm not joking about this. I really might need an occasional reminder that this is a long game, not a lost cause.

Do I even believe that? I look at Demetri again, asleep on the couch in a mansion he's never seen before but will wake up to discover is ours. Still wearing a uniform he'll never need again. He'll be so happy to learn that, won't he?

"It's been quite a day. I'll leave him in your care."

Tom leaves quietly. I stare at Demetri's beautiful face through my tears and exhaustion. The floor is more comfortable than it should be as I lean against the couch holding his hand. I don't want to leave his side for even a moment. I'll just rest a bit.

And so thinking, I drift off, still crumpled beside him.

Chapter Thirty-Four

Out

Demetri

Nothing feels quite right in the moments before I open my eyes.

The first thing I know is I'm not in my bed. Quarantine? But no, based on the position I'm in, this isn't any kind of bed at all, even a shitty hospital one. I'm still in uniform too. What the hell?

The mystery triggers enough alarm to drag me over the threshold of consciousness, and yet, opening my eyes answers none of my questions. This is a place I've never seen before. And the weirdest fucking thing is there's sunlight pouring through the windows.

I push myself up to sitting, and holy shit. *Stella.* She's on the floor right by this couch I've been sleeping on—is she okay? How did either of us get here?

I lean over and touch her cheek. "Stella?" *Please be okay. Please just wake up and tell me you're okay.*

Her eyes flutter open, and she goes from confusion to elation in a heartbeat. "You're awake."

"Why are you on the floor? Where are we? How did—"

"Shh. In a minute, okay?"

I nod and take her hand to help her up, then wrap my arms around her and hold on tight.

"Are you injured at all?"

It's a confusing question, but it forces me to pay attention to my body, and sure enough, my right knee's a little sore, like I landed on it. Also, I might actually die if I don't take a piss.

"Um, yeah, maybe. I gotta take a look. There a bathroom nearby?"

"Yeah. I haven't had a chance to look around, but—"

"I'll be back."

This place is big and weird and way too nice for me to have the slightest clue what I'm doing here, but it's still a house, so I hurry along the hall and find the bathroom behind the third door I check.

How the fuck long was I out? It feels like I could irrigate a fucking farm.

Once that's out of the way, I push my pants down around my calves to get a look at my knee. Seriously, what happened?

When I come out of the bathroom, I hear water running in the first door off the hallway and find Stella in the kitchen, filling a glass. It's the most normal thing I've ever seen her do. Wherever we are, whatever's going on, it feels so peaceful right now.

She turns and catches me staring, and she offers me the glass.

"I skinned my knee or something, and maybe a bone bruise like my mom used to say. But I don't know how it happened."

She sighs. "I'm so sorry. My... sponsor or mentor or... frenemy. He thought it would be funny to drop you the way the Genneros did me."

"The implant."

She nods, frowning sadly, and I pull her into my arms again. I stroke her hair and enjoy the mussed, second-day feel and smell of us both. The way I'm in need of a shower and it's not stopping her from leaning up on me like this, breathing me in.

When my dick starts to swell, she makes another, sweeter kind of sigh and pulls herself tighter against me.

"What is this place? Is it his? The um, frenemy?"

The idea doesn't feel quite right even as I say it, but we're clearly in a fancy Illustris home. *Old Illustris*. Just a few nights ago, my friends were holding me back when I wanted to knock down the door of a place like this to find her, and now I'm here on the other side of it with her.

She looks up at me again, and she has this shy, hopeful smile forming on her mouth. I wanna kiss it.

"It's ours."

"I must've heard that wrong. I was all distracted staring at your lips," I confess, going in for a kiss to demonstrate.

"It's our house, Demetri."

The words actually stop me. "*Our* house. Yours and mine."

She nods again, still looking hopeful but nervous, like I'm gonna take this badly. A million questions are crowding my brain, and I have to pick one, preferably one that won't prove she's right to be this worried about my reaction.

In the end, all I can settle on is, "How?"

"I'm on the Council now. It's a very long story, and I'll tell you everything, but part of it affects you. And I'm sorry. I don't think it's a bad thing," she rushes to add, "but it still should have been a choice you got to make, and—"

I drag her mouth into mine and kiss her all the way out of this spiral she was starting on. She only hesitates half a heartbeat at the start, because I know she was trying to tell me something big, but I also know this is bigger. We needed this.

We need a lot more.

"Whatever it is, I choose you," I remind her, gently stroking her cheek and loving the pressure of my dick against her belly.

And once again, I'm not hearing things right, because I think she just asked me to marry her.

Chapter Thirty-Five

Peace and War

Stella

"I know this isn't the way anything is supposed to happen, but... will you marry me?"

Demetri was about to kiss me again, but he stops halfway to my lips and I watch his brain process the words.

"I know I didn't hear that right," he says with a wild smile. "Did I?"

His kiss pushes me back against the counter, and his hardness invites me to accept a change of subject. Fortunately, he's got more words for me as well.

"You're all mine now, aren't you? No more humoring Illustris douchebags and hiding in dark corners. You've got me now, and I've got you. Is that what you want, Stella?"

"Yes."

"You want to be my wife."

"Yes."

"You want to have my babies."

He presses harder into me. A throbbing emptiness inside me cries out *yes* even as I speak the word through a heaving gasp.

Demetri shrugs off his uniform, shoving it down and away. The moment his cock is free, I take hold of it, grasping, stroking. It's so stiff, and it's all mine.

"I need to be inside you, Stella."

Glancing around the room, I spot a breakfast nook with a banquette. I lead him there, never letting go of his cock, and urge him to sit.

"Your knee," I remind him. "You should keep your weight off it."

He looks almost dazed with love, desire, and something else. Something I can't put my finger on right now.

"God, you're going to be so beautiful riding me." He grips himself fiercely. "Get that dress off so I can watch your tits bounce."

I watch his face as I undo my dress and let it fall. He's so hungry. *For me.*

I place my knees on either side of his hips to straddle him, and he rubs the head of his cock against me from clit to labia and back.

"Take it, Stella. It's all yours. Take it."

I sink down onto him, marveling at how much of him there is and how quickly I've come to love this powerful fullness. When my inner thighs land snugly against his hipbones, I feel it deep within, the delicious pressure that's all Demetri.

"I've never felt anything like this," I murmur, holding still and relishing the sensations.

"Neither have I, Stella."

In his voice, it's clear he's not talking about sex. I open my eyes and take in the raw, soulful sincerity of his gaze.

"I'm so in love with you, Demetri."

My lips chase the words into a deep kiss, and his tongue in my mouth sets the pace for my hips and thighs as I start to move. As my orgasm draws within reach, I lose the sense of controlled rhythm and just ride the feeling with wild desperation, trapping him tight with needy, shallow, erratic motion.

Gripping my hips, he says, "That's it. Take what you need. You're gonna come for me. I'm gonna fill you up so deep, Stella. That's what you want, say it."

"Yes—yes, come in me, do it, I'm yours."

He pulls me down on him, hard, grinds into me, practically growling as he fills me. The quaking of my own fading orgasm begs for his seed and pulls it deeper.

"I'm not playing, Stella. I want a family with you."

"Good."

"How long before they switch your birth control off?"

I flinch and lean back to watch his face as I break the news.

"It turns out... I was never on it. Illustris default."

He chuckles. "So all this time—"

"All this time," I confirm.

"I guess it makes sense. They trap military women into making babies by letting them fall in love. For civilian women they just do it the old-fashioned way."

"Hmm," I agree vaguely. An errant thought has peeled off from his words and is trying to get my attention, but now is not the time.

"Funny you should mention civilians... because you are one now."

I know it's not bad news; after what Tom confided in me last night, I'm confident it's good news. Yet it's still a life change I'm presenting to him as a fait accompli, and I can't help feeling awkward about that.

I explain it much the same as Judah brought the matter before the Council.

"And I am sorry, again, that this isn't a choice I can offer you. I never would have—"

He places a gentle finger against my lips.

"Stella. You're telling me I get to be... a dad?"

I nod. The quietest, simplest smile finds his lips, and his head drops forward a little, like a massive knot of tension just released. When he looks up again, he's so peaceful. He reaches up and strokes my hair, staring at me with affection and gratitude.

"Don't ever apologize for that," he assures me.

Demetri's long arms wrap around me tightly, and his face disappears into my hair, which I know is now absorbing very manly tears.

"I thought I'd be fighting till it killed me," he confesses.

"I need you to live a long, peaceful life, Demetri."

A moment later, he shakes with a chuckle that seems to surprise him, then explains, "Guess there is such a thing as a trophy husband."

His happy laughter eases softly into another kiss. One hand slides into my hair, cradling the base of my skull as he gently holds me close. The other explores my hip, my waist, moving up to cup my breast. I can already feel him thickening again inside me. My nipples prickle with sensation, seeming to reach for the gorgeous man I'm riding. A deep inhale becomes a hungry sigh.

A knock at the front door freezes us like an erotic tableau.

"That's an angry sound," I whisper.

"Your ex's family?" Demetri guesses softly.

"Or Maxwell," I agree, regretting that I haven't had time to explain in full detail all the minefields we'll be navigating together.

The second knock is less aggressive, slower and more deliberate, which only makes it more ominous. Not a *bang-bang* like the first but a *thunk. Thunk. Thunk.*

I slide off of Demetri with regret that's equal parts emotional and physical. We hadn't properly undressed, so it's a simple matter of smoothing and buttoning that restores our presentability. When Demetri stands, he winces, favoring his right leg.

"Are you—"

"I'll be fine," he assures me with a mild grimace. "Might have to wait a few days to take you against the wall again, that's all."

I'm moving more quickly than he is right now, and that may be the primary reason I reach the door first, but I realize as I reach for the knob: This is the right order to present, at least for an initial impression. I need to be seen as the head of this house. It's going to matter, at least to the people who present the greatest danger to us.

And sure enough, here's one of them.

"Commander," I say without stepping aside to invite him.

Demetri appears beside me a moment later and puts his arm around my shoulders. Maxwell barely suppresses a sneer as he regards his former subordinate.

"Congratulations," he snarls through gritted teeth.

"Thanks," Demetri says hesitantly, clearly not quite sure how to file this overt hostility.

"It's a nice place. I'm sure you'll be very happy here. Meanwhile I'm down a Helmet, not that either of you care about—"

"That's your problem," I interrupt. "Though if you'd care to argue in favor of relaxing admission criteria, I'll be more than happy to support any number of proposals."

The look in his eyes could melt steel. "Don't you dare patronize me. I know you don't believe you have any actual power here."

"Maybe not," I agree equably. "Maybe all I'll ever actually accomplish is what I already have: freeing myself from the Genneros and Demetri from the military. That will always have been worth it. But don't underestimate me. As an ally," I add after a pause just long enough to make sure he has time to take it the other way too. "It's still conceivable, in my mind, that we could work together. Surely we can move past the mutual history of distrust when there are greater issues in play."

Demetri's hand on my shoulder flexes protectively, but he stays quiet, aware he's not fully informed.

"It was good of you to stop by and offer your well wishes. Take time to consider whether we can work together. Right now, I'd like to be alone with my... husband," I say with only a breath of hesitation about applying the word.

The arm around me tightens in a brief squeeze that feels affectionate and happy, and I dare to glance over to confirm. His smile is radiant, loving, and utterly disarming, which is what I was afraid of. I didn't want to relax while Maxwell's eyes are still on me, but Demetri's effect on me is undeniable and, no doubt, visible.

I can't bring myself to face the Commander again right away, or maybe I don't quite want to. In the corner of my eye, he's shaking his head slightly, perhaps with disgust or resignation, but I don't need to turn my attention his way and absorb whatever energy this is.

"Enjoy your new life, Sandeaux," he grumbles. Half a step into turning to go, he adds tartly, "Or is it Vernon?"

As I give the door a sudden, solid push, I see the malicious humor he's aimed at me with this final barb toward Demetri.

"That was a low blow," I acknowledge quietly after his shadow moves off the doorstep. Turning to face Demetri, I look him in the eyes and place my hands on his hips. "I'm sorry. That may not be the only such insinuation you'll have to deal with. We're in a unique position, you and I. There may be numerous attempts to sow discord between us, and implying that there's something necessarily emasculating about our household is—"

He kisses me, pulls me close, lets me feel his erection as it eagerly returns to full attention after our disruptive visitor.

"I still feel plenty masculine."

"Yes, you do," I confirm, melting against him.

"Think we have a bedroom in this place?"

I grin against his lips. "I haven't gone exploring yet, but bedrooms are pretty standard, yes."

"Then let's find one. I need us farther from the door in case anyone else decides to knock on it. I need these clothes off for real."

Taking his hand, I lead him to the stairs and up, mindful of the pace with his injury. "Don't worry, there are only two floors, not nine."

When we find a bedroom and walk inside, he gasps in sudden realization. "Windows. Sunlight."

I nod. "We're far enough from the walls there was no rush to close everything off, and the homes aren't tall enough to present remote targets even from the tops of the walls—that was the initial thinking. There was discussion of flyover threats, but, well, if someone drops a bomb on you, windows are the least of your problems. And after a time, everyone started to relax about that because jet fuel has a shelf life.

"Anyway, yes, windows. It's comforting, isn't it?"

"I *need* these clothes off," he says again with quiet urgency. As he grins down at me, he holds me close, letting his hands roam my body and explore my curves. "I need to see you in the light of day, like the goddess you are."

I'm on the way to kiss him when I have a realization of my own to share.

"After you take off that uniform, you'll never need to put it on again."

His mouth takes mine in a powerful kiss that carries us across the room. I encourage him to sit on the edge of the bed, and we both start the business of undressing, reluctant to break eye contact for long at a time even to ease the process.

When he winces again bending his right knee, I start to ask if he's okay, but he waves it off. "It's nothing. Come here, beautiful."

He slides further back on the bed, his cock proudly inviting me to follow. As I start climbing up to join him, I am once again taken by the sight of him.

His tall, lean body reclining before me. His arrestingly handsome face that only grew more beautiful as we fell in love. The floppy silk of his dark hair and the wiry trail of even darker hair narrowing from his chest to his belly and pointing at his cock. It looks so big, and I wonder if part of that is in contrast with his overall leanness; this is the rare part of a man's anatomy where girth doesn't derive from body weight.

His hipbones jut more than they will after a few months here with me, I think as I straddle him here in our new bed. They're sharp against my inner thighs, but that could change. I've bought his freedom, his peace. His chance to grow old. To be happy.

I lean over him and let our chests press together as we kiss. He grips my hips and guides my pelvis in a sliding motion that drags the tip of his cock deliciously up and down at my entrance. I can feel how wet I am, how he would slide in like velvet. I try to push back onto him, but those firm hands at my hips keep me from taking him in.

A frustrated whimper accompanies a helpless wriggle that only deepens the tease, not the penetration.

"No," he says softly against my ear. "You're on top because of my knee. But I'm fucking you."

Chapter Thirty-Six

Gravity

Demetri

Another adorable little wriggle on me, and it feels so crazy good I'm aching to let her win. But my girl needs proof I'm still me. She needs to know I'm not intimidated by her strength, I'm in love with it. I'm turned on by it. I have to let her feel how much.

Right now, she's got just the tip of my dick, and she doesn't want to let it go, gripping like she's afraid the world will reverse gravity and she'll go flying off if she's not holding me tight inside her.

"You're all mine now. I'm gonna be at your side, holding your hand, you hear me?"

Her eyes are wet as she stares down at me, momentarily distracted from how wet she's making my dick. And that's perfect. That's exactly what I needed. I kiss her again, softly, and hold her hips right where they are as I rotate mine, letting her feel all that need again just as she'd started to lose focus on it. Her eyelids slip halfway shut and she moans hungrily.

"You want this?" I give her just the slightest push, partly to tease her but mostly to feel how hard she tries to keep me.

"Demetri," she breathes. "Please."

She strains against my hands, grabbing the top two inches of my dick and aching to take it all.

"It's yours, baby. I'm yours."

But I don't move, just let her roll and struggle against my grip, trying to take me deeper.

"I never doubted you for a moment when Maxwell said you were engaged. I want you to know that."

She whimpers, nods, makes a little sound: *yes* in the language of pure need.

"But when you disappeared, I really thought I might lose you, Stella. Never again. You're mine."

She arches and wriggles and tries to spear herself on my cock.

"You sure you can handle it? 'Cause I'm gonna love you, and I'm not gonna stop—"

A desperate sound as she realizes I've let go, finally freeing her to take me in. I'm lost inside her, buried to the hilt, locked into her warmth. She moans as I hit her so deep, that aching mix of pleasure and pain. You'll get used to me. You'll wonder how you ever lived without it. And you'll never have to live without it again.

She falls forward and sucks my lips into a hungry kiss, and I take hold of her hips again to keep her just where I want her. I bend my good leg for leverage and thrust up into her.

That's right, Stella. Feel it. Know it. I don't have to be on top to fuck you this hard.

Deep inside, she pulses in a steadily growing rhythm. She's almost ready for me.

"Fuck, yes, Stella. Come for me, beautiful."

Her cries grow faster, shallower, and her head tilts back as she leans almost fully upright, pulling me into just the right angle, and as she clenches hard around me, the drenching thrill of her deepest orgasm explodes around me. She was silky wet before, but now she's soaked me, and it feels and sounds wetter than anything I've ever known as I take her for my final thrusts and pull her onto me hard to give her my come.

She's still shaking, alternately heaving breaths and excited sighs as she slumps down on me, weak and slick with sweat. My arms slide around her, keeping her here just in case she might have felt the impulse to move away. Girls are like that, worried they're sweating on you, worried you're thinking they're heavy, worried about so many goddamn things. I'm grateful right now for all the women I've known and all the ways I've known them, because I know so well how to treat this woman. And how lucky I am to be holding her like this.

"Stella," I whisper, feeling another pulse where our bodies are still locked together, like my dick wants to let us both know it could rally for another run. I kiss her hair, and I realize it's in her face. Probably not comfortable for her, so I relax my hold on her enough to use one hand to clear her hair away before encouraging her to rest her cheek and stay right where she is.

What was I saying? Oh yeah.

"Stella, I'm so proud of you. I'm so proud to be the man who gets to make love to you. And kiss you. And fuck you. Come inside this beautiful body and make gorgeous babies—that hopefully get their smarts from you," I add with a chuckle.

She lifts her head and looks in my eyes. "You need to stop that. You're so much smarter than you admit to yourself. The biggest difference between you and me or you and your *best friend*?" She raises her eyebrows meaningfully to drive home her point. "Your willingness to be happy. It might take the rest of my life to learn that." She gently swipes my sweaty hair from my forehead and drops a sweet, tender kiss on my speechless lips. "But I've got the right man to learn from."

The showers in the barracks were awesome, and I don't know what I was expecting here, but it's kind of underwhelming. The function is about the same, just a fancier presentation. I liked the simple version better, actually, not that I'm complaining. This place is so much bigger and nicer, it's fucking insane to think I live here.

Growing up, we had a perfectly nice home. Lenora and I had our own rooms, and there was a basement for watching movies without light pollution. No complaints.

Okay, some complaints, but only because we were kids and that's what kids do. But overall, we were good with our lives and grateful for what we had.

My kids are gonna grow up in a frickin' mansion in the ultimate gated community. Unreal.

Granted, they're gonna be born into a zombie apocalypse. Win some, lose some.

We're all cleaned up, and I'm dressed in civvies for the first day of the rest of my life. It doesn't feel like a real change yet, because I'd've been off today anyway. Tomorrow is where I get to see how weird it feels. Will I get all itchy, jump up at random moments, like when you realize you're late for school in a dream?

When the second knock at the door comes, it's evening, and based on the time, I pretty much know who it's gonna be. I throw my arms around Tom right away. Stella told me all about how he stayed by my side no matter what after I hit the ground yesterday. I hug him hard and fast, and when I let go, we just kind of nod at each other.

He puts a hand on my shoulder. "Congratulations, my friend. I see it took far less debilitating an injury than you may have envisioned." A tiny smile rides the corner of his mouth, and his eyes twinkle.

My exhale is almost a laugh of relief as I think back on the conversation he's referencing. Can that really have been so recent? It was just before I discovered Stella had been taken. So much has changed so quickly, it's like a distant dream.

"Nah," I say, a little shakily. "Stella did a magic trick is all. The knee was more like a punchline."

He nods, glancing toward the door which has now shut, all our friends present and accounted for.

"Your friend from the Council," he says to Stella, who looks a little emotional after being hugged enthusiastically by Nina, Monica, and Davy in turn—the last of which probably surprised her most of all, since they barely know each other. He's just still a little shook up she got taken on his watch. Manny kind of hangs back and gives her a little wave in acknowledgment of how awkward it must be to be the only one not flinging his arms around her. As far as I know, they've never even spoken.

Stella nods. "Judah. And friend isn't quite the right word."

I reach out to her, and she takes my hand gratefully, moving into the shadow of my left arm, then glancing with concern at my knee.

"Let's all sit down," she says, moving me toward the couch I spent last night passed out on.

Once we're all basically on the same footing in terms of information (though a couple of glances between Stella and Tom make it clear there's still stuff the rest of us might not ever know), Monica says, "I need a very clear answer on one thing. Do we trust Maxwell or not? He's still got all our lives in his hands, in more ways than one."

Tom's mouth presses tight in a grimace. "Whether or not we trust him, we have no choice but to proceed as if we did. We can't afford his thinking we've turned on him, not for a moment. With apologies, of course," he says, glancing my way, "as you're no longer quite one of us. Maxwell may or may not see us as all on the same side in the coming days."

Stella adds quietly, "We'll see. I gave him something to think about at least."

"Well, we're back where we started on one level," Manny notes. "We can't all just be hanging out here all the time. Half of us aren't supposed to be at the barracks. The library is probably not safe anymore."

"We can use our place sometimes," Nina offers.

"Spring hits in random, early waves," Monica says. "We're not far off from being able to visit Remembrance Hill."

"Good enough," says Tom. There's a conclusiveness to his tone before he turns to Stella and asks, "Might I have a word?"

Chapter Thirty-Seven

Comfort

Stella

I lead Tom into the kitchen for whatever private moment he needs to have. There's a troubled knit to his brow just before he speaks.

"Stella, I hate to ask this. It's weighed on me, and I'm not sure I have the right, but..."

"Go on. After everything, if I can help, I will."

His fretful expression fractures with reluctant gratitude.

"The implant. The things you've told me it can do—"

"I don't know if there's any way to prevent its being used against any of us, if that's what—"

"No," he says, waving the idea away, "I fully understand the limitations of your access, particularly at this stage, and I know if you could take such an action, you'd hardly need me to have suggested it. It's not the future I'm asking about but the past. The way your former fiancé used the implant... was that widely implemented, to the best of your knowledge?"

His vulnerability as he voices this fear, for that's what it clearly is, stuns me briefly into silence.

"I don't know," I admit. "I can try to find out... but maybe it's a question for Maxwell."

Tom's eyes flash with seeming admiration, acknowledging the strategic potential of the suggestion.

"That's good," he agrees.

If Tom has to ask Maxwell for information I couldn't provide, it may help shore up their connection and even imply to Maxwell that I don't hold our friends' full trust. It may mean the difference between maintaining good will and being shut out, even endangered.

With a nod, he turns toward the door again, and we return to the group.

The mood in the living room is lighter, and Monica seems to be teasing Demetri about something, based on her playful grin and his uncontrollable blush. I settle in beside him, and he holds me close, pulling me tight against his side.

"Demetri's going to need a wardrobe upgrade," Monica informs me. "I was asking who we need to take out around here that's about the right size so we can raid their closet."

Nina gives her a wry, knowing smirk as Demetri continues to blush, and I know it's not the full story. When it strikes me that Davy's also blushing, I look at him and raise an eyebrow.

He instantly caves. "Monica suggested I take his measurements and do some knitting on our next backup shift."

Multiple snickers erupt around the room, and Manny adds, "You offered to start by making him a 'cock sock.' I can't let you get away with leaving out that detail."

The laughter bursts forth freely from all of them, and I smile at my handsome man, who smiles back and kisses me.

A disquiet fills me as our lips part and I stare into his eyes. "What if I've already done all the magic I'm ever going to pull off?"

It's barely louder than a whisper, but it still shuts down the fun, and I have time to regret doing that before Nina says, "I don't believe that. When Maxwell recruited me, he said the mistake these people made was underestimating him. Seems to me these people underestimated you plenty, and now they think you're contained, which means they're primed to go right back to it."

Tom's smile is full of pride and desire as he strokes her hair. She sits beside him, resting her cheek on his thigh, and it strikes me there were other places she could have sat. He seems like a king on a throne. It's unmistakable. She worships him, and he revels in it.

His question comes back to me, and I suddenly understand the reason for his distress. My hand twitches in Demetri's. I wish I could have given him comfort. At least I gave him a move to make in this wearisome game.

"Right you are, darling," he tells her, then looks up at me. "I believe Stella's demonstrated they underestimated her at their peril, and that will make it even sweeter when they do so once more, and again pay the price."

He nods slightly to reinforce the sentiment, and perhaps to remind me of his words from last night.

After they're gone, Demetri and I head back upstairs. I keep eyeing his right leg.

"I'll be fine," he says with cheerful impatience like he can't believe I'm still thinking about this.

"If you're not, I'll kill Judah," I mutter. "Probably shouldn't rule out doing that either way, actually."

Demetri stops and gently turns me until we're squarely facing each other.

"Don't even joke," he says soberly. "If violence needs doing, point me in the right direction and then get out of the way. You're taking zero chances from now on, you hear me?"

A slow, grateful smile drives the remaining distress from my face, if not my mind. "You're going to take care of me," I say wonderingly.

"We'll take care of each other," he affirms, pulling me into a deep kiss.

His hardness against me quickens my heartbeat. I reach into his waistband and take hold.

"I've been sick, poisoned all the way to my blood. Only you can cure me. Come in my mouth," I murmur against his lips.

He practically staggers, and I lead him the rest of the way up the stairs by the head of his cock. I slide his pants down to his thighs and gently push him into a soft chair, then sink to my knees before him and run my hands up the gently furred muscles of his thighs.

Just before I take him in my mouth, I look in his eyes for a long moment. This man is mine. I'm on my knees before him, and I know I was just thinking how powerful it made Tom look to have Nina kneel at his feet, but right now, I feel powerful. Because he's mine. Because I'm the one he's looking at with such passion.

I slide my mouth down onto him, again mindful of the depth, and stroke the lower half with my fist as I lick and suck. He tastes so clean right now, recently showered, the pungent tang of his precum a subtle overture to the main act.

His hips begin flexing, seemingly helpless not to participate in the nearing wave of pleasure, and I suck harder, letting him take control of the rhythm as he plunges into my mouth from below. I feel it just before it happens, and I focus my effort, sucking, flicking my tongue just below the tender frenulum as he spasms, filling my mouth with heat.

"Oh, Stella," he moans as his fingers flex in my hair. The gentle tug at my roots mimics the twitching of my throat as I swallow him down.

I continue to suck an extra moment past the point when I know he's done, prolonging the sensation as much as possible, wanting to show how hungry I am for all of him. When I finally look up, he's staring at me all dozy and satisfied.

"Come lie down with me," I say, standing and offering him my hand.

We shed our clothes for the final time today and slide between the cool, silky sheets. Our bodies press together as he pulls me into his arms for a loving kiss that quickly intensifies.

"I've got the rest of my life to explore this body," he says almost reverently as his hands roam over my curves.

"It's yours," I promise.

"Yeah?" He pulls my thigh to rest on his hip, opening me to his fingertips as they dance at the edge of my entrance. "All mine?" A long finger slides in and presses against the front wall before slowly dragging back out.

"All yours." I moan in agreement and flex my hips toward him needily.

"You like that? Want more?"

I whimper something close to yes, my head bouncing in a tiny, helpless nod against his lips.

He slides his hand between our bodies and plunges two fingers into me, pulling me to him from inside.

"Don't think I don't know what you just did. You've got nothing to prove to me. You're my girl. I know it. Everyone's gonna know it. Know how? 'Cause I'm gonna come inside you and make beautiful, genius babies with you. You feel me, Stella?"

My eyes have slipped shut. My hips rock with the steady pressure his fingers are building.

"You're my girl. Now come on my fingers before I fill you up again."

He adds a third, and the fullness takes me to immediate, gasping climax. I barely reach the end of the orgasm before he slips into me, slick and deep.

Demetri keeps us on our sides, sparing his knee without placing either of us in a superior or subordinate position. He makes slow, steady love to me, accompanied with kisses rather than words. When he comes, he pulls gently at my hair and strains to push even deeper into me, making sure I feel it.

"Don't doubt you've got plenty of magic left," he says softly as we drift off after.

Chapter Thirty-Eight

Tomorrow

Stella

Our host tonight is Linwood Burroughs, Greta's husband. Nominally, that makes her our hostess, but she barely put in an appearance before being exiled upstairs to be with their newborn. She looked exhausted, yet oddly less diminished than our past encounters. Whatever has changed about her, I don't for a moment believe it has anything to do with her husband, a man who appears beneath her concern in some ineffable way.

Quickly, it's clear he's not troubled by Greta's absence either, based on the leering manner with which he regards their household help. My skin crawls, more so now than it did before I was officially aware of the arrangement. Marie's fortunate enough to be kept by a man she seems to genuinely want, but most of these women are just accepting placements—and likely tolerating sexual relationships—with men they neither like nor want.

All for the right to keep their birth control on.

I don't know what I'll ever be able to do for them. Or indeed, about any situation that preceded my joining the Council.

In my darkest moments, I fear I'll never substantively affect any future decisions either. As Judah so plainly put it, a Council majority is unlikely to side with me on any point.

Before Tom's words revived my hope that night, I was looking at this as a deal with the devil, accepting that I had sold my soul for Demetri's.

But Judah's not the devil. He's just a man. No ersatz devil's bargain is the final word on our future.

Demetri looks only slightly nervous about his first night among the Illustris elite. His knee is still a little tender, but he's not favoring it too obviously, and he looks almost as good in his new hand-me-down suit as he looked in his uniform—though nowhere near as good as he looks out of it. My eyes drink him in for another long moment. Sometimes it seems I get stuck when I turn to gaze at him. His beauty grabs and holds me in place as the rest of the world fades into the background.

"Demetri, welcome to the other side. You clean up good. Funny to see Jackass Morton's suits on a man who's not trying to fuck everyone's wives. Presumably."

"Judah," I say stiffly, halfway between a greeting and a request to kindly shut the hell up as Demetri goes rigid at my side, plainly enraged at the suggestion.

"He was a tall, handsome guy too. Very popular with the ladies. Didn't love being Delia's pet, but he did enjoy the benefits."

"His clothes are comfortable enough. Shoes were a little small for me," Demetri comments with a barely restrained glare.

Judah gives Demetri an evaluating look, then turns to me. "No attaching at the hip here, Stella. You are actually required to mingle. Make friends, or at least allies. You can't be seen as the sort of woman who never leaves her husband's side."

"Nor as the sort who only mingles among the other wives, yes, Judah, I actually do understand the politics."

He holds out an arm, and I reluctantly take it, allowing him to lead me away from Demetri after a kiss.

"You may not be able to mingle among the wives, but he can. Hope you can trust your stud unattended," Judah taunts.

I can't help but laugh. "Of course I can," I say without defensiveness or artifice.

It's true. After Greg, I didn't know if I would ever trust my judgment again, let alone trust a man to be the same person today as he was yesterday. I trust Demetri with everything I am and ever will be.

Making small talk with these people is so much easier now. I asserted my place, challenged them, and won. It's mostly honorary, this token acceptance Judah has bestowed, but it got us here—it may yet bring us further.

Every so often throughout the evening, I catch a glimpse of Demetri. He's more at ease than he expected to be, no doubt enjoying the benefit of that pretty privilege he unselfconsciously acknowledged before. Rich people wanted you around to be pretty and charming, he said. Now we are rich people, in a sense, yet still here on invitation. Special dispensation from the king, as it were.

"Tell me the truth," I challenge Judah as the evening is winding down. "You spread the word that men should ignore him, didn't you?"

A slight smirk at the right side of his mouth, a mischievous twinkle in his eyes.

Shaking my head wearily, I ask why.

"It's for your own good, Stella. Let everyone see you're not threatened or jealous or weak, for one thing. Give him a chance to prove himself, for another. In case the subtleties of the Morton situation were lost on you, we sent a man into the wilderness to die because he didn't show respect for certain ethical boundaries. And

I said he was a tall, handsome guy, but let me be clear, he wasn't in your boy's league."

With a sigh, I conclude, "So you're testing him to make sure you don't need to have him killed for trying to fuck everyone in sight."

"Nah," he says easily. "I don't currently have a dog in that race, in case you've forgotten. But there are plenty of other people who do. I'm not testing your husband, Stella. I'm making sure you understand the danger he could be in."

"If he slept with someone else?" I scoff. "He wouldn't."

Judah leans a little closer and murmurs, "If someone thought he was."

Jerking back in anger and alarm, I bristle as he grabs my wrist to keep me close.

"I'm still working out what your deal is with Maxwell. I love your girl boss energy, Stella, really I do, but I never believed for a moment that you randomly selected him because you heard someone at my level talking shit. Know why? Because the people at my level care so little about the people at his level, there's no shit to talk."

The words ring horribly true; isn't that basically what I said to Sarah Maxwell that day in the library? I knew her husband was utterly insignificant to the people at the top.

"So this is your warning shot across my bow?"

He laughs. "No! Jeez, always so sincere. And I love that. There are no warning shots. If you draw fire, *my* fire, it will land on target."

Then why are you afraid of me?

The words flash in my mind like a sputtering neon sign.

The sheer number of times he's bothered to threaten me like this, to assert his control and my helplessness... he's afraid of me. Or finds me far less predictable than he likes to imply, wonders what I might yet do to surprise him.

Judah Basher considers me a threat of some sort. A wild card. A resource to be locked down and contained. That's reason enough to have hope.

Demetri pulls me into his arms and kisses me as if we've been separated for days rather than mere hours. He doesn't so much as glance around us after, just puts an arm around my waist and moves us to the door.

We walk home in silence. It's not far anyway, and in this part of town, there are likely no friendly ears.

Once safely inside our own front door, he kisses me again with even greater fervor.

"I felt like Magic Mike tonight, Stella. Pretty sure half those women thought I should tear off my suit and start bump-and-grinding. It's not just that I'm a man, either. It's the outsider thing. They look at me like, I don't wanna say a piece of meat, but—"

"I know what you mean." I gently stroke his furrowed brow. "And I'm sorry. For what it's worth, I'm pretty sure you'll be able to interact with men next time. Tonight was Judah's doing."

"Of course it was," he grumbles. "I kinda wish he just wanted to fuck you."

Recoiling at the suggestion, I pull back in shock.

"I don't mean—it's just, that kind of thing, I would know what to expect, you know? He's got angles I can't read, and it makes me nervous. My instinct is to protect you, and I don't even know what I'm supposed to be protecting you from."

I feel the muscles of my face relax back into an affectionate smile, and I pull him back into a slower, deeper kiss.

When we reach the top of the stairs, I ask, "Your knee didn't give you too much trouble tonight, did it?"

His gorgeous grin presages his reply in a way that sends tingles through the secret bundles of nerves at the center of my body.

"My knee is good," he confirms. "And I've been dying to put you up against a wall in this fancy joint."

"While you still can," I blurt as he moves in for a kiss.

He pauses barely a breath from my lips. "Meaning?"

Our eyes are locked. His instinctively follow mine to dip down to my breasts.

"I don't know anything for sure, but... getting dressed tonight, I had trouble. They're bigger. Aren't they?"

He doesn't have words to answer me. Only a deep, delirious kiss and his strong hands exploring my dimensions as if appreciating the tiniest changes only he can get close enough to feel.

His fingers slide into my underwear and dip into me before swirling around my clit, making me rock into his hand with a soft moan.

"First test for the knee," he murmurs as he smoothly kneels before me.

Removing my stockings with gentle urgency, he kisses down the insides of each leg. When he leans up to move into position, his beauty stops my breath yet again.

"Demetri." I catch his silky hair between my fingers as his mouth disappears from view. The word dissolves into a helpless sigh of pleasure just before his efforts send my gaze skyward.

It's not long before I'm on the precipice of an orgasm like to collapse my legs if he doesn't catch me, and that's when he stops, drawing a needy whimper out of me as he stands.

"This is how I want you. Ready to come, but you're gonna come on me."

Every time Demetri slides into me, my entire body reaches for him. Pressed to the wall, my thighs braced by his powerful arms, I pull at him with my lips, my tongue, my cunt. He's more than I ever dared to imagine. Handsome, strong, protective, and so warm. So true.

He powers into me faster and faster as I urge him on with every sound, every touch. When I clench around him, there's a feeling of mutual explosion as my body propulsively releases a flood of giddy liquid heat just before his release deep inside.

The strangest thought lands in the sudden shaking of our post-orgasm breaths. He's the love of my life. But if what my mother told me is true, he won't always be, will he?

"What's going on?" he asks comfortably upon seeing my odd expression.

When I explain, he laughs. With the radiant, loving smile that, it strikes me joyously, our children may inherit, Demetri tells me, "Stella, baby, that's how it's supposed to be."

Thank you for reading!

This was a journey to write, and I am grateful to everyone who came along for the ride. What's next for the Stronghold: Monica has some work ahead, as do they all, but hers is the heart. And then there's Judah... he seems to just keep surprising everyone, and I love that about him.

Besides reading the book, reviewing, rating, and/or recommending are among the kindest things you can do for any author. Best of all is reaching out, so if you enjoyed Trust in Tomorrow, I would love to know that! If you didn't, that's totally fine, but I'd rather be excluded from that kind of conversation :)

You can find me on my website, danasweeney.com, which has links to my social media.

Acknowledgements

Thank you to: Lisa Sullivan, who helps keep me sane IRL, the Despair Icon family, who keep me sane every hour of the day from afar. Poppy Fitzgerald for alpha reading, Kit McKrae for testing the potential of Trust to stand alone, Kate Raven (hashtag goals <3) and Aspen Kilgore for letting me throw random pieces at them to see if they worked, and Kerri Andrews, Madeline Thorne, Kathryn Klammt, and Emma Craven for beta reading. Ariel DeWinter for telling me to let Demetri yap at me. Nenia Campbell for being one of the kindest people and biggest cheerleaders in the indie community and the book world in general. Kayla and Amanda of Erotically Neurotic and Katie of Cheap Smut, hilarious and delightful podcasts that chose Lust for Tomorrow to talk about. Kristina Carmela whose superhuman energy, drive, and organizational skills brought the Indieverse Awards to life, and everyone who nominated Lust for Tomorrow.

To my dear Sparkle for being a sunbeam every day, and Sarah Linkert for being the Reader in my head.